Susi Osborne has led a varied career, mostly in libraries but also as a classroom assistant, craft worker, fundraiser, telesales adviser and carer. Along the way teenagers, trying to adopt, physically handicapped children, gay friends, neurotic dogs and a mother with Alzheimer's have kept her on her toes, and equipped her with more than enough material for her career as a novelist. Susi lives in Winsford, Cheshire with her family.

'Susi Osborne's sense of humour shines throughout *Grace and Disgrace* and at one point I laughed so much tears rolled down my cheeks.'

Diana B. Tackley, Artist and Broadcaster


By the same author

*The Ripples of Life*, Book Guild Publishing, 2008

# GRACE AND DISGRACE

*Best wishes*

Susi Osborne

*Susi Osborne*

Book Guild Publishing
Sussex, England

First published in Great Britain in 2010 by
The Book Guild Ltd
Pavilion View
19 New Road
Brighton, BN1 1UF

Typesetting in Baskerville by
Norman Tilley Graphics Ltd, Northampton

Printed in Great Britain by
CPI Antony Rowe

A catalogue record for this book is available from
The British Library

ISBN 978 1 84624 463 6

To my very lovely friend Bernice ... with whom I seem to laugh constantly! She is not only an inspiration but also one of the kindest and most thoughtful people I know.

Thanks to ...

| | | |
|---|---|---|
| My mother | – | Alzheimer's and humour don't always go together but it helps when they do. |
| Robert, Nik, Sophie and Naomi | – | my family, my life ... crazy as it is! |
| Jennie | – | for having my gorgeous grandson, Alexander Percy. |
| Will, John and Robert | – | for equalling me in insanity! |
| Hazel | – | for her friendship and her proof-reading prowess. |
| Helen | – | for teaching me how to say 'no'! |
| John T. | – | a true gentleman and a wonderful friend. |
| The Daniels, Rays and Minshulls | – | for their unfailing support. |
| Everyone at Book Guild | – | for publishing my second novel! |

# 1

'Mum! He's in the bathroom again! How am I ever supposed to be ready on time?' Cleo's outraged voice echoed through the hallway as she thudded down the stairs to confront her poor unfortunate mother who was attempting to revive the charred remains of toast from the non-pop-up toaster yet again.

'Me want toast! Me want toast!' chanted three-year-old Izzy, her hands beating on the kitchen table like a drum.

'Mum! Did you hear me? Zak's been in the bathroom now for twenty minutes! I can't wait any longer – the bus leaves at half past.'

''Morning, young lady.' Charlie, Grace's long-suffering husband, breezed into the room and kissed the top of Izzy's neatly braided head.

'Ow, mind my hair, Daddy. Mummy did that and it took her ages and ages.'

Cleo was about to erupt. 'Is anybody listening to me?'

'No need to shout, dear,' retorted Gran, sipping her tea.

'Wouldn't it be easier to make some fresh?' asked Charlie, peering over Grace's shoulder, his arm sliding around her.

'It's the last of the bread, although I'm sure I bought another loaf yesterday.'

'Hello!' yelled Cleo.

'You did, dear, I put it away for you,' said Gran, dunking a biscuit and having to retrieve the soggy end from her cup with a teaspoon.

'Errgh, Gran, that's yuk,' exclaimed Izzy, covering her eyes with her hands.

'*Grrr!* It's so unfair!' Cleo was steaming.

'Sorry, Cleo – what did you say?' Grace turned to see her daughter stomping back down the hall and heard an explosion at the top of the stairs followed shortly by the slamming of the bathroom door. Whatever was wrong with that girl just lately?

Her thoughts were echoed by Zak as he drifted into the room and dropped his rucksack onto the kitchen floor. 'Cleo in a mood again?'

'Just being Cleo I think, love. Move your bag, somebody's going to fall over it there.'

'Sorry, Mum. Any toast going?'

'There would be if we could find the bread – Gran's been up to her old tricks again.'

'Why is it, whenever anything goes wrong around here, it's always my fault?' slurped the old lady.

'Good question,' whispered Charlie, hot on the trail of the missing loaf. 'Aha! In the laundry basket under the stairs! Why ever didn't I think to look there first?'

Gradually the house emptied and peace was restored once more. Gran had wandered off to her room to watch *The Jeremy Kyle Show*. Grace could never understand the fascination, but her mother sat glued to the screen each morning watching people with problems she could never even have imagined in the sheltered life she'd led.

Grace settled down to read the newspaper and drink her tea, relishing the tranquility. There were plenty of things she should be doing while Izzy was at nursery but sod it, it would all still be there tomorrow. Her eyes scanned the headlines as she slowly flicked through the pages, coming to rest on an article about troubled teens. She thought it was just her age that was making Cleo act the way she did lately – a phase she was going through. But recently things seemed to be going from bad to worse. Perhaps she should start watching *Jeremy Kyle* with Gran! No, seriously though, she was worried about Cleo.

Any hope of Grace gaining helpful advice from the article was short-lived: the writer lived in cloud cuckoo land. '... often caused by a crisis in their lives ... divorce ... new baby ... make time for them ...' Did they think she didn't realise that already? She'd like nothing better than to be able to devote more time to Cleo but she already felt pulled in about fifteen different directions and there were, after all, only twenty-four hours in a day. It was true, though, that Cleo's problems had started when she and Richard separated.

In the beginning Grace and Richard had been so in love – spending all their time just with each other, planning for the future, a blissful existence. But then, as with so many couples before and since, life had got in the way. Mortgage, children, work, never enough time for anything. They simply grew apart. Sex, conversation, fun – all became a distant memory. There were never particularly major arguments, they were just stuck in a rut, each plodding along in their daily lives, getting on with what they had to do. Until one day Richard had said, 'Enough.'

The word had stopped Grace in her tracks. She hadn't even considered just how far they'd drifted apart until that moment. Enough. That one word had changed their lives completely. It wasn't as though there was anyone else involved. Extramarital sex? What a joke. They hadn't had time for each other, never mind making time for someone else. Why had life always seemed like a whirlwind, a never-ending treadmill? They could have been so happy; were, at one time.

Thankfully the split had been amicable enough. They'd both been so worn down by the drudgery of their lives that

3

they felt numb. In a way, that one word had been a lifesaver, a glimmer of hope on the horizon. Of course Grace had felt scared at first, left on her own with the responsibility of bringing up the children, but Richard hadn't moved far away and was always there to help whenever she had a problem.

And problem number one had soon appeared, in the shape of her mother. No, that was a cruel thing to say. It was just that, immediately after the split with Richard, Grace's mother had been a great support to her. A widow herself, she was glad to be able to help out. But gradually she'd started to take over and make herself indispensable. Grace didn't particularly notice at first and was just glad of the help so that she could continue with her part-time job at the local florist's. Her mother would stay over for the odd night here and there and Grace never minded at all. But then one day her mother announced that she would like to come and live with them permanently. She explained how she was struggling to cope on her own and how lonely she was. What else could Grace do but say yes? Richard did warn her, but did she listen? No.

Cleo hadn't minded too much at first. Grace had discussed it with the children – they'd been ten and twelve at the time – but Zak had been the only one to raise any objections. 'What about when I want my music on?' 'What about when my mates are round?', that sort of thing. But they'd managed to reach a compromise and fitted out the dining-room as a sort of granny flat so that Gran could have her own space and hopefully not spill over too much into theirs. Initially it hadn't worked out badly – Gran was careful not to inflict herself on them too much. But as Cleo reached her teens, Gran couldn't seem to help herself; no matter what Cleo did, it was never right for Gran. Grace couldn't understand what had brought about this change in their relationship; they'd got on so well when Cleo was younger.

And then there'd been the arrival of Charlie in their lives. An absolute joy for Grace, who'd never in a million years thought she'd ever marry again. Who in their right mind would want to take on a woman rapidly approaching forty who lived in a deteriorating house with two teenagers, a mother showing the first signs of dementia, and an ageing, neurotic dog? Well, Charlie did. To Grace he was an angel in disguise. But to Cleo ... well, he was okay, and she wanted her mum to be happy, but deep down inside, although she told no one, she felt he was taking the place where her dad should have been and she didn't like that one little bit.

Grace and Charlie were sensitive to the situation with Cleo. Grace had tried to talk to her about it on numerous occasions, as had Charlie, but she merely shrugged it off and said it didn't bother her. Nevertheless it was clear that it did. They'd worried as well how it would affect her when Grace became pregnant with Izzy, but they couldn't put their lives on hold forever and Charlie was desperate to have a child of his own. But actually Cleo loved Izzy, Grace was sure of it. Who couldn't love Izzy?

'Grace! Didn't anybody let the dog out this morning?'

Problem number one had emerged from her room and was on her way to the kettle.

'You did, Mother. I asked you and you said he'd been outside.'

'How did I know I'd get the blame again? Well I've stood in it now and it's all over my slipper.'

With a sigh Grace reluctantly made her way into the kitchen.

'Oh Mother! You've trodden it all across the floor!'

'Well if you'd let him out in the first place it wouldn't have happened.'

'But you said ... oh never mind. Take your slipper off.' Grace took a deep breath and went to get a cloth. It was easier just to get on with it.

5

Alfie sat looking at her, his big brown eyes full of worry. He knew he'd been naughty.

'Poor boy.' Grace gave his troubled head a reassuring pat. 'It wasn't your fault was it?'

His tail moved gingerly from side to side on the floor. His mum still loved him.


Izzy skipped along happily, holding tightly to Grace's hand as they made their way home from nursery school.

'Mrs Clarke said my painting is brilliant.'

'Well it is.' Grace glanced across at it, clutched tightly in Izzy's other hand.

'Mrs Clarke said I'm a very good girl.'

'And Mrs Clarke is right,' said Grace, smiling at her beaming little daughter.

'Mrs Clarke read us a story today about The Very Hungry Caterpillar.'

'Oh, the story we've got at home?'

'Yes. And Mrs Clarke said what did we like to eat best of all and I said pizza. So can we have pizza for lunch today, Mummy, please?'

'I suppose we'd better then, if Mrs Clarke thinks you've been such a good girl.'

'Goody, goody!' Izzy jumped up and down, clapping her hands with excitement. It didn't take much to please Izzy.

'Mind your painting.'

'Will Daddy be home for lunch?'

'Not today, Izzy, he's at work. He'll be back at teatime.'

Charlie was a painter and decorator, although really he could turn his hand to almost anything. It had been his father's business before him and, although it didn't earn a fortune, it kept them comfortably in their modest lifestyle. Grace was sure he could have built up the business if he'd wanted to, he was always having to turn away customers, but Charlie was a bit of a plodder and was happy with the way things were. What was the point of working yourself into an early grave? He was happy spending time with his family now. He did have two young lads who worked for him though, which was good as they could be trusted to get on with a job if ever he needed any time off.

Charlie had never even considered marriage until Grace had come into his life. He'd had a few relationships in the past but nothing that serious before. He'd met Grace through a mutual friend who'd introduced them, knowing they'd get on, and right from the beginning there'd been a spark of interest between them. Grace had been longing for someone to share her life with again, and Charlie got on well enough with her family as he got to know them, so when he asked her to marry him, she'd been delighted to accept. Charlie was devoted to Grace and when she gave birth to his beautiful baby daughter, Izzy, his happiness was complete. Here he was, three years down the road from bachelordom with a wife, three kids, a loopy mother-in-law and a crazy dog – and he loved it.

In fact Charlie *was* there when Grace and Izzy got home.

'We weren't expecting to see you.' Grace kissed him lightly on the cheek, removing her coat simultaneously.

Alfie bounced up and down, panting with the excitement of seeing them again. 'Alright Alfie, get down! I only left you half an hour ago.'

'Daddy!' Izzy threw herself at him as he lifted her up into his arms and hugged her tightly.

'Hey, pooch. Had a good time?'

'Oops, squashed it now … look at my painting!' she beamed, retrieving it from between them.

'That's fantastic Izzy.' He looked at it admiringly. 'Go and show Gran, she's in her room.'

He put her back down and she skipped out of the kitchen in search of Gran, Alfie following eagerly, not wanting to be left out.

'So why are you home?' asked Grace when peace had descended.

'Had to do a quote for somebody in Maybury Grove, so I thought I might as well pop home for lunch.'

'Pizza okay?'

'Fine. Want a hand?'

'No, it's okay.'

Grace washed her hands, turned on the oven and searched the freezer. Oven chips, fish fingers, beefburgers … they were here somewhere … aha!

'Something wrong, Gracie? I can feel the stress oozing from you.' Charlie left the table and came over to Grace, his hand rubbing her back soothingly.

'Oh, I don't know, just Cleo – again. I seem to worry about her all the time just lately. Sorry.' She stayed with her back to him, tearing off the packaging, putting the pizzas into the oven.

He turned her to face him, tilting her chin so her eyes looked into his. 'Don't shut me out, Gracie. We're in this together, remember?'

'Sorry.'

'And stop apologising. I may not be Cleo's real dad but I want to help. How can I if you shut me out all the time?'

'Sorry. Oops, sorry, I said it again.' Her face broke into a tremulous smile as she leant against him, his arms around her, her solid dependable Charlie.

Grace was in the kitchen making a curry when Cleo returned.

'I'm home.'

Grace looked up to speak but the footsteps thudded straight up the stairs and on went the music. Grace washed her hands and followed, knocking on the bedroom door.

'Cleo?' No response. 'Cleo?'

The door flew open, the sound of music quadrupled and

8

an angry face appeared.

'What?'

'I only wanted to say hello, welcome home, nice to see you, stuff like that.'

'You being sarcastic?'

''Course not. I just never seem to see you these days that's all. Anyway, how was school? I'm making your favourite for tea – curry,' said Grace, not waiting for an answer to her question.

'School was rubbish as usual.' Cleo rummaged through her wardrobe, haphazardly, her back turned to Grace. 'God, you can never find anything in this place, bet it's still at the bottom of the washing basket buried under everyone else's rubbish.'

'Lost something?' Grace ventured into the room, glancing briefly at the chaos that lurked inside.

'My red top.'

'Here,' said Grace, retrieving it from beneath a plate of uneaten toast from goodness knows when, on the floor.

'Ah, brill! Thanks, Mum.' Cleo turned with a smile of gratitude, a rare thing these days. But it was short-lived.

'Oh, look at the state of it, it's all creased!'

'Well it will be if you leave it lying on the floor. Here, it looks clean enough, I'll take it down and run the iron over it for you. Will it do after tea?'

'No, I need it now, I'm going out.'

'But not until after we've eaten, surely?'

'Yeah, I'm meeting Cassie and then we're going to Lisa's.'

'But you've not had anything to eat yet.'

'Oh stop fussing. I'll get something when I'm out.'

'And what about your homework?'

'Not got any.'

Grace raised her eyebrows reprovingly.

'I haven't!'

9

Grace sighed and turned to leave. 'I'll go and iron your top.'

'Thanks, Mum.'

Grace glanced back at her wayward daughter as she left the room but Cleo was now on her hands and knees, dragging things out from under the bed in search of some other lost item, and didn't see the worry etched on Grace's face. Not that she would have done anything about it even if she had. Why did mothers always have to nag?

'But she came home on time, didn't she? Give her some credit. You said nine o'clock and she was there right on the dot.' Charlie climbed into bed and snuggled up beside his wife wondering, what all the fuss was about.

'Under protest.'

'Well, maybe it was a bit early ...'

'Charlie! She's only fifteen and she's got school tomorrow!'

'You worry too much,' he said nibbling her ear, trying to get her undivided attention for once. His hand moved slowly down her body, dispelling any further thoughts from her mind as she gasped with ...

'Charlie!' Her body was rigid.

'What?' He was a man on a mission, not wanting to stop.

'The door!'

'What?'

Flustered, Grace shot up in bed. 'Izzy, come here. What's wrong?' she panted, to the forlorn figure who stood in the doorway sucking her thumb.

'Can I come in your bed?'

A groan came from the prostrate figure laid next to her. 'Looks like she's the only one who will,' he sighed.

'Charlie! Of course you can, darling. Come and get in next to me.'

Charlie shuffled along, his displeasure plain to all.

10

'It's only for a little while, Charlie, don't be so mean. She'll soon fall asleep again then I'll carry her back to her own bed.'

'Hmmph,' grunted Charlie.

Peace was restored. Sleepy little snores came from Izzy. Grace, warm and relaxed now, was drifting into the land of Nod. But Charlie's ardour was not so easily assuaged.

'She's asleep.'

'What?'

'She's asleep.'

'So was I.'

'You said you'd take her back,' he said, running a finger down the spine that lay facing him, pressing himself up against her – an action that had the desired effect.

'Okay, okay, I'm going.' Grace dragged herself out of bed and, gathering her sleepy bundle of daughter in her arms, disappeared out of the door, leaving Charlie in happy anticipation of what he'd been waiting for all night.

# 2

It was the last thing Zak expected to see as he scuffed along, bent over from the weight of his rucksack, making his way through the park on his way home from college. He'd only had History this morning, had frees for the rest of the day. It was meant to be English but there was some staff meeting or other so Zak had decided to come home and get some work done so that he could go out tonight.

Zak loved college. His mum had wanted him to stay on in the sixth form at school for his A levels but even she could see now that he'd made the right choice. It was a whole new world, a stepping stone towards going to university, and that was definitely what he wanted to do next year.

He wanted to be a teacher, he'd known that for years and had never wavered from the idea. He loved kids and he loved English, and that was what he wanted to teach. Zak knew he had a lot of work ahead of him but he was determined and had every confidence in himself.

It wasn't all work, though, he was a popular lad with more mates than he knew what to do with. His phone never stopped ringing – well, texting anyway – and being a sixth-form college there seemed to be eighteenth birthday parties practically every week.

Home was equally as chaotic as his social life in many ways just lately, and it seemed to be getting worse. Some days he couldn't wait to get away to uni to escape, although at the same time he knew he'd miss everyone like mad, miss being a part of the chaos that was family life.

He'd miss his mum most of all; they were very close, closer than most of his mates were to their mums – in fact they used to tease him about it sometimes. But he could take it. Anyway they all thought she was cool – they were just jealous. He'd always got on well with his mum, but when his parents had split up he'd been twelve and had felt the need to take over as the man of the house in a houseful of women. He'd grown up very quickly that year – not that he regretted anything. His parents were happier apart and he loved both of them.

He'd been pleased though when his mum had met and married Charlie. Cleo had been a bit unsure but, for him, it took some of the weight of responsibility from his shoulders. He got on well with Charlie; it was good to have another man in the house. Besides, Charlie coming to live with them had resulted in Izzy, and who couldn't love her? A smile spread across his face involuntarily as he thought about his mischievous little sister with her impish ways and her infectious giggle. Izzy: she was one person he'd miss big time when uni came around, although if he let that slip to his mates he really would be thought of as a total wus.

Zak looked at his watch. Twenty past two already? He knew he shouldn't have hung around with Bainesy and all that lot, he should've come straight back. A sudden movement in the bushes caught his eye. Cleo? Surely not. He slowed his pace to look more closely, trying hard not to appear to be a pervert. Sure enough, there she was, back against a tree, lips locked with … he was trying his best to see who, but whoever it was had his hands everywhere and he looked far too old for his sister – who should have been in school anyway.

'Cleo!' Like, obviously, that was going to stop her. 'Cleo!' One eye opened and looked at him. 'Sod off, Zak.'
'I'll tell Mum!'
'Like I care.'

'Cleo!'

But the lip-locking and body-groping had resumed. Zak was totally ignored. Short of dragging Romeo bodily off his sister, he was fighting a losing battle, which is what he would have been doing even if he'd tried. Romeo was about seven feet tall and obviously worked out.

Defeated, Zak carried on home, but he worried about Cleo. They'd been so close at one time but now she was like the sister from hell. Should he tell Mum? He hated having to snitch on anybody, hated to be thought of as a dobber. Mum seemed to be getting nowhere with Cleo recently, anyway. Perhaps he'd just try having a talk to her himself – if she'd listen, which didn't seem very likely.

Grace was sitting at the kitchen table talking to Gran when Zak came in through the back door.

'Hey.'

'Hello, love, I wasn't expecting you home this early.'

'I know, but …'

Zak was stopped mid-sentence as Izzy and Alfie launched themselves at him simultaneously, overjoyed to see him.

'Hey, you two,' he smiled, hugging Izzy with one arm and stroking Alfie with his free hand.

'Do you want a game of football in the garden with us?' Izzy looked up at him, turning on the charm.

'I've got work to do, Iz, that's why I came home early.'

Her gaze never faltered.

'Oh, go on. Five minutes, that's all. Go and get the ball out ready, I'll be there in a sec.'

'Yeay!' Izzy clapped her hands with excitement and shot out into the garden, Alfie hot on her heels.

'She's got you just where she wants you that one,' said Gran, dunking a chocolate biscuit into her tea.

'Any news?' asked Mum.

His heart skipped a beat. He couldn't dob, he couldn't.

'God, you're so nosy,' grinned Zak.

'That's what mothers are for.'

By the time he came back in from the garden Cleo had returned. She was sat talking to Mum and Gran – amazingly.

'Hey.' She couldn't even look at him.

'You're back early,' he said, only half accusingly.

She stared at the table, arms folded in front of herself, protectively. 'Free period.'

'Hope you get one next month,' he said under his breath, but just loud enough for her to hear as he walked past her.

'What did you say, love?' asked Mum, temporarily distracted by a tug-of-war with Alfie.

'Just going up to text Ruth.' Zak was quite proud of his quick thinking.

Cleo looked anything but impressed.


'More chicken, anyone? There's plenty left.'

Grace glanced around the table, her eyes coming to rest on Alfie whose ears had pricked up expectantly at the very mention of the word, and who was feigning invisibility as he wriggled across the floor on his stomach towards the delicious aroma that had wafted over to his bed in the corner of the room. Sussed.

'Alfie! Basket, now!'

His cover had been blown. Head down and tail between his legs, Alfie turned and walked slowly back to his corner.

'Bad dog!'

All he'd wanted was a piece of chicken. He lay down despondently and gave a sigh, simulating sleep, but keeping one eye alert to any falling morsels.

'Zak? I know you won't say no.' Grace scooped some onto his already mountainous plate. 'Cleo?'

'No thanks, Mum, I'm bursting already.'

'But you've hardly eaten a thing.'

15

Cleo just seemed to be moving the food around on her plate without actually consuming any of it.

'I had some crisps before and they filled me up. Sorry. I'll get something later if I'm hungry.'

'Oh Cleo, you're always doing that just lately.'

'I so am not! One day last week, and then today, that's all! Anyway it's your fault for making tea so late, we didn't used to have to wait until this time. Just 'cos Charlie's in late.' Cleo stabbed the tiniest piece of chicken with her fork and rammed it into her mouth with a grimace, her eyes brimming with unshed tears.

'Okay, sis, calm down.' Zak hated all this aggro.

'Shut it, you,' glowered Cleo.

'Fight! Fight! Fight!' chanted Izzy, banging her knife and fork rhythmically against the table.

'Alright everybody!' Charlie had had enough. 'Can we just enjoy the rest of our meal in peace please?'

Grace squeezed his hand gratefully. This masterful side of Charlie wasn't revealed very often, but she liked it. However, not everyone did.

'You're not my dad – you don't tell me what to do!' Cleo threw her knife and fork down onto her plate, leapt to her feet and ran upstairs.

'Cleo?' said Grace, about to follow.

'Leave her, Gracie, get your tea. She'll come round in her own time.'

But Grace was not so sure.

Later that evening when Izzy was safely tucked up in bed and Charlie was washing up, ably – or otherwise – assisted by Gran, Grace ventured upstairs to Cleo's room. All seemed to be quiet. She knocked gently on the door.

'Cleo?'

'Come in,' a sad voice responded.

Grace entered the room, closing the door quietly behind

her. Cleo was laid on her bed, eyes red-rimmed, a photo of Richard in her hand.

'Darling, what's wrong?' Grace sat on the bed beside her.

Cleo sat up and fell into her arms, sobbing as though her heart would break. 'I hate Charlie,' she spluttered. 'He can't tell me what to do.'

Grace stroked her hair back from her tear-stained face, soothingly. 'But he doesn't, he just tries to keep the peace, that's all.'

'I wish Dad was here.'

'I know you do, Cleo, but we've talked about all this before. You know your dad and me were never going to get back together, we're happier apart. And you know you can see him any time you want to – this weekend probably, if you like. Shall we give him a ring?'

'No point.'

'What do you mean "no point"? You know he loves having you round.'

'I mean "no point" because he's got a girlfriend now. I saw them in town. Didn't see me, though, they only had eyes for each other.' Cleo's downturned mouth quivered as she spoke. 'It'll be the same as you and Charlie: nobody wants me any more.'

Grace wiped away the tears that spilled down Cleo's face. 'Darling, don't ever think that, you know we love you. You and Zak and Izzy are the most important people in our lives, and I mean *all* of our lives. As for Dad, he's bound to have girlfriends, you can't expect him to be alone for the rest of his life. But that doesn't mean any of them are serious, I'm sure he would have told us if they were. In any case, even if he does meet someone one day you're still going to be your daddy's girl, you know you are. You know he loves you, don't you?'

Cleo nodded, a tremulous smile hovering on her lips. 'Thanks, Mum.'

Grace hugged her wayward daughter tightly, feeling closer to her than she had in a long time. 'Now, do you want to ring Dad about the weekend or shall I?'

By the time Grace came back downstairs everyone had disappeared. She thought she'd heard the door bang; Charlie must have taken Alfie for his nightly walk around the block – or the other way round, more like. He really did need training, that dog.

It was good to get a bit of peace at last and even better to think she'd managed to break down a bit of a barrier with Cleo tonight. She definitely should try to spend more time with her; it was just a question of organising herself.

'Gracie!' Charlie and Alfie were back. 'Could you do something with his feet, they're really dirty?'

'But Charlie, I've …'

'Sorry, but my feet are muddy as well, I need to scrape off my shoes.'

'Where on earth have you been? Oh Alfie! Naughty boy, get down!'

'Took him for a run on that field at the bottom; didn't realise how wet it was.'

'Evidently not.'

Into the chaos came Zak.

'Mum?' The worry of seeing Cleo that afternoon was still preying heavily on his mind. Grace looked up from her tangle of towel and wet dog. Can I have a word with you?'

'Not now, Zak, can't you see? Alfie! Sit!'

'It's about Cleo.'

'She's alright now, I had a talk to her earlier.'

'But Mum.'

'Not now Zak, okay?'

'But …'

'Zak! Alfie!'

And in came Gran, resplendent in pink hairnet and

quilted dressing gown. 'Would anyone like a nice cup of tea?'

'I thought you'd gone to bed, Mother.'

'I didn't want to miss anything, did I?'

'Not for me, thanks, Gran.'

'Not for you what?'

'Tea. You just asked if anyone would like a cup of tea.'

'Did I? Yes, that would be very nice dear, thank you,' said Gran, sitting at the table expectantly.

Sighing, Zak went to put the kettle on, his sister still filling his thoughts.

'About Cleo …'

'Zak! I said not now!'

'Disgrace, that one. That's who she takes after. Disgrace.'

'Mother!'

'What do you mean by that, Gran?'

'Nothing. She means nothing, do you Mother?'

The old lady remained silent, but Zak had never seen such a look of hatred on his grandmother's face before.

After the chat she'd had with Mum and then the telephone conversation she'd had with her dad, Cleo was feeling somewhat happier. Mum had been right about the woman she'd seen Dad with. It was nothing serious, just somebody he'd met through an Internet dating agency; there'd been a few of them apparently. Cleo had teased him about it mercilessly when he'd told her. They'd always got on so well together, shared the same sense of humour. She was a real daddy's girl.

He'd asked her whether she'd like to spend the weekend with him if she wasn't doing anything. He might even take her shopping into Manchester, Zak too if he wanted. Cleo didn't need any persuasion, it would be good to escape this madhouse. But she was sure Zak would be busy this weekend; she just wanted her dad all to herself.

Silence had pervaded the house, everyone must have gone to bed. Cleo looked at her watch: ten past eleven already? How did it get to that time? She tiptoed across the landing to the bathroom, startled as she came face to face with Zak outside the door.

'Hey, sis, been meaning to talk to you.'

'Not now, Zak, it's late.'

'Who was that you were with in the park?'

'None of your fuckin' business!'

Undeterred, Zak ploughed on. 'Well, that was obviously the only thing on his mind. He's way too old for you, whoever he is. You're fifteen, for God's sake! And why weren't you in school, anyway?'

'Who the hell do you think you are? My dad or something? You're not exactly Mr Innocent yourself, are you?'

'Well at least I'm over sixteen and haven't got the reputation for being a slag like you.'

'Cheeky sod. What about that slapper I saw ...'

'Cleo! Zak! What on earth is going on? You're going to wake up the whole house in a minute!' A sleep-bedraggled Grace had appeared from her bedroom. 'Can you please keep the noise down? What's the matter with you both, anyway?'

'Nothing Mum, sorry.' A crestfallen Zak gave his mother a hug. 'Go back to bed. We were just talking, that's all.'

'Well could you find a better time and place to do it next time, please? Goodnight!'

''Night Mum. Sorry.'

Zak turned back to look at Cleo, but too late. She'd taken the opportunity to sneak into the bathroom. The door was firmly closed.

Saturday morning arrived and so did Richard, on the doorstep to collect his daughter, who ran excitedly down the stairs, overnight bag in hand, at the first sound of his voice. After fending off Alfie, Richard hugged both her and Zak.

'You not coming with us, Zak?' Richard asked.

Cleo stared at her brother threateningly. She wanted some time alone with her dad.

Zak caught the look. Who wouldn't? 'No. Thanks anyway, but I've got a party to go to tonight over the other side of town. Maybe next time.'

'Okay, if you're sure. Perhaps we could meet up one night in the week. Go for a beer, or a Coke or something,' Richard grinned, not wanting his son to feel left out; he knew how possessive Cleo could be.

'Thanks, Dad, I'd like that. Give me a ring.'

'Will do, son. Ready?' he asked Cleo.

'That skirt's too short,' said Gran as they waved goodbye at the door. 'And how you could let her stay all night on her own with him I'll never know.'

Grace looked puzzled. 'He's her father.'

'He's a man, isn't he?'

'Mother, don't be so ridiculous!'

'Disgrace.'

'Mother!'

# 3

And so the all too familiar chaos of family life continued, with Grace in the pivotal role, trying to keep everyone happy. It was exhausting at times; well, all of the time, when she stopped to think about it. But despite everything she loved them all dearly and wouldn't have it any other way. She knew there'd come a time when they would all have flown the nest, and she couldn't begin to imagine what her life would be like then. Dull and boring, probably. Just imagine a home without children. But at least she'd still have Charlie. No, life as a singleton did not appeal to her at all. Grace loved the warmth and cosiness of family life. When she read of city pads and singles bars she could only feel sympathy for these people, wealthy or not. To her their lives sounded futile and desolate, a facade of success masking the emptiness within. Nevertheless, something was about to happen that would give her an unexpected insight into this alien world.

It started off as the usual kind of Monday morning. Charlie late for work, Zak hogging the bathroom, Cleo in a mood because she couldn't get a shower, Izzy covered in butter and marmalade, Gran confusing everyone with her own confusion, Alfie simulating sleep but with one eye firmly focused on any food that might come his way. And Grace? Grace running around after everyone, trying to keep the peace and looking forward to her *Jeremy Kyle* moment when she would be able to relax for half an hour with her cup of coffee and the newspaper.

The clang of the letterbox welcomed the day's post as it landed on the doormat with a thud.

'I'll get it! I'll get it!' Izzy shouted excitedly, scrambling down from her chair and depositing a trail of stickiness in her wake.

'Izzy! Get back here now!' The firmness of Charlie's voice stopped her in her tracks.

'You know you don't leave the table until you've asked, and you certainly don't go anywhere with hands like that!' Grace added.

'Sorry.' Izzy was subdued for a moment. 'But I've finished my breakfast now and I only wanted to get the letters.'

'Okay,' Grace relented. 'Get down and wash your hands first, though; nobody wants sticky letters to read.'

Izzy climbed down again, a marmalade-covered fragment of toast descending to the floor with her. Alfie's luck was in, his patience had paid off. Stealthily, surreptitiously, he slid swiftly from his …

'Alfie! Basket!'

Foiled again.

Hands washed, Izzy skipped down the hall, chanting, 'I'm being the postman! I'm being the postman!' returning with the bundle of letters like a prize trophy. 'All for Mummy,' she declared, depositing them proudly on Grace's lap.

Yes, Grace had actually sat down by this time. She flicked through them casually. Bills, bills, Charlie, junk mail, Zak (girlie writing – who's that from?) and me. Me? I don't usually get letters, not letter letters anyway. A London postmark? She slit open the envelope with her thumb and pulled out the contents inquisitively. Handwritten. She was intrigued. But not half as intrigued as she was when she turned it over to see who it was from. The name almost leapt off the page at her: Anna.

23

Her heart was beating so fast she thought she was going to pass out.

Charlie looked across at her with concern. 'You alright, Gracie?'

'Y-yes, f-fine,' she said, putting the letter back into its envelope and hiding it away in her pocket for later. Her left hand stroked her forehead in confusion.

'Pour your mother a cup of tea,' Charlie said to Zak, who appeared just at the right moment. 'She looks as though she's seen a ghost.'

Little did he know.

Grace could think of nothing but the letter as she completed everything she had to do in a trance-like, almost robotic state. But it was not until she returned from taking Izzy to nursery school that she had the opportunity to retrieve it from her pocket. Even then …

'Grace, I've put the kettle on, would you like a cup of tea?'

Mother.

'I thought you'd be watching *Jeremy Kyle*.'

'Not on. Cricket or tennis or something.'

Typical.

'Here, have this magazine to read, *This Morning* will be on soon.'

Her mother took it from her, tutted a few times as she saw the front cover and read what was in it, but thankfully headed towards her room.

Grace sat down heavily at the table, the letter in her hand.

'Grace?'

'For God's sake!'

'Have you seen my glasses?'

Letter back in her pocket, Grace searched around. She seemed to spend half her life searching for her mother's possessions just lately; no wonder she never got anything done.

'Here, in Alfie's basket of all places.'

'That dog'll be the death of me.'

'More like the other way round if they'd broken and cut him.'

'Why do I always get the blame for everything?'

'I'm not blaming anybody it's just … Oh, never mind, go and read your magazine.' Gran sat down at the table. 'Mother, I thought you were going to sit in your room for a bit like you usually do of a morning.'

'Oh, I see. Not wanted, am I? It's alright, you'll be old yourself one day then you'll know what it's like being on your own.'

'Mother, you're hardly on your own.'

'Alright, alright, I'm going. Keep your hair on. I'll head for the river if you like; that'll make everyone happy.'

'Don't be ridiculous, Mother.'

'Oh, ridiculous now, am I? Have you looked in the mirror lately?'

'Look, I don't want an argument. All I'm asking for is a bit of time on my own, half an hour. Is that too much to ask?'

Grace had the patience of a saint, it was a well-known fact, but she had to be on her own to read the letter. She couldn't possibly read it when anyone else was around, and it would be time to go for Izzy again soon; she'd need time to compose herself before then.

Finally, gums clenched, Gran stomped off, leaning on her walking stick. 'Oh, don't worry about me, I'll just sit in here on my own.'

Peace at last. Grace took the letter from her pocket and opened it once more. Her eyes skimmed over the address: 'Lavender Hill, Battersea', she read:

*Dear Grace,*

*I realise this letter has come completely out of the blue. Hearing from me again after all these years must have come as a bit of a shock to say the very least. I wasn't sure how to find you so I contacted the Salvation Army where we used to live. It was surprisingly straightforward, somebody there actually knew of you. Luckily, she said, you still live in the same village and she gave me your address. I hope she was correct and that this letter reaches you. I would so love to be able to make some form of contact.*

*What I would really like to do though, although I realise you may not want this, is …*

'Grace! Has that kettle boiled yet? I've been waiting all day for a cup of tea. But of course if it's too much trouble …' sniffed Gran.

The saint's patience was almost at breaking point. 'I'll bring it to your room,' she snapped. 'Just give me five minutes.'

'My, my, temper, temper,' huffed Gran. 'What's that you're reading?'

'Nothing. Now go and read your magazine, or watch *This Morning* or something. I'll be there in five minutes.'

'Exactly like your father you are. Never think of anyone but yourself.'

Grace refrained from responding, merely muttering, 'Yes, and I realise now what he had to put up with', under her breath as the heightened tap-tapping sound of the walking stick reverberated along the hall.

Somewhat flustered, Grace returned to the letter:

*What I would really like to do though, although I realise you may not want this, is to come and see you – get to know you again. You were only eight years old when I saw you last; so much has happened since then – to both of us, I'm sure.*

*It was all my fault that things happened the way they did and I should never have let it drift on for so long. But believe me when I tell you that I love my little sister and not a day has gone by when I haven't thought of you. You must wonder why I never tried to contact you before and I can only admit that I was a coward. I was afraid of being rejected by you as well as by our parents. You were too young at the time to understand all that happened to me but I can only hope that, given time, I can explain it all to you, and I pray that within your heart you will be able to forgive me.*

*I don't know how you would feel about this, but in a couple of weeks I have some leave from work and I should like nothing better than to come and stay with you for a few days if that's possible. Perhaps you could have a think about it and let me know. I would so love to see you again. Nevertheless I will equally understand if you never want to see me again having taken off like that. Abandoning you to a life of what? I don't know. And you will never know how much guilt that causes me to feel.*

*I hope above hope that I shall hear from you soon, although I will totally understand if I do not.*
*Be happy.*
*All my love*
*Anna*

The letter blurred before Grace's eyes. A tear overflowed, rolled down her cheek and plopped onto the table. It was followed by another. What had made Anna try to make contact after all this time? Alfie, sensing her sadness, left his basket and came over to her. Leaning heavily against her leg with a sigh, he nuzzled her lap, looking up at her with big sad eyes. Grace stroked his head absent-mindedly, drawing comfort from the warmth of his soft furry body.

Anna had been sixteen when she'd left home. Her departure had been sudden and was shrouded in mystery. When

Grace had asked her parents where Anna had gone, she was told to mind her own business and not to ask questions about things that didn't concern her. She never got answers to her questions, no matter how hard she tried. Her parents just seemed to have drawn a line under the fact that her sister had ever existed, and if ever Grace tried to cross that line she found herself severely punished. Anna's name was never mentioned at home again, and eventually Grace came to accept that that was the way it had to be. She could only think that her sister must have done something really evil, as she submitted to living life as an only child.

The only time she was able to mention her sister's name was when she was with her friends, and for a time after Anna's disappearance they would concoct stories and make-believe games about Anna the murderer, Anna the burglar, Anna the kidnapper, Anna the whatever. Stories of her infamous sister gave Grace great street cred amongst her peers for a while, although the novelty of hearing about the disappearing sister soon wore off after little Billy Banks's father robbed the local post office using a sawn-off shotgun. Anna became yesterday's news and Grace was glad; the stories she'd been telling, the games she'd played, were all bravado. Underneath it all she really missed her sister and desperately wished she'd come home.

Eventually the pain of separation had become less; Grace had got on with her life, she had no choice. But home had become a much duller place without …

'Grace! I take it you do know what time it is?'

Grace reined herself back to the present in an instant and focused on the clock.

'Mother! Why didn't you tell me?' Hurriedly she folded the letter back into her pocket and ran to get her coat from under the stairs, Alfie hot on her heels. 'Sorry, Alfie, not now, I'm in a hurry. Why didn't you tell me, Mother? I'm going to be late for Izzy now.'

'Well, I might have known. My fault again. Can't win with you, can I? I did tell you, if you remember, otherwise you'd still be sat there now with your head in the clouds. Always have to blame somebody else, don't you? And it's usually me. Have you seen my teeth?'

'*Your teeth?* Oh Mother, for goodness sake, I haven't got time now. Have a good look for them while I'm out.'

'Do I have to do everything around here? I don't know how you'd manage without me, I really don't.'

'Just find your teeth, Mother,' said Grace through her own gritted ones. 'Nobody's going to be happy if they turn up in the biscuit barrel again.'

'You know, I think you might be right. I took them out when I was dunking that biscuit this morning …'

Grace was oozing with guilt as she rushed to nursery school. Bad mother … abandoned child … Breathlessly, she burst in through the door to see Izzy sitting with her coat on, clutching a picture and chattering happily to Mrs Clarke. Even the stragglers had gone.

'I'm so, so sorry,' gasped Grace, 'I didn't …'

'That's alright, you're here now.' Mrs Clarke's face said that her lunch break was long overdue.

'Nice picture, Izzy. Some sheep in a field.'

'No, silly. That's Gran's teeth in the biscuit barrel. She put them in there when I was eating my toast.'

'The things they come out with.' Mrs Clarke's starving features rearranged themselves into something approaching a smile.

'Indeed,' grimaced Grace nervously, taking her daughter's hand and bidding a hasty retreat through the door.

Outside, she was helpless with laughter.

'What are you laughing at, Mummy?'

'I'm laughing at you, Izzy,' gasped Grace, 'painting a picture of Gran's teeth.'

29

'That's not funny, Mummy. It's a good picture, Mrs Clarke said so.'

'Sorry. It is a good picture, Izzy, I shouldn't have laughed.'

'Why are your eyes all red?'

Did nothing get past this child?

For the remainder of the day Grace, understandably, could think of nothing but Anna. Of course she had to see her, no question about it. She was desperate to see her, in fact, desperate to know why she'd left under such a dark cloud of mystery, why she'd never made contact during all of those intervening years, why her name had never been allowed to be mentioned – so many questions. The jumble of thoughts raced round and round inside Grace's head, making it impossible for her to concentrate on anything else. She could feel herself being unfairly short-tempered with Izzy's constant questions, and her mother's inane ramblings were driving her insane. She sent Izzy out to play in the garden with Alfie and suggested her mother might like to try doing a bit of knitting in her room where the light was better. Izzy was easy and raced out of the door. Her mother was somewhat more reluctant.

'Okay, I get the message. I know when I'm not wanted. You'll know what it's like one day.'

But at least she went.

Grace took out the letter again; postal address, e-mail and phone number. Anna was certainly giving her all the options. She'd just have to discuss it with everyone later and then … send her an e-mail maybe? A letter would take too long, and to phone up – she didn't feel quite brave enough to do that yet; an e-mail seemed a lot less confrontational. Just have to discuss it first. That sounded so simple and straightforward, as she was sure it would be, or relatively so anyway, with all of them. But her mother? That was going to be horrendous. Strange, when you came to think about it, how her mother forgot everything else and yet, when it came to Anna, her mother's mind was sharper than Carol Vorderman's used to be on *Countdown*.

Well, whatever. This was Grace's house and if she wanted Anna to come and stay, then stay she would. Grace was not a little girl any more and her mother couldn't tell her what to do. If she didn't like it then that was her tough luck. The trouble was, her mother still did have that capacity to make her feel like a naughty child again and she knew exactly how scared she was at the prospect of telling her of the impending visit. Guilty about the secretive way she'd hidden the letter and petrified of informing her of its existence.

'Hey, Mum!'

The slam of the front door heralded the arrival of Zak back from college. Oh, and Cleo too.

'It's not often you two arrive home at the same time,' Grace babbled, trying to gather herself together quickly and forcing a smile. 'Had a good day?'

'Is that your only question, Mum? You're slipping, it's usually "What do you know?" "Who did you pull?"'

'Cheeky sod!' Grace smiled, more relaxed now. 'I like to keep up, that's all, and keeping track of your ever-changing line of girlfriends takes some doing. They'd have more luck catching a Virgin Train. Get it?'

'Mum! That's bad, even for you! What's that you've got anyway? A letter from a long-lost lover?'

Grace, temporarily distracted, had forgotten the letter was still on the table in front of her. Hastily she picked it up and furtively returned it to its envelope.

'Aha! I was right! I was only joking then but you should see your face – guilty or what?'

Cleo came over from the fridge where she'd been pouring a drink for herself. 'Isn't that the letter that came for you this morning, the one that made you turn a funny

31

colour, and then you hid it in your pocket? Big secret, I'd say!'

Secrets around here? They must be joking!

'Stop it, you two, of course it's not a secret. It just came as a bit of a shock this morning, that's all. It's a letter from my long-lost sister, your Auntie Anna, who I haven't seen since I was a little girl. She wants to come and stay.'

'Wow!'

'I know. You see now why it was such a shock?'

'What are you going to do? Is she coming? What about Gran?'

Zak and Cleo were full of questions. They'd been told, over the years, different things about their aunt, but to them she'd just seemed like a character from a storybook. They'd never expected actually to meet her.

Cleo sat down with her glass of orange juice. 'So when is she coming?'

'When is who coming?' Izzy had sneaked in through the back door unnoticed, unusually silenced by the seriousness of their conversation.

Grace was flustered, not really wanting Izzy to know at this stage, not before she'd thought of how to explain it to her mother and discussed it with Charlie. Izzy's mouth did have a tendency to run away with her at times, like all children's.

'Oh ... er ... um ... Daddy. What have you been up to with Alfie?'

But Izzy wasn't stupid. 'Not Daddy, silly. You said "when is *she* coming?"'

Izzy scrambled up onto Grace's knee and looked into her eyes. Oh, where was the harm? She'd have to know sooner or later.

'Auntie Anna. She wants to come and visit us.'

'Auntie Anna? Who's Auntie Anna?'

'My sister. Remember? I told you I had a sister but I

hadn't seen her for a very long time.'

Izzy looked thoughtful and fiddled with Grace's earring. 'Like Cleo's my sister?'

'That's right, just like that. She wants to come and stay with us for a while. That's okay, isn't it?'

'S'pose.' Izzy concentrated on the earring. 'Will I like her?'

'I'm sure you will, Izzy. You like everyone. Anyway, as I was saying' – Grace turned her attention back to the other two – 'she's hopefully going to be here in a couple of weeks and I'm really looking forward to seeing her again. It's going to seem weird, though. I'd practically forgotten I'd got a sister. After all I was only eight when she left and she … well, she was about the same age as Cleo is now.'

Izzy's eyes rounded. 'Will Cleo go as well?'

Cleo laughed. 'Pea brain! I'm not going anywhere, am I? Although I wish I could sometimes, with a sister like you.'

'Cleo! That's not very nice. Say sorry to her now!'

'Sorry, Iz.'

Izzy slid down from Grace's lap and danced around the kitchen chanting, 'Pea brain, pea brain, Cleo is a pea brain!'

'Izzy!'

Why did everything always have to descend into chaos?

'Anyway, all I wanted to say was, please don't mention any of this in front of Charlie or Gran, not until I've had a chance to talk to them about it properly. That goes for you too, Izzy. Don't tell Daddy or Gran, okay?'

'Your secret's safe with us, Ma,' winked Zak, gathering his things together and disappearing up to his room.

'Secret, secret, we've got a secret!'

'Izzy!'

It wasn't until they were in bed that night that Grace got a chance to talk to Charlie but, as she'd anticipated, he was quite amenable to the impending visit. He knew how the departure of her sister all those years ago had left a huge gap in her life. Although she hadn't talked to him a lot about it, he sensed her loss, saw the sadness in her eyes on the odd occasion when the subject cropped up.

He'd sometimes wondered why Grace had never tried to trace Anna, He was sure he would have done in her situation. But then, he was an only child, so what did he know? He sure as hell knew one thing, though. He loved this woman. Would do anything for her. He turned to look at her sleeping form, watching the rise and fall of the sheet on her breast with each breath as she slept. His Gracie.

He tried to focus his mind instead of his body. Think about her mother, that should soon quell any flames of desire. How on earth was Grace going to break the news? 'Oh, by the way, Mother, Anna's coming to stay', 'Very nice, dear'. He didn't think so, somehow. Gran had always been so domineering: he could understand Grace's trepidation. Whatever had happened all those years ago must certainly have been big to have caused such a family rift.

Talking about big. He put his hand under the bedcovers and felt himself, he'd explode in a minute. He shuffled up next to Grace, breathing heavily, hoping the movement might disturb her. No such luck.

Pressing himself up against her, he whispered, 'Gracie?'

'Mm?'

'I love you.'

'Me too, go to sleep.'

'But Gracie I ...'

She yawned and ... was that her body writhing with desire or just a stretch? Just a stretch.

'What time is it?'

'Time to make love to me,' he groaned, his passion all-consuming.

'Oh Charlie,' she smiled, turning her head to face him.

He loved her so much, this big teddy bear of a man.

And as he found relief in her welcoming flesh she realised how lucky she was to have found him.

# 4

Of course, how else would the news have been broken except in the form of a bombshell dropped by Izzy?

'We've got a secret.' Izzy's smug little face beamed across the table.

'Izzy!' Grace threatened, 'strict mother' style.

'That's nice, dear.' Gran concentrated on her dunking, bereft of teeth.

Undeterred, Izzy continued. 'Auntie Anna's coming.'

Bomb dropped. A two-second silence. The half-dunked biscuit dropped into the tea with a plop.

'*What* did you say?'

Spoonfuls of cereal that, prior to this moment, were being hastily shovelled towards mouths, suddenly stopped mid-flight.

'Erm … time to go, I'm late.'

'Charlie!'

'Sorry, Grace, but I am. I was meant to be there half an hour ago.' Charlie hated confrontation.

'Well, tough. Sit down.'

Cleo spluttered nervously into her cereal, splattering milk onto the table. Zak gave her a warning look. Gran, amazingly not deaf on this occasion, had heard Izzy loud and clear. Her beady eyes scanned the faces around the table.

'Could somebody please tell me what's going on?'

Grace appeared amazingly calm. 'Izzy's right, Mother, although I didn't mean you to hear it quite as bluntly as that. I've had a letter from Anna and she wants to come and

36

stay with us for a few days.'

'Over my dead body.'

Grace just hoped it wouldn't be. She knew her mother had problems with her blood pressure and she was looking extraordinarily puce. Nevertheless, she was determined to stand her ground. She was nearly forty years old, for God's sake; time she took control.

'Mother, Anna is my sister whether you like it or not. You drove her away and kept us apart for all these years. She's been brave enough to take that first step towards us getting to know each other again by writing the letter. If she wants to come here, and I want it too, then come here she will no matter what you say. You don't rule the roost any more.'

It was an emotive speech from Grace; the tears welling in her eyes threatened to overflow, but somehow she managed to keep control.

'Go Mum! Go Mum!' chanted Zak under his breath.

Cleo emitted a tiny giggle of embarrassment.

'There is absolutely no way that that … that disgrace ever crosses this doorstep!' Gran snorted in fury.

'Then she'll just have to come in through the other door,' retorted Grace haughtily, 'because, if you remember, Mother dear, this is my house not yours and what I say goes. You are, in fact, just the lodger here and if you don't like it you know what you can do.'

There was a stunned silence around the breakfast table. Taking a deep breath, Grace rose to her feet and started to clear away the dirty dishes. Gran also got up from her seat or, rather, tried to. Playing for sympathy, she suddenly seemed to have lost the use of her limbs.

'Could you help me up, Zak, if you don't mind? You're such a good boy, the only one that's got any sense around here. I've never heard anything like it! Talking to a poor defenceless old woman like that. She should be ashamed of herself. Thinks she knows it all, she does – but just wait.'

As Zak helped her to stand she turned to Grace. 'I'm going to my room until you come to your senses.' Then, hobbling down the hall in true drama queen style, she said in her best old-lady voice that was reserved for special occasions, 'Could somebody bring me a glass of water? I won't trouble you for tea.'

Grandma didn't emerge from her room for the rest of the day. Grace felt an enormous amount of guilt but knew she couldn't back down. For her own peace of mind she had to see Anna again and hear her story. Lunchtime came and went but Gran did not appear. Grace knocked on the door with a plate of sandwiches but the only response she got was 'Go away'. She said she'd leave them outside the door and, miraculously, they disappeared within seconds. (No, it wasn't Alfie.) Teatime brought a similar performance with Zak delivering her meal ('Bless him'). How long was she going to keep this up?

Despite the guilt, Grace remained undeterred. Nervously, she sent an e-mail to Anna saying how pleased she'd been to receive the letter, and that of course she could come to stay. It was hard to word the message, difficult to know exactly what to put into it. She was sure Anna would be just like she was herself: dissecting each sentence, searching for hidden meanings. Best to keep it brief, she thought, the basic facts. Welcoming but not overpowering; she didn't want to frighten her away. She told her about Charlie and about Zak, Cleo and Izzy. She told her that Father had died a few years ago. But Mother? Grace didn't know what to say about her. Just told her she was living with them now – what more could she do?

Next morning when Grace came downstairs, Gran had actually left her room and was in the middle of her tea and soggy biscuits ritual. Old habits die hard. Maybe she'd be somewhat more compliant today. One could but hope.

'Good morning, Mother. Sleep well?'

'Hmmphh.'

Well, maybe not. Grace set the table for breakfast and put some bread in the toaster.

'Has Alfie been out?'

No response.

Grace let him out anyway, and filled the kettle. 'Nice day.'

No comment.

'You're going to have to speak soon, Mother. She is coming and that's an end to it.'

'I don't know how you can be so cruel.'

'Cruel?! Do you think that wasn't cruel, banishing my sister and keeping us apart for all those years?'

'Think you know everything, don't you?'

'I know I would never do anything like that to my children, that's what I know.' Grace took out her anger on the tea caddy as she replaced the lid with a resounding thud, and then on the cutlery as she slammed down the place settings on the table.

'What's that smell? Mum! The toast's on fire!' A timely entrance from Zak.

Once again, Grace tipped out the charred remains. They really must buy a new toaster.

'Mum … back late tonight … won't need any tea.'

'Cleo? What do you mean? Where are you going? Come here a minute, you've not even had any breakfast.'

'In a rush, Mum,' said Cleo, struggling into her coat and flinging her rucksack over her shoulder. 'Here, I'll take a piece of this to eat on the way if it makes you happy,' she said, looking with some disdain at the least-blackened piece on the heap. 'See ya.'

'But Cleo …!'

Too late. The door slammed behind her.

Zak lifted the cereal boxes down from the cupboard. 'I'm

worried about Cleo, Mum. She's hanging around with all sorts of oddballs just lately.'

'What d'you mean "oddballs"?'

'Dunno. Different lads. Even tried it on with one of my mates the other day. Then last week, I saw her in the park with this older guy, hands all over her.'

'Zak! Why didn't you tell me?'

'Sorry, Mum, I didn't like to dob. But it was in the afternoon so she must have bunked off school as well.'

'Zak!'

'I know. I did try to stop her but she told me to ... well, you can guess what she told me to do. I tried talking to her later but ... sorry Mum.'

'Huh! Think yourself a good mother do you?'

'Mother!'

'I shall be in my room,' sniffed Gran, painful limbs forgotten, as she marched haughtily towards the door, head held high.

As if Grace didn't have enough problems. She tried Cleo's mobile but, predictably, it was switched off. Other than discussing it with Richard there was nothing more she could do for the moment. Charlie didn't seem to understand. He thought she was making a fuss about nothing and that she shouldn't play the heavy mother all the time. It was all part of growing up, just a rebellious teenager phase, she'd get over it. But then, Cleo wasn't his own flesh and blood, so maybe he didn't feel this protective instinct quite so intensely. She was only fifteen for God's sake!

'Do you want me to take Izzy this morning? I've got a late start.' Charlie came downstairs, Izzy in his arms stretching his mouth into strange shapes with her fingers as he spoke.

He removed her probing digits and put her down. She rushed over to give Grace a good morning kiss and then shot out into the garden in search of Alfie.

'Izzy don't ...' but it was too late. Alfie gave Izzy an overly

40

affectionate greeting but, having been out in the wet garden for the past half-hour, this was not the best of ideas.

Izzy rushed back in, closely followed by her filthy four-legged friend. 'What did you say, Mummy?'

'Just look at the state of you! You're covered in mud! What did you let him jump all over you for?'

Izzy looked down at her clothes. 'Oops,' she bit on her bottom lip and rolled her big blue eyes. 'Mrs Clarke'll not like that.'

Charlie could see Grace was furious; she was so stressed out just lately. 'Here,' he said, taking charge, 'sit down and get your breakfast, I'll sort her out.'

Whatever had she done to deserve this man? She pushed Alfie back out through the door and headed back to the toaster.

'Mum?'

'God, Zak! You were so quiet I'd almost forgotten you were here!'

'Sorry, I wanted to ask a favour. Would it be okay to ask a few mates round on Saturday? Watch the footie and have a few cans?'

'Zak! D'you think I haven't got enough to put up with? No you cannot! Now get to college and leave me in peace.'

'Sorry,' he gathered his things together. 'See ya later.'

'See ya,' she said, feeling guilty, her tear-blurred eyes following him as he went out through the door.

Perhaps she wasn't the good mother she'd thought she was.


Grace decided to pamper herself with a long relaxing soak in the bath once Charlie had headed off to work, dropping Izzy off at nursery school on his way. She poured in some of the bath oil Richard had bought her for Christmas. Funny, they still bought each other Christmas presents even though they'd been divorced for all this time. Calming, soothing, a promise of tranquility – everything she needed in a bottle of bath oil. She tested the water temperature tentatively with her toe. Perfect. Into it she slid, and lay back, languishing in the luxury of it all. This was the life. The cares of the day just floating away.

Her thoughts drifted back to Richard. She wished he could find someone to share his life with like she had; he always looked so lost on his own. He'd tried Internet dating a few times but it never seemed to work out for him. Still, maybe one day … She smiled to herself as she thought of how he always rang her to report on his latest conquests. Funny, that. They'd actually been closer in some ways since the divorce than they had during the final few years of their marriage. It was good that they were able to talk to each other, though: it certainly made it easier with Zak and Cleo that they were still a team when it came to parenting. Perhaps she should try ringing Richard today actually; she could really do with his input into this Cleo situation. Charlie reckoned it was just a rebellious teenager phase she'd grow out of, but to Grace, things seemed to be going from bad to worse.

Time, unfortunately, was ticking by. Reluctantly, Grace realised she must relinquish her relaxing aromas and get herself ready for the day ahead, whatever that may bring. It certainly hadn't got off to the best of starts so hopefully things could only get better.

Quickly she got dressed and went downstairs, where a scratching at the back door led her to investigate. Poor Alfie, she'd forgotten all about him. A by now drip-dried dog sat dolefully on the doorstep. But she was his very favourite person, and soon forgiven, as he bounded into the house all tongue and tail to give her a rapturous greeting.

Sitting with Alfie lolling lovingly against her, Grace texted Zak. She hadn't meant to snap at him like that when he hadn't done anything wrong and she felt better for apologising. She'd talk to him later about having his mates round; he didn't ask for much. Conscience slightly assuaged, she tried ringing Richard's mobile, hoping he might be able to meet up with her later in the day to discuss the problem of Cleo – yet again. But Richard had troubles of his own at the moment. He was late for a business meeting in Birmingham and had been stuck in a traffic jam on the M6 for the past three-quarters of an hour. There must have been an accident or something. Nevertheless, he was pleased to hear another human voice over his hands-free, even one with problems, and Grace was glad to be able to offload some of her worries about Cleo onto him. They agreed to show a united front and sit down together with Cleo on Saturday for a serious talk about her behaviour. That's if they could get her to sit down with them in the first place. Richard reckoned Cleo wouldn't be able to resist him cooking a meal for just the three of them at his place. Grace had her reservations, although Richard could be quite persuasive – he wasn't in sales for nothing. Charlie wouldn't be happy, but he'd simply have to understand that it was for the good of Cleo.

Feeling much happier, Grace glanced at the clock. She'd just got time to check her e-mails quickly before going to collect Izzy. Poor Alfie. He got pushed to one side yet again and headed for his basket where he scratched up his bedding into a comfortable heap and lay down on top of it with a groan, one eye still following Grace, who was moving some unwashed dishes from the table into the sink. The minute she disappeared through the door Alfie was behind her, as if he was attached to her heel by an invisible thread, padding down the hall to the study.

Grace turned on the computer and clicked on Hotmail.

'Anna Chapman. My visit.'

Grace's heart turned a somersault and leapt into her throat as she clicked again to read the message:

*Hi Grace,*
*Thank you so, so much for getting in touch, you don't know*
*what this means to me. Can't wait to see you and meet your*
*family – I'm so excited! Mother's living with you now? Is she*
*okay about me coming? If it's alright with you I'll be coming a*
*week on Saturday (25th) and should be there about 2-ish (I'm*
*driving up so that's traffic permitting).*
*See you soon (that sounds so odd!!)*
*Lots of love*
*Anna xx*

Emotion swept through Grace like a tidal wave. Her
sister! She was actually going to see her sister! Late as she
was (again) to collect Izzy, she just had to reply:

*Hi Anna,*
*I can't wait either! Excited is an understatement!! Yes, I'm*
*afraid Mother is living with us and no, although I hate to say*
*it, she's not happy about your visit. She's suffering from*
*dementia now but she has her own little granny flat within*
*our house and hopefully she'll be okay when you're here. She*
*has the option of staying in her room if she's not so don't let*
*that put you off at all. We're all desperate to see you – 25th*
*can't come soon enough for us!!*
*Counting the days.*
*Lots of love*
*Grace xx*

Elated by the anticipation of seeing Anna again, Grace
turned off the computer, locked Alfie back in the kitchen
and quickly grabbed her coat. Why was she always late? But
she was too excited to feel guilty today. Mrs Clarke could
give her all the 'bad mother' looks she liked – it wasn't
every day you were reunited with your long-lost sister.

44

Saturday worked out quite well in the end, despite Charlie being a bit miffed at the prospect of Grace spending time with Richard. He didn't understand why they were making such a big deal out of it: Cleo was just being a teenager, that was all. There was no point in arguing with him; he could be so stubborn at times. Basically, though, as Grace realised, Charlie was jealous of Richard. She could understand to a certain extent his jealousy of their shared parentage of Zak and Cleo: that must make him feel excluded at times, but it was unavoidable. Richard was their father and wanted to be involved in their welfare. It was not up to her to push him away and, besides, it wouldn't be fair on the children. Children? They were hardly that any more. But still full of problems nevertheless.

Grace had relented with Zak. Of course he could have his mates round for the football – as long as they didn't wreck the house in her absence. No, she trusted them ... pretty much, anyway. They were a nice bunch of lads, Zak's mates. They'd asked Charlie to watch the match with them, but he'd opted to take Izzy to the zoo. It would be nice for him to spend some quality time with her on his own, he didn't get the chance very often. The boys could have Gran instead, she'd keep them entertained; although Zak was praying she'd be staying in her room. Grace couldn't imagine why.

The offer of Richard cooking a meal for just the three of them had, as predicted, been too good for Cleo to resist. He'd made a lasagne with salad, amazing even Grace with his skill.

'See,' he said, when Cleo had gone to use the bathroom, 'nothing wrong with her appetite there. She ate nearly the same amount as the two of us put together. I think you worry a bit too much sometimes.'

Maybe he was right, she did have a tendency to panic and she'd convinced herself that Cleo was anorexic on top of everything else. But she'd been fine today, wolfed down everything in sight.

'Okay, okay, it's probably just me being paranoid.' She hated that smug look he had when he was right. 'That doesn't get rid of the other problems though.'

'Talking about me?'

Grace looked somewhat shamefaced; she didn't want Cleo to think they'd been talking about her behind her back as soon as she'd left the room. But Cleo was all smiles. What a changed person she was today. Cleo sat on the arm of her father's chair and hugged him.

'It's really good us all being together – I love it,' she said, looking happier than Grace had seen her in a long time.

'Well, maybe we can spend a bit more time together if you start behaving yourself, young lady. No more bunking off school and chasing after every male in sight.'

'Dad!'

'You know what I'm talking about. You're getting yourself a bit of a reputation and your mum and I worry about you. We just want what's best for you, that's all. You get your act together and there'll be more days like this, I promise.'

'Sorry, Dad,' said Cleo, tears welling, 'I know I need to sort myself out.'

'Come here, daftie,' he said, holding her close.

Looking at the two of them together, Grace realised just how much Cleo was missing her dad as she grew up. It probably was at the root of most of her problems. Searching for a father figure in all these guys she was chasing, though, was certainly treading on dangerous ground. Grace knew Charlie was not going to be happy at the prospect of her spending more time with Richard, but if it was for the good of Cleo, it would have to be done.

# 5

And so the day dawned. Grace's eyes sprang open with the sudden realisation that it was finally here. She was going to see her sister *today*! A shudder of trepidation rippled down her spine but was quickly overpowered by the excitement that coursed through her veins. Her heart pounded furiously and she put a hand on her chest to quell its beating. She couldn't have a heart attack, not today.

'Charlie!'

'Hmmphh.'

'Charlie!'

She tapped him, not gently, then jabbed at his leg with her toe.

'Wassupp?'

He couldn't believe his luck, she wasn't usually this eager. Her initiative sparked his arousal as he stretched to wake himself and turned to face her, his protuberance prodding purposefully towards her.

'Charlie!'

'What? I thought that's what you wanted,' he said, eyes half closed with euphoria.

Grace tried to disentangle herself from his desirous arms and deflate his ardour. Her libido was not in full flow. She did not succeed.

'But Charlie, my sister …'

His mouth came down on hers as his body moved above her. She was helpless to resist and submitted to his needs, although her mind was anywhere but here. Hopefully he

47

wouldn't be long … and he wasn't.

As he came to a juddering halt and rolled off her, he caught his breath and said cheekily, 'You were saying?'

'I said, my sister is coming today.'

'And you?' he asked, grinning like a Cheshire cat, melting her somewhat.

'Nowhere near it yet,' she said, turning towards him. She wasn't made of stone, after all.

'Mummy! Mummy! Mummy!' Izzy bounded in through the bedroom door and landed on top of them with a thud. 'Cleo said to tell you it's eleven o'clock.'

'Oh my God!' Grace sat bolt upright in bed. 'We must have gone back to sleep!'

Izzy stared at her inquisitively. 'Where's your nightie?'

Grace glanced down at herself, suddenly embarrassed by her nakedness. 'Oh, I was hot in bed last night,' she said, bashfully.

'Indeed you were,' piped up a voice from the pillow next to hers.

Grace shot him a withering look, thinking it was a pity she hadn't done that earlier. 'Tell Cleo I'm coming in a minute.'

'Again?' grinned the voice.

Izzy looked confused. Her mummy and daddy had gone mad. She jumped off the bed and ran back down the stairs to the insanity of grandma.

Grace leapt out of bed. 'Charlie, get up!'

But Charlie lay there, a bemused look on his face. 'You want more? I'm not sure that I can, so quickly.'

'For goodness sake! She'll be here soon … my sister. I can't believe it!' grinned Grace, rushing to the shower in a flurry of excitement.

By the time Grace got downstairs, Cleo had everything

under control. She'd been a changed person since that day they'd spent with Richard.

'Aw Cleo, thank you!' Grace gave her a hug. 'Whatever time did you get up this morning? You must have worked really hard – the place looks immaculate.'

'I can be good sometimes,' grinned Cleo. 'Zak helped as well. Oh, and Izzy,' she added, noticing her little sister standing with hands on hips, looking somewhat disgruntled. 'We thought it'd be a nice surprise for you, I know how nervous you must be feeling about today.'

'Well thanks, love, you've all done a really good job. You too, Izzy,' she said, kissing her youngest. 'Where's Zak?'

'He went to take Alfie for a walk, tire him out a bit.'

'My, my, we are organised.'

Gran remained silent, sitting at the table with a face like thunder, not even dunking today.

'And how are you today, Mother? Looking forward to the visit?' Grace couldn't help herself sometimes.

'I don't know how you could,' muttered Gran, gums pursed. 'How you could let that … that disgrace walk back into our lives I shall never know.'

'What's so bad about Auntie Anna, Gran?' asked Cleo, as she finished drying the dishes.

It was a question Grace had been trying to find the answer to for years but, as usual, none was forthcoming. Gran got to her feet and stomped down the hall with her stick.

'You'd better be nice to her when she gets here,' threatened Grace to the retreating figure.

'Ann-tee Ann-na, Ann-tee Ann-na, Ann-tee Ann-na,' chanted Izzy, skipping around with excitement.

Two o'clock came and went.

'She's not coming.' Grace was feeling the strain.

It was ten minutes to three when Izzy heard the sound of

a car and raced to the window to investigate. 'She's here! She's here!' she yelled, dancing up and down.

Grace leapt to her feet and followed Izzy to the front door, her heart pounding in anxious anticipation. The others followed at a discrete distance, curiosity about this hitherto unseen relative overcoming their reticence. Gran stayed in her room.

Anna had approached the house with some trepidation but she need not have worried. She didn't even have to ring the bell. As she approached, the door flew open to a rapturous welcome, especially from Grace, who enfolded her in her arms with tears of absolute joy. It was impossible to explain how good it felt to be reunited again as they clung together in wonderment, interrupted only by the voice of innocence.

'Hello, I'm Izzy.'

Reluctantly, Anna broke away from her newly discovered sister, almost blinded by the mist of emotion. She dried her eyes on the backs of her hands to clear her vision, and looked down to see the cutest niece ever.

'My, you are a little poppet, aren't you?' she smiled, as she bent down to give her a hug.

The cute niece looked mystified and wrinkled her button nose. 'No, I'm Izzy.' Then, smiling up, she studied this new auntie. 'You look just like my mummy, but she's fat.'

'Hey, cheeky,' grinned Grace. 'But you're right, I wish I was nice and slim like Anna. Look at the figure on you,' she said admiringly, looking her sister up and down. 'How do you get to be so trim?'

Anna shrugged off the question with a smile. 'Never mind about me, are you going to introduce me to the rest of your family or what?'

Formal introductions over, they adjourned to the lounge to get to know each other a little better. Charlie felt a bit uncomfortable about the situation; he'd never come across anything quite like this before. He carried Anna's suitcase up to her room and then went to put the kettle on.

'Tea anyone? Anna?' he asked, popping his head around the lounge door. Izzy was right, she did look remarkably like Grace, but a bit too skinny for his liking.

'Thanks, that would be lovely. Do you have herbal?'

'Herbal?' She might as well have asked Charlie to fly to the moon.

'Sorry, Anna,' smiled Grace, 'you're back up north now, nowt like a good old fashioned cup o'tea. Or there's coffee, if you'd prefer it?'

'See, Mum, I've been asking you to get me some of that herbal stuff for ages.' Cleo shot her aunt a conspiratorial glance.

Anna could see she'd acquired a fan and gave her a wink. 'We'll go to the shop together and get some tomorrow – they don't know what they're missing, do they? I will have a tea though, thanks Charlie. Black, no sugar.'

Black? No sugar? No wonder she was so skinny. He wandered to the kitchen, knocking on Gran's door as he passed.

'Making some tea, would you like a cup?'

'No thank you.'

Blimey, things must be bad.

Grace, on the other hand, just couldn't take her eyes off her sister. It was surreal being together again after all this time, and yet it was as though they'd never been apart. She couldn't wait to ask her about the intervening years, to know how her life had been and how it was now, to find out why and where she'd gone – so many questions. But now wasn't the right time. Anna looked exhausted after her journey. Grace had survived this long without any answers; she could surely wait a bit longer. Anna was going to be staying for a few days, there would be time enough.

Despite herself, Anna couldn't help watching Zak. He was beginning to feel a bit embarrassed by the way her eyes kept wandering back to him and his cheeks reddened under her gaze. She suddenly realised she was the cause of his blushes.

'Sorry, Zak, I didn't mean to stare, but you bear an uncanny resemblance to someone I know,' she said, flustered by her admission.

'Someone from work?'

'No, just someone,' she said, guardedly.

Charlie returned with the tea, putting any further questions in abeyance. Anna expressed her gratitude, which was not just for the tea.

And Izzy? She expressed her approval by perching herself on her auntie's knee and giving her a hug. 'I love you, Auntie Anna,' she said.

Anna's eyes welled with the emotion of her acceptance as she hugged her back. 'And I love you too, poppet.'

Izzy leant back from the hug and put her hands firmly on her hips. 'My name's Izzy, not poppet,' she said, instigating laughter all round.

'Izzy, I shall remember that in future,' smiled Anna, unashamedly letting the tears trickle down her cheeks.

All afternoon Grace was desperate for everyone to go away so that she could spend some time alone with Anna. Selfish as that seemed, they needed to talk. That was the trouble with this household, it was always so full of people. Constant comings and goings and never any privacy. But, after their meal this evening, she'd gladly agreed when both Cleo and Zak had asked if they could go out. Cleo was going to Lisa's, or at least that's what she said. Grace was trying hard to trust her and give her a bit more freedom. After all, she had been so much better lately, so hopefully it was simply a matter of give and take. They'd sat down together and negotiated a curfew and so far it seemed to be working just fine. As for Zak, he'd apparently got a hot date with a girl called Genevieve. According to Bainesy and the rest of the gang who arrived to pick him up, she was 'well fit' and they'd been running some sort of contest amongst themselves to see who could be the first to pull her. Lucky Zak! Grace had found herself laughing along with them when they'd been talking about it earlier but then she'd realised her double standards. She'd hate to think of a gang of lads leching over Cleo like that, but then Cleo was only fifteen. To lecture Zak on respect for women at that point in time would not have gone well. But she did warn him yet again to stay safe and use a condom – much to the delight of his mates and the embarrassment of her son.

Anna had been listening to the banter in fascination. She knew nothing of today's teenage world and felt quite envious of Grace having everything she'd missed out on in her life. She'd felt quite insular, set apart from these young people by her lack of knowledge of their culture, their language. Everything was so different now. She really had lost so much. But then Cleo had flown in, in a whirl of adolescent insecurity, and rescued Anna from her moment of morbidity.

'Could you help me with my make-up please, Auntie Anna? Yours looks really nice and I'm rubbish at it,' she said, depositing a dusty heap of cheap cosmetics on the kitchen table with a clatter.

Anna was flattered by the admiration showered on her by this newly acquired teenage niece. She'd never been used to having someone look up to her before.

'Sure it's only Lisa's you're going to?' asked Grace suspiciously, despite knowing she should be trying to show some trust.

'Mum!' growled Cleo.

Baines didn't help. 'Go on then, Cleo, who is it tonight? Not Petey-boy again? He's a right loser.'

Cleo blushed furiously. 'Shurrup you! I'm so over him. Not that it's any of your business.'

With some constraint, Grace bit her tongue and refrained from commenting, keeping her worries to herself.

Anna flashed Cleo a conspiratorial smile. 'Let's have a go at this make-up, then. If you get my handbag from the lounge for me you can see if I've got any in there you'd like to try.'

Cleo responded appreciatively, mini tantrum forgotten. She was liking having Auntie Anna here more every minute.

Eventually the turbulence subsided and the torrent of teens flowed out through the door in its usual hormonal haste, with a brief cry of 'Laters!'

'How do you cope with that lot?' smiled Anna in amazement.

'That was relatively peaceful,' responded Grace, her eyes still following the trail of the whirlwind, motherly pride written all over her face.

'Quiet in here,' Charlie breezed in, resplendent in jacket over his usual T-shirt. 'Got to pop out for a while, love. Sorry, but I've got a couple of estimates to do on Kingsmead. I've seen to Izzy and read her a story so, hopefully, that'll be her down for the night now. I'll take Alfie when I get back – shouldn't be too long.'

Ever alert, Alfie pricked up his ears at the mention of his name combined with the word 'take' and abandoned his basket, giving himself a thorough shake from head to tail in excited anticipation.

'No, Alfie. I said when I get back. Basket.'

Alfie drooped despondently and settled back down with a groan of disappointment, two sad brown eyes beaming guilt onto Charlie.

'I'm sorry, okay? I will take you later, honestly. Later. See you in a bit, girls, I'll leave you in peace,' he said, kissing

Grace on his way out. 'Just leave the mess, Gracie, I'll sort it out when I get back.'

Anna looked on with envy. 'You're so lucky, you know. Wherever did you manage to find him?'

'I know.'

But Anna had spotted the fleeting glimpse of resignation that flickered across Grace's face, even though now was probably not the time to query it.

'D'you want tea or something stronger?'

'To be honest, I think I'm in need of some alcoholic sustenance. You might be too, when you hear my story.'

Grace glanced round worriedly. 'Wine okay?'

'Anything.' Anna looked very pale and drawn, her skin almost transparent.

'Go and sit down, you must be exhausted. I'll just take Mother her tea and biscuits or I'll never hear the end of it. I'll be there in a minute.'

Anna retreated gratefully to the lounge, where she sank into the depths of the sofa, suddenly drained of all energy. She battled with herself. Now was not the time to give in. Grace had to be told the truth, and she had to be told now, before it was too late. From the other room she could hear the sound of raised voices, the unmistakable vitriolic tones of her mother, still so agonisingly familiar even after all this time. Should she go in now, just interrupt and confront her? But Anna knew she simply hadn't got the energy, not at this moment. And besides, she needed to explain it all to Grace first. She couldn't just walk in there and drop it like a bombshell in front of her. If only she didn't feel so exhausted …

'Told you then, has she?' Gran glowered at Grace, her beady eyes narrowing antagonistically.

Grace put down the tea and biscuits and stood facing her, arms folded. 'As a matter of fact she hasn't yet, no. In case you haven't noticed, some of us have other things to do, no time to sit and gossip like you. A couple of Zak's mates called round, we've had a houseful.'

'Well, lucky you. Nobody bothered to come in here and talk to me though, did they? But then, I'm just a poor old lady, all on my own.'

'Mother! For goodness sake!'

'It's alright, you'll be old yourself one day. It's not much fun when you're on your own.'

'Mother! You're not even on your own. It was your choice to shut yourself away in here because you refuse to see your own daughter, your own flesh and blood. Poor Anna, I don't know how you could.'

'Poor …!' Gran's eyes widened with horror, she couldn't even bear to say her name. 'Well just you wait until she tells you what she did, my girl. See what you think about her then. An absolute disgrace, that's what she is!' Gran dunked a biscuit furiously.

'Oh please yourself.' Grace turned and headed for the door. 'You just stay in here and be miserable if that's what you want. I'll see you later.'

# 6

Grace was surprised to find Anna asleep on the sofa by the time she managed to escape from Gran. Alfie was snuggled up on the floor next to her but leapt to his feet at Grace's entrance and lolloped over to greet her in his usual waggly sort of way.

The sudden movement roused Anna from her nap and she rubbed her eyes, disorientated for a moment. 'Oh, sorry, I must have dozed off,' she said, embarrassed to have been caught sleeping.

'You must be exhausted,' said Grace, concerned by her pallor. 'Would you rather we left talking until tomorrow? After all, I've waited this long, another day won't make much difference.'

'No, I'm fine, honestly. Too many late nights catching up with me, that's all,' she smiled. She'd convince herself in a minute. 'Get that bottle opened, that'll wake me up.'

Grace did as she was bade and poured them both a glass, handing one to Anna. 'Here's to sharing the rest of our lives as sisters again,' she said, joyously chinking their glasses together.

Unfathomed depths of emotion threatened to overflow from Anna's eyes. 'Sisters reunited,' she guardedly replied.

An uncomfortable silence filled the room for a while, a silence filled with trepidation. Grace sipped nervously at her drink and glanced across at Anna. Her sister, and yet someone she really didn't know at all.

Anna struggled with her emotions, struggled to break

free from this supposedly self-imposed exile. For what would happen if her sister was to blame her too? She'd have nothing left to live for at all then … except for Hugo. She caught her sister's glance and their eyes locked.

'What happened when I'd gone, Grace. Did they hurt you?' It was a question she could wait no longer to ask. It just fell from her mouth without warning.

'Hurt me? What do you mean? I was only hurt by them taking you away from me. The silence, not knowing where you'd gone.'

But Anna had to be certain. 'You're quite sure nothing ever happened to you? Nobody ever did anything you didn't want them to do? They left you alone?'

'Yes, like I said, I was just left alone. Nobody would ever tell me anything. They used to argue a lot, or there would be complete silence. I wasn't even allowed to mention your name.'

An ominous silence filled the air once more until a horrendous thought lurched into Grace's head.

'Anna? Please tell me this isn't what I'm thinking. Hurt? As in … oh my God!' The sudden realisation hit her like a sledgehammer as she clasped her hand to her mouth. 'Dad?' she asked, in a horrified whisper.

Anna nodded silently, for the moment unable to speak.

'And Mother?'

Anna choked back her nightmarish memories. 'She knew what was going on, I'm sure she did. I told her anyway, begged her to do something, but she just said I was a stupid little liar and I must never say anything like that again. She'd always hated me, remember? I was Dad's favourite. He was always buying me presents, making me feel special. How was I to know where it was leading? I just thought he loved me, I was his girl, that's what he said. And it made me happy. After all, Mother never had any time for me whereas he … he'd hug me and kiss me, tell me I was his special girl.

'I was small and skinny as a child, if you remember, which was probably why I was quite a late developer. But when I was thirteen my body started to change. I'd catch Dad looking at me sometimes. "What?" I'd ask, but he'd not answer, just give me a hug which invariably ended up as a tickling match with us rolling around on the floor. I loved it, loved the way he played around with me ... and maybe that does make me to blame in a way, maybe I did lead him on, as Mother said.'

'Anna! You can't possibly think that! You were just a child whereas Dad, he ...' Grace's voice faded out in disbelief, not of what Anna was saying but of her father, the person she'd grown up loving and trusting, the person she hadn't known at all.

'Anyway, Mother never noticed my developing body or, if she did, she didn't mention it at all. When I think back she probably did notice but tried to ignore it. She'd probably been aware of Dad's wandering eye and didn't want to encourage any burgeoning sexuality on my part. She just busied herself with all her pointless pursuits and buried her head in the sand.

'So it was Dad who took me to buy my first bra – unusual I know, but not to me. It was Dad who was there watching when I brought it home and put it on, Dad's hands fastening it for me when I had difficulty, Dad's hands moving over my breasts to check it was the right size – supposedly. And it was Dad that I turned to when my period started, that frightening moment when I went to the toilet and found blood in my knickers. Nobody had ever really explained to me about that; to Mother it was one of those "dirty" subjects that nobody discussed. We'd had a talk about it in school of course but it had been very basic and factual with the majority of the class sniggering and the teacher wanting to get it over with as quickly as possible. I'd heard other girls talking about how they'd "come on", but to me, that day, it

59

just seemed really scary.

'So Dad sorted me out. He even felt me to make sure I was okay, said he didn't want me losing too much blood. I must have been so naive. Well, I was. He got me some sanitary towels – must have been some of Mother's – and slid one inside my clean knickers for me.' Anna's face contorted with disbelief at the memory. 'Why didn't I just tell him to bog off? I can't believe I was so trusting! Just listening to myself now – could I really have been that innocent? Sometimes I think maybe Mother does have a point …'

'Anna! How can you even remotely think that? He was a fully grown man for God's sake! Your father – you trusted him, of course you did!'

Anna's face, etched with the pain of remembrance, turned to her sister. 'And none of this happened to you? You're quite sure he never touched you in any way?'

'Quite sure,' replied Grace firmly. 'He always seemed to steer clear of me. But I must have been the innocent one, I never knew any of this. How could I not have known?'

'You were only young, Grace, too young to have known. Always off out playing with your friends – and you had loads of them. Quite the Miss Popular you were, and I'm glad.' She smiled, tentatively. But the smile faded as her thoughts turned back to herself. 'Me? I was a bit of a loner, hanging around at home most of the time. No wonder Dad saw me as an easy target.'

'Stop it, Anna. Stop trying to lay the blame on yourself all the time. You were a child, you did nothing wrong.'

'He used to talk to me as well, "just a bit of fatherly advice" he'd say and he'd warn me not to hang around with the lads from school, or "those pimply youths" as he'd call them. He reckoned they'd only be after me for one thing and that I was worth more than that. I was his special girl, after all. Why did I listen to him? Why did I not go off out and hang round on street corners like everyone else?

Mother was always off out at her meetings. W.I., choir, Ladies Guild – she was a member of so many groups she was hardly ever at home. Remember? Dad and I were quite often in on our own.

'Thinking back, I reckon Mother was starting to become a bit suspicious of things about that time. Although I wasn't one for going out much, I did love fashion and make-up and would spend hours in my bedroom trying out different styles. I'd roll my skirts over at the waistband and hitch them up to my bum – I was a great follower of the mini skirt! As for my face, it'd be plastered in pancake and that revolting blue eyeshadow. I even had false eyelashes.'

'God, I do remember that! I used to think you looked fantastic, like a model. In fact I used to ask if I could put some on but you'd never let me.'

The light-hearted moment brought a fleeting glimmer of a smile to both of their faces, even though it was short-lived.

Anna lowered her head in shame, any trace of gaiety gone. 'I was asking for it, wasn't I? A cheap tart. Mother's right.'

'I wish you'd stop saying that. You were just being normal. All girls dress up, experiment with make-up. Look at Cleo.' Yes, look at Cleo. That must be why Mother went on at her so much. It was beginning to make sense now.

'What are you thinking?' Anna didn't miss a thing.

'Just thinking how Mother goes on at Cleo now, about her make-up and short skirts. They used to get on, but now she never leaves her alone. I'm beginning to understand a bit more …'

'That she's scared she's turning into a tart like me – asking for it,' retorted Anna, cuttingly.

'Hey, that's not what I meant at all, you know I didn't,' said Grace, smarting from the sting of the remark.

'Sorry, I didn't mean to snap at you. Just a bit tense, that's all.'

'Understandably. So I take it things got even worse?'

Anna groaned and leaned forward on the sofa, her head held in upturned palms as she stared at the floor. 'Time moved on, but one night when I was thirteen, Mother was out at one of her meetings and you were fast asleep in your room. I'd gone to bed early that night and was lying there reading when Dad came upstairs and popped his head round my bedroom door. "Can I come in?" he asked, smiling. I can see his face now. Why didn't I just send him away? Tell him I was reading? Anything. But no. In he came.

'He sat on the edge of my bed next to me, pretending to be interested in my book at first. He'd been drinking, I could smell it on his breath. "What's it about?" he asked, closing the book slightly so he could see the front cover. "It's about this girl, Lucy. Her mother's had to go away to look after her sick auntie and Lucy's left at home with her dad. They get …" "Does he look after her?"

'I remember feeling a bit odd about his question, the way he suddenly interrupted me. Looking up from my book, I noticed beads of perspiration had formed on his top lip and there was a wildness in his eyes I'd never seen before. A flurry of fear rippled up the hairs on the back of my neck. I threw back the covers to get out of bed but his hand came down to stop me. "Hey, what's the matter? Where are you going?" he asked. "Erm … dunno," I answered nervously. He said, "I've got something special I want to show you but you have to promise this will be our little secret, okay?"

'I swallowed hard at the lump of fear that had knotted in my throat. Was I just being stupid? After all, he was my father, he looked after me and I loved him. He would never do anything to hurt me. But he could. And he did.'

Grace tried to speak, to comfort, she could hardly bear to see the pain her sister was going through as she relived her ordeal. Anna put up a hand to stop her.

'It seemed to last for ever, his weight crushing my still childlike body, my flesh tearing apart. But finally it was over, and he rolled off me, eyes closed. I remember thinking for a moment that perhaps he was dead, that I'd killed him; he'd certainly cried out in pain. But no, he looked at me and smiled. "You're a very special girl," he said, "do you know that?" I could do no more than whimper, in terror and disbelief of what had just happened to me. He kissed me on the cheek and said "Goodnight, special girl. Sweet dreams. And remember, this is our little secret." With that he turned out the light and was gone through the door, closing it softly behind him.

'In the bed I lay shivering, too traumatised to move. A soreness and burning inside me like I'd never known and a hot stickiness between my legs. What had he done to me? This was my father, he loved me. I didn't even dare to move again that night. I just lay there in the dark, silently sobbing, until I fell into an exhausted sleep ... and oblivion.'

Anna was silent again now as she relived the memory. Staring into some distant past life that seemed like it was only yesterday. That moment had been the pivotal point of her life. From then on, everything had changed direction.

Grace's voice broke through the trauma she was reliving. 'How could he? How could he have done that to you, his own daughter?' Tears were streaming down her face. 'And to think I never knew anything, never suspected a thing. He was my dad and I loved him and yet I didn't know him at all – he was a monster, a pervert! To think, as well, that I used to defend him, stick up for him against Mother. I thought she was the bossy one, always telling him what to do, him just the meek and mild underdog. What a sham! Oh Anna, I'm so sorry. I should have been there for you, helped you. How did I not realise something was wrong?' she sobbed. 'I'm so stupid.'

Anna dragged herself back from her nightmare. 'You

63

were just a child, Grace. How could you have known? It's Mother that I blame for not helping. I told her. Dad said I had to keep it a secret, but it was wrong, I knew it was wrong, and I told her. I told her every time, hoping against hope that she'd do something, make it all stop. But it never did. She just called me a dirty little liar and said I should stop trying to cause trouble, so I did.'

'So it continued?' Grace's eyes were rounded with horror. 'For over a year.'

'Oh Anna.' Grace moved over to the sofa next to her and encircled her in her arms, wanting to protect her beloved sister even though it was too late. The help she'd needed had been long ago; no one had been there for her then.

The hard protective shell Anna had woven around herself over the intervening years began to unravel. 'Why did he do it, Grace? Why did he do that to me?' She sobbed as if her heart would break. 'He said he loved me. That …'

'… wasn't love, Anna. That was incest, perversion, whatever. I hope he rots in hell.'

'How did he die?'

'Prostrate cancer. He really suffered. I used to feel sorry for him, hated seeing him in so much pain, but now I'm glad. He deserved to suffer for what he did to you.'

'Just taking Alfie!' shouted Charlie.

'Okay.' Grace hadn't even heard him come back.

Charlie put his head round the door. 'Where …?' But Alfie was off like a rocket as soon as the lounge door opened to let him escape. *He* had heard Charlie.

'Walkies! Don't think he needs telling.' Charlie glanced worriedly at the two sisters clinging together on the sofa. He was unaccustomed to silence in this house. A miasma of tension hung in the air. 'Everything alright in here?'

'Fine, Charlie. Just leave us would you?' snapped Grace.

'Only asking.' He really did feel like an intruder in his own house sometimes.

'So all this went on for over a year? What happened then?'

'Well, after that first time I used to try and stay out of his way. I started hanging out with some of the kids from school, going off out at night instead of sitting around the house, just trying to keep out of his way basically. But I couldn't escape, not really. He was still there when I came home, watching, staring. I used to not want to go to bed, not knowing when he was going to follow. It was only on the nights Mother stayed in that I felt relatively safe. When she was out I'd lie in the dark, shaking with fear beneath the covers, praying that I wouldn't hear the tread of his foot-steps coming up the stairs, the creaking of my bedroom door as it opened.'

'Oh Anna, I just can't imagine how bad it was for you – and there was I, fast asleep in the next room, no help to you at all. I feel so awful.'

'You were only a child, seven, eight years old. What could you have done? I'm only glad that he never turned to you too. You are sure … you would tell me, wouldn't you?'

'Of course I would. He never touched me, you can be certain of that.'

'Not even after I'd gone? That's what used to worry me, that after I'd left he'd transfer his so-called "affections" to you.'

'Well, that never happened. Things did seem to change, though, between Mother and Dad.'

'How d'you mean?'

'Like, I know Mother was always a strong character, but it was as though she had some sort of hold over him, he had to do whatever she said. He became her meek and mild little lapdog almost, a shadow of his former self.'

'Can't say I feel sorry.'

'So why did you suddenly disappear? What happened to …?'

'I'm home!' Cleo. ''Night.' Footsteps thundered up the stairs.

'Cleo?' Grace leapt to her feet and rushed into the hall where her heightened mother-senses were greeted by a trailing waft of alcoholic fumes deposited by her hastily disappearing daughter. 'Cleo!'

'What?!'

'Come here please.'

'Toilet.'

This was all she needed, tonight of all nights. Grace went upstairs and waited outside the bathroom door. 'You okay?'

'Mm.' She was so obviously not.

Eventually she emerged, face white, eyes red, and headed for her bedroom. Grace followed.

'You've been drinking.'

'Ten out of ten.'

'Don't speak to me like that, please!'

'Sorry.' Cleo stumbled about, getting ready for bed.

'You're early.'

'God! Thought you didn't like me being late and now you don't like it when I'm early! Can't win with you, can I?'

'Oh, get to bed, and I'll talk to you tomorrow. Remember Dad's coming to pick you up in the morning, I'm sure he'll have a few words to say about this as well.'

'Yeah, yeah.'

'Cleo!'

'Sorry.'

'Goodnight.'

''Night Mum. Sorry.'

Grace headed back down to the lounge only to find her sister asleep on the sofa.

'Anna?' she tried to wake her gently.

'Oohh! Sorry, I must have drifted off again then.'

'You must be exhausted. Now, what were we saying? I know, you were just going to t...'

'Listen, I'm really sorry, I know you're desperate to know everything, but I really am absolutely shattered. All that talking, remembering, well I feel completely drained. Any chance we could carry on with the rest of this conversation tomorrow?'

'Of course we can.' Grace couldn't help but register a certain amount of disappointment, she'd waited so long for this moment ... But she was being selfish. 'We'll talk tomorrow. You go to bed and get some sleep. It's been a long day.'

Grace was sitting alone in the lounge, staring into space, when Charlie returned with Alfie. Once again, she hadn't even heard him come in.

'Penny for them.'

'What? Oh Charlie, don't sneak up on me like that!'

'Where is everybody?' he asked, hurt by the way she kept speaking to him ever since Anna had arrived.

'Bed, where do you think?' she answered crossly.

'Coming up?' he asked hopefully, persuasive look in his eye.

'Later,' she replied, blind to his needs.

For what seemed like hours she sat there alone, going over everything in her head. Her father. How could you live with someone like that for all those years and not know what was happening, not know them at all? She thought back to her childhood, how little time she'd actually spent alone with him, as opposed to her sister. Anna was right, she'd always been off out playing with her friends, leaving them alone together, unknowing. But then, she'd just been young and innocent, she'd simply thought that Anna liked staying at home, being with Dad – she was his favourite after all, or so Grace had thought. But not in that way. Never in that way. Her father ... It made her flesh crawl to think about it.

'Hey!'

Zak. She hadn't even realised he was still out.

'What are you doing up? Everyone else asleep?'

'Far as I know.' Grace tried to rein herself in from the horrific thoughts that filled her head.

'What's up?' asked Zak, sensitive to his mother's fragility.

'Oh, nothing for you to worry about. How did it go with Genevieve?' she asked, almost visibly trying to paint a smile on her face.

'That's more like it,' he grinned, giving her a hug. 'Don't like to see you sad. Genevieve? Fantastic! Seeing her again tomorrow.'

'Two days in a row? Must be love,' teased Grace, used to the errant ways of her stud of a son.

'Yeah, yeah,' he grinned. 'Anyway, I'm off to bed before the interrogation – besides, I need to be up in the morning, we're meeting for lunch.'

'Lunch?' Grace's eyes rounded in amazement. 'Lunch?'

'Yes, you did hear me right the first time. Any more questions?'

'So …?'

'I'm going to bed,' he groaned, rolling his eyes. 'Good-night, Mother!'

''Night, Zak,' she smiled at her roguish son.

Her past may not have been what it seemed, but at least she was blessed to have some semblance of normal family life now. She gathered herself together and wandered slowly up the stairs.

# 7

Bark, bark, bark! What was wrong with that dog? Grace tried putting the pillow over her head in a vain attempt to drown out the noise, but it failed. She'd only had about two hours' sleep. After the evening's revelations she'd tossed and turned all night. Surely somebody else would get up and see to him? But no, just Izzy.

A wide-awake child came round the door. 'Mummy, why is Alfie barking?'

Grace gave up. Who needed sleep anyway? 'I don't know, Izzy. Shall we go and find out?'

Leaving Charlie still snoring contentedly, Grace grudgingly abandoned her nice warm bed and, scrambling into her dressing gown and yawning loudly, she followed Izzy down the stairs.

Alfie stopped barking and turned briefly to greet them with a mini waggle of his tail, panting and dribbly, dancing around in a panic, staring at the closed kitchen door.

'Alfie! What are you doing locked out in the hall? You're meant to be in your basket.'

'Well, why do you think I'm barking?' his brown eyes seemed to say.

Grace opened the kitchen door. 'Mother! What are you doing locking Alfie out in the hall?'

'Don't tell me! It's my fault I suppose. Go on, you might as well say it. I can never do anything right around here.'

'Well didn't you hear him, poor dog?'

'Poor dog! It's poor everyone round here, even the dog,

69

but it's never poor me is it? Oh no. A defenceless old lady, but nobody cares.' She slurped her tea meaningfully.

'I'm surprised to see you in here anyway, I thought you'd still be locked in your room.'

'Yes, I bet you did. That's what you like, don't you? Me locked away in my room.'

'Mother, stop being silly.'

'Breakfast please! Breakfast please!' chanted Izzy, clambering up onto her seat at the table.

A battle for the bathroom could be heard from the landing. Alfie scratched at the back door to be let out – all that stress had played havoc with his bladder. Grace sighed and let him out, any longings she'd had about returning to her nice warm bed disappearing through the door with him.

'Anyone for toast?'

'Me, me, me!' sang Izzy.

'Can't chew it, Grace, I thought you would know that by now.'

'Well put your teeth in.'

'Pass them to me, then.'

'Well *I* haven't got them, have I?'

'Ooh, temper, temper. You want to control that, my girl.'

'Grrr!' Grace managed to hold her tongue, just about.

Izzy gobbled up her breakfast in an instant. 'Please can I go and find Daddy?'

Yes, why should he be left in peace? 'Okay then, but don't disturb Auntie Anna.'

''Kay.' Izzy was off like a rocket. Oh for half of her energy.

She was back down a few minutes later. 'Auntie Anna's getting up in a minute.'

Gran spluttered into her tea.

'I thought I told you not to disturb Auntie Anna.'

'I didn't 'sturb her. I just went to see if she was getting up. She called me poppet.'

Grace couldn't help but smile. 'And Daddy?'

'He's doing a poo.'

'Izzy!'

Charlie was just coming downstairs as the doorbell rang. He opened the front door to Richard.

'Alright?'

'Alright?'

Men of few words.

Charlie headed towards the kitchen; Richard followed. Grace was looking flustered, still in her dressing gown.

'Is it that time already? Sorry, Richard, I hadn't realised. Cleo won't be long, hopefully, although she's probably suffering a bit this morning.' She told him about the state their daughter was in when she'd come home last night.

Charlie shook some cereal into his bowl and banged the packet back down onto the table with a thud. Gran raised her eyebrows and slurped noisily.

'Don't worry, I'll talk to her,' Richard said, putting a re-assuring hand on her arm.

Charlie cleared his throat, meaningfully. Richard received the message loud and clear, and removed his hand. Grace adjusted her dressing gown more tightly around herself.

For someone with dementia, sometimes Gran could be quite astute. Her beady eyes weighed up the situation. 'For goodness sake, Grace, go and put some clothes on. Just look at you, flaunting yourself. You're as bad as that ... that disgrace.'

'Mother! Don't be so ridiculous! Richard's my ex-husband, he's seen me in my dressing gown before.'

In the chaos, nobody had noticed Izzy sneak upstairs, but she bounced back into the kitchen, beaming with a sense of achievement. 'Auntie Anna says she'll be down in ten minutes.'

'Izzy! You didn't wake her up again, did you?'

'No, I just climbed on the bed to see if her eyes were

71

closed. Hello, Uncle Richard. Can I come to your house with Cleo, please?'

Charlie almost choked on his last spoonful of cereal, pushed his chair aside, and went to pick up Izzy, encircling her protectively with his arms.

'No you can't, Izzy, not today, because you and I, we're going to … to the seaside!' he said, latching on to the first idea that came into his head. This was *his* daughter, not Richard's.

'The seaside?' chorused Grace and Izzy, shocked and in unison.

'Yeah. Erm … thought she'd enjoy it, give you some time with Anna …' he muttered, stumbling over his words. What had he let himself in for?

Grace saw right through him but still, it *would* give her a chance to talk to Anna again. 'Thanks, Charlie,' she said, giving him a kiss on the cheek, although this green-eyed monster of his was getting ridiculous.

'We're going to the seaside! We're going to the seaside!' danced Izzy. 'Ooh, can Alfie come?'

'Suppose,' said Charlie. He'd backed himself into a corner now.

Peace descended. Zak out with Genevieve, Cleo with Richard, Charlie with Izzy and Alfie, and Mother back in her room before 'that disgrace' put in an appearance. Grace cleared away the dishes from the table and went up for a shower. She still hadn't heard any movement from Anna, but didn't want to disturb her again.

Grace showered and dressed, taking her time, not in a rush for once. In her head she kept going over and over everything Anna had said last night. It made her feel sick even to think of her father now. You really never did know anybody. If you couldn't trust your own parents, who could you trust? Her mother? She'd been as bad. She'd known all about what was happening and not done a thing to prevent it. Little snippets of things kept coming back to Grace now. Like when her mother had said Cleo shouldn't be allowed to spend the night with Richard at his house. Grace remembered thinking that was an odd thing for her to say – Richard was her father, what was wrong with that? 'He's a man isn't he?' her mother had replied. It was all becoming clear now. Just to think what Anna had gone through … it made her flesh crawl. To go on for all that time as well, with no chance of escape. But what had happened to change things? Why had Anna disappeared so suddenly? It was a mystery that had puzzled her for over thirty years. Hopefully, today, she'd find some answers.

Grace dragged the brush through her hair, suddenly filled with a sense of urgency. Out on the landing the door to Anna's bedroom was still firmly closed. Unable to wait any longer, Grace quietly turned the handle and peeped inside. Empty. Bed neatly made. Not a thing out of place. Panic did a double somersault inside Grace's stomach. Surely she hadn't disappeared, not again. Maybe she couldn't face telling her any more. Maybe she … Grace's footsteps gathered speed down the stairs and, breathless, she almost flew into the kitchen.

''Morning. You okay? You look as though you've seen a ghost.'

Grace clasped her chest with relief. 'Sorry, but just for a minute I thought …'

'You thought I'd disappeared again, didn't you? Oh Grace, I'm not going to do that. I just heard you in the shower so I thought I'd come down and help myself, if that's okay.'

'Of course it is,' said Grace, sinking onto a kitchen chair. 'I want you to feel at home. It was just that when I looked in your room and you'd gone … I know I'm being silly, but it brought it all back. That day you disappeared.'

'Well I'm not going anywhere, not today at least.' Anna tried to muster a smile, make it at least seem like a joke.

They discussed trivialities for a while, getting to know each other. It was the perfect opportunity while they had the house to themselves; apart from Gran that is, and there was no chance she would emerge from her room, not while Anna was there. Eventually, Grace felt able to steer the conversation in the direction she wanted it to go, even though she could sense a certain amount of reticence on her sister's part. Anna was gabbling away nervously about nothing in particular, trying not to leave a gap for any probing questions to leap into.

But Grace could wait no longer. 'Anna, why did you leave?' Her voice sounded almost like that of a child, as if the memory had transported her back through time.

Anna's heart contracted, her mouth was dry. 'I was pregnant.' Not so hard when you say it fast.

The words hit Grace like a stone. 'Pregnant? Surely not Dad's? Was there …?'

'Well of course it was Dad's. It couldn't have possibly been anyone else's. After all I'd been going through, having sex with someone for pleasure was the last thing on my mind.'

'Pregnant by Dad? Oh my God! So you went away to have an abortion?'

'Amazingly enough, no. For some reason I didn't understand at the time, Mother and Dad were both dead set against the idea.'

'*You had the baby?* But what happened? Was it a normal baby? It was Dad's … incest … surely there would be something wrong with it? Did it die?' Grace's head was filled with questions, she could hardly take in what she'd been told. Wasn't it illegal?

Anna's face contorted with the pain of remembering. She

74

was reliving it all in her head. That rollercoaster of fear and terror, pain and separation she'd been on, with no one to turn to, no one to make it stop. Up to that point she'd thought her life was bad. She'd never realised it could get even worse.

'Yes, I had the baby,' said Anna hoarsely, her voice sounding a lot calmer than she felt. 'No discussion ever took place to the contrary as far as I'm aware. Although I was never involved in any decisions that were made about it anyway,' she said, her voice now filled with bitterness. 'Who was I? Just a female body for my father's pleasure, a receptacle for his sperm, an incubator, a chance to make money. Didn't they know I was a person with feelings? I was their daughter. None of it had been my fault. The last words Mother said to me were "You're just a cheap, common prostitute. Get out of this house, I never want to see you again!"'

Tears were running, unchecked, down Grace's face. 'Oh, Anna, I don't know what to say. I just never knew all this was happening to you – and yet there I was, living in the same house.'

'You were young, Grace, just a child. How could you have known?'

'So what about Dad? Did he help?'

'Him? He was squirming with guilt. About me, and about Mother knowing. For a fraction of a second I may even have found it in my heart to feel a little bit sorry for him. Mother really had the upper hand now, she had him jumping through hoops. And me, I was feeling ill, throwing up, traumatised … almost on the verge of a breakdown.

'Anyway, he sorted out a plan that at least made Mother happy – and me too, briefly, as it meant me getting away from them. The only downside, or so I thought, was being separated from you, and that just broke my heart. But go was what I had to do, there was no other choice. It was only later that I learned the full extent of the plan, and by then it was too late, the deal had been done.'

'The deal?'

'Remember Auntie Alice?'

'Dad's sister? I think I only ever saw her once – can't really remember though. What was her husband called? Uncle Frank, that's right. Don't think I ever met him at all.'

'Well, unfortunately, I did. They'd been wanting a baby for years. Tried to adopt but it didn't work out. So Dad thought he could solve all his problems in one go. He arranged for me to go down and stay with them while I was pregnant and then, after the birth, they would keep the baby as their own and arrange somewhere for me to go and live for a couple of months while I sorted myself out.'

Grace was horrified. 'Take your baby and then just abandon you, a sixteen-year-old girl?'

Anna's voice shook with emotion, tears ran unchecked down her face. Memories of that day … reliving the moment when they'd snatched her baby from her arms. His crying. Her screaming as she was dragged from the house to her uncle's waiting car and driven away.

'How could they, Grace? After all I'd been through, how could they take my baby away and then desert me? Just thrown away like a heap of old rubbish, like trash, discarded when its use is over. But more than that, my baby. My whole body ached for him. They tore my heart out when they took him away.' Anna was sobbing openly now.

'A boy?' asked Grace gently.

Anna nodded, trying to continue despite her grief. 'Hugo, I called him. I thought they'd change his name, but they didn't.'

Grace looked puzzled, but didn't want to interrupt. Anna was finding this hard enough.

'They took him away from me and drove me away. Miles and miles, the distance between me and my baby growing further every minute. It felt like the end of the world, I'd never see him again … We stopped eventually, Uncle Frank taking me up to some godforsaken bedsit that was to be my new home. A pokey little cubbyhole in Tooting, South London. My rent was paid for two months, he said. He gave me some money for food and then after that, it would be up to me. He left shortly afterwards, but not until he told me never to try and contact them again and never, ever to come looking for my baby. They were moving the next day anyway, he said, so I wouldn't stand a chance of finding them.'

Grace's head was in a whirl, she'd never heard anything like it. This was her family, they'd behaved like monsters. 'And Mother, what did she have to gain from all of this? How did Dad manage to win her round?'

'Money, what do you think? That was all part of the deal. Auntie Alice and Uncle Frank would see I was looked after while I was pregnant and for two months afterwards. They would have the baby, and our dear parents would receive ten thousand pounds for their trouble.'

'A pay-off, oh my God!'

'I know. Ten thousand pounds was a lot of money in those days. Mother was always very money-orientated. I'm sure it went a long way towards helping her to get over father's misdemeanours.'

'Oh Anna, I can't begin to imagine what it must have been like for you. The baby, was he okay? I mean …'

'A child from an incestuous relationship, I know what you mean. There was a chance he could have been handi-capped, anything. I have at least that to be grateful for – he was perfect. I don't know what would have happened if there *had* been something wrong: would they still have taken him? But then, I had no knowledge of these things, I was only sixteen after all.'

'Thank God he was alright. Hugo, his name, how d'you know they didn't change it?'

'Because,' a glimmer of a smile played on Anna's lips now 'when he reached his eighteenth birthday he came looking for me.'

'Anna! You've met him! How amazing is that?'

Anna's smile broadened, her face beaming with pride. 'He lives near to me now, in Clapham. I see him all the time. He's thirty-two, and a fantastic young man. I would say that wouldn't I?' she grinned. 'No, but really, he is. When you think of the start he had in life ... well, I think he's unbelievable. I hope you can meet him one day soon, judge for yourself.'

'I'd love to. What's he like?'

'In looks, he's a lot like Zak. In fact I couldn't stop staring at Zak when I first saw him, the resemblance is uncanny.'

'Family genes I suppose – as long as he hasn't got Cleo's temper!' joked Grace.

'No,' smiled Anna, 'he's actually the kindest, gentlest person you could wish to meet. Although he does have a wicked sense of humour.'

'Mr Perfect, eh?'

'That's my boy!'

'What happened to Auntie Alice and Uncle Frank?'

'Still around. They're living in Eastbourne somewhere. I've never had any contact, wouldn't want to, but Hugo still sees them. I think he feels a bit torn actually. To all intents and purposes they're his parents, they're the ones who brought him up, I'm just his birth mother. But that's fine, we have a fantastic relationship and that's all that matters to me now.'

'I'd love to meet him.'

'He wants to meet you too. In fact, I know it's difficult for you to get away, but I was kind of hoping you might be able to come back with me when I go. Meet my son, sample life in the big city. What d'you think? Would they cope without you?'

'I'm sure we could work something out. Charlie's pretty good – most of the time, anyway.'

'Yes, I've noticed he's been a bit quiet. Is it to do with me being here?' Anna had quite a complex about not being wanted, understandably.

'No, it's not you,' Grace reassured her. 'I think he just feels a bit excluded sometimes. It's all about second marriages, stepping into someone else's family – especially with Richard still being around. Jealousy, I suppose, in a way.'

'Ah, the mythical Richard. Will I get to meet him while I'm here?'

'Probably tonight, when he brings Cleo home. He usually pops in for a chat and I know he'll want to see you.'

'Still like him, don't you? No wonder Charlie's jealous!'

'Anna! That was over a long time ago. Things just didn't work out.' A flush spread across Grace's face as she changed the subject. 'Anyway, back to Hugo. He knows about me, then, does he?'

'He knows about everything, Grace; knows the full story.'

'How on earth did he handle that? What a thing to have to take on board! It's a wonder it didn't send him crazy.'

'He did go off the rails for a while – drink, drugs, the lot. Spent a lot of time in rehab actually. It was a bad time for both of us, but we came through it. And when I look at him now … well, you'll see for yourself.' Anna simply glowed with pride as she thought about this perfect specimen of a man that she'd given birth to all those years ago. Hugo, her son.

# 8

'We're home! We're home!' Izzy burst in through the door like a force nine gale, closely followed by Charlie, a sand-encrusted Alfie dangling dolefully under one arm.

'Oh Charlie, look at the state of him!' Grace cried in alarm.

'Okay, okay, I'll put the hosepipe on him outside. Nice to see you too!'

'Sorry, but …'

'I know, I'm going,' said Charlie, as doleful as the dog as he went out through the back door.

'You are awful,' said Anna. 'Poor Charlie, you don't realise what a good man you've got there.'

'I know, I don't mean to snap. I'll make it up to him later.'

'Too much information.'

The two sisters giggled together like two mischievous children. A third mischievous child stood in front of them.

'Hello!' How dare they ignore her?

'Hello, poppet.' Anna wiped the tears of laughter from her eyes. 'Had a good time at the seaside?'

Izzy leant with her hands on Anna's knees, staring wide-eyed at her, and loudly proclaimed, 'I'm not poppet, I'm Izzy!'

Anna's laughter continued, 'Oh Izzy, I'm sorry. How could I forget? A beautiful name for a beautiful girl.'

Izzy grinned in her own inimitable way and climbed up onto Anna's knee, giving her a kiss. 'I love you, Auntie Anna.'

'And I love you too, Izzy. Now tell me all about your day at the seaside. Did you go for a paddle?'

Grace wandered outside to find Charlie, feeling guilty. 'Sorry, I didn't mean to snap at you like that. Thanks for taking them out for the day, it's been good spending time with Anna. We really needed that time on our own to talk.'

'And do you know now why she left?'

'Oh Charlie, her story's horrendous. My father, my own father, raped her! He used to go up to her bedroom and force himself onto her night after night – it went on for almost three years! She ended up pregnant and abandoned and he actually *sold* the baby! How bad is that?'

'Couldn't get much worse, could it?' Charlie abandoned his dog-hosing to comfort his visibly upset wife and she leaned into his arms gratefully.

'I'm so lucky to have you,' she said, drawing strength from him.

'I love you, you know that.'

'Love you too.'

It was about nine o'clock before Cleo returned. 'Hello! I'm back!'

She opened the door to the lounge to find them slumped, comatose, in front of the television – it had been a long day.

'Dad's here. Come in and meet Auntie Anna, Dad, you'll love her.'

Cleo had been working on this plan all day. Dad was looking for a girlfriend, and who could be better for him than Auntie Anna? She was just a trendier version of Mum, and a bit thinner. Cleo knew Dad still loved Mum really, all this Internet dating malarkey was just a waste of time, a cover-up. Whereas Auntie Anna … perfect! And besides, if they got married Cleo could escape this madhouse and go and live with them. In her head, she'd moved in already.

'Sure I'm not intruding?' Richard hesitated at the door.

Cleo grabbed his hand and dragged him in. ''Course not. Auntie Anna, this is my dad. Dad, Auntie Anna,' she beamed.

Richard stepped forward to greet her. She did look remarkably like Grace. 'Pleased to meet you. You've certainly made an impression on my daughter, she hadn't stopped talking about you all day.'

'Nothing bad, I hope?' she smiled, a flush creeping into her normally pallid cheeks.

Was it in Cleo's imagination or was there a spark between them already? Something was there, she was sure of it. She hugged her arms around herself and repressed a squeak of excitement that bubbled up inside her. This was looking good.

'Move up, Mum, and let Dad sit next to Auntie Anna.'

'Cleo!' Grace knew just what her daughter was up to. She was so transparent at times.

She moved up nevertheless, and Richard sat down between the two sisters, looking somewhat bewildered. They could have been twins, they were so alike. He turned his attention to Anna who, by now, was quite pink in the face.

'So when are you going back to London?' Bollocks! What a stupid question! He sounded as though he couldn't wait to get rid of her – and that certainly wasn't the case. 'Sorry, I didn't mean …'

She grinned at him, impishly. 'I know. Not for a few days at least.'

'Perhaps you'll let me show you around a bit while you're here? If you have the time, that is.'

Boy, was her father a fast worker! Cleo was well

impressed. Grace looked somewhat taken aback and went to put the kettle on. Charlie followed. Cleo hung around for a second or two, but started to feel like a gooseberry. She loved it when a plan came together but even she hadn't expected it to happen that quickly. Just look at them! Sorted!

Grace snuggled up to Charlie in bed that night as she recounted Anna's story to him.

'It's so hard to take in. How could anyone do that to their own daughter? It makes you feel sick,' Charlie grimaced.

'I know, he must have been pretty sick himself to behave like that.'

'And the boy? He's alright?'

'Hugo. Thankfully, yes – luckily.'

'Amazing, how he just turned up out of the blue.'

'At least something good came out of it all. Anna reckons he's fantastic.'

They lay in silence for a while, each lost in their own thoughts. But Charlie's thoughts moved on to other things as his hand moved slowly down over her belly. She was aroused, but not in the way he'd intended. She covered his hand with her own as if she was pressing the pause button on a video.

'Charlie?'

'Mm?'

'Would I be able to go back with Anna when she goes home? Stay in London for a few days so I can meet Hugo?'

'Mmm.' He had other things on his mind.

'You sure that's okay? Would you manage?'

'Yeah. Be fine.' He'd agree to anything at this moment.

'What about work?'

'No worries. Sort it.' His need all-consuming, he pressed fast forward.

'Oh Charlie!' She showed her gratitude to excess, her

mounting pleasure blocking out all, as she rode to an orgasm second to none.

Anna lay in bed, staring at a cobweb on the ceiling above her. Its delicately woven thread stretched all the way across from the light fitting and swayed gently in the breeze from the open window. What clever creatures spiders were to create such intricate patterns. She could never understand why so many people were afraid of them. Surely the spider had more to fear from human beings? Webs destroyed, bodies stamped on, lives crushed. A bit of a parody of how her own life had been in a way, although she was luckier than the spider: at least she was still alive. She had survived this far and had a lot to be thankful for – not least of all, Hugo.

Her heart melted as she thought about him, her amazing son. He'd enriched her life so much since they'd been reunited, despite the problems which were obviously going to have been there. At eighteen, when he'd come looking for her, he was already in a state and wanting answers. High on drugs, alcohol or whatever, shouting the odds as he'd forced his way into her hitherto peaceful apartment needing to know why she'd abandoned him, never tried to make contact. She'd been filled with a mixture of emotions from ecstasy to trepidation. This was her son, her son, and the day she'd been longing for. It should have been a euphoric moment, and yet who was this creature? How could that sweet innocent baby, whose return she had longed for, have turned into this ... this wild, manic young man, without her knowing?

Her first thoughts had been to blame Alice and Frank. After all, it was them who had brought him up, their influence that had made him this way. What had they done to her beautiful baby boy? But then her thoughts reverted; it was totally her own fault. He was her baby, how could she have just let him go? She was his mother, she should have fought for him. Why had she let all this happen? How could she have deserted him?

The intensity of that first meeting had been almost unbearable. Screams, sobs and more, as previously unplumbed depths of emotion were painfully explored in the hope of finding some semblance of explanation. The police were called at one point, by a concerned neighbour from the flat below, although Anna had managed to spin them some story and get rid of them. Interference from a third party at that point was something they did not need; that's where it had all gone wrong before.

Anna's face was awash with tears as she relived that day, the sense of failure she'd felt towards her son. Almost the same sense of failure she was feeling towards him again now. But surely this couldn't be her fault? Surely it couldn't have been caused by something she'd done? Life throws things at you that's for sure, but Anna certainly felt she'd had more things thrown at her than most. Still, no point in feeling sorry for herself, just have to make the best of it. 'Live life to the max', as Hugo says. Hugo. What was to become of him now?

'Can Auntie Anna walk me to school today?' asked a pensive Izzy, as she drew patterns in the butter on her toast with her finger, tongue out, in deep concentration.

'Let's leave Auntie Anna to have a lie-in, Izzy. You eat your breakfast and stop playing around with it.'

'But I love Auntie Anna.'

'I know you do, but she'll still be here when you get back.'

'I've got tummy ache.'

'Nice try, Izzy,' sniggered Cleo, grabbing herself a piece of toast and stuffing it into her mouth on her way out of the kitchen.

'Cleo! You're meant to sit at the table and eat your breakfast properly!'

'Soz, Mum, bus due in a min,' Cleo mumbled through a flurry of crumbs. 'Laters!' The front door closed with a resounding slam.

Another door opened simultaneously. Gran hobbled down the hall with her walking stick, checking out the kitchen, furtively, with her beady eyes before settling herself at the table.

'Oh, decided to join us have you?' Grace couldn't help herself.

'I could die of starvation in that room and no one would notice I'd gone. Any toast for me? And a cup of tea would be nice. It's over a week since I had anything to eat or drink, no wonder I'm so ill.'

Grace grimaced and passed her the toast. Zak poured her a cup of tea.

'Look at that! He's such a good boy, bless him, the only one who does anything for me around here. Grace, where are my teeth?'

'Oh for God's sake!'

'Ooh, temper, temper!'

'In the sugar bowl,' piped up Izzy, much to everyone's horror. 'They are! Look!'

Sure enough, smiling sweetly amongst the sugar, there they were, the missing set of dentures.

'Oh my God! I've just had some of that sugar on my cereal!' gasped Grace, almost retching at the thought.

'Well they won't do you any harm, they're perfectly clean, I only gave them a soak yesterday,' said Gran, as she retrieved them from the bowl, not understanding what all the fuss was about. Painstakingly, she licked off every last grain of sugar and popped them back into her mouth. 'Hmmphh. That's better.'

Izzy clasped both of her hands to her own mouth, eyes

alight with mischief. 'My tummy ache's gone now. Want to go to school and tell Mrs Clarke. I can do a picture!'

Grace grimaced, trying desperately to keep the contents of her stomach in place. 'Mother! That's absolutely disgusting!'

'Oh, and I suppose you'll be saying it's my fault in a minute, won't you?' Gran huffed haughtily.

Grace opened her mouth to reply, but Charlie leapt in. 'Leave it, Gracie. It won't get you anywhere. D'you want me to take Izzy this morning?'

'Thanks, but no. I'll be glad to escape this madhouse.'

Anna was up and dressed by the time Grace returned, Alfie snuggled up at her feet as she glanced through the newspaper. The sound of Grace's entrance soon roused him from his slumbers, he waddled waggily across to welcome her.

'Good boy,' Grace hugged him lovingly. ''Morning. Sleep well?' she asked her sister, pushing the bouncing dog aside.

'Bit of a sleepless night, if I'm honest. Talking about everything yesterday rakes it all up. Just kept going over it again in my mind.'

'Oh Anna, I'm sorry. We don't have to talk about it, you know, not if you don't want to.'

'I know, I know. But I want to tell you, all of it, so you understand how it was. It's important to me, and important for Hugo's sake.'

'Grace!' Guess who.

'I take it you've not come face to face with her yet?' Grace grimaced.

'No, thank God. That's one thing I really don't think I could face today.'

'Listen, I'll go and see what she wants then let's go out somewhere for a bit, get away from this madhouse. Get away from Mother, at least.'

'Sounds good to me,' smiled Anna gratefully.

They didn't have long, as Grace had to be back for Izzy, but the two sisters enjoyed their walk in Delamere Forest. Alfie accompanied them, joyful to excess, chasing invisible rabbits, which made a refreshing change from chasing his tail.

It felt good to get out in the fresh air, the invigorating smell of the forest filling their nostrils as their feet scuffed along through the pine needles, in step with each other, arms linked. Two sisters reunited, secrets shared, in harmony once more.

Anna talked about Hugo, told Grace how it had been when he'd sought her out, about his time in rehab, her therapy. She told of all the traumas they'd gone through to reach the relationship they had today. How Hugo had gone from mixed-up angry young man to being the best son any-one could hope for. They'd been to hell and back but their hard work had paid off, their lives enriched because of it.

'Oh Anna, I'm dying to meet him.'

A look of panic flitted across Anna's face. Her eyes flick-ered as she gave a sharp intake of breath. 'I really need you to get to know him too,' she breathed plaintively.

'You okay? You've gone very pale.' Grace glanced worriedly at her sister.

Anna swallowed nervously. 'I'm fine,' she said, forcing a smile. 'It's all this fresh country air, it's not good for me. I'm a townie you know, probably getting withdrawal symptoms from the carbon monoxide fumes as we speak.'

Grace squeezed her arm. 'Come on you, let's get you back. You can come with me to collect Izzy if you like – face Mrs Clarke, that really will make you turn pale.'

Grace had actually thought she was on time for once, but the lack of mothers with chattering offspring along the path that led to the nursery, suddenly gave her an uncomfortable feeling in the pit of her stomach. She glanced at her watch. How did it get to that time? Her feet gathered speed in rising panic.

Anna trotted along behind. 'I'm sure they'll understand. We're only a little bit late.'

'Hmmphh.' Grace pushed open the nursery door, guilt oozing out of her every pore. She was met by a stony wall of disapproval.

'So sorry,' muttered Grace, 'we didn't …'

'This seems to be becoming a bit of a habit,' Mrs Clarke interrupted, sternly.

Why do teachers always make you feel as though you're about six years old? Grace almost felt as though she should go and stand in the corner. But hey, she was the mother here, not the naughty schoolgirl.

She pulled herself together. 'I realise I have been late a couple of times recently and I apologise, it won't happen again.'

'Let's hope not,' replied Mrs Clarke, stone wall not crumbling in the least.

Izzy gathered her things together and rushed over to Anna, who lurked guiltily in the doorway. Mrs Clarke gazed across in horror. Surely there couldn't be two of them?

'This is my mummy's sister, Auntie Anna.'

Mrs Clarke's face said it all. 'Izzy, don't forget your picture.'

Izzy retrieved it from her teacher and dashed across to show Anna.

'That's lovely Izzy. What is …?'

Grace had a sudden flash of remembrance. 'I think we'd better be going, Izzy,' she hastily interrupted. 'Daddy will be waiting for his lunch.'

'He's not the only one,' Mrs Clarke was at great pains to point out.

As they came in through the back door, Gran's stooping figure retreated rapidly down the hall, leaning heavily on her walking stick.

'Don't mind me, I only live here,' she huffed, although she was unable to resist a furtive glimpse at the daughter she'd turned her back on so long ago. 'I'll go to my room, I know when I'm not wanted.'

'Stay if you like, Mother, but only if you're going to be pleasant.'

'Hmmphh,' grunted Gran, as she disappeared into her room and closed the door firmly behind her.

Grace turned, sensing the panic emitting from her sister. 'Sorry, that must have been a bit of a shock for you.'

'Not your fault. It was bound to happen sooner or later.'

The impact of seeing her mother again after all these years had hit her like a bolt out of the blue. Icy fingers seemed to grip her by the skull and run down her spine. She sank gratefully onto a kitchen chair, elbows on the table, supporting her head in her hands.

Izzy skipped over to her, completely oblivious, picture in hand. 'I did this for you, Auntie Anna,' she said, almost pushing the picture into her face.

But, to Anna, Izzy's voice seemed to come from miles away, as she took some deep breaths, trying to pull herself together.

Grace intervened. 'Go and show it to Gran, Izzy, I'm sure she'd like to see it first.'

'But …'

'No buts, just do as you're told.'

'But …'

'Izzy!'

Subdued by the strict tone of her mother's voice, the child slunk off sulkily to show her masterpiece to the owner of the sugar-encrusted teeth. After all, this picture wouldn't even have existed if it hadn't been for Gran.

Grace put a glass in front of Anna. 'Here, have a sip of water. You okay?'

'Mm. Just didn't expect it to hit me like that, that's all. Stupid really, I should have known. Knew she was in the house, knew we'd come face to face soon, so why do I feel like this? Got anything stronger?' she asked, glancing at the glass of water.

'Seriously?'

'Seriously.'

Later that afternoon the phone rang. Izzy hurtled through to answer it, almost tripping over Alfie in her haste.

'Uncle Richard wants to speak to …'

Grace leapt to her feet, a smile on her face. He was so thoughtful, he'd be wondering how they were getting on.

'… Auntie Anna.' finished Izzy.

'What?' Grace stopped in her tracks, startled.

'Uncle Richard wants to speak to Auntie Anna.'

'Me?'

Izzy rolled her eyes and sighed. Adults. They could be so thick sometimes.

Anna took the handset and disappeared into the kitchen with it, closing the door.

Mm. Interesting.

'Why does Uncle Richard want to talk to Auntie Anna?'

'I don't know, darling, but I'm sure we'll soon find out.'

Some time later Anna emerged, pink and flustered. 'He's asked me to go out for a meal with him tonight,' she babbled excitedly. 'I've said yes. Is that okay?'

A squirmy feeling whizzed around inside Grace's head. 'Of course it is. Why wouldn't it be?'

'Well you know, ex-husband, all of that.'

The squirmy feeling persisted. 'Don't be daft. You go – you deserve a night out.'

'You sure?'

'Of course I am.'

But, in her heart of hearts, Grace was jealous. She knew Richard was her ex, that she didn't have exclusivity of him, that she had Charlie. She knew Richard had had lots of other dates since their divorce, but they'd been with face-less other women, nobody she'd known, insignificant other beings. But Anna? This was a different ball game altogether.

Anna was excited. She twittered on, almost like a teenager on a first date. Grace's head came back halfway through the conversation.

'... such a long time, I don't know. What d'you think?'

'Sorry?'

'Grace, are you sure you're alright about this? You've gone very quiet.'

'Hello! Where is everybody?'

Cleo.

'In here, love. You're back early.'

'God, there you go again! Late, early, can't win, can I?'

'Sorry, love. Had a good day?'

But Izzy could contain the secret no longer. 'Auntie Anna's got a date! Auntie Anna's got a date!' she chanted, as she skipped around the living room.

Cleo's eyes rounded with excitement. 'With my dad?' she shrieked, bouncing on the balls of her feet and clasping her hands together, prayer-like.

'The very same,' smiled Anna.

'Yes!' gasped Cleo.

Only one person not happy, then.

# 9

'What am I going to wear?' babbled Anna nervously. 'Trousers? Skirt? Dress? What do you wear for a first date?'

'Auntie Anna! Surely you must know! gasped Cleo. 'What d'you usually wear when you go out with someone for the first time?'

'It's so long since, I can't remember,' laughed Anna, still pink with excitement.

'But you live in London!'

'And your point is?'

'Surely you must have men queuing up to take you out.'

'You'd be surprised, young lady. Anyway, come upstairs and help me find something. I can't even remember what I've brought with me. Coming, Grace?'

'No, you go. I'd better start dinner, Charlie will be in soon.'

Anna caught the hurt in Grace's voice and momentarily came back to earth. 'You go on up, Cleo, I'll follow you in a minute.'

Cleo was hesitant until Anna said, 'Have a root through my clothes, see what you can find.' And up the stairs she flew.

'You're sure you're alright about this? I won't go if you don't want me to,' said Anna, concerned.

'Of course I am,' lied Grace. 'What is there not to be alright about? You go and have a good time,' she said, noisily dragging pans from the cupboard, a lid clattering to the floor.

'Grace, look at me! You still like him, don't you?'

Grace turned slowly to face her sister. 'He's my ex, of course I've got feelings for him. But I'm with Charlie now and Charlie's a good man. Honestly, Anna, you go. I'm fine about it, really I am.'

Anna bit her lip, hesitantly. 'Well, if you're sure. It's been a long time since anyone asked me out and, as Hugo always says, you should live life to the max. It *is* only a dinner date, Grace, nothing more. I'll be going home in a few days.'

Izzy was the first to spot him pulling up in his car outside. Not surprising really, she'd been glued to the window for the past hour. Grace got up to let him in but a euphoric Cleo flew down the stairs and beat her to it.

'Oh Dad, wait till you see her, she looks gorgeous,' Cleo exclaimed, clasping her hands together with delight.

Calm down, Cleo,' her father said as he gave her a hug. 'It's just a dinner date.'

'Yeah, yeah,' replied Cleo knowingly.

Zak put in an appearance at the top of the stairs. 'Hey! Sorry, but I'm in a bit of a rush.'

'Going out?'

'Yeah, meeting Genevieve in town.'

'Want a lift?'

'No, you're okay thanks, I don't want to cramp your style!'

'You two!' exclaimed Richard. 'Like I keep saying, it's just a dinner date.'

'Yeah, yeah,' they chorused.

Grace wandered out from the lounge. 'Stop teasing your father, you two!'

But Richard had eyes for no one else as down the stairs, looking every inch a superstar, glided Anna.

'Hi,' she said, shyly.

'You look amazing,' he said, almost bereft of speech.

The squirmy feeling returned to Grace's head in an instant. 'Have a good time,' she forced herself to say.

Charlie came up behind her and encircled her with his arms. She stiffened at his touch.

'What time will you be back?' she found herself asking.

'Mum!' warned Cleo, not wanting anything to spoil this. Ooh, it was so exciting!

Grace watched from the doorway as they drove off in Richard's car. Richard's car ... a big, flash, sporty model. When she'd been with him he'd driven an old banger but ... those were the days.

'I love you, Gracie,' Charlie whispered in her ear.

Her silence spoke volumes.


'Grace!'

Typical. Anna gets to go on a romantic night out, she gets left at home with Mother.

'Coming, Mother.'

Grace grudgingly opened the door to Gran's room.

'What's happening?'

As if she didn't know. There was absolutely nothing wrong with Gran's ears when she wanted to hear, it was just convenience deafness that she suffered from occasionally.

'Anna's gone out.'

'Gone out?'

'Yes, gone out.'

'But I thought I heard Richard?'

Wait for it. 'You did. It's Richard she's gone out with.'

'Gone out with Richard?'

'Yes, Mother, gone out with Richard.'

'What did I tell you? She's an absolute disgrace that one. Not been here five minutes and she's gone out with your husband!'

'Mother! Don't be ridiculous,' snapped Grace, the squirmy feeling going into overdrive. 'Richard is my *ex*-husband, not my husband – remember? She's perfectly entitled to go out with him if she wants to. She's doing nothing wrong.'

'Why do you look so upset about it then?'

'Because of you winding me up, that's why.'

Gran's beady eyes narrowed. 'I'm telling you, you want to watch that one. No man is safe with her around.'

'Mother! They've only gone out for a meal, nothing more.'

'Yes, and if you believe that you'll believe anything.'

Infuriated, face burning, she turned to leave the room, coming face to face with Charlie.

'Gracie?'

'Mother! She's driving me insane!'

'You mark my words, my girl,' muttered Gran.

Charlie touched Grace's arm tenderly. 'You go and sit down. I'll make us all a nice cup of tea.'

Grace left the room in silence, anguish all-pervasive. Cup of tea? Cup of tea? Is that all anyone ever thinks of around here? They think it solves everything. She sank into the sofa, Alfie leaning dolefully against her, concerned.

'Off now, then! See you later!' shouted Zak, on his way out to meet Genevieve.

'Me too, I won't be late!' shouted Cleo.

That didn't help. Was everyone out having fun except her? She wasn't old. Charlie was just happy with his cup of tea and the television, as was her mother who – good timing – came hobbling through the door at that moment. Charlie followed closely, with the tea.

'Anything on?'

She'd scream in a minute.

As Anna studied the menu, Richard studied Anna. It was uncanny how much she resembled her sister. And yet that wasn't the reason he was attracted to her, he was sure it wasn't. Fair enough, he still did have feelings for Grace.

After all, she was the mother of his children, they had a shared history. But it was over for them; had been a long time ago.

Anna felt his eyes on her and glanced up, self-conscious. 'What?' she asked, shyly.

'Nothing,' replied Richard, embarrassed at being caught staring.

'There so obviously was something,' she said, coyly. She was starting to enjoy this now.

'Just thinking how beautiful you are.'

'Flatterer.' Definitely enjoying it. 'Bet that wasn't what you were really thinking though. Bet you were thinking that I look just like Grace.'

'Okay, truth. I *was* thinking how much you look like Grace but I was also thinking that that isn't the reason I'm attracted to you.'

'So what is?'

'Don't take compliments easily do you?' he joked. 'Okay, you're absolutely gorgeous, good sense of humour, intelligent ... what more do you want? I haven't known you for long enough to find out the rest yet – although I'm hoping I might get the chance.'

Anna panicked a little. 'I'm only here for a few days, you know.'

'I know. Just have to make the most of it, won't we?'

Anna panicked a little more.


'Grace?'

Grace lay in silence, her back towards him, feigning sleep.

'Grace? Can we ... you know?' He shuffled about, living in hope.

Grace remained still, the stress of avoidance making her breathe faster. She really did not want to make love to Charlie, not tonight. She tried to slow down the rhythm of her breathing to convince him she was asleep, she definitely did *not* want any other kind of rhythmical things taking place in the bed that night.

Too late. He nibbled her ear. 'You avoiding me?'

'I've got a headache, Charlie.' Lame, I know.

'This'll make it better,' he said, rubbing himself up against her.

'But Charlie ...' she felt about as sexy as a plate of cold porridge.

His hand moved up the inside of her thigh, aiming for hot. Could this man not take no for an answer? Obviously not.

He prodded up behind her, a man on a mission, entered her, pounding away. But nothing could float Grace's boat tonight. Charlie's needs were soon satisfied, Grace's prayers answered.


'Would you like to come back to my place for a bit?'

'A bit of what, did you have in mind?' Anna smiled, rolling her eyes at his confusion.

'For a coffee, is what I meant to say.'

'Mm, that's what they all say,' she said, still teasing.

'Oh, *all* eh? There have been that many?' he asked, teasing reversed, taking his eyes off the road for a moment to glance at her.

'Watch where you're going, Richard.'

'Ooh, bossy as well. I like it.'

'Okay.'

'Okay what?'

'Coffee.'

'Coffee?'

'Coffee, but that's all.'

He grinned at her as he pulled into the drive of his house, confident of what was about to happen.

'I mean it, Richard.'

'Sure you do,' he said, locking the car.

But she had willpower.

'I'll put the kettle on,' he said, expecting them to reach boiling point before it did. 'Or would you prefer something stronger?'

'Something stronger,' she said, taking off her coat.

His eyes mentally undressed her. 'Don't stop there.'

'Richard! I told you! Just a drink.'

'But you moved on from coffee to something stronger.' He moved towards her. 'How about …?'

'Gin,' she said, a little too quickly, 'and, um, tonic.' She handed him her coat.

She had willpower, she had willpower … okay, it was weakening.

He hung up her coat, poured them both a drink, and sat down on the sofa beside her.

'Don't forget you're driving.'

Definitely bossy. 'Driving?'

'Me, home.'

'Home? But I thought …'

'No, Richard.' Desire mounting, she wrestled with herself, a battle that could not be won. It had been so long … The next minute, her tongue was down his throat.

'I thought you said no,' he mumbled through the passion.

'That was then,' she muttered, urgency all-consuming as they struggled out of their clothes.

Wet, throbbing, and pretty desperate it has to be said, a vague distant memory of willpower flew right out of the window as she grabbed him with some urgency and guided him into her. Gasping with pleasure as he entered her, sensations that she'd thought she may never experience again rippled through her body, reawakening it from its long period of abstinence. His thrust deep inside her made her cry out with long-forgotten feelings of ecstasy as he moved, slowly at first, and then gradually building up to an almost unbearable climax. He'd lit fireworks, she could have sworn it.

They lay back in a post-ejaculatory haze for a moment or two, covered in sweat, gasping.

'Wow,' he said, as he turned his head to look at her. 'I wasn't expecting that.'

'Liar,' she said, smiling, sated.

'You were so adamant.'

'I know, then I turned to mush. It's been so long ... nearly five years actually. I'm not usually that forward.'

'Five years!' he gasped. 'How on earth do you manage without sex for all that time?'

'Have you ever heard of Jessica Rabbit?' she asked, grinning mischievously.

'Mmm,' he said, turned on by the thought.

'Hey, I must go,' she said, scrambling to get up.

'Don't go,' he said, visibly aroused.

'I have to, I'm sorry.'

'Please ... it's Jessica Rabbit's fault.'

'She has a lot to answer for, that one,' said Anna, straddling him, desirous again herself. This was so out of character.


'Oh! Mum! You made me jump! What are you doing down here sat in the dark?' asked Cleo, as she turned on the kitchen light.

'I could ask you the same question.'

'Couldn't sleep.'

'Me neither.'

'Want a brew?' asked Cleo, filling the kettle.

'Might as well.'

'Keep wondering how Dad's getting on with Auntie Anna, do you?'

'Dunno, I expect she'll be back soon.'

'Back? Tonight? I don't think so, they'll be shagging.'

'Cleo!'

'Oh, sorry. But they will. Be at it like rabbits tonight.'

'Cleo!'

'Well, didn't you see them? Definitely fancy each other – and they are adults. What's to stop them?'

'Self-respect, that's what. You don't just go jumping into bed with every man you meet. And it'd do you good to remember that, young lady.'

'Okay, okay, calm down.' Cleo glanced over her shoulder at her mother as she put the tea in the pot. 'Are you jealous? Do you still fancy Dad?' Cleo spun round to see the reaction.

'Cleo! Don't be silly. You know I don't.'

'I only know what I see,' said Cleo, brain in overdrive.

They both turned as they heard the front door.

'Anna?'

Zak.

'Hey! Wassup?' he asked, not in full control of his limbs, or anything else for that matter.

'Zak, you're drunk,' said Grace, stating the obvious.

'Soz. Goin' to bed,' he said, staggering back down the hall and swaying up the stairs. ''Night.'

''Night Zak.'

'How come he gets away with it and I don't?' seethed Cleo.

'Because he's older and has a bit more sense.'

'It's so unfair.' Cleo was about to stomp out of the room, but then remembered that she might miss something. 'I'll pour the tea,' she said sulkily.

Grace yawned. 'We should go to bed.'

'In a bit. I've made it now. And anyway, we were just talking about Dad.'

'Were we?'

'You know we were.'

Front door again. Anna, dishevelled.

'Oh, I wasn't expecting a reception committee.' A trifle sarcastic that, but she was used to living on her own, coming and going as she pleased.

'Evidently.' Sarcastic too. Look at the state of her, she looked as if she'd just rolled out of bed.

Cleo smiled welcomingly. Result! 'Had a good time? Just made a brew if you want one.'

'No thanks. Think I'll go straight up if you don't mind.'

But Cleo was bursting to know, even though it was blatantly obvious. 'So, did you …?'

'Cleo!' the sisters chorused, in agreement on that one.

# 10

'Got any paracetamols, Mum?' Zak, decidedly hungover.

'Have you tried the bathroom cabinet?'

'Can't get in the bathroom.'

'Here, good job I keep an emergency supply,' said Grace, rooting through her handbag and passing him the packet.

'Me want toast! Me want toast!' chanted Izzy, as was customary for this time of day.

Zak held his head with a groan. 'Izzy, please don't,' he said feebly.

'You know you really shouldn't go out drinking, not when you've got college the next morning,' she scolded.

'I know, it's just ... well, I dumped Genevieve last night. Discovered some things about her I didn't like.'

'Oh Zak, I'm sorry. What sort of things?'

'Drugs, actually. Found out just how dependent she is on them. Thought I was pathetic when I wouldn't ...'

'Drugs?'

'Drugs! Drugs! Me want drugs!'

'Izzy!'

Charlie came in at precisely that moment. '*What* did she just say?'

'I know, I know. I was just talking to Zak and forgot she was there.'

'Gotta go, Mum. Speak to you later.' Zak swung his rucksack, gingerly, onto his shoulder.

'Sure you don't want anything to eat?'

'Couldn't Mum, honestly. Don't worry, I'll be fine. Just a hangover.'

Grace watched him go, a worried frown on her face.

'What's up with him?' asked Charlie, pouring himself some cereal.

'Woman trouble.'

Gran was at the kitchen table alone, dunking and slurping, when Grace got back from taking Izzy.

'Thought I might as well stay out here and have a bit of company while she's not in. Stayed out all night with your husband, did she? Well, I did warn you. Disgrace, that's what she is. Disgrace.'

'Mother, for the last time, Richard is *not* my husband. And it's absolutely none of your business what Anna does, you washed your hands of her years ago – remember? But, if you must know, she *did* come home last night.'

Grace lifted the teapot and poured out a cup, stirring it noisily. Leaving her mother moaning away to herself, she carried the cup of tea upstairs, mutterings of 'I'm a poor defenceless old lady' ringing in her ears.

Grace knocked gently on Anna's bedroom door. 'Anna? Can I come in?'

''Course. What time …? Ten past ten! I'd no idea! Sorry.'

Grace put down the cup on the bedside cabinet. 'Peace offering.'

Anna rubbed her eyes and yawned, trying to wake up. She felt exhausted. 'Don't be silly.'

'No. That's what *I* was being,' said Grace, sitting down on the edge of the bed. 'I've had time to think now. I don't want Richard, but I didn't want anyone else to have him either, especially my sister. Can you understand that? It's like he's one of my best friends: we have a special bond and I didn't want anyone else butting in to break that. It's different with those faceless people from the Internet site that he's been out with, I didn't know them. But you're my sister, I love you. You were a threat, I was excluded. Do you understand what I'm saying?'

'Oh Grace, I think you're being a bit paranoid.'

'That's not the only reason I felt grumpy, though. I just feel so stuck in a rut.'

Anna sat up and took a sip of the tea, trying hard to wake up. 'How do you mean?' she asked, plumping up the pillows to support her aching back.

'Exactly that, really. Everybody out having a good time, me stuck at home. I mean I'm not old, time enough for that then. Charlie's happy enough staying in every night watching TV, but me, I want more. As it is, my life feels that it's over.'

Anna cringed. 'Be grateful for what you've got, Grace,' she said poignantly. 'Many people would be glad to be in your position.'

'I know, I know. Anyway, enough of me. How did it go with Richard?'

'A lot further than I intended it to, if you must know. A relationship is the last thing I came here looking for. Been on my own for too long and like it that way. I don't trust men usually, but Richard …'

'… is tried and tested,' smiled Grace.

'Suppose,' she answered, deep in thought.

Grace looked at her inquisitively. 'So?'

Anna brought herself back to the moment. 'I still don't want a relationship. Anyway, I'm going home in a few days,' she said, resignedly.

'London's not that far away.'

'I can't have a relationship.'

'I don't understand.' Grace was puzzled.

'You will one day.'

Later that morning, as she walked to nursery to collect Izzy,

Grace mulled over what Anna had said about not wanting a relationship. Strange, the way she seemed so adamant about it; strange and yet understandable. After all she'd gone through in her past it was no wonder she didn't want to get close to anyone; trust would be virtually impossible, barriers up. Having said that, she could certainly see that Anna was deeply attracted to Richard, definitely a chink of light breaking through there. Perhaps, given time …

Weird. It was only yesterday that she had hated the thought of Anna with Richard and now, here she was thinking of ways to encourage it. They would make a lovely couple and they could all be close – one big happy family. Who was she kidding? Well, close-ish anyway. She'd love them to get together, and for Anna to move up here permanently.

Maybe that would help her own situation too, give them a bit more fun in their lives. She hated the way she criticised Charlie sometimes. After all, he was the perfect man in many ways, the ideal husband. Kind, thoughtful, hardworking, patient, what more could she possibly want? Excitement, that's what, fun and frivolity before it was too late. Oh well, she was going to London with Anna in a few days, that was something to look forward to. And how could she ever begin to criticise Charlie? There she was, waltzing off to London, leaving him to cope with everything in her absence. And did he complain? Not one iota. As Anna said, she should be grateful for what she'd got.

'Ah, could I have a word? In my office, if you don't mind.'

Mrs Clarke. Now what? She wasn't even late. She glanced around anxiously to try and spot Izzy, but noticed her painstakingly tidying up the jigsaws in the corner unaware of her mother's arrival, probably presuming she'd be late. Grace followed Mrs Clarke into the office.

'Take a seat.'

Serious stuff then.

Mrs Clarke cleared her throat. 'It's about Izzy.'

Oh God, what's she done now?

'Izzy was in the play kitchen area today and had some dolls sitting around the table, feeding them each in turn. I stopped to talk to her, and asked what she was giving them to eat. I wonder if you can tell me what she said?'

Was this a trick question? How was she to know the answer to that? She felt like a child about to fail an exam and made some mad, random guess, hoping that humour would save the day.

'Fish fingers, chips and beans followed by apple crumble and custard?' This was one of Izzy's favourite meals; she thought she might be on to a winner. She grinned hopefully at Mrs Clarke.

Mrs Clarke did not return the grin, in fact her face seemed to have turned to stone … marble actually. Grace had never really studied Mrs Clarke's face before but it did in fact have quite a mottled appearance, shiny as well. Did it always look like that or was she just having a bad day? Maybe …

'I don't think you realise the seriousness of the situation,' continued Mrs Clarke, breaking through Grace's train of thought. 'The answer Izzy gave to my question was, "I'm giving them drugs. They like them."'

Grace couldn't manage totally to suppress a nervous giggle, even though she tried hard. 'Drugs?' she spluttered.

'I don't think you quite realise the seriousness of the situation,' repeated Mrs Clarke, annoyance radiating. 'Fortunately none of the other children were near to Izzy at the time, so the remark was not overheard or repeated by anyone else. Nevertheless I am extremely concerned about the incident and have to consider whether any action should be taken.'

'But …'

Mrs Clarke raised a hand to deter Grace from speaking. 'Obviously the welfare of the children is my top priority. If any of the other parents got to hear about this, I can assure you, heads would roll.'

'But ...'

'Do you have any idea why she should say such a thing?'

'She ...'

'A child learns by example. Now I'm not saying that Izzy has witnessed drugs being taken in your house, but this would imply ...'

'This would imply *what*?' It was Grace's turn to interrupt now, like a mother lion protecting her cubs. *Nobody* attacked her family – not even Mrs Clarke.

'Well, I ...'

'I sincerely hope you are *not* implying that any one of my family has been involved in any way with drugs. I know exactly where this has come from. I was having a conversation with my son this morning about a girlfriend from whom he'd split up the previous evening due to his discovery of her drug habit. My son did not want to become a part of that scene and I'm proud of him for having had the strength of character to walk away. I also feel proud of the way he feels able to discuss these things with me which, I think, proves that I'm not the useless mother you seem to think I am.'

'I ...'

'Let me finish! I realise Izzy overheard part of the conversation and picked up on the word without having the slightest idea what she's talking about. If I make a big fuss about it now and reprimand her for using the word it will stick in her mind. I think the best thing I can do is keep her at home for a few days, let her spend some time with her new auntie, and give her a chance to forget that she ever heard it. As for you, Mrs Clarke, I would really appreciate it if you didn't display such a pious attitude towards me in future. Do you even have children of your own?'

'I ...'

'No, I thought not. So do not judge me when you know absolutely nothing about me or my family. Good day to you, Mrs Clarke. I shall collect my daughter and go. Izzy will be back at the end of the week.'

Tables well and truly turned.

It certainly seemed to be a morning for confrontation. Grace could hear raised voices coming from inside the house as she approached the front door with Izzy. The sound of Alfie barking didn't help. He bounded down the hall to them as they came in, panting and wild-eyed, a dog in a panic, in need of protection.

Anna and Gran had met.

'Izzy, take Alfie upstairs with you and play in your bedroom for a while.'

'But Alfie's not allowed upstairs.'

'He is today.'

Adults. They could be so confusing sometimes. First Mrs Clarke and now Mummy. She took Alfie by the collar and led him up the stairs, shaking her head and sighing with bewilderment. On top of everything else, Mummy said she hadn't got to go to school for two whole days, and it wasn't even the holidays. She couldn't work it out at all.

Meanwhile, Grace entered the war zone that was the kitchen.

'I just find it impossible to understand why you would never believe me, why you'd never protect me, make it stop.' Anna's voice was broken and raw.

The anguish that emanated from her almost over-powered Grace. She wanted to step in, protect her sister, tell them to stop, but she knew she had to hold back.

'Because it was your fault, you whore!' growled Gran through clenched gums. 'When I married your father it was till death us do part, and that's the way it had to be. But then you came along. Always trying to please him, weren't you? Even as a little girl. Then, as you grew up … well! Disgusting! Skirts up to your backside, plastered in make-up, flaunting yourself, no wonder he weakened. Nothing but a trollop. And then, to top it all, to go and get yourself pregnant! An absolute disgrace. The neighbours would have been horrified if they'd ever found out …'

'Horrified? They would have been, but with Dad, not with me. I was just a child. How could you send me away?'

'A child? Huh! An evil little bitch more like. Why did I send you away? Because I had to. I couldn't stand the sight of you. You were a disgrace and tried to bring the rest of us down with you.'

'Nothing to do with the money, then?' spat Anna.

'Money?' asked Gran, feebly.

'Oh come on! Don't play the innocent now! I know all about the pay-off you received from Uncle Frank. Ten thousand pounds for my baby. How could you?'

'Ten thousand pounds? That was nothing for all I'd gone through.'

'All *you'd* gone through? You're unbelievable, do you know that?'

'And you're a disgrace. Off with somebody else's husband now and you've not been here five minutes.'

'What?'

'Mother!' Grace could intervene now. 'I keep telling you, Richard is no longer my husband. Anna is perfectly entitled to go out with him if she wants to.'

'Well, you'd better keep an eye on Charlie. Zak as well, because no man is safe with her around.'

'Mother!' Grace's cheeks were burning with indignation.

Anna glanced at her gratefully. 'No point, Grace. Leave her to stew in her own little world, bigoted old bat. Alone and angry, like she deserves.'

110

'I've got my family, they love me.'

'Put up with you, more like. Anyway, they're my family too again now, and I've got Hugo.'

'Hugo?' Gran asked, inquisitive now.

'Yes, Hugo. The person you sold for ten thousand pounds.'

There was a knock on the kitchen door. 'Mummy!'

Izzy.

'Go back upstairs Izzy, I'll be up in a minute.'

'But Mummy …'

'Izzy!'

'But Mummy, Alfie's pooed, and it's everywhere.'

'Oh God.' Grace disappeared on a mummy mission, leaving Anna alone with hers.

By the time she came back downstairs, child and dog in tow, the two had separated. Silence pervaded. Izzy clung to Grace's skirt, sensitive to the atmosphere. Alfie slithered into his basket, where he settled, unasked, with a sigh.

'Okay?' Grace asked her sister, who sat at the kitchen table, her head in her hands.

'As I'll ever be,' she replied sadly.

'Want a drink?'

Anna got to her feet, looking pale and exhausted. 'No thanks, I'm okay. Think I'll go up to my room and lie down for a while, though, if you don't mind.'

Izzy left Grace's side and rushed to give Anna a hug. 'I love you, Auntie Anna,' she said.

'I love you too, poppet,' Anna replied, tears not far away.

Izzy didn't even bother to correct her this time. She really did love her auntie, and if she wanted to call her 'poppet', then it was fine by her.

'Hey.' Zak, home early.

'Feeling better?'

111

'A bit.' He still looked glum.

'You did the right thing, you know.'

'What? Getting drunk?'

Still had his sense of humour then.

'Idiot,' smiled Grace, giving him a slap. 'I meant all that stuff with Genevieve – walking away. I'm proud of you,' she said, hugging him now.

'I know. I know it was the right thing to do. Anyway, I'm going out on the pull tonight with Bainsey. Plenty more where she came from … sod her.'

'Good boy.' Good boy? What am I saying? 'Don't go out getting bladdered again tonight, you've got college in the morning.'

'Chill, Mum, it's fine. I'm not going to be drinking much anyway. On the pull, remember?'

Cleo followed shortly afterwards. 'Where's Auntie Anna?'

'Nice to see you too,' said Grace, feeling invisible.

'Sorry, Mum,' she said, giving her a hug (yes, things were definitely improving here – a hug from Cleo!), 'but Dad wants her.'

'What?'

'He's been trying to phone her mobile but she's not answering, so he tried mine.'

'He didn't ring the house.'

'Said he did. You didn't answer either.'

Come to think of it they wouldn't even have heard the phone with all the shouting that was going on.

'Anna's having a lie down. She had a confrontation with Gran today. It didn't go well.'

'Oh fuck!'

'Cleo!'

'Sorry. Is she very upset?'

'Well of course she is. I think she needs some time on her own.'

'Can I go up?'

'What have I just said?'

But this was not a firm enough answer in the negative for Cleo, who bounded up the stairs two at a time.

'Cleo!'

At least she had the decency to knock on the door, even though she was undeterred by the lack of response from within. 'Hi,' she breezed, smilingly.

Anna was not used to this invasion of privacy and sat up hurriedly, embarrassed by her soggy-nosed, red-eyed state, 'Cleo, I ...'

'It's okay, Mum told me. She also told me not to disturb you, but this'll cheer you up.'

'Cleo! I told you not to come upstairs!' Grace had followed to reprimand her disobedient daughter, Izzy clung to her legs and Alfie close behind.

All eyes were on the squirmingly self-conscious figure who sat huddled on the bed. Anna was used to her privacy and found the intrusion hard to deal with.

Cleo bounced on the balls of her feet, contrastingly joyful. 'Dad rang you but you didn't answer your phone. He wants to know if he can take you out tonight.'

'Tonight?' Anna snuffled. 'You can see the state of me. And anyway, I really don't ...'

'Oh, go on, pretty please! He really likes you. And I'll help you get ready,' Cleo pleaded.

The row of eyes continued to stare, Cleo's in particular bearing persuasion in bucketloads.

'Oh, what the heck,' she rallied, noisily blowing her nose. 'Is the bathroom free?'

'We'll make sure it is,' Cleo grinned. Result.

# 11

Richard was early.

'Keen or what?' asked Cleo, as she let him in.

'Alright, Grace?' he asked, as he came into the living room. She hadn't looked happy about him going out with Anna when he'd collected her yesterday. Understandably so; he was her ex, Anna her sister.

'Mm, fine,' she smiled warmly, seeming okay about it now.

'Why wouldn't she be alright?' Charlie asked sharply, jealousy creeping in.

'No reason, mate, just a figure of speech. Anna ready?'

'I'll give her a shout,' said Cleo.

But there was no need. Anna was just coming down the stairs, resplendent in dark glasses.

'Didn't know the sun was still out?' Richard teased, he already knew of her predicament, she'd spoken to him on the phone earlier.

'Don't be so mean,' she admonished.

Grace was pleased to see how comfortable they seemed with each other and, when Anna mentioned that she may not be back until morning, Cleo was over the moon.

'Where are we going?' asked Anna, as she got into his car.

'Nowhere,' he smiled.

'We so obviously are going somewhere,' she said, curious as to why he looked so smug.

'Okay, okay,' he gave in. 'You said you didn't feel up to seeing anyone tonight so I thought I'd take you to this really high-class restaurant …'

'Richard!'

'… called Ricardo's, where the chef is the best in the world.'

'Richard, I told you …!'

'Perfect setting, perfect wine, and as for the after-dinner entertainment …'

The penny dropped. 'Richard, you are a torment! You can cook?' she asked, suddenly feeling stupid.

He loved winding her up. 'Well of course I can cook! How else do you think I've survived these past few years?'

'Takeaways?'

He turned to give her a withering look and was suddenly filled with a pang of … was it love? 'Take off the sunglasses,' he said, eyes back on the road, his voice soft and caring, 'you don't have to pretend with me.'

Drawing up outside his house, he turned off the engine and came round to open the car door for her. What a gentleman. He held out his hand to help her, and she took it, feeling an unexpected tingle of excitement at their skin-to-skin touch. Was this love or lust? She fervently hoped the latter. There was no way love could be on the agenda, no way at all.

A mouthwatering aroma drifted towards them as they entered the house.

'Mmm, something smells nice.'

'Indeed it does,' he said, taking her coat, nuzzling her neck.

Oh God. Lust. Please, lust.

'Can I get you a drink?' he asked, trying to control himself.

Ignoring his question, her eyes locked on his. 'Um, how long will dinner be?'

'Long enough,' he said, smouldering as she made the first move.

'You sure?' she gasped, as his fingers hit her G-spot.

'Hot dinner, hot diner – I know which I prefer,' he joked, before abandoning himself completely to her all-encompassing flesh. This was one special woman.

Despite all of his culinary efforts earlier, food had not been high on their list of priorities this evening and, by the time they came to eat, it had lost its intended tastebud-tempting appeal and now resembled the charred remains of a last week's barbecue.

Richard apologised profusely as he rescued all that he could.

'No worries, I like charcoal,' she grinned impishly.

He glanced at her, still scraping. 'And it was going to be delicious as well, it took me ages.'

'Sorry, my fault.'

'Hey, don't think I'm complaining.'

Amazingly, he did manage to rescue enough of it for them to eat, filling up with cheese, garlic bread and olives in addition – a virtual feast, in fact. They gobbled up eagerly, hungry after their lovemaking.

'What are you staring at?' she asked, popping an olive into her mouth and removing an unexpected stone.

'You,' he said, gaze never faltering.

'Well, I know that. What I meant was, why are you staring at me?'

'Because … I think I'm falling in love with you.'

The olive stone dropped to the plate with a chink. Anna's heart missed a beat. 'Don't be ridiculous, we've only just met. It's that daughter of yours putting ideas in your head. And anyway, love isn't possible, I'm going home next week. I live in London, for God's sake. I've got work. I've got Hugo.'

'And I think you love me too.'

'Have you gone completely insane? This time last week I

didn't even know you. Nobody falls in love that quickly. And anyway, I don't want a relationship, I like my life as it is. I like being on my own. I like living in London.'

'What are you scared of?' he asked, moving round the table towards her.

'Scared? Who says I'm …?' She was silenced by his lips on hers, as he knelt down before her, hand fondling her breast.

She flinched ever so slightly, and pushed him away. 'Richard, we can't do this,' she said, panic rising. 'We can't fall in love, we can't let it happen.'

Anna lay in the empty bed, sleep a zillion miles away. In her panic earlier she'd wanted to go home, back to Grace's house, anywhere but here. But Richard had been drinking, couldn't drive, and to have got a taxi back at that time would have undoubtedly triggered an inquisition from Grace and Cleo. Nothing escaped their notice as far as she and Richard were concerned; there would have been raised eyebrows all round.

How had she got herself into this? She'd been fine as she was, single and carefree. Well, not carefree exactly. Single and independent, not having to answer to anyone. Now, every move was scrutinised, every statement dissected. She loved being part of a family again but was finding that some-times it could be a bit stifling, especially at this point in her life when she needed to shield them from the truth. Perhaps she should just come out with it and be honest, but that had not been part of her plan. No, to waver now and give in would change everything. It was up to her to be strong and keep her secret. It was better for them all that way.

But Richard: what about him? He must be totally baffled by her behaviour, one minute all over him and the next keeping him at arm's length. Actually it was the only time in her entire life that she'd found some reason to be grateful for the abuse she'd suffered as a child. Richard was under the impression that this was the reason for her behaviour, and to a certain extent it was. But now that other things had happened to compound the situation, it was impossible for her to have a serious relationship. He would just have to understand that without knowing the full facts, because if she told him, she knew he would find it impossible to keep to himself.

But love? He'd said he was falling in love with her and, much as she was reluctant to admit the truth even to herself, she knew that the feeling was mutual. This was more than she'd ever felt for anyone else before. Just thinking about him now, despite her worries, made her nether regions turn into hot mush. She realised they'd been starved of activity for a long time and that could have something to do with them screaming so loudly for action. But it wasn't a simple case of lust, she was sure of it.

What a gentleman he'd been when she'd had her panic, his calmness just what she'd needed. She'd been ranting away about going home, ringing for a taxi, walking even. He'd simply stated the facts – too drunk to drive, too far to walk, Grace and Cleo's undoubted questions – in such a calm, unflustered manner that it had made her see sense. He was right, she had to stay overnight even if they didn't share a bed. The whole idea must have seemed ludicrous to him, but if it did, he didn't let it show. He simply suggested that he should sleep on the sofa, an offer she'd accepted gratefully.

She pictured him now, under his blanket, his comfortable bed vacated for what, to him, must seem like some sort of crazy woman. What on earth had she been thinking, turning him out of his own bed? She groaned and turned over, covering her head with the duvet. Thinking of him, thinking of him … how could she sleep? Uhh! It was so hot! She threw back the duvet and turned onto her back, trying desperately to quell the flames of desire that were threatening to engulf her. Love, lust, whatever it was – she had to have him or she'd spontaneously combust.

Feeling like a harlot on the game, she sat up, swung her legs out of bed and, propelled by desire, made her way quietly to the lounge, hoping he'd be awake and understanding. Well, he certainly wasn't the former. Open-mouthed snores emanated from his prostrate form, which could well have been off-putting to any long-term partner, but which only served to be infinitely endearing in this starry-eyed case.

She could have just sat there and watched him sleep. His rugged, chiselled features, early-morning stubble breaking through, strong muscular arms and shoulders protruding above the blanket. The rise and fall of his chest with each breath. She could just have sat there … but on him she leapt. How could she do otherwise?

'Jeezwassat!' he didn't usually have dreams this good. But this was for real. He opened his eyes with a start to find her staring down at him, her body laid on top of his. 'I thought …'

'I know, I'm sorry. It's the "L" word I can't cope with. I'm fine with lust but just don't mention the other one, okay?'

'I'd agree to anything at this moment,' he groaned, eyes closed again, as her hand brought him to life – it didn't take long.

'Wait for me!' she cried, straddling him, anxious to assuage her throbbing desire, moaning with pleasure as she lowered herself onto him and rode the waves of delight. Screaming out, they climaxed together, satiated and as one.

Almost too exhausted to move, she rolled off him and he grabbed her, laughing, as she very nearly landed on the floor.

'We would have been so much better in bed,' he laughed, tucking the blanket in behind her.

119

'Better than that? Didn't think it was possible,' she said sleepily.

'We could try, compare the two,' he said, fully awake now.

'Oh Richard, think I've used up all my energy there. I was the one doing all the work.'

'Then allow me, madam,' he said, carrying her through to the bedroom. 'Just lie back and enjoy.'

As the early morning light filtered in through the curtains she woke with a start, disorientated for a moment, until sudden realisation made her turn over. There she was, awake, watching her with a smile on his face.

'Good morning, beautiful.'

She grimaced, but in a smiley kind of way. 'There's nothing beautiful about me of a morning. What time is it?'

'Seven. Plenty of time.'

'I thought you'd got work.'

'Mm. Don't have to be up until half past,' he said, his fingers already having reached their target, playing with her emotions as well as her body.

'Ohhh, Richard, I love …' she panted, sense almost abandoned as excruciatingly mind-blowing sensations rippled through her.

'What did you say?' he teased, tantalisingly withdrawing his hand.

'Ohhh – don't stop!' she gasped, eyes closed, not wanting to leave that pleasurable place.

His fingers returned, tormenting only briefly, then moving rapidly, rhythmically. Within seconds her body shuddered to orgasmic heights. Panting, her eyes opened as she reached out for him, his penis pulsating at her touch. He almost came as she guided him into her, but somehow managed to hold back. Moving slowly above her he was practically seeing stars.

'Anna ... I ...' he breathed, his face looking tormented.

She visibly stiffened beneath him. 'Don't ...' she gasped.

But the tensing of her body added to the overwhelming pleasure he was already feeling. To delay was no longer an option, his body convulsed to a climax.

'Sorry,' he gasped, hovering briefly, his limpness now sliding from her.

She looked at him mischievously, anxious to prevent him from seeing the panic she felt inside. 'Just remember, the word is lust. Okay?'

Lying back down with a post-orgasmic sigh of fulfilment, he turned his head lazily to look at her. What was it with this woman? He was utterly, completely in love with her. How could he go back to how things were before ... was it only last week? It seemed like a lifetime ago. He couldn't let her just slip away now, back to her life in London, back to a life he knew nothing about.

'What are you thinking?' Her voice cut through his thoughts.

He knew he had to tread carefully, he didn't want her bolting again. 'I'm thinking I don't understand you,' he said, gazing into her eyes.

Love, plain to see, gazed back at him briefly until, avoiding further eye contact, she snuggled up against him, her head on his chest, the windows to her soul no longer in his line of vision.

'Nobody does, not even me,' she joked, trying to lighten the moment.

'But ...'

'Lust, remember,' she said firmly.

Richard dropped her off at Grace's on his way to work. A reception committee consisting of Grace, her mother and Izzy met her in the kitchen. Izzy jumped down from her seat and ran to give her auntie a welcoming hug.

'Errgh, you smell funny,' she said, in her own inimitable Izzy way.

'Izzy!'

'It's okay, I know I do. I've not had time for a shower yet.'

'How come you're allowed to sleep at Uncle Richard's house and Cleo is too, but not me?' Izzy, in with both feet again.

'Good question,' grunted Gran.

'Izzy! Leave Auntie Anna in peace. Go and see to Alfie, he's scratching at the door to come in.'

Amazingly obedient for once, Izzy skipped off to the rescue of her four-legged friend and took him back up the garden, leaving Gran to take over.

'What did I tell you? Only been here five minutes and she's spending the night with the first man she sees – who just happens to be your husband.'

'Mother! Go to your room!' Grace was furious.

'Go to my room? Who do you think I am? One of your children?'

'Well you certainly act like one. Leave Anna alone – now!'

'You can tell Izzy to stop all you like, my girl, but you can't tell me. Just look at the state of her! Like I said, she's nothing but a whore, a disgrace to our family!'

'Mother!'

'It's okay, Grace, I'll get out of the way. I need to have a shower anyway.'

'Hmmph. Tarnished you are, no matter how hard you scrub.'

Anna shook her head sadly at Grace to deter her. It was no good prolonging the argument, it would never get anywhere and only made her feel depressed. She left them glowering at each other and went upstairs to get herself washed and changed before Izzy had a chance to comment again.

When she thought about it, maybe her mother was right

in some ways. After all she had only just met Richard, and he was once Grace's husband. Staying out all night, coming in smelling of sex and stale alcohol – what must they be thinking of her? They'd only accepted her back into the family a few days ago. What kind of an impression was she giving? A harlot ... like she'd been with Richard last night, throwing him out of his own bed and then hunting him down in the middle of the night, demanding sex.

The trouble was, the impression they were getting was so far from the truth of who she really was. Back in London, her friends actually considered her to be a bit of a prude. Well, not prude exactly, she was broad-minded enough, it's just that she didn't enjoy being flirtatious and throwing herself at men like most of the others did. Which is probably why she'd been starved of sex for such a long time, come to think of it.

She needed to get back there, that was the only answer. As it was she was causing nothing but bad feeling in this household. Her mother, she knew, would never forgive her and would always be stirring things up, causing upset for everyone. Charlie as well. He was the easiest bloke in the world to get on with, but she could see that understandably he was feeling pushed out since she'd come to stay with them, occupying so much of Grace's time. Grace and the children had been fantastic; she'd loved spending time with them. But then there was Richard. Richard, Richard, Richard, that was the crux of the matter. She was falling in love with him, try as she might to persuade herself otherwise, and that was only going to lead to complications. It wasn't fair to him either, leading him on like this, knowing it could never come to anything. It was her own fault. Why had she agreed to go out with him in the first place? She was single, unattached, and that was the way it was going to stay.

'You decent?' Grace knocked on the bedroom door.

'Yeah, come in. I've not even made it to the shower yet.'

'Sorry about Mother, you know what she's like. Try not to let it bother you.'

'I know, she'll never change. Made me think, though, that I really should be going home. What with her and with Richard and everything, I seem to be causing chaos.'

'But Anna, you can't go yet, you've only just got here! We're only just getting to know you, we love having you to stay.'

'You and the kids, maybe, but I'm worried, Grace, about Richard.'

'Richard?'

'I feel as though I'm leading him on. The more I see him the worse it'll be. He says he loves me.'

'Loves you?' Grace's eyes rounded in surprise. 'But that's good, isn't it?'

'No!' she snapped. 'No, it's not good. I told you, I don't want a relationship, that's not what I came here looking for.'

'I don't understand.'

'I'm happy as I am, that's all. Happy being single.'

'Well, I must say, you don't look it.'

Anna shot her a withering look. 'All I want to know is, do you still want to come with me when I go? Sample life in the big city for a few days?'

Grace's heart gave a nervous back somersault. 'Um, well yes, I suppose. When were you thinking of?'

'Tomorrow.'

'*Tomorrow?* I couldn't possibly go that quickly. I'd have to organise … Charlie'd have to … It's like deserting a sinking ship!' Headless chicken time had arrived.

'Sorry, I didn't mean to throw you into a panic. You don't have to come if you don't want to, I just thought …'

'I do, I do! I do want to, it's just that there are things I'll have to do, things to sort out. Could you not wait a few more days?'

'I suppose,' Anna said resignedly. She wasn't used to this idea of having to take other people into consideration. She usually just made a decision and went with it. 'Sunday then, final offer.'

Grace steeled herself. 'Sunday it is.'

# 12

'London? You're really going?'

'Well you know I am, Charlie. You said it was okay when we talked about it before, said you'd manage.'

'I know, I know. Didn't really think you meant it, though. Didn't realise you'd actually go.'

'It's only for a few days.'

'London, though?'

'It's not exactly Australia,' she tried hard not to snap. 'You will manage won't you?'

'S'pose I'll have to. I'll take a few days off, the lads can manage, next week, we've not got that much on.'

'Thanks, Charlie,' said Grace, giving him a hug. 'I do appreciate this you know, I really do.'

'Too soft with her, you are,' chipped in Gran, with her usual words of wisdom. 'You want to put your foot down, show her who's boss. She'll be off gallivanting all over the place with that trollop of a sister of hers. Who knows what they'll be up to? Too trusting for your own good. Letting your wife go off to that den of iniquity flaunting her wares … disgusting, that's what it is.'

'Mother, for the last time, will you please mind your own business and keep your nose out of ours.'

'But …'

'Mother!'

Amazingly enough, Gran's advice had the reverse effect on Charlie. Instead of continuing to try and make Grace feel guilty, he suddenly grew two inches taller and sprang to her defence. 'Look, could you please stop trying to cause trouble. I know my wife and trust her implicitly. Think of all she has to put up with, day after day, from everyone in this house. She works non-stop trying to look after everybody and keep things running smoothly. Do you not think she deserves a break? Because I, for one, certainly do, and it's up to us to take care of the house and each other while she's away so that she doesn't have to worry.'

A ten-second silence.

'I'll be in my room,' said Gran, huffily as she headed down the hall.

Charlie looked positively triumphant, an unexpected air of manliness about him. Grace regarded him with awe. If he acted like that a bit more often she wouldn't even *want* to go to London.

Zak's reaction to Grace's imminent departure was, predictably, the most straightforward. In fact, you could say, there was virtually no reaction at all.

'Sunday? 'Kay ... I thought I put my old trainers in the cupboard under the stairs,' he said, hunting around in a chilled sort of way.

'You did, but I put them in your room when I was cleaning it out last week.'

'Cool. I'll get them when I go up.'

'Did you hear what I said before?'

'Yeah, Sunday.'

'Gonna miss me, then?' asked Grace, fishing for 'How will we manage without you Mum?' 'The house won't be the same without you Mum', or any 'without you Mum'-type compliments at all.

'You'll only be gone a few days.'

Hmmph!

Cleo, on the other hand, turned into some kind of whirling dervish.

'You're going to London? On Sunday?'

'You know I'm going, I told you before.'

'But on Sunday? blazed Cleo, hands on hips.

'What's wrong with Sunday? You know I want to go and spend some time on my own with Auntie Anna, see where she lives, meet Hugo.'

'Auntie Anna's going too?'

'Well of course she is. I'm hardly going to be going on my own, am I?'

'But what about Dad? I was hoping they were going to move in together.'

'Cleo! That's up to them. You can't orchestrate people's lives.'

'Ohhh! This is so unfair!' she said, stamping her feet, marching up and down the kitchen in fury. 'What if I need you? Who will I talk to? What if I have a problem?'

'*Have* you got a problem?'

'No, but I might have. Then what?'

'I'll only be away for a short while. You'll hardly even notice I've gone, the amount of time you spend at home these days.'

'Uhhh!' grimaced Cleo in frustration, banging the kitchen door behind her as she stomped up the stairs to her room, and slammed the door so firmly shut that the house almost fell down.

Hormones, it had to be. Grace couldn't weigh her up at all ... she'd been so much better recently, somewhere almost approaching affectionate in fact – well, once anyway. She could understand Cleo not wanting Anna to go and leave Richard, just as she'd thought she was getting them together, the thought of a peaceful alternative home for herself on the horizon. But Cleo was going to miss *her*? Surely not, she hardly said two words to her most days, and they were usually 'See ya' as she disappeared out through the door. Guilt galloped in gung-ho and attacked the gullible Grace. Why do the words 'guilt' and 'mother' always seem to go hand in hand? Should she even be going to London? What was she thinking of? She had a family to look after, she should be putting them first, they needed her.

'What's Cleo in a strop about?' Anna, awakened from her nap by all the noise, came downstairs and joined her sister. This whole family thing drove her mad at times, if she was honest, everything seemed to descend into chaos. How did they cope with it on a regular basis? She just thanked her lucky stars she was single.

'Cleo? She's upset about me going to London. I feel really guilty now.'

'Oh for God's sake! How often do you go away and leave them? Never! It'll do them good to learn to stand on their own two feet for a while, give them a bit of independence.'

'You don't know what it's like being a mother, you ... Oh! I'm so sorry, Anna! I didn't mean ... I just didn't think.' Grace was mortified.

'Don't worry about it. It was an easy mistake to make.' Anna registered sadness, nevertheless. 'Go up and see to your daughter. I don't think she's as tough as she makes out.'

Her and her big mouth, what a thing to have come out with! Apologising profusely, Grace went in search of Cleo, following the trail of sobs that descended the stairs.

'Cleo?' No response when she knocked on the door.

'Can I come in?' Again no response, other than a few anguished sniffles, but she went in anyway.

'Go away!'

'Not until you tell me what's wrong.'

'Nothing.'

'Well something obviously is.'

Silence.

'I won't go to London if that's what's bothering you.'

129

''Snot that.'

'What is it, then?'

'Nothing.'

'Oh Cleo, I wish you'd talk to me.'

Silence.

'Is it Dad and Auntie Anna?'

'A bit.'

'Well, we can't do anything about that, that's up to them. You do see that, don't you?'

'S'pose.'

'So you're okay about me going to London? It'll not be for long.'

'Mm.'

'Come here and give me a hug.' Grace held out her arms and Cleo, amazingly, acquiesced.

'I do love you, you know that don't you?' said Grace, enjoying this moment of closeness with her wayward daughter, wishing it would happen more often. 'And remember, while I'm away, if you do have a problem I'm only on the other end of the phone. Don't suffer in silence, okay?'

''Kay. Thanks, Mum. Sorry.'

When she got to the bottom of the stairs, Grace could hear what sounded like a very serious conversation going on between Anna and Izzy, Alfie's snores providing the backing track. Grace was intrigued and didn't want to interrupt. She tiptoed down the hall and stood quietly near the doorway in order to eavesdrop, seeing Izzy sitting on Anna's knee, gazing up at her intently.

'Why?' asked Izzy, her voice filled with curiosity.

'Because I wasn't really old enough to be a proper mummy to him.'

'Where was his daddy?'

'His daddy had to go away,' answered Anna, battling her emotions.

'For ever?'

'For ever.'

'Poor Hugo.'

Silence reigned for a while. Grace was about to go in and interrupt, but Izzy piped up again.

'Did he like living with your auntie and uncle?'

'He did, Izzy, yes.' What else could she say?

'Did you go and see him?'

'No,' her voice was cracking now.

Grace hovered, should she stop them?

'Why?' asked Izzy, in all innocence.

Anna caught Grace's slight movement and signalled with her eyes for her to stay where she was, out of the room.

'It was too far away.'

'Like Australia?'

'Something like that, yes.'

Silence again, longer this time.

'Does he live at your house now?'

'No, he doesn't. He has his own house not very far away from me, though. I see him all the time.'

'Will you bring him here to see me?'

'I would love to, Izzy. Or he might even come on his own.'

'On his own?' Izzy was shocked.

'Yes, he's a big boy now, even older than Zak.'

'Cor!' giggled Izzy, covering her mouth and nose with both of her hands, eyes wide. Then she was silent for a moment or two. 'Auntie Anna?'

'What, Izzy?'

'I don't want you to go back to London.' She sounded nearly in tears.

Anna too. 'I promise I'll try my very best to come back and visit you soon.'

'When?'

'That all depends, Izzy, we'll have to see.'

131

'I love you, Auntie Anna.'

'I love you too, poppet.'

Definitely time for Grace's entrance now. 'Hey, you two, what are you up to?'

Two tear-stained faces gazed back at her in silence. Alfie, the only happy one, stretched, shook from head to tail and greeted her as waggily as if she was returning from her week in London already. Grace bent to make a fuss of him, suggesting to the other two that they might all go and take him for a walk to cheer them up a bit, they looked in need of some fresh air. Cheer *them* up a bit? It certainly had that effect on Alfie. The word 'walk' and he was whizzing round in circles like a spinning top, tongue drooling at the prospect.

How to break the news to Richard, that was Anna's greatest problem. How could she possibly tell him that she was going back to London on Sunday and didn't want to see him any more? Didn't want to see him – well, that was a lie for a start. Didn't want to? There was nothing she wanted more. But she couldn't, she knew she couldn't, and that was that. No point in even thinking about it.

Grace didn't help. No matter how many times she told her, she couldn't seem to grasp the fact that Anna would not be seeing Richard at all once she'd gone back to London. Grace was looking at it from her own point of view: she wanted them to be together, and couldn't understand what the problem was. London was only a couple of hours away by train – if she'd said that once, she'd said it a hundred times. Anna just wished she'd butt out and mind her own business. It was good having a sister, but sometimes … She supposed she'd been on her own too long; she wasn't used to having to explain herself to anyone, and now was not the time to have to start.

But Richard. What on earth could she say to him? Just

have to continue the love–lust theme that she'd used so far she supposed, even though he did see right through her and said he knew how she felt about him. To keep on denying it was all that she could do.

Grace was also worried about Richard. He'd been looking for love for so long, and now he'd finally found it, it was about to turn around and kick him in the teeth. She felt sort of responsible, Anna being her sister, and urged her to let him down gently. She'd actually wanted the four of them to go out for a meal together, as a persuasive ploy rather than a final farewell, but Anna had been adamant that this could not possibly happen. The intensity of emotion between Richard and herself was going to be bad enough; they certainly didn't have any need for an audience before their final curtain, despite Grace obviously still hoping to see a happy ending.

He picked her up that evening, blissfully unaware of what the outcome would be. Grace hovered suspiciously, looking as though she was waiting to wave them off. They were only going out for a meal, what was wrong with her?

'Alright Grace?' he asked, curious.

'Ye-ah, fine,' she stuttered, making a strange little half-wave gesture with her hand.

'Hmmph,' grunted Charlie.

Cleo ran upstairs.

'Am I missing something here?' Richard was completely baffled.

'No, but you will be if we don't leave right now,' Anna whispered seductively into his ear.

'The table's booked for half-eight, we've got ages yet,' he said, still perplexed, but less so.

Her smouldering look penetrated through to his soul, the intensity of feeling giving part of his anatomy a sudden unexpected wake-up call.

'Come,' she said, opening the door, anxious to get him away from here. Mesmerised, he followed.

They drove to a quiet country lane, her hand on his crotch, he on autopilot.

'You shouldn't ... that was dangerous,' he gasped as he stopped the car and her mouth came down on him, tongue flicking around.

'Sorry,' she mumbled, her mouth suddenly full as his body convulsed with excruciating pleasure. He was seeing stars, and not just the ones outside.

'Hey,' she said, sitting back up and smiling at him as he came back down to planet earth. 'Let's go and eat.'

'Thought you just did,' he sighed, contented now.

'Only the starter. I'm starving.'

'But what about you?'

'I'll keep,' she said, smiling, yet filled with sadness. This had to end, and soon.


It did. Abruptly.

'When are you going back to London?' asked Richard, in all innocence, in the middle of the main course.

'Sunday,' she said, appearing to give her full concentration to the cutting of her steak.

'Sunday as in the day after tomorrow?'

'Mm.'

'When were you going to tell me?'

'Tonight ... later,' she mumbled, sawing away.

'Do you have to go back?'

'Well of course I do! I have a job, a house, a son ...'

'What if I asked you to marry me?'

'You *are* joking.'

But Richard was down on one knee. 'Anna, will you m ...?'

'Richard! Please get up! You're embarrassing me now. Everybody's looking.'

'And if I get up you'll say "yes"?'

'Just get up. Please, can we go?'

'But you haven't finished your steak,' he said, getting back into his seat.

'I've lost my appetite, let's go,' she snapped, struggling into her coat.

He paid the bill and they left, each huffily in their own world.

'You coming back to mine?' he asked eventually, as they got into the car.

'I don't think I should.'

'Please,' he begged, not knowing what he'd done that was so wrong.

She hesitated for a second or two. 'Suppose I would get a major inquisition from Grace and Cleo if I went back this early.'

'And that's the only reason?'

'You know it's not.'

She was a sex maniac. Had to be. Her mother had been right all along. Here she was back in bed with him. She was meant to be saying goodbye. But instead his head disappeared under the duvet bringing with it a dalliance of delights

'O-h-h-h!'

Goodbye would have to wait.

They made love (or lust) for hours that night, each knowing that for whatever reason and without further discussion, they would soon be parted. Each clung to the other in desperation, not wanting the night to end, until eventually they fell asleep in each other's arms, exhausted and bound together by love (or lust).

Richard was the first to wake, or so he thought. He turned his head to watch his beloved girl as she slept, wanting to savour every moment. But asleep she was not. How could she sleep, knowing she had to leave him the very next day? Deep in thought, she didn't notice him stir as a silent tear trickled down her cheek.

'Anna! What's wrong?'

'You know what's wrong. I won't see you again after today.'

'Plan Lust' seemed to have flown out of the window.

'It doesn't have to be like that.'

'Oh Richard, please don't start proposing to me again,' she grinned tearfully, trying to lighten the moment, joke her way out of the situation.

It didn't work.

'I don't mean marry me. Think I learned my lesson about overzealous proposals last night,' he said, a rueful smile playing on his lips. 'But there's nothing to stop us still seeing each other, London's only a couple of hours away by train.'

Errgh! He'd taken Grace's words right out of her mouth. 'I don't do part-time relationships.'

'Nor full-time either, apparently. Think about it, it's perfect. I could come down and see you at weekends, there's nothing to keep me here.'

'There's Zak and Cleo for a start.'

'I can see them any time. You could show me around London, we could explore it together, and then at night we could …'

'No, Richard!' She said, firmly pushing away the hand that was creeping up her inner thigh. 'Once I've gone, I've gone. Back to my old life, back to …'

'Your fella. You've got somebody else haven't you? This has just been a bit of a fling for you. Was that all I was, eh? A bit on the side?' He sat up in bed, head in his hands, his back rigid with tension.

She ran her index finger down his spine, sad that he could think she would do that to him. 'You know that isn't true,' she said softly. 'I told you, it's been almost five years since I've been with anyone. The only thing I've got at home is Jessica Rabbit, not some big hunky male,' she said, trying to lighten his mood.

But not succeeding. 'This is not a joke, Anna. I love you. How can you just lie there and make light of it? Anyway, I don't know that I can believe you. You say there's nobody else, say it's been five years since you've been with anyone, and yet there you are, constantly jumping on me like an old pro!'

Anna sat up, horrified. 'I can't believe you just said that! Is that what you think of me? Some kind of slapper?' Anger, frustration, hurt, beamed from her eyes like lasers as she jumped out of bed and struggled into her clothes. 'You believed what you'd heard about me all along didn't you? Believed what my mother said, believed that I must have been asking for it when my father had sex with me.' Grabbing her bag, she rooted through it for her mobile. 'I'm going home. I'll make my own way,' she said, as she rang for a taxi.

'But ...'

'Go to hell!'

She rang the doorbell impatiently, Grace came to let her in.

'Anna?' Grace was stunned by the ravaged face of her sister, so drastically transformed since yesterday. 'I take it you told him.'

Anna nodded briefly, aware of several pairs of beady eyes watching inquisitively from the kitchen. She dashed up the stairs, choking back the sobs, needing some time on her own. Grace watched her go, feeling her pain. She so wanted to go after her, help her, give her a hug, but she knew Anna was a private person, she needed her space. Turning worriedly back to the others, she returned to the kitchen.

'What a trollop!' Gran declared victoriously, 'I told you

what she was like and now you've seen it for yourselves maybe you'll believe me.'

'Mother!'

'You can "mother" me all you like but you have to agree. Off with the first man she saw. How many nights has she slept here in the bed you provided for her? One, was it? And what about Richard now? What sort of a state has she left him in? Oh, she can turn on the tears alright, crocodile tears they are. A real drama queen, always was.'

'Mother, I really wish you wouldn't talk like this. She's my sister and I love her. She's had a dreadful time in the past, it must have damaged her. Things like that scar you for life, it's not something you get over, like an illness or whatever. She was traumatised by what happened to her and that was partly your fault. How can you be so mean to her now? She needs our support and our love, not criticism.'

'Hey, sis, what's wrong?' asked Zak, suddenly realising Cleo was in tears.

'It's my fault. It was me that got them together and now it's just a big mess.'

'Cry baby, cry baby,' chanted Izzy, banging her spoon on the table, not really understanding what was going on.

'Izzy! Say sorry to Cleo.'

'Soz.'

'Properly!'

'Sorry, Cleo.'

'Now eat your breakfast like a good girl.' Grace turned her attention to her other daughter. 'Cleo, you're not to blame at all. Okay, so you got them together, so what? Like I said to you before, you can introduce people to each other but you can't orchestrate their relationship. What happens next is up to them.'

'But look how upset Auntie Anna is now and … and I bet Dad is too. If I hadn't pushed them so much to go out with each other they wouldn't have been.'

'That's what happens in relationships sometimes, people do get upset when they split up. You should know that more than most. How many times have you come home in floods of tears, thinking the end of the world has come just because some lad's dumped you?'

'Suppose,' sniffed Cleo, a glimmer of a smile hovering.

'And how long does it take you to move on to the next one?'

'Few days,' replied Cleo, smile broadening now.

'There you go, then. Nothing for you to feel guilty about at all.'

'Mummy?'

'Yes, Izzy. Have you eaten your breakfast yet?'

Izzy moved it round the plate trying to make it disappear. 'Mummy, what's a trollop?'

Zak choked on his cereal; Gran feigned innocence.

'Is it like the troll in *The Three Billy Goats Gruff*?'

'Sort of, Izzy, sort of,' said Grace, trying hard to keep a straight face.

'It's what your Auntie Anna is,' asserted Gran.

'Mother!'

'Auntie Anna's an ugly troll? That's not very nice. I'll tell Mrs Clarke what you said.'

'Izzy! Get on with your breakfast!'

# 13

It was almost noon before Anna reappeared. Grace had been intent on going up to check on her all morning but, as usual, there'd been one crisis after another and she just hadn't been able to. On the other hand she knew Anna needed some time alone, so in a way it was good that she'd given her some space.

'Hey. How are you feeling now?' Grace hardly needed to ask, she looked dreadful.

'Not good. Please don't ask me what happened, I can't even bear to think about it at the moment. All I know is I have to go home, back to London, today.'

'*Today?*' Grace's eyes rounded like saucers – well, plates actually … spinning ones, a thousand and one problems whirling around in her head. 'But …'

'You don't have to come with me if you're struggling, you can always follow on the train another day.'

'Er-ooh-wha …,' headless chicken time had arrived again.

'It's just … I've got to get away. I can't cope with this.'

Grace was in a turmoil. Anna looked terrible, she couldn't just abandon her when she so obviously needed help; she'd been left to cope alone too often already by her family. But Grace wasn't organised, not for leaving today. How could she just drop everything and go? Charlie wasn't even back yet, he'd gone out to look at a job ages ago. Where was he? And Cleo, she was out, goodness only knows

140

where. Gran was in a mood. Alfie needed a walk. Zak – was he in his room?

'I …'

'It's okay, don't worry, I understand,' said Anna, a look of resignation on her already exhausted face.

'It's just … I haven't packed or anything. And … and I was going to make sure all the washing and ironing was up to date, stock up with food for them, make sure they're okay.'

'For God's sake! I'm sure they'd survive. Do they not know how to use a washing machine, or where the nearest supermarket is?'

Grace was a bit taken aback by the sharpness of Anna's tone, hurt in fact. 'I know, I've made a rod for my own back. I can't help it, it's the way I am.'

Anna was so full of her own pain that she didn't even notice the pain she had inflicted on her sister. 'Suit yourself, I'm going to get ready.'

'Okay, I'll come.' An amazingly speedy decision for such a ditherer.

'Two o'clock,' said Anna, not even batting an eyelid as she went up the stairs.

'Two o'clock?! Two o'clock?!' spluttered Grace, her head in a whirl, panicking in the sudden frenzied realisation of what she'd just committed herself to. No backing out now. 'Zak!'

Two o'clock came … and went.

'I really, really need to get going, Grace,' said Anna, patience running thin.

'He'll be here in a minute, he promised … Cleo too,' replied Grace, throwing random items haphazardly into a suitcase, feeling as though she had suddenly grown fifteen hands and two heads. Which was fortunate, as she needed them all. 'D'you know, I have absolutely no idea what I'm packing here? My head's all over the place.'

Anna merely gave her a withering look and shook her head in despair. The concept of having a houseful of people so totally reliant on just one individual was totally alien to her. In her own world, you could just drop every-thing and go, without another thought. Independence was a wonderful thing. However, today she did have someone to worry about – Richard. He'd tried phoning three times already and she'd just ignored his call. The last thing she wanted was him turning up on the doorstep pleading for forgiveness. In her opinion, it was better that they'd split up acrimoniously. At least this way she could dwell on what he'd said, the truth of what he thought of her, to get her through moments of weakness when she would be wanting to take him back.

'Have you seen it?'

'Sorry?' Anna was miles away in her head, desperate to be so in reality.

'The eye make-up remover. Can't find it anywhere.'

'Oh, for God's sake!' snapped Anna. 'There are shops in London, believe it or not. Buy some when you get there, or use mine – anything. But can we please go?'

Tears welled in Grace's eyes and threatened to overflow. This was a side to her sister she hadn't seen before. Okay, so Anna had a problem with Richard. But she didn't have to take it out on her. A little consideration wouldn't go amiss; after all she had everyone to sort out, not just herself. She struggled to close the lid of her suitcase, but in vain. Why had she packed so much stuff?

'Here,' Anna relented, 'you sit on the lid to squash it down while I fasten the locks.'

'Thanks,' said Grace, gratefully.

Task accomplished, Anna looked at her, shamefaced. 'Sorry for sounding like a complete bitch. I didn't mean to be horrible to you, it's not your fault.'

'It's okay, I know you're upset about Richard and I'm faffing about like a wet lettuce. Suppose it's all part of learning how to be sisters again, we've just been being polite so far, like people who don't really know each other.'

'Yeah, now we can have sisterly spats.'

'Ooh, I can't wait,' laughed Grace.

It was in fact nearer to three o'clock by the time they set off. Charlie had got back as quickly as he could and was so supportive of Grace's trip that she almost didn't want to leave him at all … an emotion that was soon overcome when Anna reminded her how amazing it would be to escape this humdrum existence for a while and see a bit of life.

But Cleo was the real reason for their delay. Zak had rung her mobile several times, telling her to hurry home. Grace couldn't possibly leave without saying goodbye to her, Anna neither. Eventually the ever-recalcitrant daughter returned, an aura of angst abounding.

'This is so unfair,' she stomped, 'why can't I come with you?'

'Come *with* me?' Grace responded in shock. 'But I didn't think you liked going anywhere with me!'

'But I can't stay here with Charlie, he's not my dad.'

'Well go and stay with your dad then if you'd rather. I'm sure he'd love to have you.'

'He wouldn't. I've just asked him, he said no. He's dead upset … So that means I've got to stay here if I don't come with you.'

'Well I'm sorry, Cleo, but that's just the way it is. I can't take you, you've got school. And besides, Auntie Anna and I want to spend some time together, just the two of us. Surely you can understand that?'

'So you're saying you don't want me either, then?'

'Cleo! You know I'm not saying that at all. You know I

love you and that I'm always here for you but, just for once in my life, I want to take a few days away to get to know my sister. You'll be fine here with Charlie and Gran, and Zak and Izzy.'

'Yeah, what on earth would they all do if you went away as well?' interrupted Anna. 'They need you to be the substitute mum to keep them under control.'

Cleo gave a half smile. Anna put an arm around her niece's shoulders. 'Think you're up to the job?'

'Suppose.'

'That's my girl.' Anna gave her a hug, tears in her own eyes. 'Look after your dad for me too, won't you?'

'I'll try,' said Cleo. She was going to miss this auntie of hers.

They were quiet in the car, each lost in their own thoughts. Anna's heart felt ripped to shreds. She'd never meant to fall in love, just a bit of excitement was all she'd wanted. But now all she wanted was Richard. It was no good thinking about what could have been, common sense told her that, but common sense flew out of the window when cupid's arrow struck. She'd never really understood before when she'd heard people talk about the pain of a broken heart at the end of a relationship, but then she'd never been in love like this before. Prior to Richard, she'd always trod warily as far as men were concerned, unable to trust after all that had happened to her in the past.

In a way, what she was feeling now reminded her of that heart-wrenching torture she'd suffered when her baby had been snatched away all those years ago. Tears came into her eyes and she blinked them away, trying to concentrate on the road. She couldn't cope with any more pain, she had had enough. The only way she'd get through this was to build up on the animosity she'd felt when she'd run out on him. An old pro! How could he have even thought that of her? It was so hurtful …

'Anna? You okay?'

Anna brushed away a tear hurriedly. 'Mm,' she said, eyes on the road ahead.

'We can stop if you want,' said Grace, valuing her life. Anna looked dreadful.

'Next services is fifteen miles.' Anna felt like shit.

'I wish I could drive.'

'Me too.'

'There's always the hard shoulder,' said Grace nervously.

'Don't look that bad, do I?' Anna mustered a smile.

'You do, actually. Why don't we stop?'

'I'm fine, honestly.'

Somehow they reached the service station where Anna sank gratefully onto a chair while Grace went in search of coffee and cake, chocolate, anything to perk her sister up a bit. Grace was really worried. How was she going to manage to drive all that way? They were only at Oxford, still about an hour and a half away yet according to Anna.

Carrying the tray back towards their table, Grace could see Anna apparently taking tablets although, on glancing across and seeing her sister approaching, she seemed agitated as she scooped the packets back into her bag.

'Headache?' asked Grace, putting down the tray and lifting the contents onto the table.

'What?' Anna responded nervously.

'Thought I just saw you taking tablets,' said Grace, sitting down and propping the now empty tray against the table leg.

'Oh, that … yeah, headache.'

'Hope they're alright.'

'What?'

'At home, hope they're managing.'

'For God's sake! Of course they'll be managing. It's a pity

145

that's all you've got to worry about.'

Stung by the sharpness of Anna's tongue yet again, Grace was mortified. 'I should never have come.'

'Give me strength! Think about yourself for a change, it'll do you good to have a break – if you can stop worrying about them all for long enough, that is.'

'Did you see Cleo's face? I can't believe she wanted to come with me. I feel really guilty now, like I've let her down.'

'Grace! Stop it! I can't believe what I'm hearing.' Even Anna was smiling now.

'Sorry, but ...'

'No buts.'

'But at least it's made you look better, was what I was going to say,' smiled Grace, with a sense of relief.

'Feel heaps better now, actually. Let's go. London, here we come!'

Grace registered mini panic.

'Where's your sense of adventure?'

'Lost, a long time ago.'

'Well, better find it quickly, we're about to hit the town.'


'I can't believe all this activity,' said a stunned Grace as they drove through Tooting.

'Bit of a difference from sleepy Cheshire, eh?' laughed Anna.

'You can say that again, I'm loving it!'

'Thought it might all be a bit much for you ... *get out of my way, idiot*!' fumed Anna, horn blaring as someone cut out in front of her and blocked the road.

'Not at all, apart from the traffic,' said Grace, gripping onto her seat. 'Is it always this crazy?'

'Sure is.' Anna attempted to manoeuvre the car to the left as a police siren sounded behind them.

'Oh my God, how's he going to get through?'

'He will, they're used to it.'

'Blimey.' Grace relaxed a little and loosened her grip on the seat. 'Much further?'

'Only ten minutes or so now. Nerves can't stand it?' grinned Anna.

Parking spaces were in short supply as usual when they arrived although they did, luckily, manage to find one. Anna looked exhausted, Grace exhilarated.

'Can't wait to go exploring.'

'Think that might have to wait. I'm knackered after that drive.'

'Sorry, I wasn't thinking. Just really excited, that's all. Here, let me carry the cases.'

Back home chaos reigned. Grace would have returned on the next train if she could have seen them. Charlie had always known Grace was superwoman, but how did she cope with this lot every day? She must have the patience of a saint – well, she did, he knew she did. Gracie … he hadn't realised how much he'd miss her.

Since she'd gone, Gran had been impossible. There was absolutely no reasoning with her at all. Whatever he said to her seemed to go in one ear and out the other, although most of the time she simply feigned deafness altogether and ignored him completely. He'd always considered himself to be a patient man and occasionally, although he wouldn't have dreamed of telling her, thought Grace was a bit harsh with her mother. Let's just say his opinion had changed somewhat.

The trouble with Gran was that now Grace was away, she thought she was in charge. In a way, Charlie could see some sort of logic in this thought. After all, she'd been the one to look after them in days gone by; Charlie hadn't even been around then. In Gran's head she thought nothing had changed and she was still perfectly capable but, in reality, she couldn't even look after herself, never mind anyone else.

Okay, so the evening meal incident had been his own fault – in a way. Izzy had asked him earlier in the afternoon what he was going to cook that night. Grace had pointed out some casseroles and various other meals in the freezer that he'd just have to heat up, but because Izzy was missing her mummy, he'd said they'd have fish fingers, chips and beans – Izzy's favourite.

Some time later Gran had been in her room and he'd wandered into the lounge to check on the football score, where he'd unintentionally nodded off to sleep. It was a strange cooking smell suddenly filling his nostrils that woke him with a start.

'Wassat?'

Charlie rushed into a steam-filled, deserted kitchen to see a pan bubbling away on the hob. A closer inspection revealed fish fingers, oven chips and baked beans all being boiled together in a large saucepan of water.

'Oh my God, *Gran!*' He could hardly believe his eyes. What a revolting mess.

'What?' She came hobbling in on her stick. 'Is it ready?'

'Ready? You surely don't expect us to eat that, do you?'

'That's what you said you wanted, had you forgotten?'

'Forgotten? I … What a waste of good food! I've never seen anything like it.'

'There's nothing wrong with it, Charlie. Get the plates out,' said Gran, giving it a stir.

'Plates? You must be joking! We can't eat that, it's disgusting.'

'Well,' said Gran, drama queen style, 'I won't pretend I'm not hurt, because I am. Talk about ungrateful! But never mind, we'll just go straight for the pudding.'

'Pudding? Where's the pudding?'

'In the oven, Mr Know-It-All.'

Overcautious, or maybe not, Charlie opened the oven

door. 'Oh my …'

It took him a while to work out exactly what it had been, but at least he had something to be grateful for – it was on a baking tray rather than all over the bottom of the oven. He lifted it out gingerly.

'Pooh! What's that?' asked Izzy, drawn by the smell.

Alfie whimpered, and scratched at the back door to escape.

'Yoghurt, I believe. Five melted plastic pots of it.'

'Yuk!'

'Gran must have thought it would be nice to eat it hot and mixed with melted plastic for a change.'

'Errgh!'

'Why do I always get the blame for everything around here?' huffed Gran, heading for her room. 'Expect me to do all the work, and then complain when it's not to your liking. Well, you can sort yourselves out from now on because I've had enough.'

Charlie lifted the baking tray and its gooey contents out of the oven to cool off before he could throw the whole lot into the bin.

'Oh Daddy,' said Izzy knowingly, arms folded, viewing the scene with some distaste. 'Shall we go to McDonald's?'

# 14

Miserable and alone, Cleo sat on a swing in the park. The place was deserted except for her – a bit like her life felt really. She was leaning forward, staring at the ground, her arms wrapped around the chains, hands tense and gripping on. Her toes swayed backwards and forwards, left and right, lackadaisically, on the ground, giving her the kind of momentum one might expect from someone deeply troubled.

How could she have been so stupid? Everyone had warned her, seen she was heading for a fall, but she'd just been her usual pig-headed self and carried on regardless. She'd thought she was invincible that was the trouble. Thought she'd show them all, that she was tough, nothing could hurt her. How wrong could you be?

The trouble was, nobody knew the real Cleo, and that was the saddest thing of all. On the outside she was this hard, stroppy teenager who rebelled against everything and argued with everyone. What a false impression she'd created, a hard shell that she'd built up around herself for protection, keeping everyone else at bay. And, so far, it had worked.

She hadn't used to be like that. When Mum and Dad had been together she'd felt safe and protected, happy with the world. But then they'd split, and gradually her world had spun out of control. The arrival of Charlie in their lives had been especially devastating to Cleo, as that had destroyed any glimmer of hope she'd harboured that her dad might one day come home.

Having Gran living with them had also been difficult. Zak was so obviously Gran's favourite, like the son she'd never had. She idolised him and, in her eyes, he could never do anything wrong. She, on the other hand, could never do anything right. Gran criticised her every move, her clothes, her make-up, saying she was becoming a disgrace like Auntie Anna.

Well, maybe Gran was right … and how she would gloat when this news came out. Not that Cleo minded being compared to Auntie Anna, in fact in some ways she took it as a compliment. Auntie Anna was someone to look up to, in her opinion. She was the first adult in a long time to have treated her with a bit of respect and shown an interest. If only she was still here …

Mum tried her best, but she was always so busy running round after everyone. Mum still treated her like a kid, as well, and bossed her about instead of taking time to talk to her and treating her like an adult. She had a really negative attitude and always expected the worst, which was quite often what Cleo gave her, just to fulfil expectations. But Mum wasn't all bad, and Cleo so wished she was here today. Mum never went away … why now? This was so typical of her luck. An unexpected tear trickled down her cheek. She scrubbed it away with the back of her hand. Blubbing wasn't going to help anything.

Okay, there was Dad. Normally he might have been the one she turn to today but she'd tried talking to him earlier on the phone – not about this, but just generally sounding him out. She had been hoping he might ask her to go and stay with him while Mum was away, but no such luck. He sounded in a real mess over Auntie Anna, although he'd never confide in her fully. Like Mum, to a certain extent he still viewed her as a child, not as someone to share his problems with. But maybe she couldn't have coped with them anyway, not today.

151

Zak? You must be joking! Charlie? Equally! There were her mates of course. She could always talk to them. Although even they'd been excluding her a bit just lately. That was the trouble with girls, they could be so bitchy. Not that she could talk. It wasn't that long ago that she'd gone off with Lisa leaving Cassie on her own. Now it was her turn. Just bad timing, that's all.

Oh Mum, I wish you hadn't gone away. Her lips wobbled this time, threatening more waterworks. She pursed them together defiantly, refusing to turn into a cry baby. Baby.

'Hey sis! What you up to?'

Oh God, where did he spring from?

'Hey,' she said, blinking away, biting her bottom lip firmly into control.

'On your own?'

'Well, I can't see anyone else, can you?'

'Okay, cut the sarcasm. You okay?'

'Mm.'

'You been crying?'

'No!'

'Okay, okay. Don't snap at me. Only trying to help.'

'Well I don't need your help.'

'Fine. Coming home?'

'Nope.'


Refreshed after a nap, Anna came down from her bedroom to find Grace snooping about in the kitchen.

'This has to be the craziest fridge in the world,' marvelled Grace, turning her eyes from ogling its contents to face her sister. 'It's full of perfumes and skin creams instead of food. What on earth are they all doing in there?'

'Keep better, don't they. Perfume evaporates at room temperature.'

Grace closed the fridge door, shaking her head in disbelief. 'But what about food? You've nothing in at all, not even in the cupboards. No wonder you're so skinny.'

'Did I judge your way of living?'

'Sorry, it's just that I'm starving.'

'We'll eat out. I usually do.'

'Usually eat out?'

'Grace, you're judging again. Let's go.'

'But I'm not even ready.'

'You're fine as you are.'

They wandered along Lavender Hill, Grace in awe of everything. She was like a child in a sweetshop, eyes darting this way and that, relishing all that came before her. In her excitement she found it impossible to choose where she wanted to eat so Anna took her to a Thai place she knew. Grace ate everything in sight; she could diet when she got back home.

'Wonder how they're getting on without you?'

Grace felt a sudden pang of guilt. 'To be honest, I've been having such a good time I'd forgotten all about them. How bad is that?'

'Sorry I mentioned it now. Just continue to forget about them, they'll be fine. You enjoy yourself. More wine?' asked Anna, bottle poised over her sister's empty glass.

'Don't mind if I do,' giggled Grace gleefully. 'Are we going on somewhere after this?'

'On somewhere? Tonight?'

'Well, this is London, I thought everyone went out in London.' Grace was up for anything now.

Anna gave in. Well, it was her first night after all. 'Okay, there's a bar just down the road where we hang out some-times.'

'We?'

'Mates.'

'Mates?'

'I do have some, you know.'

Back home, Charlie was not having such a good time. For one thing, he'd lost Cleo. Not lost exactly, mislaid would probably have been a better word. For goodness sake! Grace had only gone this afternoon and already she was one child down. At this rate there'd be none left at all by the time she got back. Zak had told him he'd seen her on a swing in the park, looking pretty miserable, but he'd had a walk down there with Izzy and there was no Cleo in sight.

'Probably kissing boys – yuk!' Izzy certainly knew how to wind him up. 'Uncle Richard will know what to do.' Yes, Izzy certainly *did* know how to wind him up.

Actually Charlie had phoned Richard, several times in fact, putting his pride aside for the sake of Cleo. But Richard's phone was switched off, he didn't want to speak to anyone today, other than the one person who didn't want to speak to him.

'Mummy will be cross,' piped up mini-motormouth.

Jesus! Understatement of the year.

'It's okay, Izzy, we'll find her,' he said, with more confidence than he felt.

Eventually, even he had to admit defeat. They'd detoured to McDonald's for the takeaway. He'd have to sort out something for Cleo later, when she decided to return … *if* she decided to return. God, Grace would kill him if anything had happened to her, but what was he to do? He could hardly stop her going out, lock her in her bedroom until her mother got back. At last he was beginning to understand why Grace always worried so much. A piteous cry broke through his thoughts.

'Daddy!'

He turned to see his daughter in a crumpled heap on the pavement. She'd been trailing behind him and, although he hated to admit it, he'd forgotten for a moment that she was there.

154

'Izzy!' he ran to pick her up, dropping the takeaway to the ground.

'Hurt knees,' she cried, 'and hands – look.'

Sure enough, skinned and bleeding.

'What were you doing?' asked Charlie, rooting through his pockets for a clean handkerchief, but in vain. (See, that's why women carry handbags.)

'Yuk! That's dirty!' For Izzy, a moment of disgust traversed her diva-style sobs.

'It's not that bad,' soothed Charlie.

'It is, it is! I fell off the little wall. Mummy always holds my hand.'

Guilt-tripper.

'Sorry, that's my fault. Come on, stand up. Let's get home, then we can clean you up.'

'Carry me.'

'But Izzy, you're heavy, it's a long walk, I've got …'

'Want Mummy,' she wailed, heart-tuggingly.

'Okay, let me pick you up,' he said, giving in gracefully, the takeaway abandoned to some other fate; Charlie had completely forgotten about it being on the ground behind him. He was a man, after all: multitasking was not his thing.

By the time they got home, Charlie was exhausted. But things didn't get any better. Zak, usually such a calm and patient soul, was bent over with his head in the fridge, stress oozing from him in bucketloads.

'Wassup?' seemed to be Charlie's favourite word just recently.

'Can't find anything to eat and I'm starving. Got to go out in a minute.'

'Sorry, that's my fault,' said Charlie, full of remorse. 'I did get us all a McDonald's but I seem to have lost it on the way home.'

'How can you lose a McDonald's?' questioned Zak, not even faintly amused.

'Don't ask.' Charlie reached into his pocket for his wallet. 'Here, take some money, get something while you're out.'

'Don't bother!' snapped Zak, totally out of character. 'I'll manage without.'

'But Zak …' pleaded Charlie.

'Be late back,' said Zak, slamming the front door on his way out.

'Oh Daddy,' exclaimed Izzy with a roll of her eyes. 'You in big trouble.'

Why did this child have to state the obvious? Okay Grace, you only went today, entrusting your three precious children to me. So far I've lost one, injured one and upset the most placid one of all. Oh and incidentally, your mother's locked herself in her room in a huff. And Alfie? Oh yes, he's done a puddle on the kitchen floor because nobody remembered to let him out. Great job, eh?

But Grace? She'd discovered a whole new world. While Charlie was left at home like Cinderella, she was having a ball, or trying to, anyway. It was difficult, to be honest, to transform herself from a mumsy creature with a country bumpkin lifestyle into a jet-setting girl about town without appearing obviously fake, but she was giving it her best shot. They were a nice crowd, Anna's friends, but from another planet. Barristers, accountants, single, child-free – what could they possibly find interesting about her? They seemed to find something for all that, and gave her their undivided attention. Maybe they were just being polite, fascinated to discover that Anna had a sister.

They talked about holidays, yachts off the south coast of France. She wisely kept her thoughts to herself: the nearest she'd got to a yacht was their little rubber dinghy off the south coast of Cornwall. She smiled, trying to look knowledgeable, cringing inside at her own unworldliness. Nervously, she glanced around for Anna but she'd disappeared, maybe gone to the loo. Perhaps that's where she should go too, escape for a while, all this nonchalant talk about travel was doing her confidence no good at all. As she turned to go, she was waylaid by a really pretty woman she hadn't noticed before.

'Hi, I'm Kate, we haven't been introduced, I'm a stranger here too, just on holiday.'

'Oh hi, I'm Grace. Really pleased to meet you. I was just beginning to feel a bit … well, you know, everyone seems to know each other and they're all so …'

'Rich? Intelligent? Super confident? Tell me about it,' Kate giggled.

'Oghh! It's so good to meet someone on my wavelength.'

Kate smiled in acknowledgement. 'I recognise that accent, where are you from?'

'The good old north – Cheshire actually.'

'Oh me too …' her smile faded momentarily, 'well, I'm actually based in Cornwall now, St Ives. I'm an artist, I have a studio there.'

'Wow, that's amazing. What a fantastic place to live. And how funny you should say that, I was just thinking about Cornwall, we holiday there a lot.'

'It is beautiful.'

'The kids love it, especially my son. He still comes with us at eighteen – for the surf of course, not to be with us.'

Kate's smile held a tinge of sadness. 'How many children have you got?'

Grace groaned, rolling her eyes. 'Three, for my penance – Zak's eighteen, Cleo fifteen and then Izzy's just three. Do you have children?'

'Just the one. Jessica's six now.'

As mysteriously as she appeared, so she disappeared. Grace was simply distracted for a moment by the reappearance of Anna who had finally returned from the loo and was wanting to go home. Grace discussed it for a moment or two then turned to say goodbye to Kate, only to find that she'd vanished.

'Sure you weren't hallucinating?' teased Anna. 'You have had a fair bit to drink after all.'

'No she was there, I swear she was. How very strange.'

It was almost eleven before Charlie finally heard the front door slam and footsteps disappearing up the stairs. He dragged himself reluctantly from the comfort of *Match of the Day*.

'Cleo? Is that you?'

'Sod off.'

So that's a yes, then.

'Don't speak to me like that, please. Come downstairs, I want to talk to you.'

Think you're heading for a fall here, Charlie.

'No.'

'Please.'

Don't beg. Who's the boss here?

'Going to bed.'

She is, obviously.

'Okay, I'll talk to you in the morning.'

Saving face, or what?

Charlie retreated back to the match but his concentration had gone. There seemed to be more tackles in this house than on any football pitch and his skills were sadly lacking. With a look of defeat he turned off the television and remembered to let Alfie out for his final bladder-emptying session of the day. He stood sadly at the door as the dog snuffled his way excitedly around the garden, leaving no blade of grass unsniffed. Oh to be a dog, life is so simple. Satisfied that his territory was safe, Alfie scampered back into the kitchen, giving himself a joyous shake from head to tail before pawing at the cupboard door for his customary Bonio. Creatures of habit are dogs: routines are not to be broken, demands have to be met. Charlie acquiesced and threw one for him to catch, waiting while he gobbled it up greedily.

'Right then, basket,' commanded Charlie.

Alfie knew the routine and slunk in, tail between his legs, turning to sit and face Charlie with his sad brown eyes.

'You pining for your mum too, fella?' asked Charlie, patting him, drawing comfort from their mutual missing of the woman they both loved best in the world.

With no idea what time Zak would be home, Charlie turned out the lights and made his way upstairs. Gracie, Gracie, Gracie, how he needed her tonight. He climbed into bed in a world of his own, not even noticing the slumbering figure sprawled in his way. What is it about children? So small in stature and yet, when they invade your bed, their arms and legs seem to double in length and spread everywhere.

'Wassat?' Charlie rebounded in surprise, emitting his customary response.

'Ow!' Izzy sat up, rubbing her eyes. 'You squashed me!'

'Sorry, Iz, I didn't know you were there. What are you doing in here anyway? Come on, let's get you back to your own bed.'

Nice try, Charlie.

'Want Mummy.' Izzy's lip quivered.

'Okay, okay, stay there just for a little while then.'

'Want a drink.'

'I'll go and get you one.'

Downstairs Charlie came face to face with Gran in the kitchen, making tea and dropping sticky pieces of Jammie Dodger for Alfie all over his freshly washed kitchen floor. He bit his tongue, it wasn't worth the hassle.

'Izzy wants a drink.'

'Is she awake?'

'Yeah, she's in my bed.'

159

'*In your bed?* That's disgusting! You men, you're all the same.'

'But …'

'Grace is not going to like this.'

'But …'

'Not one little bit.'

'But …'

'I can't believe it.'

'But …'

'The one man I thought I could trust.'

'But I haven't …'

'I'm going to bed.'

'But …'

'Can't even bear to look at you. Goodnight!'

Ogghhh! Grace, it's a madhouse. How can I cope with this lot for a whole week?

# 15

Two weeks ago he hadn't even met her. But then she'd spun into his life like some kind of hurricane, whirling around inside his head, spinning out of control, sucking the life from him, eating his heart. And where was she now? Gone.

The blackness invaded, swamped his mind, crushed his soul, tugged at his heart strings. Floods of despair, drowning in sorrow. She was gone. He would never see her again.

Richard poured himself another Scotch although he knew it wouldn't help, nothing could help, but at least it numbed the pain just a little bit. He swirled the golden liquid around the glass a couple of times before downing it in one, the strength of it almost taking his breath away as it hit the back of his throat. Goddam woman, why did she not answer his calls? He needed to talk to her, had to talk to her, had to know what was going on. What the hell was wrong with her? He rang her number again, knowing full well it was a pointless exercise but still living in hope. Switched off, switched off … why was she doing this to him? Groaning with pent-up frustration, he felt like throwing his phone across the room but managed to restrain himself – that would be no good to anyone.

The thing was, he'd never met anyone quite like Anna before. Well, Grace, obviously, but although he hated to admit it, even she hadn't had this effect on him. He'd loved Grace, of course he had, still did in a way, but with Anna … Well, it was as though sparks of electricity shot between them as soon as they came into the same vicinity. How could she bear to go away and break that connection? She must have felt it too; he knew she had, it was impossible not to. She was everything he wanted in a woman, mischievous, fun to be with, sexy, gorgeous, strong, independent …

Strong and independent. Yes, that was definitely where she differed from Grace. She'd had to be that way to survive all the things in her past. The abuse, the torment of having her baby taken away from her; he couldn't begin to imagine what she must have gone through. A lone tear trickled down his cheek and caught him off guard. It wasn't usual for him to become emotional and it took him by surprise. He wiped it away hurriedly, reaching out for the whisky bottle once more. It was the road to nowhere, he knew it was. But what the hell.

Two hundred miles away, Anna was feeling equally depressed. Why had she got herself into this situation? She'd known what the consequences would be, known it could only end in tears. She lay in bed, unable to sleep despite the sheer exhaustion that was weighing her down.

It had been such a stupid thing to do in the first place, to sleep with her sister's ex. Totally off-limits, was what she should have told herself. If she'd been that desperate for sex, why couldn't she have just gone out and pulled some random guy? But no, in with both feet as usual, and now the whole family were involved. Grace had been on at her tonight: 'Why don't you call him, it can't do any harm?' Oh, can't it?

The sex had been good, there was no denying that. If they could just have kept it to satisfying their lust it would have been amazing, in fact. The problems had only begun when feelings started to creep in, uninvited. She'd tried to build a barrier to keep them out, but that had stood about as much chance as a picket fence against a tsunami.

Her whole body ached with longing for him. Would it be so wrong to ...? Of course it would, there was no point in even thinking about it, absolutely none. She'd made a decision about how things were going to be and she could not waver now. It was just that she hadn't expected such temptation to come her way. After all, it had been five years since she'd had any sort of love life at all, prior to Richard. Although she'd certainly made up for it this past week. She smiled briefly at her recollections: he must have thought she was some kind of nymphomaniac, no wonder he'd called her an 'old pro'.

That wiped the smile from her face, although she couldn't feel anger with him any more. He'd just been lashing out in frustration, unable to understand why they couldn't be together, why she couldn't commit to him, knowing the intensity of their feelings for each other. One day he'd understand, although by then it would be too late.

'Anna! Can I come in?'

Anna was startled back to reality by a knocking at her bedroom door. She'd almost forgotten Grace was here, so used was she to being on her own.

''Course. Come on in,' she replied, dragging herself back into the present.

Grace tottered in somewhat unsteadily, still a little on the tipsy side from her foray into the fun-filled world.

'Oh my God, think I'm a bit drunk,' she said, collapsing in a heap of giggles on the bottom of the bed. 'Sorry, that your foot?' she asked, sobering a little at Anna's expression.

'No, you're okay.'

'Was a good night, wasn't it? Makes such a change to go out. Wonder what happened to Kate?'

'Kate who?'

'You know, the artist.'

'What?'

'The one who disappeared.'

163

'That all you came to say? Only I really would like to get some sleep.'

'Oops sorry,' giggled Grace, hand over her mouth by way of apology. ''Night then,' she said, tripping over her feet as she aimed herself towards the door.

'Goodnight, Grace.'

'Oops, nearly forgot,' she said, hovering in the doorway. Now what. 'What?'

'Richard phoned my mobile. He said please, please, please will you ring him? He loves you, Anna.'

'Go to bed Grace.'

'But he loves you. L-l-l-loves you.'

'Butt out, Grace.'

'Well I think …'

'… you should go to bed, Grace. Now. Goodnight.'

Back in Cheshire, Cleo tossed and turned, having a similarly sleepless night. She should have spoken to Mum before she'd gone away, it's just that it was so difficult to broach the subject, especially in this house. There always seemed to be other people around, demanding Mum's time. It was almost impossible to get her on her own and, if you did, you could virtually guarantee you'd be interrupted within twenty seconds. Gran, Izzy, Charlie, Zak, Alfie, they were all as bad as each other. Grace this, Mum that – where was she meant to fit in? Last in the queue, that's where.

But deep down, Cleo knew that wasn't true. It was her own fault for pushing people away all the time, especially Mum. It was so hard being a teenager, trying to prove you were tough and independent, that you didn't need anyone, that you were fine on your own, perfectly capable. Parents were out of touch with reality, knew nothing, lived in the past. But even Mum had been a teenager once, she would understand … hopefully. Cleo's hard exterior had been struck by a blow from harsh reality and was well and truly cracked.

She heard the front door open and close and Zak, presumably, stumbling up the stairs. It was Zak: she heard him curse as he lost his footing. Cleo glanced at her clock, 2.15 a.m. He could get away with murder, that boy. Here he was, coming in drunk at this time of night, and nobody said a word and yet she – she'd come in at 10.30 p.m., never even had a drink, and Charlie was on her case. It was so unfair! One rule for Zak and another for her; they should both be treated the same. Just because he was a boy ... and they were worse, she should know. The trouble was, it was always the girls who were left with the consequences. Left holding the ...

'*What?*'

Zak had stumbled into her bedroom.

'*Get out!*' she screamed at him, pulling the bed covers up tightly beneath her chin. 'Don't you know what time it is?'

'Yeah, soz,' he slurred. 'Just came to see if you're okay. Worried about you.'

'Well don't be. Get to bed, you stink of booze.'

'Soz. Love you, you know,' he mumbled, sitting down heavily on the bottom of her bed.

'Yeah, yeah.'

'No, I do. You're my kid sis and I worry about you, specially with Mum away.'

'Go to bed, Zak,' she said, pushing at him with her feet to get him off her bed.

'Okay, okay, I'm going,' he said, standing, if somewhat unsteadily. 'You would tell me though, wouldn't you, if something was wrong?'

'Yeah, yeah. Go to bed, Zak, and leave me alone.'

''Night then, sis.'

''Night.'

Charlie heard the sound of voices but just couldn't be bothered. He'd only managed to get Izzy back to her own bedroom about an hour ago and he was missing Gracie so much. He'd heard Zak come in, obviously drunk, and as for Cleo … What the hell was wrong with that girl? Oh well, tomorrow was another day. He'd sort them out tomorrow.

Tomorrow arrived, as did Richard, banging on the front door as if his life depended on it.

'Wassup?' greeted Charlie, feeling half dead from lack of sleep and added responsibility.

'God, you look as rough as I feel. Mind if I come in?'

Charlie would have liked to say that yes he did mind, but given his lack of energy, he knew he wouldn't be able to muster enough strength for an argument.

'Sure,' he said, heading towards the kitchen.

'Where is everyone?' asked Richard, amazed at the lack of kitchen hubbub.

'Zak and Cleo are both still in bed, Zak with a hangover and Cleo … well I can't work out what's wrong with her. Something on her mind, but won't talk to me at all.'

'Not more teenage angst. She rang me yesterday but I was in no fit state. I'll go up and have a word with her in a bit – if that's okay?'

'Go for it. Glad of any help I can get this week. Don't know how Grace copes with them all. Want a cuppa?'

Charlie being friendly to Richard? That's a first.

'Yeah, sure, if I'm not stopping you.'

'Relief to see a sane person, if you must know. Grrr, this damn toaster! What the hell's wrong with it?' exclaimed Charlie, sticking the knife in to try and fix it.

'You might want to unplug it before you do that.'

'Okay, okay, you don't have to tell me what to do, Grace says I'm a lot better at fixing stuff than you ever were.' That sounds more like the Charlie we know, sticking the knife in again, but figuratively speaking this time.

'Dad!' Cleo almost flew into the kitchen, straight into his

166

arms. 'Thought I heard your voice. Have you come to take me to yours? Won't take me long to get ready,' she said, hopping from one foot to the other, edging her way towards the staircase. 'I won't need to pack much for just a week.'

'Hold it, hold it, Cleo!' Richard jumped in, dashing her hopes in an instant. He didn't want to upset her but 'You really can't come and stay with me this week. I'm in no fit state to cope with myself, let alone ...'

'Then I'm just what you need!' Cleo was determined, if nothing else. 'I can look after you, cheer you up.'

'No, Cleo. I'm sorry, but no.'

Charlie glanced up from his broken toaster, shocked to see such a broken man. Anna had clearly had a major impact on him.

'This is so unfair! Why is it that nobody ever wants me?'

'Stop being such a baby, Cleo. Can't you see your dad's upset? It's time you started having a bit of consideration for others instead of thinking the world always has to revolve around you!'

It wasn't often that Charlie reprimanded anybody, so when he did, the impact was great. However, in this instance, it was one of his words in particular that struck a chord with Cleo. Emitting a muffled groan, which she stifled with her hand over her mouth, she turned on her heels and ran up the stairs to her bedroom, slamming the door hard behind her.

'What is wrong with that girl just lately?' Richard scratched his head, looking bewildered.

'Wish I knew the answer to that one, mate, save a lot of aggro in this house. Hope you didn't mind me slapping her down in front of you – you being her dad, like. Just thought she needed telling and didn't stop to think.'

'Not at all, you do a good job with her. Got a lot more patience than I have, I can only thank you. Not easy bring-ing up kids – especially that one.'

'This damn toaster!'

'Here, do you want me to have a look at it for you?'

'Go for it.'


Half an hour and one working toaster later, Cleo slunk back into the kitchen, shamefacedly, and gave her dad a hug.

'Sorry.'

Now there's a first!

'I'm sorry too – that I can't have you to stay, I mean. But I only came round to find out if you've got an address for Auntie Anna.' Cleo's and Charlie's eyes rounded on him. 'I've decided I can't just give up on her, she means too much to me. I'm going to drive down there, see if I can talk to her, make her see sense.'

'Go, Dad!'

Charlie looked concerned. 'Have you tried phoning?'

'Done nothing else. She just switches off her phone when my name comes up. I've left messages, tons of them, but she never gets back to me. I've even tried Grace's mobile but she won't put me on to Anna, says she doesn't want to speak to me.'

'Not sounding good, mate.'

'Bit like me, Auntie Anna, once she's made up her mind about something there's ...' Cleo cut herself off mid-sentence, seeing the look on her dad's face. 'Thing is, we haven't got her address. I know it was on that letter Mum had from her but where that went to ... Hang on, is it in that pile on the computer desk?' she asked, racing off to check. 'She usually keeps her bills and things there.'

Richard's hopes were raised for a moment, but soon dashed.

'Sorry, not there. It's probably in her handbag, taken it with her.'

Richard looked crestfallen. 'Could you maybe ring her up and find it out for me? Or ring Mum and ask her?'

'Bit obvious, Dad. D'you not think they'd see straight through me? They know how much you want to see her.'

'Suppose … Jesus!' he said, running his fingers through his hair in frustration. 'How can I get to speak to the woman? It's driving me crazy!'

# 16

'My feet are killing me, I wish we'd got a seat,' groaned Grace, swaying about and holding on tightly as the train clattered along through the tunnel. 'I hate the Underground.'

'Oh for God's sake stop complaining!' snapped Anna. They had had a good day, but she really was exhausted now and just wanted to get home.

'Sorry.'

It still took Grace by surprise when Anna snapped like that, it always sounded so out of character. She clutched her Harrods carrier bag tightly, pleased with her purchase. She'd only bought a coffee mug, but it would be a momento of her trip and Charlie would be proud of her for spending so little. Mind you, it hadn't been a shopping trip today, more of a whirlwind sightseeing tour. With a lot of walking, they'd managed to see not only Harrods, but Hyde Park, Buckingham Palace, Horse Guards Parade, Downing Street, the Houses of Parliament and Big Ben. Unbelievable. She couldn't wait to ring home and tell them all about it.

She hated the Underground though, so claustrophobic, people packed in like sardines in a tin. It must be a nightmare to have to do this every day, no wonder they all looked so miserable. She made eye contact with a man and gave him a friendly smile, but his expression never changed, his features frozen in a frown. They seemed just like zombies, as though the tube had sucked the life out of them, leaving them in a trance until the next stop, where heads would bob up, bodies rush out and others move in, shuffle along, take their place. Mind-blowing. She felt like a country bumpkin, almost from another world.

'Next stop,' hissed Anna.

'Thank God,' responded Grace. 'Much longer on here and I'll be as comatose as the rest.'

Grace perked up again. 'I can't wait to meet Hugo. It's the day after tomorrow he's back, isn't it?'

Despite her tiredness, Anna glowed with pride at the mention of her son. 'Yes, and I can't wait for you to meet him either. I'm sure you're going to love him – almost as much as I do! You'll be amazed at how much like Zak he is.'

'Did you say he'd gone to Leeds?'

'Yes, something to do with work. Likely to be quite late when he gets back, I should think.'

'Hope he approves of his new auntie.'

'The two of you are going to get on like a house on fire,' said Anna, 'I just know it.'

They had to, it was vital to her plan for the future. The future … Anna's momentary spark was extinguished.

'Better make the most of the time we've got then, while he's still away. Where shall be go tomorrow?'

Even the thought of another day like that exhausted Anna, she felt totally drained. 'One day at a time. Let's get home first and have something to eat.'

'Are we not going out? I thought you said you always eat out?'

'Well, not tonight. Thought we'd ring for a pizza instead.'

'You okay?' Grace hadn't really noticed before, but Anna was very pale.

'Yeah, yeah, fine. Didn't feel like turning out again tonight, that's all.'

Grace just wanted to paint the town red and only had one week to do it in but she hid her disappointment well. After all, if they went to bed at a reasonable time they could be out earlier in the morning. Tomorrow was another day. Covent Garden? Trafalgar Square? Grace's mind whirred with possibilities. London just fizzed with excitement. Life back home would never seem the same again.

Little did she know how right she was.

By the next morning, Gran had apparently forgotten she wasn't speaking to Charlie.

'Charlie, time to get Zak up!'

'Charlie, have you let that dog out yet?'

'Charlie, another cup of tea would be nice.'

'Charlie, have you seen my teeth?'

It was the last straw, enough to break any camel's back.

'For God's sake!' yelled Charlie. 'Nag, nag, nag. Will you leave me alone? I'm already trying to do fifteen jobs at the same time and you're not helping!'

'Yeah, Gran,' sniggered Cleo, conspiratorially. 'Did you not know? Men are useless when it comes to multitasking. They find it impossible.'

'Cleo!' remonstrated Charlie. 'A little less criticism and a little more assistance would be greatly appreciated.'

'How greatly?' questioned Cleo, cheekily hinting at some monetary reward.

A withering look from an overstressed stepdad soon brought her back from cloud cuckoo land.

'Sorry. I'll do Izzy's hair. Come on upstairs, Iz.'

'In a minute, think there's a toy in the cornflake box,' she said, fishing it out with glee. 'Oh yuk!' she exclaimed, hurling the retrieved object across the table in the direction of Gran.

'Don't throw, Izzy, that's naughty. Oh! My teeth! Good girl! I've been looking everywhere for them.'

'Grandma!' came the horrified chorus.

'That's disgusting!'

'I feel sick.'

'Revolting.'

'Well at least they were clean,' said Gran, popping them back into her mouth and smiling triumphantly.

Meanwhile, back in London, Grace bounced out of bed full of excitement. She thought briefly of Charlie, back home and getting everyone ready in the Monday morning rush. Her thoughts didn't linger there for long, though: why should they? She felt like a bird let out of its cage and intended to stay that way for this precious week at any rate. Nevertheless, guilt made her think of Cleo, how upset she'd been ... so out of character. Should she ring? See if she's okay? No, of course she'd be okay. She had Charlie and Richard and Zak, she'd be fine. If Grace started ringing to check it would probably only upset her again. Besides, it wasn't as though Cleo wanted her when she was there, that was the weird part about it. No. it was only for a week, and out of her cage she was staying. Everything else could wait, this was *her* time.

'Anna! Are you awake?' Grace asked, peering uninvited round the bedroom door.

Her slumbering sister stretched and yawned, still snug and sleepy in her bed. 'Time is it?'

'Eight o'clock.'

'*Eight o'clock?* Are you out of your mind? What on earth are you waking me up at this time for?'

'I'm on my holidays. A week of freedom. Places to go, things to see. Get up lazybones!'

'But ...' struggled Anna, not wanting to wake up in the slightest, 'I'm still tired.'

'You can't possibly be tired, you've had your eight hours.'

Anna opened one eye with a look of disdain which Grace chose to ignore.

'Tea?'

'I suppose.'

Whilst waiting for the kettle to boil, Grace's mobile rang. Richard. Again.

'Hey,' she answered, resignedly.

'Hey. It's me,' he responded dismally.

'Nothing wrong, is there?' she asked, fully aware of what he wanted.

'Yeah, I need to speak to Anna.'

'Richard! How many more times? She doesn't want to speak to you, and that's all there is to it.'

'But I can't go on like this.'

'Well you're gonna have to. She's adamant. It's over, move on.'

'Can't.'

'Richard, she says "no" and she means it. There's absolutely no point in going on about it. Anyway, I thought you'd be in a rush to get to work this morning.'

'Not going.'

'Richard! You're starting to sound like Cleo now! You've got to work, don't be ridiculous.'

'If you just give me the address I could drive down. She'd see me then. I know she would.'

'Do you realise how pathetic you're sounding? She wouldn't see you even if you did, so you'd be wasting your time. Get over it, Richard.'

'But I love her.'

'You've only known her for five minutes.'

'Long enough.'

'Look, I'll tell her you called. If she wants to speak to you she'll get in touch. But give her some space, for heaven's sake!'

'I love her, Grace.'

'But she doesn't love you.'

'I know she does, though. I know she does. It's just ... something's stopping her, making her hold back, and I need to find out what it is. Please tell me the address,

Grace. Please, I'm begging you.'

Grace hated hearing him so upset, but what could she do? Anna was adamant that she didn't want him to know where she was. She could hardly reveal the address to him now, Anna would be furious.

'Sorry, Richard, but I can't. Leave things to settle down for a while and she might come round eventually, you never know. I'll have a talk to her in a couple of days and see how she feels then, but for the moment, as far as she's concerned, the subject is well and truly closed.'

'You don't think she's got someone else, do you?'

'Not that I know of.'

'Then why? Tell me the address, I could …'

'No, Richard! I've told you. Leave it. I'll talk to her when the time is right.'

'But …'

'Goodbye, Richard,' said Grace firmly, closing her phone.


During the course of the past couple of days a fact had come to Charlie's attention that he had never noticed before. The fact was that it was beyond all realms of possibility that Izzy could be rushed. She would do things, yes, but at her own speed. And as Izzy had a habit of being side-tracked into about fifteen different directions at once, that speed tended to be somewhere between slow and hardly moving at all – otherwise known as snail's pace. Take going to nursery this morning for instance. Only down the road. Grace usually set off at 8.30 a.m. and Charlie had never been able to understand why. Half an hour? What was she on about? It would only take fifteen minutes, max. So off they set.

'Daddy, I need a wee.'

They'd only gone to the bottom of the path.

'But you've only just done one. Can't you wait until we get there?'

'Need one now. And a poo.'

'Okay, back we go,' said Charlie, turning reluctantly. 'Go on, hurry up.'

'Daddy!' shouted Izzy, moments later. 'No toilet roll.'

'Hang on, I'll get you one.'

Mission completed, Izzy washed her hands at the bathroom sink, blowing bubbles with the lather. 'Look at this one, Daddy, it's got a rainbow in it,' she said, fascinated by the shimmering colours.

'Dry your hands and let's go, Izzy. We're going to be late.'

'Mrs Clarke won't like it if we're late,' she said, hurriedly, for once, reaching for the towel.

She ran downstairs, out of the door and up the path before pausing for a swing on the front gate as it opened.

'Look Daddy, I'm flying!' she said, one arm outstretched as the other held on tightly.

Charlie looked at his watch. Nine o'clock. Late already. 'Come on, let's go,' he said, marching at speed to set the pace.

'Aaagghh!'

'What?' he turned, startled.

'You trod on a snail. Look! It's all squashed now. You broke its shell,' she said, squatting down next to it for a closer inspection. 'Poor snail. Say sorry, Daddy.'

'Sorry snail.' What on earth was he doing apologising to snails at nine o'clock in the morning? He pulled himself together and took his daughter firmly by the hand, pulling her to her feet. 'Come on, we're late,' he said, dragging her along.

'Ow!'

'What now?'

'You're treading on the cracks.'

'What?'

'Not meant to tread on cracks.'

'What?'

'I play it with Mummy – don't tread on the cracks.'

'Izzy! I haven't got time for this.'

'I want Mummy,' she quivered, bottom lip out and wobbling.

'Okay, okay.' Anything for a quiet life. 'No treading on cracks,' he said, stepping carefully.

It was almost nine-thirty by the time they opened the nursery school door. Silence pervaded. Mrs Clarke had all the children gathered around her, seated on the carpet. She had been in the middle of reading them a story, which Izzy and Charlie's untimely arrival rudely interrupted. Twenty pairs of eyes stared at them, unspeaking.

'Sorry,' said Charlie, an expression of guilt on his countenance.

'We're late 'cos Daddy killed somebody.'

Izzy, that was so well put. How does she manage it?

Mrs Clarke looked positively horrified. Her hand fluttered to her mouth.

'Quiet children,' she half-whispered, although none of them had spoken or even moved. They looked more like waxwork images. Mrs Clarke stood up and moved cautiously towards them, her face a little pale.

'What she means is,' said Charlie, laughing to cover his embarrassment, 'I stood on a snail, squashed it … dead. Just a snail,' he emphasised.

'Thank you for clearing that up,' said Mrs Clarke, 'although this is no laughing matter. We're all God's creatures, you know, isn't that right children? Now, say goodbye to your daddy, Izzy, and sit on the carpet with the others. I must just get myself a glass of water.'

Grace and Anna sat sipping gin and tonic in a bar in Leicester Square. It felt almost decadent to Grace to be doing so at two o'clock in the afternoon. But then, decadence was the name of the game this week – if only Mrs

Clarke could see her now!

They'd spent the morning in Covent Garden, exploring, watching an opera singer give an amazing performance out in the street for one thing. But, finally, Grace had spotted Pineapple Dance Studios and had been drawn to it, almost licking the steam from the window with envy, reading the list of classes, drawn into the ambience.

'I so wish I'd done something like that when I was younger,' she said longingly, as she sipped her gin and tonic.

'What?'

'Been a dancer.'

'Bit late for that now,' smiled Anna.

'Or anything, really. Sometimes I just feel I've wasted my life.'

'You've brought up three fantastic kids, how can you say that?'

'I know, but nothing for me. What have I achieved for myself? It's all about other people, what I do to support them.'

'Then do something about it before it's too late. Although, when it comes to dancing, I think it probably is too late,' grinned Anna, teasingly.

'Bloomin' cheek!'

'Be grateful for what you've got though, Grace, there are a lot of people who would quite willingly swap places with you right now – one not too far away, in fact.'

'You? What d'you mean? You've got a great life living here, being independent.'

'Grace, not everything is what it seems, you know.'

A cloud of sadness crept over Anna's face. Grace looked at her questioningly. Anna pulled herself together.

'Right, let's go and hit the shops on Oxford Street. It's this gin, it always makes me maudlin.'

When Charlie brought Izzy home from nursery school they were surprised to find Richard waiting outside the house. Izzy ran to greet him, her latest picture grasped tightly in her hand.

'Uncle Richard! Uncle Richard!' she shouted excitedly, as he got out of the car to meet her.

'Hi, Izzy. You just back from school?'

'Yes,' she said, hugging him. 'Do you like my picture? It's the Queen in the palace. Mummy and Auntie Anna went to see her yesterday.'

'I don't think they actually saw the Queen, Izzy, just Buckingham Palace,' said Charlie, smiling as he reached them and caught the tail-end of the conversation. 'How's it going, Richard?'

'Not bad. Had to come up to the shop, so thought I'd call in. Could use a bit of company if you're not too busy.'

'Sure,' said Charlie, opening the front door. 'You'll have to excuse the place, though – bit of a mess.'

'Give you a hand if you like, nothing better to do.'

'Not working today?'

'Off all this week – couldn't face it.'

Alfie was torn between greeting them ecstatically and staying glued to Gran as she dunked a biscuit at the kitchen table. He reached a compromise – greeted them ecstatically whilst keeping his eyes firmly glued to the biscuit.

'Could somebody let the dog out?'

'I'll take him for a walk if you like,' volunteered Richard.

Oh no! Biscuit – walk? Biscuit – walk? What's a dog to do? The decision was made for him.

'That's great. Thanks, Richard. I'll make us a sandwich for when you get back.'

Alfie shuffled about nervously as his eyes darted backwards and forwards. Lead – biscuit – lead – biscuit. He jumped up, wagging apprehensively, as Richard attached him to the lead, his eyes still firmly attached to the biscuit, and then … yeay! Gran threw him her last piece of Jammie Dodger! He would love her for ever.

It seemed a surreal situation for Charlie, Izzy and Richard to be sitting around the table eating lunch together, exchanging pleasantries. Grace would have been astounded. Gran had chosen to eat in her room, men not being her favourite species of the human race, and two of them together, definitely too much.

Charlie's mobile rang mid-meal, interrupting the proceedings. He got up and moved into the hall as he answered it.

'Daddy!' reprimanded Izzy. 'You're not allowed to leave the table until you've finished eating.'

Charlie turned and gave her a withering look as he continued with his phone conversation.

'But that's what you say to me,' continued Izzy, not easily silenced.

'This is about your daddy's work, though,' said Richard, stepping in to Charlie's defence, unable to avoid eavesdropping on the conversation. 'He can't ignore calls like that or he wouldn't earn enough money to buy nice things for you.'

Izzy looked thoughtful for a moment. 'Like toys and presents?'

'And food and clothes and this house.'

'Just want lots and lots of toys and presents. 'Bout this much,' she said, stretching her arms out wide.

'Greedy,' laughed Richard, smitten by this feisty little character that he'd never really taken much notice of before.

Charlie returned to the table, putting his phone back into his pocket, frustratedly.

'Problem?' asked Richard.

'Just some stupid woman,' said Charlie, uncharacteristically. 'She wanted an estimate doing this afternoon or not at all. I said I could do it next week, but would she listen? I wouldn't mind, but I've done jobs for her before so she knows I'm reliable, it's not as though she thinks I won't turn up. Oh well, she'll just have to find somebody else.'

'I can look after Izzy if you want to go.'

Charlie looked a bit taken aback by this unexpected offer. 'You sure?'

'Nothing better to do, have I?'

'Thanks, mate, I owe you one.'

Such bonhomie! Grace certainly *would* be astounded.

When Charlie had left, with heartfelt thanks and promises of not being very long, Izzy turned on the charm. She'd never had Uncle Richard all to herself before and he seemed like he could be good fun.

'Uncle Richa-a-ard,' she said, gazing into his eyes, 'do you want to play a game with me?'

'I think we'd better wash up first, don't you?'

'Wash up? Me?'

'Yes, you little rascal,' he said, tweaking her nose. 'I bet you help your mummy, don't you?'

'Ow!' she said, rubbing her nose but grinning nevertheless. 'No, Mummy does it. *Please* can we play a game?'

'Come on. Help me wash up and then we'll see.'

'O-o-o-k-a-y,' she sighed, rolling her eyes and getting down from the table.

Richard had almost forgotten how much longer each job took with a small child helping, but he enjoyed her company and, eventually, the task was completed.

'Can we play now?' she pleaded, wrapping him around her little finger with her wily charm.

'Sure we can. What do you want to play?'

'School,' she said, the game already planned. 'I'll go and get everything.'

181

Izzy disappeared upstairs before he changed his mind. Richard wandered into the lounge. He had thought he was in for an easy afternoon, but he'd forgotten exactly how exhausting young children could be.

'Uncle Richard!' shouted Izzy from the top of the stairs. 'Can you help me to carry them please?'

'Okay, I'm coming,' he replied, getting back up from the chair he'd just that minute sat down upon. It was all coming back to him now.

Izzy loaded him up with a random selection of dolls in various stages of undress, plus a pile of dolls' clothes so that they could all be got ready. She herself carried pencils, paper, books and anything else they might need. It was a mammoth task and Richard was sure Charlie would be delighted by the havoc they were about to create in the lounge. It had been so tidy when he'd left.

They came face to face with Gran in the hall.

'Richard? Have you just been upstairs? What were you doing up there?'

'He came up to my bedroom,' said Izzy, answering for him.

'Your *bedroom*? That's disgusting! I don't know what the world's coming to, I really don't. I'm going back to my room. My nerves can't take much more of this.'

'But I ...'

He was silenced by the slamming of Gran's door.

Izzy looked puzzled. 'You're not naughty, Uncle Richard,' she said.

Out of the mouths of babes ...


They seemed to have been playing for hours. Surely Charlie couldn't be much longer, this was beginning to get a bit boring.

'Shall we play a different game Izzy?'

'No, I like this.'

That was him told. He looked at his watch. Half an hour, is that all it had been? Seemed more like half a day. His eyes were stinging, wanting to close, lack of sleep catching up with him in the monotony of the game. Playing with dolls was not really his forte.

His mind wandered. Anna. There had to be a way of seeing her again, holding her in his arms, feeling her soft lips on his. And it wasn't just about sex, although, he had to admit, it was good: amazing, in fact. The spontaneity, the urgency ... he had never ...'

'Uncle Richard! Wake up!'

Jesus! What was he thinking? He was meant to be looking after an innocent child, not having sexual fantasies.

'I'm awake, I'm awake,' he said, guiltily adjusting his position in the chair as if to prove it.

'You've been a very naughty boy and you have to take this letter home to your mummy.'

'Okay. Sorry, teacher, I'll be good now.'

'Don't go to sleep again,' reprimanded a serious teacher, Izzy, wagging her finger at him, 'or you'll be in b-i-i-g trouble.'

Richard repressed a smile with some difficulty; she looked so much like Grace at times. He turned the letter over in his hand, not really taking much notice at first. But then something about it caught his attention. Handwritten envelope, addressed to Grace, London postmark ... surely it couldn't be ... could it? Izzy was busy with her dolls. Surreptitiously, he slid the letter out of its envelope, feeling guilty at invading the sisters' privacy, but overwhelmed by the desire to know. It was, it was! There it was! The complete address for Anna's flat in Battersea now printed on his mind in indelible ink. He was beside himself with excitement. He could go, he could find her, he could see her!

But not yet.

'Uncle Richard! You're a very naughty boy! That letter's

for your mummy and you've opened it!'

'Sorry, teacher,' he said, smiling all over his face and looking about as far away from sorry as it was possible to get.

Anna. His Anna. There was no stopping him now. Should he ring and say he was coming? Bad idea. Should he drive down tonight? Bad idea. No, wait until morning, go about it calmly instead of rushing down there like some kind of lunatic. Then arrive on the doorstep and surprise her. How could she resist?

He didn't tell Charlie or Zak or Cleo of his plans when they returned, thinking it better to keep them secret. If nobody knew, then nobody could let it slip to Grace or Anna, and he certainly didn't want them pre-warned. Under the pretence of sheer exhaustion from looking after Izzy, he went home to pack an overnight bag. Although, hopefully, he'd be staying a lot longer than that.

# 17

Anna woke up feeling like shit. No other word for it. She took her tablets, waited a while, and then tried to drag herself out of bed, but it was a physical impossibility. Her legs felt as though they were made of cotton wool, unable to support the rest of her body. She lay back down again with a sigh, her mind anxious to keep going, her body unwilling to let it. Drowning, drowning, drowning in a sea of exhaustion.

Grace breezed in through the bedroom door bearing tea and biscuits, so sure of their grateful reception that she didn't bother to knock.

'Wakey, wakey, rise and shine. What a beautiful morning. Would you like me to open the curtains and let the sunshine in? It's really gloomy in here.'

'Goes with me, then,' came a faint voice from the bed.

'Can't keep up the pace, eh,' teased Grace, putting the tea and biscuits on the bedside table. 'Where are we off to today, then? I thought maybe the National Gallery. We won't have much time tomorrow with Hugo coming back,' she babbled, opening the bedroom curtains without waiting for a reply, 'so we'd better do something special today. Ooh! I can't wait to meet him!'

Turning back to the bed at the lack of response from its occupant, Grace was shocked by the pallor of her sister. Her skin looked almost translucent.

'Anna! What's wrong? There's me rabbiting away ... you should have stopped me, I didn't realise you were ill.'

'Not ill, exactly,' snapped Anna, with as much energy as she could muster. She didn't want anyone thinking she was ill.

'Well, you don't look well, that's for sure. What's wrong?'

'Period.' Anna said the first thing that came into her head.

'Oh, didn't realise you had trouble. Can I get you anything?'

'Had tablets.'

'D'you think you'll be okay for going out later?'

'No.' It was an effort just to speak.

'What about if I go on my own? Will you be okay?'

'Mm.' Please. Just leave me in peace.

Grace was in a bit of a quandary as she closed the bedroom door behind her. Should she go out and leave Anna on her own? She did look ill. Still, period pains. Not a lot she could do if she stayed here, was there? And, after all, she was on her holidays. Would she be able to cope on her own around London, armed with her *A–Z*? Sod it, of course she would. She was out of her cage, confidence sky high, and she was flying!

Richard was just about to step out of the door when his house phone rang. Cleo.

'Dad?'

'Cleo? I thought you were in school. How come you're ringing me at this time?'

'In the toilets.' Throwing up if you must know, but best not mention that. 'Wondered if I could come and see you after school? Need to talk to you.'

'Not today, love, I'm busy.'

'Too busy to talk to me?'

'Another time, Cleo, just not today. I've got something very important to do.'

'But Dad, *this* is important.'

'Nothing is as important as this, Cleo. Listen, I've got to go. Give me a call later in the week, on my mobile if I'm not at home. We'll talk then.'

'But Dad, I …'

''Bye, darling. Be good. Love you.'

Yeah, sure. Sounds as if you do. Great parents, then. Dead supportive. Life sucks. Shit.

Amazingly enough, after Grace had gone, Anna started to feel a bit better. She catnapped for a while but then reclaimed one of her nine lives, gingerly sitting up, pausing, unsure. But no, she felt stronger, able to get up, shuffle to the bathroom and use the toilet before she wet herself. How bad would that have been? Who knew what the future held in store? How bad would things get?

At that depressing thought she walked slowly back to the bedroom. She couldn't be bothered with a shower, or even to wash her face. It required too much energy, energy that she just didn't have. Anyway, nobody was going to see her today other than Grace, and even she wouldn't be back until tonight.

She pulled on an old tracksuit and dragged a comb through her hair, not really caring how she looked. It was how she felt that mattered. She made her way through to the living room, turned on her iPod and settled herself down with a good book to read. That was as much as she intended to do today.

In complete contrast, Grace was filled with an almost overwhelming sense of freedom and adventure. This was her day and she intended to make the most of it. In a way she was glad that Anna had stayed at home. Not that she would have wished the period pains on her, of course, but if she could find her way around London on her own it would prove to herself that she was capable of doing anything. If.

That was a very big word. But she had her *A–Z* and a tongue in her head: she was sure she'd be fine.

She tried not to get sidetracked by the interesting-looking gift shop she spotted in the entrance to Clapham Junction Station. Maybe later, on the way back. For the moment this was about her and what *she* wanted, not about which presents to buy for everyone at home. Forget them for once, this was her time.

The train arrived at the platform within minutes and Grace managed to get a seat with no trouble at all. She sat back, surveying the other people in the carriage, glancing out at the scenery they were passing by. It felt good to be Grace today.

As Grace's confidence blossomed, Cleo's was draining away. She used to be quite a cocky individual, but now she sat slumped on the wall outside Zak's college looking as though she had the weight of the world on her shoulders. Zak was her last hope of someone to talk to. If he turned her away as their parents had, she didn't know what she would do.

'Cleo!'

She raised her eyes from staring at the pavement to glance in the direction of the vaguely familiar voice. Pete. Great, that's all she needed.

'What you up to?' he asked, approaching swaggeringly.

How could she ever have …? It turned her stomach even thinking about it.

'What's it to you?'

'Thought you might like to meet up later … now if you want?'

'And do what, precisely?' As if she didn't know.

'Hang out, whatever.'

'Yeah, I know exactly what you wanna do. Leave me alone, Pete.'

'Not what you were saying a few weeks ago. Come on, you know you love it,' he said, coming closer, sliding his arm around her, his foul-smelling breath in her face.

'Gerroff, sleazeball,' she said, pushing him away.

He was persistent, you could give him that.

'Aw, c'mon, Cleo, give a guy a break. Look,' he said, thrusting his pelvis forwards, 'I'm getting horny just looking at your tits – they getting bigger, or what?'

Slowly Cleo stood up, smiling seductively into his leering face, before swiftly kneeing him firmly in the crotch.

'Aaaggghhh!'

'That'll teach you not to mess with me, pervert!' she said, walking away with an air of triumph, leaving him writhing in pain. If only he hadn't been such a strong contender for the title of Daddy, she need never have thought of him again.


Victoria. A bit busier than the station back home. Grace glanced around nervously, confidence waning, trying to spot any potential muggers and then realising she was just being ridiculous. There seemed to be three distinct categories of people actually, almost equal in numbers. The first group stood in a line, heads held back as their eyes scanned the ever-changing departure board above the platform entrances. The second group lounged about, almost comatose, waiting for time or waiting for people, as the third group rushed about amongst them, anxious to get to their destination.

As for Grace, she supposed she belonged to the third group, until she spotted a fourth on a balcony above Wetherspoons. That's where she'd go first. Have a drink and study her A–Z again. At least she could use their loo. Purposefully she strode towards the escalator, confidence restored. Gin and tonic during the daytime, again? Charlie would never believe his ears, but it would give her a bit of Dutch courage.

She settled down at a table with her drink, street guide open before her. It looked straightforward enough. She could go past Buckingham Palace and then walk down The Mall, or Birdcage Walk. Birdcage Walk! She felt like a bird out of its cage flying for freedom, and, here she was heading for Birdcage Walk! Yes, she'd have to go down there, couldn't possibly resist with a name like that. Then along Horse Guards Parade, through Admiralty Arch, past Nelson's Column to Trafalgar Square. Simple. National Gallery? Not a problem. She knocked back her drink, a trifle more quickly than she intended, visited the Ladies and then joined the swarming masses on the streets of London, A–Z gripped tightly in her hand.

Cleo let herself in. 'Anybody home?'

'Kitchen.' Where else?

'Cleo!' shouted Izzy excitedly, running up the hall to meet her, grabbing her by the hand.

'Hey, trouble,' said Cleo, kissing her affectionately. 'Is Zak home?' she asked Charlie, still in desperate need of someone to talk to.

'No, not seen him yet,' replied a stressed-sounding Charlie, up to his elbows in potato peelings. 'Good day at school?'

'No,' she said, flopping down at the table, dejected.

'Couldn't take Alfie for a walk for me, could you?' asked Charlie, expecting a negative response.

'Suppose.'

Blimey!

'Thanks, Cleo. I wouldn't ask, but he's not been out all day, I've just not had time.

Alfie's ears pricked up and he lolloped over to Cleo with an air of expectancy (he was a very intelligent dog). He sat anxiously in front of her, eyes like saucers, tail sweeping the floor from side to side as he waited for the magic word.

'Walkies.'

Yikes! He was off.

Halfway down the road they met Zak, rushing along with his hands in pockets, stooped forwards to support the over-loaded rucksack on his back. Alfie bounded all over him joyously, slobbering, lead or not.

'Where you off to?'

'Where's it look like?'

'Down, Alfie! I'm covered in dog hairs now … and slobber. Get him off!'

Cleo wound the lead more tightly around her hand, dragging him down. A rejected dog, but still with a waggly tail and panting with excitement.

'Can I talk to you?'

'When?'

'Now, if you like. Come for a walk with us.'

'Can't now, I've got stuff to do.'

'Later, then.'

'Sorry, Cleo. Can it wait until another day? It's just that I'm meeting up with some lads from college tonight. Bainsey's calling round for me at seven.'

'Okay.'

'Sure?'

'Mm.'

'Laters, then,' called Zak, already on his way home.

'Laters,' replied Cleo, sadly dejected.

Alfie spun with excitement, then pulled her along. It's a dog's life, it's true!

As the day progressed, Anna felt much better. The rest had done her good. To be truthful, she was enjoying spending some time on her own and having a bit of peace and quiet; she wasn't used to all this frenzied activity of the past couple of weeks. She actually liked solitude and enjoyed her own company. It was good to be spending time with Grace and getting to know more about her and her family, but at the same time she felt a certain amount of resentment at the invasion of her privacy even though she, herself, had been the one to instigate it all. Grace was so inquisitive about everything, that was the problem, and there were certain things that Anna just did not want her to know.

She pottered through to the kitchen to make herself something to eat, and was in the process of filling the kettle when she heard the doorbell ring. Strange, Grace surely couldn't be back that quickly and Hugo wasn't due until tomorrow. She wasn't in the habit of receiving unexpected guests. Curiously, she opened the door.

'Jesus!'

'No, it's Richard actually,' smiled the figure on the door-step, overnight bag in his hand.

'How did …? Where …?'

'Are you going to let me in or do I have to stand here all day?'

'But …'

'Please.' He'd beg if he had to.

But he didn't have to. Anna turned and walked back into the living room, leaving the front door open for him to follow. Confusion, embarrassment, anger and desire – emotions chased themselves around inside her head, leaving her breathless, dry-mouthed and shaking. Her heart pounded in her chest, its sound echoing in her ears and for a moment she thought she would faint. Richard came in and closed the front door, depositing his bag in the hallway. He was startled by the way she looked when he followed her into the living room. He tried to take her hand in an attempt to lead her to the sofa.

'Here, come and sit down before you fall down,' he said, concerned.

But his touch only served to ignite her anger as she snatched her hand away in fury.

'Get off me! I don't need you or anybody else!' she screamed. 'What the hell gives you the right to track me down and follow me like … like some sort of lovesick puppy? I *told* you it's over! I *told* you to keep away from me!'

Which is exactly what wasn't happening. As Anna continued to hurl abuse at him, his face seemed to grow larger as he came closer, lips parted, breath on her face, mouth locking on hers, blocking out all thoughts other than her need for this man.

They almost ripped off each other's clothing in their desire for each other, unable to wait another moment. Groaning as he entered her, frantic and almost animal-like, never had their lovemaking felt so desperate as this. They rode high on their urgency, shouting out with pleasure, tensions released as they climaxed as one.

'Jesus!' he exclaimed, still seeing stars as he rolled off her and lay on his back.

'Hey, that's my line,' she teased.

He opened one eye and looked at her. 'Not angry with me now, then?'

'How could I be after that?' She licked a little rivulet of sweat as it trickled from his forehead down towards his ear. 'Still only lust, though,' she grinned cheekily. 'Don't think you're about to become a permanent fixture.'

It was a stab that went straight through Richard's heart. She had such power over him and he was completely and utterly in love. But hey, so far so good, he knew he'd just have to play it cool. He couldn't risk losing her again and, after all, she'd let him come this far. The pun wasn't lost on him. His body was far from cool.

'What?' she teased, knowing full well, her own ardour not yet dampened.

'Should we go somewhere more comfortable?' he asked, vaguely aware of the carpet burns on his knees, although not really caring, desire uppermost in his mind.

'No time,' she gasped, as her tongue ran slowly down his body, tantalisingly tormenting, taking him in her mouth. Within seconds she felt him starting to pulsate and, equally desirous of her own pleasure, moved swiftly to straddle him, riding to his orgasm, her own still yet to come.

'Sorry,' he gasped, fulfilled, but looking up into a face of frustration.

'No worries,' she panted, sliding from him, still burning with sexual need. 'Bedroom. Now! I need to do this in comfort.'

'But I can't ...' he said, totally drained.

'Then let your fingers do the walking,' she said, desperation throbbing now, 'or your tongue, or anything. Just come,' she said, dragging him up in her urgency. 'Jessica Rabbit's redundant for today.'

# 18

Well, Grace had made it, no problem at all. The National Gallery ... it was incredible. And as she stood gazing in awe at Monet's *The Water-Lily Pond* she felt almost as though she'd come on a pilgrimage to Mecca.

There was a repressed artist within Grace. She'd always been entranced by the subject at school but had never taken it any further, having been told by her mother to 'forget all those namby-pamby ideas' and get out into the real world and make a living. So where had she ended up? Working in a florist's. Great. The trouble with Grace was that she'd never had the courage of her own convictions. She should have stood up to her mother, gone on to art school as she'd wanted, followed her dream. In a way, Grace supposed, her mother had been right. She could have ended up struggling through life as a poor starving artist; at least at the florist's she'd earned a regular wage, contributed to the pot to support them all. She could have done it later, of course, but as always, life got in the way, ambitions remained unfulfilled and were almost forgotten.

But this picture was a poignant reminder. Grace had always loved Monet, the dabbed blobs of paint and the hazy reflections of light. She particularly loved the paintings he'd done of his garden in Giverny, and as she stood looking at the Japanese bridge over the waterlily pond, tears of emotion came into her eyes.

Isolated in her own little world with the painting, she was totally unaware of someone approaching her, and was startled by a sudden tap on her shoulder. She brushed away her tears hurriedly, feeling guilt, perhaps it was against the rules to show emotion in here.

'Grace?'

She turned around at the sound of the vaguely familiar voice, not recognising the person at first … another time, another place …

'Kate! What a surprise!' she said, as they hugged each other in friendly recognition. 'What brings you here? Stupid question! You're an artist, of course you'd come here.'

'More the sort of thing I'd ask you – I didn't realise you had a passion for art,' said Kate, noticing Grace's teary eyes.

'Too emotional, I know,' said Grace, turning back to the Monet, 'it's just that I've admired this painting for so long, and seeing it in reality, well …'

'It's okay, you don't have to explain.'

They gazed at it together in silence for a while.

'I've been there,' Kate whispered.

'To Giverny?'

'Mm. With Tom before we had Jess. Had our photo taken on that very bridge.'

'How amazing that must have been,' said Grace in awe. 'Tom – he's your husband?'

Not getting an answer to her question Grace turned, shocked to see tears streaming down Kate's face, which had panic written all over it.

'Oh I'm so sorry, I didn't mean to upset you! What's wrong?'

'I've got to get out of here, got to go. You stay. See you later,' Kate gasped breathlessly, almost running for the exit, people staring at her sudden retreat.

Grace followed, concerned. She couldn't just let her go off on her own like that. She found Kate sitting on the steps outside, shaking, sobbing, still gasping for air. Trying to instil some calm, Grace sat down quietly beside her and put an arm around her shoulders.

'It's alright Kate, I'm here for you. Just try and take some deep breaths ... slowly, that's it. I'm sorry, I didn't mean to upset you. Here, have another tissue,' she said, producing a clean one from her bag.

'Thanks ... not your fault,' gasped Kate, drying her tears, gradually recovering.

'I used to have panic attacks too, lots of people do, but I got over them eventually.'

'Mm ... used to get ... them ages ago ... then they went ... just came back ... again, with Tom ...' she said, dissolving into floods once more.

Grace sat quietly for a while, waiting for the tears to subside before she spoke, then suggested they went and had a coffee somewhere. 'You can talk about your troubles or not, it's entirely up to you.'

Kate looked at her gratefully. 'Thanks, Grace, that would be good. I don't want to talk about Tom but I would appreciate your company. I know we haven't known each other for long but I really value your friendship already.'

'Me too,' replied Grace, 'in fact I feel almost as though we've known each other for years.'

Back home, Cleo lay on her back on her bed, staring reminiscently at a photo she held in her hand. Mum and Dad, her and Zak, just the four of them. A family. Life had been so good then, her smiling face was so innocent, with not a care in the world. Until Dad had gone. He'd promised her he'd always be there for her, but where was he now? 'Something important,' he'd said. What could possibly be more important than this? She'd tried his mobile but it was switched off, Mum's too. 'Ring if there's a problem,' they'd said. Well, she'd tried. How come they were both switched off? Sex with her auntie for one, and visiting an art

197

gallery for the other – but she didn't know that, how could she? All she did know was that they couldn't care about her one little bit or they'd be here for her now when she needed them.

Tears rolled down her face unchecked, trickling sideways through her hair and forming damp patches on her pillow at each side of her head. It was so unfair. Other girls at school slept with lads all the time and never got caught out. How come this had happened to her? She ran a hand down over her belly. There was a definite mound now, she couldn't ignore it. People would begin to notice soon. Even Pete, of all people, had said today about her boobs looking bigger, and he was right, they did: she'd thought so herself when she looked in the mirror. What a mess.

Grace and Kate chatted animatedly over coffee. Each was appreciative of the bond they'd formed in such a short period of acquaintance. Friends come and go throughout life but a friendship such as this was one to be treasured.

'I have to say, Grace, I'm so glad we met. I've been going through a really tough time recently and just talking to you … well, it makes me realise life still goes on. No point in sitting around brooding all the time, got to get on – with my painting *and* with my life.'

'You're so right, life's too short. Stay still for a minute and it's gone. I've wasted years just looking after everyone else instead of doing the things that I've wanted to do for me. But no more! This trip to London's done me the world of good. I'm out of my cage and I intend to stay that way! Oh, and by the way – me too.'

'What?'

'I'm really, really happy that we've become such good friends.'

Grace thought about Kate as she walked back up Lavender

Hill. She had such a sad aura about her despite the laughter they'd had. But at least she'd managed to cheer her up a little bit and they'd exchanged mobile numbers to keep in touch. Hopefully they'd meet up again while they were both still here in London, maybe tomorrow night in fact ... although, no, she was due to meet Hugo tomorrow, it might have to be the night afterwards. Maybe Kate would feel able to confide in her a bit by then, offload some of her problems. It was always better to talk about things than to keep them bottled up like she seemed to be doing.

'Hello!' Grace shouted, as she let herself into Anna's flat.

No response. Anna must still be in bed. Grace cursed under her breath as she tripped over a bag that was standing in the hallway. Strange, that wasn't there when she'd left. Perhaps it belonged to Hugo, perhaps he'd got back early. Odd that Anna should have stayed in bed all day, it was only period pains for God's sake. Concerned, Grace made her way to the bedroom to check that Anna was okay.

Was she okay ... Two startled heads popped up from the pillows simultaneously, wide-eyed and wide-mouthed, hands frantically scrabbling for anything that would cover their naked forms.

'Oh my God! Richard?'

'Do you ever think of knocking before you come barging into my room like that?' snapped Anna in her embarrassment.

'But I didn't ... What are *you* doing here?' Grace stormed at Richard.

'What's it look like?' growled Richard, not seeing why he should have to answer to his ex-wife.

'Was this a set-up just to get me out of the way? I thought you weren't feeling great.'

'She feels great to me,' said Richard, good humour restored as he groped Anna's naked flesh underneath the bedcovers.

199

'Richard!' Anna pushed his hand away, understandably embarrassed in her sister's presence.

Grace was not to be silenced. 'You told me you had period pains,' she said, accusingly.

'Period pains?' questioned Richard. 'But …'

Anna silenced him with her eyes before turning her attention back to her sister. 'Grace, could you please get out of my room? You're standing there gawping at us like some kind of pervert.'

Grace turned on her heels and fled to the kitchen feeling, suddenly, very much the odd one out. Feeling cheated also. Had Anna known Richard was arriving today? Is that why she'd pretended to be ill and let her go off to central London on her own? She felt hurt and angry, let down by both of them, and in desperate need of a hug. She phoned Charlie, solid, dependable Charlie.

'Hey. Didn't expect to hear from you until later. Thought you'd be off out, living it up.'

'Well I have been, sort of, but on my own. Richard's here.'

'Richard? But …'

'I know, it was a shock to me too. I just walked in on them.'

'How d'you mean?'

'At it … you know.'

'Bet they were pleased,' sniggered Charlie.

'Charlie! Don't laugh, it's not funny.'

'Sorry, Gracie, you okay?'

'I was, but now I don't know what to do. If Richard's staying I feel a bit like a gooseberry. I just want to come home. Missing me?'

''Course I am, you know that. Everybody is, especially Cleo. She's been in a really strange mood ever since you left.'

'Nothing new there, then – Cleo in a strange mood,' said

Grace, smiling fondly at the thought of her tantrum-torn daughter.

'Wish you were here.'

'Me too,' said Grace, tears in her eyes. 'Listen, I'm going to stay and meet Hugo tomorrow, but if Richard's still here by the next day, I'm going to get the train home. No point in my staying here with these two lovebirds.'

Meanwhile Anna had some explaining to do.

'Period pains?'

'So?'

'But you're not even having your period.'

'So?'

'Explain.'

'Okay, I didn't want to go out today so I told a little white lie. Nothing wrong with that, is there?'

'Not on its own, no. It's just that when you add it to every-thing else, the mystery deepens.'

'Richard, there *is* no mystery.'

'Oh, but I think there is. You're just running away all the time, hiding the truth. What is it with you? I've got to know now, you've got to tell me. I can't take it any more. I don't think you realise just how much I love you.'

It was the first time Richard had cried in front of anyone for years and, once the floodgates were opened, there seemed to be no end to his grief. Anna felt overpowered by guilt as she held him in her arms. What had she done to this man? She loved him so much, and to have hurt him like that was almost more than she could bear. Should she tell him the truth? But then that wouldn't ease his pain, would only serve to make it worse. And Grace would find out, and the rest of her family – that was the last thing she'd wanted. She'd had it so well planned and now it was all going horribly wrong. Love has a lot to answer for.

'I love you too, you, must know that,' she sobbed, letting

201

down her guard. 'I wanted to tell you, but how could I? If I'd told you it would have changed everything.'

Richard glanced up at her, embarrassed by this baring of his emotions but unable, now, to stop himself from picking away at her protective shell. He had to know, and he had to know now, today. The truth had to be told.

Poor Grace. She'd been on a high all day, flying free, confidence soaring, but now she could feel herself fluttering back down to the ground. The cage beckoned. She shouldn't be sitting here on her own like this: she was in London, for God's sake, she should be out there enjoying herself while she had the chance. The trouble was, she didn't much feel like enjoying herself any more, the mood had been broken. She felt lied to, cheated. She'd come all this way, organised everything, so that she could spend some time getting to know her sister, and then that same sister had locked herself away and left her on her own. Great.

She'd moaned about Charlie being predictable and boring, but at least he was dependable, there was a lot to be said for that. Grace had been craving for excitement, but was that really what she wanted at the end of the day?

Her mobile interrupted her thoughts. Charlie. Again. Grace smiled as she held the phone to her ear.

'Hey you. Can you read my mind? I was ...'

'Gracie, this is serious. I've got something to tell you.'

Grace felt the colour drain from her face, the phone shook in her hand. 'It's one of the children, isn't it? Something's happened to one of my babies! Or is it Mother? Tell me, Charlie! Tell me!'

'Calm down, calm down, nobody's hurt, we're all okay ...'

'Then what ...?'

'It's Cleo. Just dropped a bombshell. She reckons she's pregnant!'

'Pregnant? Cleo? But ...'

'I know. She's in a mess, Gracie, really upset. Says she's been trying to phone you and Richard all afternoon but your phones were switched off. I don't know what to do with her, I think she only turned to me as a last resort.'

'Oh God, Charlie, I feel awful. Poor Cleo, I should never have left her, I should have known there was something wrong when she didn't want me to go. Where is she? Can I speak to her?'

'She's here now, I'll put her on.'

'Mum?' Such a little voice, she sounded about five years old, not fifteen.

'Darling! Are you okay? I'm so sorry I left you, I would never have come away if I'd known.'

''S okay,' Cleo was crying too much to speak.

Grace made a snap decision. There was no other option as far as she was concerned. 'Listen, Dad's here too. He came down today to see Auntie Anna, but we'll come home. I'll tell him what's happened and we'll drive straight back, tonight if possible.'

Silence, punctuated by snuffles, was all that could be heard from the other end of the phone.

'Okay, Cleo?'

'Mm.'

'Right, then, I'm going to go now and tell Dad, but we'll be back soon, alright?'

'Mum?'

'What, darling?'

'Are you really cross with me?'

'Just worried about you, Cleo, not cross. But don't *you* worry, you're not on your own, we'll help you all we can and we'll be with you very soon. We both love you very much, you know that, don't you?'

'Mm, I love you too. Thanks, Mum.'

Tears welled in Grace's eyes, almost as much from Cleo

saying 'I love you' as from the fact that her teenage daughter was pregnant. Cleo, pregnant, at the tender age of fifteen. It was almost too much to contemplate.

Somehow Anna had still managed to avoid telling the truth – sex was a wonderful thing, and a great distraction in addition to the insurmountable pleasure it gave. Richard gasped in excruciating pleasure as her soft, moist tongue teased him mercilessly, probing, flicking, a myriad of delights. She raised her head momentarily to see the expression on his face, raised her game and climbed upon him, moving slowly, in control. But gradually her need became an urgency and she bounced in wild abandon, hearing a knocking in the distance but not caring from whence it came.

'Yes!' shouted Richard, in the orgasmic ecstasy they rode together.

'A-a-aagghh!' groaned Anna from her pleasurable place.

'Oh, sorry!' gasped Grace, as she walked in through the door at the most inopportune moment she could possibly have chosen.

'What the fuck …?' spat Richard, astounded at the sudden appearance of his ex in his line of vision behind Anna. That sure must have been some orgasm, he was hallucinating, having kinky thoughts of a *ménage à trois* … they were sisters, for God's sake.

Even Anna didn't realise what was happening for a moment, she really thought she'd died and gone to heaven until she turned and saw, through a post-orgasmic haze … Grace, rooted to the spot.

'Jesus!'

'Sorry.' What more could she say?

'I can't believe it! You again! What the hell do you think you're doing? Does it never occur to you to knock? You could see the door was closed!'

'Sorry, sorry, I'm really, really sorry, but I did knock, honestly. It's just that when I heard Richard shout "yes" I thought that he meant I could come in.'

'Suppose that's one variation of the word "come" anyway,' muttered Richard, under his breath.

'But even now you don't seem to have the decency to turn around and go out again. What is it with you? Get out and give us some privacy!' yelled Anna, totally uncomfortable now, still perched astride Richard and limply attached to his now flaccid penis. She had no other option, she could hardly climb off and reveal absolutely all to her already goggle-eyed sister, she'd seen enough already. 'Go, for God's sake! I feel like I'm in some sort of porn movie!'

'In a minute, but this is urgent.'

'So's this, believe me.'

'It's Cleo,' said Grace, looking beyond Anna to Richard. 'She's pregnant.'

'Pregnant?' Richard sat up in shock, sliding slipperily out of Anna and almost knocking her onto the floor.

'Jesus!' blasphemed Anna yet again, as she rescued herself and her dignity, or what was left of it, and attempted to cover her nakedness with the duvet, even though it was a little bit late for that.

'But she's only fifteen!' Richard was horrified.

'That's not a form of contraception, Richard. You can still get pregnant at fifteen. If you have unprotected sex you have to deal with the consequences at any age,' she said pointedly.

'But didn't you warn her?'

'Well of course I did, don't be stupid, but you know what she's been like just lately, off out with all sorts.'

'And you didn't stop her?'

'I tried, you know I did. I told you how worried I was about her. Where were you, anyway? The absent father.'

'I've always been there for my kids, you know I have, but

you're the one that has them living with you, you're the one that's supposed to look after them.'

'I knew it! I knew you'd blame me for this! Why is it that everything's always my fault?'

'*Be quiet!*' screamed Anna.

To be honest, they'd both completely forgotten she was there.

'*This is my bedroom! If you want to argue, take it elsewhere!*' She was not best pleased.

They still didn't really register her presence, just headed towards the lounge, mid-altercation.

'You're her mother, for fuck's sake, you must have talked to her.'

'Ogghh! You make me so angry! What do you think I ...'

'*Richard!*' Anna glared at him from the heap of duvet on the bed, the very same one that had been such a hotbed of sexual frenzy only moments before. '*Do not* go through there with your bits jiggling in front of my sister!' her voice was firmness itself.

He did sort of half-hear her this time, it was hard not to. 'I was married to her, remember, she's seen it all before. She's hardly going to jump me, is she? We've got more important things to think about.'

Well, great. That made Anna feel just fantastic.

'Cover yourself up.'

'Strewth!'

# 19

It wasn't a decision that was difficult to make. Their children were top priority for both of them and they knew they had to go back to Cleo tonight; she needed them, and they had to show a united front. Their love for her was paramount. Without further ado they started to gather their things together for the journey home, although for Richard this was hardly a mammoth task, he'd only been there for a matter of hours.

Anna was feeling decidedly discarded, insignificant in the general scheme of things, rekindling memories of the past. Her family had abandoned her once before and now, having only just rediscovered them, they were about to do it again. Should she say something now? Should she tell them? That would certainly stop them in their tracks, they'd have to notice her then. Cleo being pregnant wouldn't seem like such a big deal, not in comparison …

But that was her just being selfish. She loved Cleo, and felt sorry for the girl. Nevertheless, when she thought back to when she'd found out *she* was pregnant, and the circumstances she'd found herself in, Cleo's situation was nothing. Cleo would have all the support she could possibly wish for. It was hard not to feel bitter.

'So I'm to be abandoned, then?' she asked of Richard, as he returned to the bedroom, still scantily clad in a towel.

'Sorry, but you understand, don't you?'

Oh yeah, sure, she understood alright. You come into this world alone and you leave it alone and, especially in her

207

case, there were a lot of lonely bits along the way too.

'Is it okay if I have a shower?'

'Help yourself.'

'Don't be like that,' he said, actually noticing her finally, perching on the edge of the bed, clutching his towel. 'Anna?'

'What?' she glowered.

'You know I wouldn't go if it wasn't for Cleo. I love you, you know that, but she's my daughter and she needs me. Bad timing, I know, but that's the way it is.'

Two silent tears trickled down Anna's face. Should she tell him the truth? Would she ever see him again?

'Please don't cry, I won't be gone for ever,' he said, covering her hand with his own. 'Oh Anna, I wish you'd tell me what it is that's troubling you so much. Whatever it is, we can deal with it together. Just tell me, tell me now before I go.'

Oh yeah, like it was something she could just blurt out. He was obviously under the impression that it was some trivial thing she'd blown up out of all proportion inside her head, something that was easy to fix. If only.

'I thought you had another man at first, thought that was the reason, but now I don't know what to think.'

'Just go and have your shower,' she said, turning her back on him and pulling the duvet firmly around herself for protection, like a tortoise retreating into its shell.

Richard sighed and shook his head sadly. There was nothing more to be said. He stood up, the towel dropping to the floor like a symbol of finality as he made his way sadly to the bathroom to get himself ready for the drive back to Cheshire.

Despite her head being concealed beneath the duvet, Anna was aware of the bedroom door opening yet again.

'Anna?'

'Jesus!'

The tortoise emerged, suddenly transformed into a British Bulldog.

'What have I said to you only five minutes ago? *Knock on the door!* I don't know what you think is going on in here, obviously some sort of spectator sport. D'you want a front row seat or something? Because if you do you'll have a long wait now. You see this supposed *ex-* husband of yours is obeying your command and leaving me tonight to drive all the way back to Cheshire with you. Got him just where you want him, haven't you?'

'Anna, please don't be like that. We've got to go to Cleo. Surely you, of all people, must understand that. She's pregnant.'

'Pregnant? Pregnant? Well I was bloody pregnant and who was there for me, eh? Certainly not my family, oh no. I had to do it all on my own, like I've always had to do everything.'

'Don't try and blame me for that, Anna. I didn't even know, I was just a child. Don't try and make me feel guilty, that was our parents' fault, not mine. I just want to do the right thing by my own child now, by Cleo, and I think Richard should come back too. She's pregnant and she needs us.'

'She's pregnant, she's not dying ...'

'Look, I know you think we're making a big fuss over nothing, but she's our daughter.'

'Just don't get me, do you?'

'What?'

'Oh never mind. Go.'

The atmosphere remained black and tense right up to the point of their departure. Grace and Richard both felt upset, and somewhat annoyed, to be truthful, that Anna couldn't even be bothered to get out of bed to say goodbye to them. Little did they know the real reason was that she felt so ill she didn't have the strength to move. Sex with

Richard had left her exhausted. Now the argument combined with the stress of trying not to reveal the truth about herself to them was all too much for her.

'See you soon, then,' said Grace, upset by her sister's apparent rejection of her and unable to understand what she had supposedly done that was so wrong. 'Keep in touch. I love you.'

'Hmmph,' muttered Anna under her breath, overwhelmed by the thought that this was probably the last time she would ever see them, and having neither the strength nor the courage to explain.

'Oh Anna, I wish you'd talk to me,' said Richard, distraught at having to leave her like this.

But Anna merely stared back at him, coldly, icy daggers piercing his heart. In a way it was all she could do. She no longer had the strength for passion, and to let him leave thinking she no longer cared was, in her eyes, possibly the kindest thing she could do.

Charlie was at his wits' end. Thank goodness Grace was coming home tonight, she deserved a medal for the way she coped with this lot. She'd said it would probably be well after midnight by the time they got back. He didn't care what time they arrived, he'd just be so relieved to see her. He really hadn't understood the meaning of the word 'stress' until the past few days. Few days? Is that all it had been? It felt like weeks.

He opened the washing machine door and put in the sheets from Izzy's bed. Alfie peered in inquisitively, nose twitching at the unfamiliar smell.

'Dirty dog – get off!' scolded Charlie, pushing him away with his knee. He didn't want to touch anything until he'd had a chance to wash his hands properly, not even a dog.

Izzy had been sick. And, okay, it was his fault. When he'd stopped to think about it he'd fed her nothing but junk food, fizzy pop, crisps and sweets since Grace had left. He hadn't meant to, it was just the way things had worked out. Anyway, she was fine now, tucked up in a nice clean bed and fast asleep. Grace need never know.

'D'you know how to work the washing machine, Cleo?' he asked, after a few failed attempts. He'd never even had to look at a washing machine since he got married. Grace saw to everything.

Cleo drifted back from the other planet she'd been on. 'Sorry, never used it. Mum does all that.'

Luckily perseverance paid off and, finally, the machine burst into action.

'Fantastic,' said Charlie, triumphant in his achievement. He was as proud as if he'd just scaled Mount Everest.

'You okay, Cleo?' he asked, turning and seeing her strained and anxious face as she sat with her elbows on the kitchen table, chin cupped in her hands.

'They're gonna go crazy at me, aren't they?' she asked, looking desperately for reassurance.

'Shouldn't think so, love, they're pretty understanding as parents go. Your mum didn't sound angry when she spoke on the phone, did she?'

'No, quite calm as it happens.'

'There you go, then. They'll be worried about you rather than cross, I would imagine.'

'That's what Mum said, but I still worry that when they see me they're gonna go mad. It's different on the phone, they'll have had time to think about it now. They had such high hopes for me.'

'Just because you're having a baby it doesn't mean …'

'Having a baby? Who's having a baby?'

Great. Enter Gran, pink hairnet, curlers, quilted dressing gown, and toothless mouth gaping wide open to match her beady eyes, eagerly receptive to the biggest family scandal to have hit her in decades.

211

Silenced wobbled nervously around the kitchen table. The washing machine droned on obliviously. Alfie whimpered and retreated to his basket.

'*Who's* having a baby?' she repeated, banging her walking stick emphatically as if to reiterate the question.

There was only one thing she could do. Like Mum had taught her, it was always best to tell the truth.

'I am, Gran,' said Cleo, bravely. 'I'm having a baby.'

Silence. She was silent! But Grandma's jaw dropped even lower, revealing the gummy cave within. She turned an extraordinary shade of puce, clashing mightily with her hairnet, as she dropped her stick to the ground with a clatter and sank onto the nearest chair.

'Please can somebody tell me this isn't true?'

Cleo remained amazingly calm, considering she was in the wrinkly face of such adversity. 'No point, Gran because it *is* true. I'm having a baby. I told Mum and Dad on the phone earlier and they're on their way back now.'

'I knew it! I knew this would happen! Just like that disgrace, I've said so all along. She should never have come here, causing trouble again. Always the same she is, always the same.'

'It's got nothing to do with Auntie Anna, Gran. How can it be her fault? She was only here for a few days, I got pregnant long before that.'

'And where is she now, eh?' asked Gran, still on her rant, ignoring all others. 'Off plying her wares on the streets of London I don't doubt, your mother with her. The whole thing's disgusting! Where did you say your father was?'

'He's with Mum.'

'With your mother *and* that disgrace in London? All three of them together? This gets worse! A threesome now is it? I've never heard anything like it!'

At least it took the heat off Cleo although, bravely, she turned it back on. 'What are you going on about, Gran?

This is about me. *I'm* the one who's pregnant, just me, nobody else.'

Gran glared at her, beady eyes narrowed. 'Well you didn't get pregnant on your own, did you? I'm not stupid, I know who the father is.'

'You do?'

'Obvious isn't it? Your father! That Richard! Comes sniffing round here, but I know his game; you think I'm daft but I'm not. He's had you there for weeks now, sleeping overnight. No wonder you're having his baby. I did warn Grace, but would she listen?'

'I think you've said enough, Gran,' warned Charlie protectively.

'Yeah. Gran, I'm not going to sleep with my own father, am I? That's sick.'

'Well that disgr…'

'Gran! I think you've said *more* than enough now. Go back to bed and I'll bring you a cup of tea.'

Gran pulled the quilted dressing gown more tightly around herself and held it firmly together under her chin. 'Don't bother. I don't want any man coming into my bedroom, thank you very much. You won't catch me getting pregnant!' And, on that note, it was amazing how quickly she got to her feet and shuffled back to her room, slamming the door firmly behind her.

Despite the seriousness of the situation, Cleo had to struggle to suppress a giggle.

'Well at least she managed to put a smile back onto your face,' said Charlie. 'And as for the baby, as far as I'm concerned what's done is done. We'll just have to get on with it and help you all we can.'

Cleo came round the table and gave him a hug. 'Thanks, Charlie. You're the best stepdad ever, and I'm sorry I've given you such a hard time.'

Charlie hugged her in amazement. Maybe he hadn't

done such a bad job after all, he'd never in a million years expected to hear those words come from Cleo's mouth. Grace would be impressed.

The next one to hear the news was Zak, who staggered in on the stroke of midnight, somewhat inebriated and loving everybody.

Dong. 'Ssshhh!' Dong. 'Ssshhh!' Dong. 'Ssshhh!' He attempted to silence the chiming clock, finger to his lips, as he tiptoed inelegantly down the hall in an ungainly manner. 'Feel like Cinderella … midnight … clock,' he giggled by way of explanation, before tripping over himself and landing awkwardly, but fortunately, on a kitchen chair. His pantomime audience did not look overly impressed.

'Zak, you've got college tomorrow and you're going to wake up with a stinking hangover. I thought you were coming back early?' reprimanded Charlie. Well, that was about as reprimanding as it got with Charlie.

'Chill Charlie … hah! Chill Charlie, chill Charlie, chill Charlie!' he laughed. 'Ch-ch-ch! Don't worry, Stepdaddy, I'll be up. I love you, did I ever tell you that? 'Cos my own dad, he went off and left us. Did you know that Charlie? Left us. But you, Charlie boy, you've been there for us and we love you, we do. Don't we, Cleo?'

'We do.'

'Well Cleo might not 'cos she's a stroppy bugger some-times, but I do, I love you Charlie. *What* did you say?' he asked, Cleo's words only just registering in his somewhat pickled brain.

'I said I love Charlie,' said Cleo, looking with new-found admiration at her beaming stepdad. He wasn't used to all this praise but he was loving every minute of it.

'You love Charlie?' slurred Zak, incredulously, trying to focus his eyes on his sister's face. 'You're not even drunk, are you?'

'No, just been talking.' Now wasn't the best time to tell him probably, but she took the bull by the horns. 'I'm pregnant, Zak.'

'Shit.' He closed his eyes briefly, as if by not being able to see her would make it not be true. It didn't do much for his head though, which seemed to have suddenly climbed onto a rollercoaster. He opened them again quickly, blinking, eyeballs rotating. 'Shit,' he repeated, making a sudden exit and heading for the bathroom.

'Great reaction there then,' said Cleo, disappointed at her brother, upon whom she could usually rely.

'Don't worry about it, Cleo, you can see what a state he's in, probably not even registered what you said. Let him sleep it off and talk to him tomorrow.'

But, in reality, the fact that his sister was pregnant *had* registered with Zak, and was equally as much a contributing factor to him throwing up as was the amount of alcohol he had consumed. He knew he should go back downstairs and talk to her; she was his kid sister and he loved her, but it was as much as he could do to stagger to his bed tonight. Nevertheless, as he lay there in his darkened room trying to gather a modicum of sense from the drunken ramblings and overpowering need for sleep that threatened to engulf him, the vision of one person's face persistently appeared before him. Pete. The bastard! He would pay for this.

As the car finally pulled into the drive, Grace fought an unexpected desire within herself to turn around and go straight back again. What kind of a terrible mother did that make her? It was just that the cage seemed to loom before her even larger now than it ever had before, and what worried her most was ... would she ever be able to find the key again? Unbeknown to her, similar thoughts were running through Richard's head. All the trauma he'd gone through these past few days when he thought he'd blown any chance he may have had with Anna, and then today had been unbelievable, they'd been so close, her almost confiding in him – until Grace's intrusion. But where did that leave him now? She wasn't even speaking to him any more.

'Come on, then,' said Richard, taking the key from the ignition with a sigh. 'Let's go and face the music.'

'Thanks for coming with me, Richard. I know I was a bit of a cow, and I know how hard it was for you to leave Anna. I really do appreciate it.'

'Hey, I'm her dad,' he said, covering her hand with his own. 'I couldn't possibly have done otherwise.'

Having seen the headlights on the drive, Charlie came out to the car to greet them, of course, not failing to notice the little – in his eyes intimate – gesture.

'Alright, Richard?' he asked, hostility prickling, as the aforementioned disentangled himself stiffly from the car.

'Been a lot of driving in one day, mate,' said Richard, not meaning that sarcastically in any way whatsoever.

'Well it's *your* daughter … *mate*,' replied Charlie, going round to open the car door for his beloved Grace.

'Charlie! So good to be back, I've missed you,' she said, throwing herself into his welcoming arms. Well, she could hardly do otherwise, could she?

But then she spotted Cleo, lurking nervously in the doorway, looking so un-Cleo-like it just wasn't true. Grace left Charlie helping Richard to unload the car and walked towards her daughter, arms outstretched. Cleo fell into them with a sob of relief, encircled by her mother's love and reassurance, the warmth of it permeating her entire body, thawing the fear that had encompassed her for so long.

An emotional mother and daughter went into the house, arms around each other, to be greeted by an ecstatic Alfie, who seemed to have developed more bounce than a kangaroo.

'I know you love me,' said Grace to him through her tears, 'but let me get in.'

And Gran. 'Oh, so you're back.'

'Yes, Mother, I'm back. Did you miss me?'

'Miss you? I've never heard anything so disgusting in all my life! Have they come back with you?'

'Richard has, yes. Not Anna.'

'Well that's something to be grateful for, then. We don't want any of that going on in *this* house thank you very much.'

'What are you talking about, Mother?'

Cleo smothered a smile through her tears. 'Don't ask, Mum,' she said.

'And as for this little minx,' said Gran, her attention turned to Cleo now. 'Have you heard the latest? I told you that disgrace would bring trouble didn't I? I did try to warn you, I said …'

'Yes, Mother,' said Grace, heading her firmly towards her room. 'Thank you very much but I think it's actually past your bedtime now, so goodnight, we'll see you tomorrow.'

'Well, charming I'm sure,' said Gran huffily. 'I know when I'm not wanted. I'll just go to my room out of the way. That's what you want, isn't it?'

Grace was in no mood to contradict. 'That would be perfect, Mother, thank you. Goodnight,' she said, firmly closing the door, hearing her mother still chuntering away to herself on the other side of it.

They sat up for half the night, the three of them plus Charlie, around the kitchen table. Well, Charlie was not about to go to bed and leave them alone together, was he? This was his family now and he was staying put to stake his claim. Funny thing was, he'd got on quite well with Richard when Grace wasn't there but then, jealousy was the root of all evil, or so they say. Still, he'd captured Cleo's heart now, at last. She sat next to him at the table, giving his hand the occasional grateful squeeze, an action that didn't escape Grace's notice. She smiled appreciatively at him, thankful for this bond that mysteriously seemed to have formed in her absence. Richard noticed it too, but didn't have the same tendency to suffer from the effects of the green-eyed monster that Charlie did. He knew his children loved him, as he loved them, unconditionally. For Cleo now, at last, to be becoming more accepting of Charlie could only be a good thing in his eyes, especially at this time in her young life. Cleo was going to need all the love and support she could get.

Cleo actually felt as though a huge weight had been lifted from her shoulders. It had been an enormous worry that she had been carrying around with her for ages and, unable to share it with anyone, she had felt as though she was drowning in a sea of responsibility. Becoming pregnant was a life-changing situation for any woman to find herself in, but at only fifteen, Cleo had been terrified. Not only, at first, had she not understood what was happening to her body but also, when she eventually did realise, she was already at such a low point in her life that she thought this would make everyone hate her even more than they did already.

She had been petrified of telling her family, knowing how disappointed they'd be in her. She'd always wanted them to feel proud of her, as any child does, but she'd been so stupid, created this hard outer shell and 'couldn't care less' attitude. How could she ever hope to make them feel proud of her now? But here they were, giving up everything that was important to them, travelling across the country to show their support. Not an angry word had been spoken, just worry and concern, as they gathered together around the kitchen table, a strong family unit filled with love for their girl.

Cleo was overwhelmed by their attitude. How could she

have been so horrible to them? Guilt-ridden, she tried to explain what had made her that way. How much she'd missed her dad and resented Charlie for taking his place. She explained how Grace seemed so busy and never had time for her and how Gran always seemed to put her down. Even at school things hadn't been easy. Cassie and Lisa had been her best friends forever, but recently they'd been really bitchy towards her, giggling behind her back and going off together, leaving her out of things. That's why, she explained, she'd been hanging around with the lads. It had been an ego boost that they all wanted to be with her; it felt good to be so popular in one area of her life and sleeping with them occasionally seemed a small price to pay. A large price now though. She'd been so stupid. A lot of growing up was done that night.

Grace was in tears, hearing Cleo talk like this. If only she'd been there for her more, listened when she wanted to talk, noticed that she was so unhappy. She could have helped, none of this need ever have happened. Another thing she couldn't get over was the fact that she had never noticed Cleo was pregnant. As the sort of mother she'd thought she was, that was unforgivable, proving just how little attention she'd paid to her daughter. Judging by the look of her now, the swell of her belly in her tiny frame, she must be four months gone at least. How could she have failed to notice? A great mother she'd turned out to be.

'I'm so sorry, Cleo.'

Cleo looked up, startled. 'What have you got to be sorry about?'

'I let you down.'

'Oh Mum, how can you possibly think that? I let you down, more like.'

'And I let you both down, probably,' said Richard, feeling quite emotional as he got up from his chair and moved around the table to give them both a hug.

219

Charlie cleared his throat, he was having none of this. 'Tea anyone?' he asked, noisily scraping back his chair and going to fill the kettle. 'Or toast even, we could have toast.'

'Mm, please,' said Grace, quite hungry now, it had been a long night. 'Watch the toaster though, don't want a fire on top of everything else.'

'It's okay, it's mended now,' mumbled Charlie. Why did he say that? Hopefully she was too distracted to notice.

No such luck. 'You? You mended the toaster, Charlie?' asked Grace, filled with incredulity.

'Well, er …'

'It was me, actually,' said Richard, quite smugly it has to be said.

'Oh thanks, Richard, that was really good of you. I thought … I'd be amazed if Charlie had done it,' laughed Grace.

'I could have, just never got round to it, that's all,' snapped Charlie.

Morning was heralded by the thunderous footsteps of Izzy bounding down the stairs, followed by Zak at a much more sedate and painful pace.

'Mummy!' shrieked a delighted Izzy, launching herself towards Grace and showering her with kisses. 'I didn't know you were here. Ooh! Is it a party?' she asked, glancing around the table excitedly.

'No party, Izzy, we're just talking, that's all. Have you missed me?'

'Lots and lots and lots,' said Izzy, rubbing her nose up against her mother's like a little Eskimo. 'Did you miss me?'

'It was very quiet without you, I have to say,' smiled Grace, tweaking Izzy's nose in return as she scrambled off in her usual haste.

'Uncle Richard!' squealed Izzy, happy to see him too and climbing up onto his knee for a cuddle.

'Right young lady, time to get you ready for school,' said Charlie, somewhat hastily.

'But Daddy …'

'Leave her Charlie, it's still early yet, there's plenty of time.'

'But you know how she dawdles …' said Charlie. Even he realised how pathetic he was sounding now, but Izzy was his, not Richard's – and so was Grace.

Izzy left Richard and returned to Grace for protection, a look of triumph on her face as Grace kissed the top of her head.

'Errgh, smells of sick.'

'I was sick in bed,' said Izzy, playing for sympathy.

Poor Charlie, would nothing go right today?

'My fault.' He might as well admit it now. 'Been feeding her too much junk food.'

'Oh Charlie.'

'I know, I know. Sorry.'

'Mum?' Nobody had noticed Zak, he was so quiet.

'Hey, how's it going? Got a hug for your favourite mother?' smiled Grace, until she saw the state of him.

'Got any paracetamols?'

'Oh Zak! You've been out drinking on a college night again! How many times …? Charlie!'

'Sorry, I know, I should have stopped him.'

Poor Charlie. Was he to blame for everything round here?

# 20

Anna felt as though she was falling down a black hole from which there was absolutely no escape. And it was true, there wasn't. In fact, falling was the wrong word. Falling would have been preferable, it would have been instant, over. Instead she was floating, drifting slowly, deeper and deeper, never reaching the end, suffering the pain, and now the heartache too. As if one thing hadn't been enough.

Why had she reacted like that? If only she could have told them the truth, let them help her. But she wasn't used to that, having to rely on other people. She'd had to be strong, independent, able to cope on her own. A survivor ... but a survivor no more. She knew she needed her family now – and what had she done? Cut them out, turned her back on them, let them think she didn't care.

Didn't care? Nothing could be further from the truth. The love she felt for Richard was so all-consuming that it was almost impossible to think of anything else. She took a never-ending supply of tablets to help mask the intensity of the pain of her illness, but no pill had been invented that would numb the pain in her heart. She had to ring him, had to get in touch. How could she leave it like this? At the end of the day it wouldn't have been fair to either of them.

She took her tablets and waited a while for them to work, then gingerly swung her legs over the edge of the bed and sat up. Not too bad. Not bad at all. She ventured into the bathroom for a shower to freshen up, and then the kitchen for tea and toast, determined to liven herself up before making the call.

Right, the time had come. Would he want to speak to her after the way she kept treating him? Of course he would, he loved her. Should she tell him the whole truth, the reason for her behaviour? Mm, not sure about this one, she'd see how it went, but he would have to be told sometime, and soon. Anna reached out to the phone to make the call but was startled by it ringing before she touched it.

Like minds …

'Richard?'

'Sorry to disappoint you, Mum, but it's me.'

'Hugo! Darling! How lovely to hear you. Are you back?' Although she could never have admitted it to him, Anna had completely forgotten that Hugo was returning home today and was supposed to be coming over to meet Grace.

'You sounded surprised. Not forgotten about me, had you?' he teased. 'And who's this Richard character, anyway?'

'As if I could forget about my ever-loving son!' Anna attempted a laugh, although she was convinced her face would crack. 'Richard? Long story. I'll tell you when you come over. What time will you be here, do you think?' Anna cheered up a little bit at the prospect of a visit from her son.

'Well, that's what I'm ringing about. I'm a bit tied up here so it's going to be tomorrow, or even the next day, before I can get back home.'

'Right,' said Anna, disappointment echoing massively in her voice. 'That's okay, I've got lots to be getting on with.'

'Are you okay, you sound a bit strange?'

'Me? I'm fine, well, fine as I'll ever be.'

'Auntie Grace still there? How are you getting on?'

'She had to go actually, last night, problems at home.'

'Oh Mum, no wonder you're upset.'

'No, no. It's nothing, truly. Don't you worry about me. I've been having a great time, honestly.'

'Sure?'

'Quite sure.'

'And the other thing – no worse?'

'No worse.' She answered, eyes brimming as she thought about all this worry she had never wanted to inflict on her beautiful son.

'Mum?'

'What?'

'I love you, you know that, don't you?'

'I know, I love you too,' she answered, tears flowing freely now.


Cleo returned from her doctor's appointment with Grace, pregnancy confirmed. Not that there had been any doubt in anyone's mind really now that Cleo had discarded the baggy jumpers and revealed the burgeoning shape of the waistline. They reckoned that she was nineteen weeks, although the doctor had referred her to the hospital for a scan which would be able to pinpoint things more precisely. Unbelievable. Almost half the pregnancy gone already and nobody but Cleo had known anything about it.

'Okay?' asked Grace, who was suffering a huge amount of guilt for the lack of support she'd been to her daughter so far.

'Guess so,' said Cleo. 'Feels weird. Like I sort of knew I was before, but now I *know* know, if you see what I mean.'

''Course I do. It still comes as a shock doesn't it? Cleo, don't take this the wrong way but I have to ask – you're quite sure you want to go ahead with the pregnancy, you definitely don't want an abortion? There's still time. Only just, but there's still time.'

'Quite sure, Mum. Look at the size of me now. It's a real baby, I feel protective of it already.'

'That's fine, then, whatever you want to do. We'll help you all we can, you know that, don't you?'

'Thanks, Mum,' said Cleo, giving Grace a hug. Pregnancy seemed to have brought out a whole new side to Cleo.

It didn't take long for the house to descend into chaos. Izzy was the first, returning from nursery school, Charlie in tow.

'Fatso, fatso, Cleo is a fatso,' she sang, skipping around the kitchen in delight for being so funny.

'Izzy,' reprimanded Grace sharply. 'Say sorry, now.'

'Soz, giggled Izzy cheekily. 'But she is, look,' she said, prodding Cleo, accusingly, in the stomach.'

'Izzy!'

'Might as well tell her, Mum, she's going to find out anyway, sooner or later.'

'Tell me what?' asked Izzy, wide-eyed.

'I'm going to have a baby,' said Cleo. It felt weird to say those words, even just to her three-year-old sister.

'But you're a girl,' said Izzy, incredulously. 'Only mummies have babies.'

'Well I'm going to be a mummy to this baby that's growing in my tummy.'

Izzy's eyes grew wider by the minute. 'But how did a baby get in your tummy?'

Grace was on standby but Cleo seemed to be coping well. 'It grew from a little seed that was in there.'

Poor Izzy, her eyes nearly exploded from her head. 'But I ate some grapes yesterday and swallowed some seeds. Does that mean lots and lots of babies will grow in my tummy?'

Cleo couldn't help but smile. 'Oh Izzy, no, it's got nothing to do with eating grapes, you're far too young to be having babies yet.'

'Phew,' said Izzy with relief. 'Can I take Alfie out and play in the garden now?'

'Of course you can, but try not to get too dirty this time,' laughed Grace, somewhat relieved at the sudden diversion from the 'where do babies come from?' questions.

Grace's feeling of relief didn't last for long – did it ever in this house? Peace was shattered by the arrival of Zak, who returned home from college somewhat dishevelled and bloody.

'Zak! What on earth happened to you?'

'Don't fuss, Mum, I'm fine.'

'Well you don't look it. What happened?'

'Nothing. Leave it, Mum.'

'How can I possibly leave it when my son comes home covered in blood?'

'This hasn't got anything to do with me has it?' asked Cleo, suddenly suspicious.

'Just had a bit of a go at Pete, if you must know.'

'Pete?' questioned Grace.

'Oh Zak, what did you do to him?' asked Cleo, horrified. 'I really wish you'd mind your own business. I wasn't going to mention this to Pete at all. It's my baby, mine alone, and I want to keep it that way.'

'I take it you think Pete's the dad, then?' asked Grace.

'I could kill him for what he's done to her,' growled Zak.

'Looks like you nearly did from the state of you,' commented Grace, sarcastically.

'Just butt out, Zak,' said Cleo. 'It could be Pete, but it could just as easily be one of the others who's the father. I know I was stupid but there it is. It's me that's got to suffer the consequences, I don't want any of them involved.'

Anna spent much of the rest of the day wallowing in self-pity. She'd tried to ring Richard's and Grace's mobiles but both were switched off. Was that because of her, because they guessed she'd try to ring and neither of them wanted to be bothered with her any more?

She could understand their reasoning if so, she had treated them both abysmally. What she should have done was to tell the truth from the beginning; things would have

226

been so different then. Instead of which she'd been covering up all this time, confusing them about how she really felt, and now it was probably too late. Now they were back in the hub of their family crisis, not even realising that she had a much worse crisis of her own to face … alone.

She had left a message on both their mobiles, an identical message, short and to the point. 'Sorry. Love you. Anna.' She'd half-hoped that one, if not both, would have got back to her by now but, despite checking for missed calls every two minutes, nothing. Richard … where was he? Despite the way she'd behaved, surely her admitting that she loved him would provoke a response? As indeed it would have done, but what Anna didn't realise was that Richard, having sat up all night discussing Cleo, was now back home and fast asleep, exhaustion precluding him checking his phone. And as for Grace, she'd turned her mobile off when she'd gone into the doctor's surgery with Cleo that morning and, with her lack of sleep and the kind of day she'd had, switching it back on was the last thing on her mind.

Loneliness engulfed Anna. She was used to solitude and normally enjoyed her own company, but whether it was because she had now discovered what it was like to be part of a family, or whether the thought of never seeing either of them again and facing her own mortality without their support, she felt lost. Never had she felt so completely and utterly alone. She cried until she had no more tears left; her misery enveloped her like a shroud. Was she just to lay there forever awaiting death? And who would miss her anyway, would they even notice she'd gone? Hugo's face appeared before her. Hugo, her beautiful son. Hugo would miss her, he loved her, and he would be back soon. She must pull herself together, she couldn't just lie there rotting away, and let him find her in such a state. She had to be positive for his sake.

Taking some more of her painkillers, she dragged herself into the bathroom and splashed cold water on her face in an attempt to feel human again. Catching a glimpse of herself in the mirror was a bit of a reality check. She certainly didn't look great, but it was the best she could do. What time was it? Seven o'clock already. There wasn't any food in the house but neither did she feel much like eating. Nevertheless she knew she should try and have something if she wasn't to fade away just yet. Perhaps she'd have a little wander along Lavender Hill, maybe have a sandwich somewhere.

Out in the street, Anna was glad she'd made the effort. The early evening air felt quite invigorating, not that she felt quite up to running the marathon or anything, but it did perk her up a bit. She decided to have a stroll through Battersea Park before looking for somewhere to eat; hopefully a bit more exercise would improve her appetite. Certainly, at the moment, she was feeling as though if she never ate again it would be too soon.

She wandered along the path, head down, hands in her pockets, a figure of desolation, heels tip-tapping as she went. If only they'd ring, tell her they still loved her, that they cared. That was all she wanted for now, to know she hadn't been abandoned again, to know she was not alone. That would give her the strength to go on. Hastily she pulled her phone from her pocket to check it again, perhaps she'd missed their calls ... but no, none. Should she leave another message, risk looking like a desperado? Why not. She pressed Richard's number. Still voicemail.

'Hey, it's me. Please get back to me, I need to talk to you, tell you everything. I know I've been impossible, but there is a reason and I want to tell you the whole truth. I love you so much, you must know that. I was just trying to protect you, but I can't do it any more. I love you. Speak to me, please speak to me.'

Anna lingered around the park, tears streaming down her face, hoping against hope that some miracle would occur, that he'd suddenly switch on his phone, hear her message, ring her back. She kept the phone in her hand, waiting, not wanting to go back to the bustle of the street in case it rang, needing to hear his voice, needing him. But she waited, and waited, and waited. Nothing. She tried to convince herself that it was simply a case of him forgetting to switch on his phone, but she failed. He'd obviously had enough of her messing him about. His family had problems and they came first. She was nothing to him now, had faded into insignificance. She had played a game with him, and lost.

In her misery Anna didn't really notice the park emptying out. The dog walkers returning to their city apartments with their canine friends, the families taking their children home to bed, the singles and couples going out for the evening, just leaving hoodies and drunks and weirdos and freaks and, more or less, Anna.

She glanced at her phone. Should she could try the number again? At least she'd know then if it was still switched off. She didn't even hear them approaching so engrossed was she in the task in hand.

'Gi's yer phone.'

Anna, in her own torturous world, remained oblivious.

'You deaf or wot?'

He finally got through. Anna lifted her head and glanced around, only to realise that she was surrounded by a gang of hooded youths.

'What?' she asked, fear mounting rapidly in a heart that was already about to explode.

'Phone! Gi's yer phone!' he repeated, agitated now.

'Phone? You're not having my phone!' yelled Anna, terrified but at the same time, determined. Her last link with Richard ... there was no way.

'Give it!' he threatened, as they moved in closer, closing ranks.

'No!' she screamed, clinging on, kicking, punching, thoughts of Richard spurring her on.

'Don't wanna get hurt d'ya?' he asked menacingly, a flash of silver catching her eye as a cold metal blade touched her cheek.

'Back off, Jez,' said another. 'Just get the phone and go.'

Fingers of iron prised open her hand and snatched the phone from her grip as though they were snatching away her life, her only contact with Richard. She didn't even have his number, it was stored in her phone.

'Give it back!' She fought like a demon, biting, scratching, punching until one grabbed her by the hair and pulled her down to the ground in the mud.

'Let's go!'

But Jez was not so anxious to leave. The others ran, taking the phone with them, as Anna struggled to her feet, almost blinded by fear and anger, gasping for breath.

'*Help!*' she started to scream to anyone who'd listen, '*My phone! They ...*'

A hand clamped firmly across her mouth, the cold steel blade held to her throat this time. Jez. His eyes blazing. Nobody argued with him.

'Something wrong, bitch?' he asked, moving the blade tantalisingly under her chin as he removed his other hand from her mouth.

'You bastard! I need that phone. You don't understand.'

'Oh I do, bitch, I understand. One more word out of you and this blade goes right through your pretty little neck. Nobody screams at me like that.'

'But I ...'

'I said nobody!' he bellowed, the flat side of the blade pushed firmly against her neck now.

Her whole life seemed to flash before her eyes ...

Richard, Grace, just fading away. She was never going to see them again. Anyway, they didn't want to know. She was dying and nobody cared, dying and nobody knew. What had she got to lose?

'Go on then, kill me, go on! But you won't will you? People like you, they're all the same, cowards. Think this makes you look good do you, to your mates? Well think again sunshine, because you're nothing, noth …'

Anna barely felt any pain as the blade sliced through her throat, just a weird sensation as she put her hand to the gash and felt the blood oozing through her fingers as she fell to the ground. She was vaguely aware of footsteps running away from her in the distance, and of Richard's face getting further and further away. And as she floated down a long dark tunnel, not wanting to go, and yet being dragged by a force beyond her control towards a bright light in the distance, she knew she had no choice. Peace and tranquility lay ahead, there was no turning back now.

# 21

'Where is everybody?' asked Gran, toothless and hairnetted, as she appeared with her walking stick at the living-room door, glaring accusingly at Charlie as though he'd done away with them all.

'In bed,' he grunted, in reply.

'Bed? But it's only ten minutes to three.'

'No Gran, quarter past ten. The news is on, look. Just catching the end of it, then I'm going up myself.'

'Might as well join you, then,' said Gran, settling herself in comfortably. 'Are you making a cup of tea?'

'No,' said Charlie, not appreciating the disturbance. 'I told you, I'm watching the news.'

'Okay, okay, I can wait. I would hate to put you to any trouble,' she said, in her best I'm-an-old-lady-and-therefore-you-have-to-feel-sorry-for-me voice.

'Hmmphh,' said Charlie with feeling, still trying to keep his attention focused on the television newsreader, who continued to drone on in a very matter-of-fact way.

'Reports just in say that the body of a woman, thought to be in her late forties, was found in Battersea Park in London earlier this evening. The woman, thought to have been the victim of a stabbing incident, has not yet been identified. Her body was discovered by a man out walking his dog. Police have sealed off the area while they carry out further investigations.'

'Battersea, isn't that where Anna lives?' yawned Charlie, struggling to stay awake.

'Who?' asked Gran, eyes narrowed, knowing full well what he'd said.

'Anna,' repeated Charlie, yawning again. 'God, I'm knackered tonight. You'll have to forget about the tea, I'm off to bed.'

At that same moment, Richard was just waking up. He'd slept for most of the day, body clock completely upside down now. He came downstairs and switched on the television, just missing the end of the news.

'Tomorrow will be cloudy, rain moving in from the east later in the day ...'

Great. Not that the weather was going to affect his day, he'd promised to go round and spend some time with Cleo. Hopefully no more storm clouds would be gathering there for a while. In fact, amazingly, she seemed to have acquired a much sunnier disposition. Perhaps it was possible to take a positive from a negative and think that this baby could be the making of Cleo. She'd be sixteen by the time it was born, not an impossible situation. She had a lot of growing up to do still, but with their help he was sure things would work out fine.

He was more concerned about Anna. Just as things had been going well they'd descended into chaos again. What was it with them? He was the kind of person who liked to know where he stood; all this passion, blowing hot and cold, was driving him insane. Now, not even a phone call.

Where was his phone, incidentally? He'd thought he'd left it next to the bed but, on going up to get it, discovered it wasn't there. It threw him into a bit of a panic for a moment. He couldn't possibly have lost it, could he? It was his contact with Anna, her number was stored in there ... Jesus! What had he done with it? But then he remembered, it was in his coat pocket from when he was at Grace's last night, he'd been so exhausted when he'd finally got home that he'd forgotten all about it. Somewhat relieved, he went to retrieve his little silver friend. Thank God for that; he couldn't live without his phone.

But then, panic number two. It was switched off! No wonder he hadn't heard from her. Why had he done that? Must have been while they'd been talking to Cleo and hadn't wanted any interruptions, he didn't even remember doing it. He switched it back on, desperately hoping that she'd tried to make contact. But if she had, had he blown it yet again?

Two voicemail messages. He pressed the button with some trepidation. This was going to lead to him being misunderstood yet again, he knew it. She'd think he'd switched it off on purpose. But then he heard her voice, a declaration of her love, apologies. *She loved him!* Tears streamed down his face. She actually loved him. She'd said so!

The sound of her voice, the longing, the words, made him ache for her. He wanted to jump back into the car right now and drive down there, take her in his arms and never be apart from her again. But reason told him he couldn't, not immediately anyway. He'd come back for Cleo, promised he'd spend time with her; he couldn't let her down even though his heart felt torn in two. Hopefully Anna would understand now that she'd had time to think. She'd finally admitted that she loved him and she knew how he felt about her. Nothing could keep them apart now, whatever it was she had to tell him. In a couple of days, when the dust had settled here, he'd go back down and they could sort everything out. Nothing was impossible, and love would conquer all. Richard knew he wanted to spend the rest of his life with her. Just thinking of her now, visualising her face, the warmth of her body, filled him with feelings of such intensity that they were impossible to ignore.

He adjusted himself with one hand and pressed her

number into his phone with the other, a smile of happy anticipation on his face. Voicemail. How could she not answer now? She'd only used it to put a message on his a couple of hours or so ago. He checked his voicemail. Yes, 7.42 p.m. it had been sent. God, surely something couldn't have gone wrong with her phone, not at this crucial point, just as everything was beginning to work out for them. That would be so typical!

He pressed the number again, with some urgency this time. Voicemail. Again. Hell! What was happening here? Consumed by frustration he thought of ringing Grace, but then realised it would be a bit of a mean thing to do, waking her up when she'd not had any sleep for the past twenty-four hours. He'd just have to keep ringing Anna; she'd have to pick up at some point. Surely fate wouldn't be so cruel as to keep them apart forever.

Grace was still in bed. She was awakened by Charlie bringing her breakfast on a tray.

'What time is it?' she sat up, startled, feeling that it must be really late.

'Just after eleven.'

'Eleven o'clock? Charlie! Why didn't you wake me?'

'Because, my love, you needed your beauty sleep. Don't worry, everything's under control.'

'But Charlie, where is everybody?'

'Izzy – nursery, Zak – college, Cleo – still asleep, and Gran – downstairs talking to Richard.'

'Richard?' Grace's eyes widened. 'What's he doing here?'

'Some problem with Anna's phone, apparently. Wondered if we'd heard anything from her.'

'Probably still sulking I shouldn't wonder. She was really horrible when we left. I wish she wouldn't be like that.' Grace sipped at the tea, gratefully. 'Oh Charlie, you're so good to me.'

'Glad to be of service,' smiled Charlie, glad to be appreciated for once. 'Anything else I can help you with?' he asked, living in hope now: it had been a while.

Grace smiled back knowingly, seduced by his attentiveness. 'But what about my egg and soldiers?'

Charlie moved the tray onto the bedside table, a man on a mission. 'I've got something else standing to attention here and it can't wait. I've only got half an hour until I have to go for Izzy.'

'Oh what a sweet-talker,' said Grace, throwing back the duvet and laying back enticingly. 'In that case, you'd better show me how good an action man you really are.'

'You might as well make yourself useful while you're here and put the kettle on,' said Gran, tipping the biscuits out of the barrel and sifting through them on the table.

'I only came to ask Grace if she'd heard from Anna,' said Richard, mournfully.

'It's over there,' said Gran, with a nod of her head.

'What?'

'The kettle.'

Richard dragged himself up from his seat and walked across the kitchen, filling the empty kettle and plugging it in. He turned back to face Gran, who was still sorting out the biscuits.

'I just don't understand why I can't get in touch with her.'

'Who?'

'Anna! Are you not listening to a word I say?' asked Richard, getting more and more irate.

'Don't know anybody of that name,' reiterated Gran, beady eyes glaring at him with hostility.

'She's your daughter, for God's sake!'

'A disgrace, that's what she is,' said Gran, attention returning to the task in hand.

'What are you doing with those biscuits anyway? They'll

not be fit for anyone to eat soon.'

'I'm looking for my teeth. Not seen them anywhere have you?'

'Jesus!'

Charlie disappeared in haste to collect Izzy, late again. But then, Mrs Clarke didn't expect any other from this family. When he'd gone, Grace wandered around in a post-coital glow, getting herself showered and dressed, ready to face the day. She popped her head round Cleo's door to check whether she was awake. Cleo, roused by the sudden influx of light into the room, yawned and stretched, peering over the duvet at her mother.

'Hey.'

'Hey, sleepyhead, rise and shine, it's nearly lunchtime.'

Cleo glanced at her clock in disbelief. 'That time already?'

'Well, I suppose we did have a lot of sleep to catch up on.'

'Suppose,' said Cleo, rubbing her eyes.

'Want a cuppa?'

'No thanks, Mum, I'll be down in a minute.'

'No hurry.'

'Mum?'

'Mm?'

'Thanks, you know, for being there for me and everything.'

'Don't be daft,' said Grace, coming into the room and giving her a hug. 'I'm your mum, that's what mums are for.'

Cleo sat up and looked at her strangely for a moment, as if giving her a quick appraisal. 'You look sort of different ... glowing,' she said, almost accusingly.

Grace gave her a wink and a self-satisfied grin. 'Well, you know what it is that makes you glow more than any face cream, don't you?' she asked cheekily.

'Mother! Too much information! Ugghh, that is so gross,

237

get out of here!' groaned Cleo, laughing simultaneously.

Mother and daughter had never been able to share moments like this before, and it felt good.

'Richard! Sorry, I'd forgotten. Charlie said you were here,' said Grace, as she was greeted, almost smotheringly, by an over-affectionate Alfie who showed his love for her in so many different ways. He bounced, licked, drooled, pawed and finally built up to the climax of his performance by attempting to have sex with her leg. 'Alfie! Stop that! I've told you before. Now get down,' she said, pushing him away until he slunk off to his basket, sufficiently reprimanded.

'I'm really worried about Anna, Grace. Have you heard anything from her?'

'Can't say I was expecting to, the mood she was in when we left. Mother! What have you done to these biscuits? You couldn't even call them biscuits any more, it's just a heap of crumbs.'

'Well, I was looking for my teeth. Can't find them any-where.'

'Ogghh! Not that again. Have you tried the cereal box?'

'Jesus! That's disgusting!'

'Mm. I know it is. Anyway, what about Anna? Why are you worried? You know what she's like.'

'Dunno, just a hunch. Something doesn't add up. Have you checked your mobile in case she's tried to ring you?'

'I haven't, to be honest. I'll do it later,' she said, busily tidying up the kitchen before Charlie got back with Izzy.

'Could you not do it now?'

'Richard! You're making a big fuss over nothing. My mobile's upstairs in my handbag, I'll get it when I go up. I just want to get all this mess cleared away first, it's not like it's an emergency or anything.'

But Richard's worries were not easily assuaged. 'She said she loved me.'

'What?'

'Left a message on my mobile, two actually, telling me she loved me.'

'Well surely that's good, isn't it?' asked Grace, scrubbing away at dried-on egginess. It had been good of Charlie to have brought her breakfast in bed, but he'd certainly wreaked havoc in the kitchen in the process.

'I know it's good, fantastic in fact, but now I can't get through to speak to her. Just goes through to voicemail all the time.'

'God Richard, is that all you've got to worry about? Here, grab a tea towel and dry these for me, will you? You know how often phones go wrong and it doesn't usually happen because there's been a major crisis. You get so panicky about absolutely nothing at times. Chill. Spend the day with your pregnant daughter – that's what you came back for, isn't it? I'm sure Anna's fine. She's a strong independent woman, used to having to look after herself. She'll phone again when she's good and ready, or as soon as her mobile's fixed.'

'I suppose,' said Richard, looking anything but reassured. His thoughts were interrupted, however, by the appearance of their aforementioned pregnant daughter.

'Hey you two. Not talking about me are you?'

'As if,' said Grace. 'Do you think we have nothing better to talk about?'

'You couldn't possibly have anything better than me,' grinned Cleo.

What a changed person! Richard put his arm around her and gave her a hug. 'What would you like to do today, princess? I am entirely at your disposal.' Grace was right. There'd be enough time for Anna, Cleo was the important one today.

Cleo's choice of what to do? Obvious. Cleo chose shopping

– and she was in her element. Grace had declined to accompany them, thinking that might be a step too far as far as Charlie was concerned, and she was probably right. So Cleo had it all today; the Trafford Centre with her ever-doting father and his ever-open wallet *and* a day off school. What more could a girl ask?

She was in fact, for once in her life, in desperate need of new clothes. With a rapidly expanding waistline, nothing seemed to fit any more. Richard was dragged around from shop to shop, his head in a whirl. Topshop, River Island, they all looked the same to him. He'd never stood outside so many ladies' changing rooms in his entire life, often standing there for so long that he was sure people were beginning to think he was some sort of pervert. How could anyone possibly imagine that shopping was a pleasure? He would never understand that in a million years.

'Isn't it amazing?' asked Cleo, twirling around in front of him in yet another mini-skirted creation.

'Far from me to criticise, but I thought you were looking for something a bit looser, something a bit more practical.'

'Practical? Oh Dad, just because I'm having a baby, it doesn't mean I have to turn into a frump.'

'Just a suggestion.'

'But look at it, it's gorgeous.'

'I agree, it is gorgeous, but it's tight on you already. In a couple of months it'll …'

'Pretty please,' said Cleo, playing on the little-girl-lost look for all she was worth.

'But isn't it almost the same as the one you bought in the last shop?'

'Dad! It's nothing like it! Pretty, pretty please.'

'Go on, get it,' groaned Richard. Anything for a quiet life. They might even be able to go home soon.

It was late that afternoon before Grace remembered to

check her mobile. She retrieved it from her handbag, realising she hadn't switched it back on since her visit to the doctor's surgery with Cleo yesterday. Two messages. The first from Anna, apologising and saying she loved her. See, what was Richard worrying about? She sounded fine, she'd forgiven them and come to her senses. The second was from Kate. God, Kate! Grace had forgotten all about her – some friend she was turning out to be. She sent Kate a text explaining that she'd had to come back to Cheshire earlier than expected due to family problems, and promising to be in touch soon. Then she tried Anna's mobile. Still not answering. Oh well, she'd sounded okay in the phone message, she was sure she'd ring them as soon as she could. Just a problem with her mobile, that's all. Anna liked her own space, she'd made that perfectly clear. She wouldn't thank them for making a fuss.

Grace went back downstairs. The house was eerily quiet. Charlie had gone to take Alfie for a walk, taking Izzy with him, and Gran was in her room. As for Zak, he'd phoned earlier to say he wouldn't be back until later. He was going straight round to a mate's house after college to work on a project they were doing together and would pick up something to eat in town.

'Lay off the drink though, Zak,' warned Grace. 'You know what you were like yesterday morning. Don't want it becoming a habit.'

'Chill, Mum, we're working, not going out on the piss.'

He was a good lad really, but it was her job to worry.

She was in the middle of loading the washing machine when the phone call came. It was the house phone. They'd had an extra bell installed in the kitchen to enable them to hear it all over the house and garden. Now, with its extra volume, it seemed to echo ominously.

'Auntie Grace?'

'Who is this?'

'It's Hugo.'

'Hugo! How lovely to hear from you. How are you? I'm so sorry I missed seeing you when I came down, but we had to get back. I expect your mother's told you.'

Silence.

'Hugo?'

'Sorry, Auntie Grace, I'm afraid I have some bad news. My mother … it's my mother, she's … she's dead.'

'Dead? But she can't be … I heard her. A message … on my phone.'

'She's dead, Auntie Grace.'

'There must be some mistake.'

'No mistake. She was found in Battersea Park last night. The police … she was … she was murdered.'

'Murdered?' Grace sank into the nearest chair, her legs no longer able to support her. 'But …'

'I know. It's horrendous. A knife … I can't believe it's happened. I only got back this morning and police were here at her flat. It's like a nightmare. I don't know what to do,' he sounded like a little boy lost.

Grace tried to pull herself together, although she was shaking so much she could hardly speak.

'Do you want me to come down?' she asked.

'If you could I'd be really grateful. The police will probably want to talk to you anyway, as you'll be one of the last people to have seen her.'

'Richard too,' sobbed Grace, realisation finally hitting her.

'Richard? Mum mentioned him.'

'He's going to be devastated,' said Grace.

# 22

As each member of the family returned home during that afternoon and evening, they were engulfed by the news of Anna's death. A cloud of mourning descended on the family, the sudden shock of her loss hard to take in. The only one unaffected by the tragedy was Gran who, even in these devastating circumstances, remained unmoved by the event.

'Well, got what was coming to her, didn't she? Got what she deserved,' she said, still dunking her biscuits and slurping away, completely oblivious to everyone else's grief. Life went on, as far as she was concerned.

'Mother! Is that all you can say? Anna was your daughter, doesn't that mean anything to you?'

'She was no daughter of mine, disowned her years ago. Better off without her, I say.'

'Mother! I don't know how you can sit there and say that!'

'Don't know what all the fuss is about. You've only seen her this past couple of weeks. Didn't even know her before that – not seen her for years.'

'Precisely. She's had such a bad life and we were just getting to know her again.'

'Good job she's gone, then. She was nothing but trouble that one.'

'Mother!'

Izzy came and climbed onto Grace's knee, snuggling up

to her tearfully. 'I loved Auntie Anna. I don't want her to be dead.'

Grace held her close and kissed the top of Izzy's head. 'Neither do we darling, we loved her too.'

'She called me poppet,' said Izzy, sucking her thumb. 'I liked being her poppet.'

Richard was totally distraught. How could this have happened? He'd met the love of his life and now she was gone. Only three weeks ago they'd never even met, and then he'd found her and been blown away. She'd ripped through his life like a whirlwind, tearing at his heartstrings, filling his head with longing for her, tormenting him with secrets unshared. How could she be gone? How could she have left him? How could he live without her? Such a short time they'd been together, and yet she was his life.

'At least you know she loved you,' said Grace, trying to console him. 'I'm so glad she left those messages. It was as if she knew, somehow, as if she knew she was going to die and wanted us to know how much she loved us.'

'Weird, isn't it? I was thinking that too. Maybe she had some sort of premonition.'

'They say people do.'

The sudden slamming of the back door announced the return of Charlie and a muddy Alfie, who was panting like a steam engine and who, being of a rather gregarious nature, bounded straight into the house to greet Grace and ravish Richard.

'Alfie! Get down! Charlie!'

Poor Charlie, in trouble again. Not only that, but the green-eyed monster was back. They were looking very cosy on *his* sofa.

'Well could you help me then? I can't do everything.'

'I'll go,' said Richard, getting up to help.

'Okay mate, see you tomorrow then,' said Charlie, seizing

the moment with glee.

'Charlie! I said Richard could stay the night, it's not very nice for him to be on his own tonight. He's going to sleep on the sofa.'

Charlie looked somewhat crestfallen. 'Oh, just thought he said he was going.'

'Sorry, mate. Meant I'd go and help you wash the dog, that's all.'

'Right,' said Charlie, dejectedly. 'You might need to do it in the back yard. His towel's under the sink.'

'Charlie, you are mean to Richard sometimes,' said Grace when he'd gone. 'He's just lost the woman he loves, have a bit of sympathy.'

'Sorry,' said Charlie, removing his muddy boots and coat. 'But you're the woman *I* love and I don't want to lose you.'

'You daftie,' said Grace, giving him a hug. 'You're not going to lose me, especially not to Richard. He's my ex, remember?'

How could he ever forget?

Charlie hovered, wanting to go to bed, as Grace fussed over Richard, making sure he'd be comfortable on the sofa.

'Sure you'll be okay on there?' she asked, concerned.

'I'll be fine,' said Richard, reassuringly.

'Would you like another blanket?' asked Grace.

'That's plenty,' said Richard.

'You coming to bed or what?' asked Charlie, plaintively.

'In a minute,' said Grace. 'Try and get some sleep then, Richard. I know it's hard. Just shout if you need anything.'

Oh, for God's sake. Charlie made his way upstairs, Grace finally following.

'I know you're struggling, Charlie, but please try and be nice to Richard.'

'Sorry, Gracie. I do try, it's just that I feel sort of pushed out sometimes when I see you together. You've got a special bond and a shared past that I was never a part of.'

'I know, I'm sorry, it's just the way it is. But you're the one I chose above Richard, remember. You're the one I chose to spend my life with, you don't have any need to be jealous, I love you.'

'Oh Gracie,' he said, holding out his arms to her as she got into bed and snuggled up next to him.

They lay in silence for a moment, each drawing strength and comfort from the other.

'I can't believe she's dead.'

'Me neither.'

'All those missing years not knowing her, and now she's gone.'

'At least she came to find you and you got to know her a little bit. At least you had some time together.'

'Weird that, isn't it? I wonder why she came to see us just out of the blue like that? Maybe Richard's right. Maybe she had some kind of premonition and knew she was going to die.'

'Oh, Richard – he's bound to be right, always is.'

Grace prodded him in the ribs. 'Stop that, you promised … Poor Anna, what a way to die, I just can't imagine what it must have been like for her, she must have been terrified.'

'Never know what's going to happen in life, do you?'

'It's so sad, to get my sister back again and then for some-body to snatch her away – and for what? Just some random stabbing. Why her? Why did they have to pick on my sister?'

'No logic in these things Gracie, just wrong place, wrong time.'

Grace had been trying to be strong for the rest of the family but now, alone with Charlie, she could let the tears flow. She needed to wash away at least some of her grief and once she had started she could not stop.

'Sorry,' she sobbed.

'Let it go, Gracie, let it go.'

'We parted on such bad terms as well. I was annoyed with

her, to be honest, she was really horrible to me. I said I loved her but she just told me to go ... We didn't even hug ... nothing.'

'She knew you loved her, though, and she loved you too. She said so on your voicemail, didn't she?'

'Suppose.'

'You weren't to know it was the last time you'd see each other. That's what happens; it's very rare that people get a chance to say goodbye.'

'I'm scared, Charlie.'

'Of what?' he asked, looking at her tenderly.

'That everyone will die and I'll be left here all alone.'

'Huh,' said Charlie, 'with the houseful that you've got I wouldn't have thought there would have been much chance of that yet awhile.'

'Charlie? You won't leave me, will you?'

'I'm not going anywhere, Gracie.'

'Charlie?'

'Mm?'

'Will you make love to me?'

That woke him up. 'Now?'

'Now,' she said plaintively, rolling onto her back in readiness for him, needing to draw comfort from the thrust of him inside her, needing reassurance that he was here to stay. They moved rhythmically together, their bodies familiar and assured and as one. Charlie was as considerate in his lovemaking, as anxious to please, as he was in the rest of his married life.

'Okay?' he asked, as he withdrew after their climax and lay back down beside her.

'Thank you,' she said, somewhat consoled.

'No need to thank me, Gracie, I love you. Now, let's get some sleep.'

Within minutes Charlie was snoring, Grace still wide awake. And as she lay there in the darkened room, tears still on her face, it was good to know that Charlie loved her and that he was always there for her. They may never reach the dizzy orgasmic heights she longed for, but at least he was reliable. Maybe this whole idea of breaking out of her cage had been just a silly dream. She should stay in it where she was loved; the cage was a safe place to be. Anna might not even be dead now, if she hadn't flown so free.

Charlie was cock-a-hoop the next morning, on post-coital cloud nine in fact. However, he was soon brought back down to earth, remembering Grace was off to London again with Richard.

'Do you have to go, Gracie?' he pleaded, his face looking as though he'd been taking lessons from Alfie in puppy-dog expressions.

'Sorry, but you know I do. The police will want to talk to us, for one thing. And then there's Hugo – I feel really sorry for him, we can't just leave him to cope with everything on his own.'

'Like you do me, you mean,' said Charlie, a trifle un-Charlie-like.

'Charlie!'

'Sorry, but I've got to get back to work, you know, the business won't run itself. There's a lady waiting for an estimate this morning – what am I meant to do?'

'I know, and I wouldn't go if I didn't have to, but it's unavoidable, there's nobody else. We'll only be there for one night though – two at the max. Get Cleo to help today, it'll give her something to do.'

'Me?' said Cleo, coming in at just the wrong moment. 'But I'm pregnant!'

'For God's sake, Cleo, you're not ill, you're only off school because of the chaos of the past couple of days.'

'I can't go back there, I told you. It was bad enough before but now everybody will know. They'll make my life hell, I know they will. You don't know what it's like.'

'Well you can stay at home for now, like I said, but we're going to have to sort something out next week; you've got exams, everything.'

'Exams? Does it really matter now? I'm pregnant.'

'Cleo, you may be pregnant but you've still got your future to think of, it doesn't all stop when the baby's born, you know.'

'I know, Mum, sorry. I will help Charlie while you're gone, I promise.'

'Thanks, love,' said Grace, giving her a hug. 'I didn't mean to snap, it's just that I've got so much on my mind at the moment.'

'I know, Mum, sorry,' said Cleo, prickliness abandoned and in full appreciation of the hug from her mum. 'I really loved Auntie Anna, you know, we had a special sort of bond,' she said, tears pouring down her face. 'It's so sad.'

'I know, sweetheart,' said Grace, choking back her own tears, trying to keep strong for everyone. 'You were both very similar in a lot of ways, it's easy to see why you got on so well. But we're just going to have to try to be brave and support each other, especially you, you've got the baby to think of as well now. Auntie Anna wouldn't have wanted us to be miserable all the time. Talking of which, have you seen your dad this morning? Perhaps you could go in and wake him – he's meant to be driving us to London, but I don't know whether he's going to be in any fit state to be honest.'

'Perhaps I should drive you,' said Charlie, as Cleo went to rouse her dad.

'Don't be daft, Charlie, there's all this lot to take care of here and Richard's got to come with me because the police will want to talk to both of us.'

'Suppose,' muttered Charlie. 'Is Izzy still going to nursery today, by the way?'

'I think she might as well, don't you? She'll only be moping round here otherwise.'

'I'll go and get her ready.'

'Thanks, Charlie.'


Apparently Zak had already gone to college, leaving early as he had to see someone, so that only left one person un-accounted for this morning, Gran – and in she came.

'Did I hear right? You're going off to London with Richard again?'

'Yes, Mother. Today. Do you have a problem with that?'

'Well it's disgusting. Have you forgotten you've got a husband?'

'Of course not, Mother. We've got to go, there are things that need sorting out.'

'Yes, I bet there are!'

'Mother!'

'It's that disgrace, still controlling everything even now she's dead and gone. Just like a bad penny, always turning up again. We'll never be rid of her – evil, she is.'

'Mother! Stop that now! If you've got nothing good to say about my sister you can go back to your room. I'm sick of hearing you going on about her. Poor Anna's dead, she didn't deserve to die, no one knows what she suffered. Let her rest in peace, for goodness sake.'

'Peace? Peace? We'd all like a bit of peace,' said Gran, leaning heavily on her walking stick as she hobbled back to her room, the mere mention of Anna's name seeming to have caused excessive deterioration of her limbs.


'You're gonna have to talk to Dad,' said Cleo, coming back into the kitchen, eyes red-rimmed. 'I've never seen him in such a state. I don't know what to say to him. Think he must have been drinking last night as well, there's an empty whisky bottle by his bed.'

'God, that's all I need. He's meant to be driving us there today.'

'Sorry Mum. I tried but …'

'I know, not your fault.'

'Richard?' said Grace, knocking gently on the living-room door.

'Go away,' came the response.

She went in anyway. 'Look, I know this is hard for you,' she said, to the prostrate figure on the sofa, 'it is for me too. She was my sister. I lost her all those years ago and now I've lost her all over again, forever this time. How d'you think that makes me feel?'

Richard turned over to look at her. 'I loved her, Grace, I wanted to spend the rest of my life with her,' he sobbed.

'I loved her too,' said Grace, sitting down on the sofa where he'd moved back to make room for her. 'We'd been torn apart, forced to live separately for all those years and now, just as we'd found each other, she's gone.'

Richard's whole body convulsed with grief. Grace held him in her arms, sharing his pain, her own tears flowing freely now.

'I'm sorry,' he said, 'it's bad enough for you without having to cope with me as well.'

'Don't be sorry, you need to cry it out. One thing you can't do with grief is bottle it up.'

'You're so strong, Grace, I don't know how you do it. I feel like such a wimp in comparison to you.'

'Me? I'm not strong at all. The only thing about me is that I have to hold it all together in front of the family. Be strong for them. It wouldn't do to let them see me falling apart. It's my job to take care of them.'

'You're an amazing woman, Grace.'

'No more so than the next person. As for you, you're going to have to try and pull yourself together. We've got to go to London today and give Hugo some support. It's what Anna would have wanted us to do, and one of the last things we can do for her.'

'I don't know whether I can face this,' he wept. 'To see her flat again, all her possessions, the bed where we made love only days ago ...'

'I know, Richard. It's hard for both of us, but we're going to have to do it, we really don't have a choice. The police will want to talk to us for one thing, we're the last people known to have seen her before she ... before she ...' Grace spluttered out the words before grief overcame her and she fell down into Richard's comforting arms, the two of them united in their sorrow. 'How will we ever get through this?' she asked eventually, as her weeping subsided.

'Get through it? I don't think I can. Getting through implies that there's somewhere to go at the other side, and for me, there isn't. My future was Anna, and now my future is gone, nothing left to strive for. I just can't imagine a life without her now.'

'Oh Richard, you'll survive – people do, people have to. You just have to take it one day at a time, and today, for a start, we have to drive down to London and do what we can to help Hugo. Imagine how he's feeling. No point in the two of us lying here being maudlin, he's grieving too ... How much of that whisky have you drunk, by the way?' asked Grace, ever the practical one.

'Oh that,' he said, looking at the empty bottle on the floor beside him. 'Not much, actually, the bottle was already nearly empty. It was last night, I just needed something to try and make me sleep – not that it did much good.'

'Sure you'll be okay for driving?'

'Have to be, won't I? Like you said, it'll be the last thing we can do for Anna,' said Richard, tears welling again.

'Oh, Richard,' said Grace, kissing him on the cheek, comfortingly, just as Izzy bounded in through the door.

'Aaahh!' said Izzy, accusingly, putting two and two together and making fifteen. 'Mummy and Uncle Richard kissing in bed!'

'Izzy! Don't be silly! Uncle Richard's upset, that's all.'

'I tell Daddy,' she said, hopping up and down with glee, hand over her grinning open mouth as though she'd just uncovered some wicked secret.

'We'll be off now ...' said a startled Charlie, coming into the room unannounced.

And indeed it must have looked pretty bad where he was coming from. His wife and her ex-husband laid on the sofa together, looking very intimate, arms around each other and guilt written all over their faces.

'What's going on here, then?' asked Charlie, green-eyed monster having suddenly grown to gargantuan proportions.

'Well what do you think?' challenged Grace, angry that such an idea could even enter Charlie's head and becoming increasingly bored by Charlie's jealousy.

'You tell me,' combated Charlie.

'Charlie! You surely can't think we're at it on the living room sofa! For goodness sake!'

'Izzy,' said Charlie, 'go and see to Alfie in the kitchen, I won't be long.'

Grace, in her anger, had completely forgotten she was there. 'I'll be through in a minute darling,' she said, as Izzy skipped off full of secrets to puzzle over. 'At it' – what did that mean? Perhaps Mrs Clarke would know.

Back in the lounge the battle continued, although it was fortunately short-lived.

'Charlie, you've got to stop being so jealous all the time. We were upset, that's all, we've both lost someone we love, we were comforting each other.'

'That's one word for it.'

'Charlie!' said Grace, getting up from the sofa and going to give him a hug. 'You know it's you I love, nobody else, but you drive me mad sometimes.'

'Sorry Gracie,' said Charlie, kissing her, 'but I love you so much, I couldn't bear it if you went away and left me.'

Tact had flown out of the window. Poor Richard, their words had only added to his grief. They turned to him in sudden remembrance.

'Oh Richard, I'm sorry,' said Grace, taking him in her arms once more.

'I'll go and take Izzy, then,' said Charlie, feeling guilty now at the hurt he'd caused.


Izzy skipped along to nursery school, holding on tightly to Charlie's hand. She was bubbling with excitement. She loved it when she had stories to tell to Mrs Clarke and today she had lots.

'Daddy?' she asked innocently, eyes wide and appealing.

'Mm?' responded Charlie, mind still on Grace and Richard despite himself.

This wasn't going to help.

'What does "at it" mean?'

'What?' That woke him up.

'Mummy said you thought they were at it on the living room sofa.'

Charlie cleared his throat, which seemed to have suddenly seized up.

'Erm ... sleeping, Izzy. I thought they'd fallen asleep on the sofa, that's all.'

'That's funny,' giggled Izzy, apparently satisfied by his explanation. But not for long.

'Daddy?' she asked again, face more thoughtful now.

'Mm?' Oh God, what next.

'You know in *Goldilocks and the Three Bears* ...'

'Mm ...?' he said, understandably apprehensive.

'You know when Baby Bear says "Who's been sleeping in my bed?" ...'

Guess what's coming.

'... Could he say, "Who's been at it in my bed?"?'

'Erm ... no. I don't think that sounds quite right, Izzy. Come on now, we're going to be late for nursery.'

'Mrs Clarke won't mind, she says I'm always late.'

'Even so ...'

'*Daddy!*'

'What?' he asked, panicking for a minute.

'Don't tread on the cracks!' she said, 'at it' forgotten for the moment.


The journey to London was pretty harrowing for both of them. A lot of it was spent in silence, each of them lost in their own thoughts. Grace felt quite nervous of Richard's silence though, unsure whether he was giving enough concentration to his driving. In his frustration he seemed to be driving even faster than usual, recklessly, if she was honest.

'Slow down, Richard, we've had enough tragedy, we don't want any more.'

'What does it matter? Nothing matters any longer.'

'Don't be ridiculous, of course it matters. I've got a family at home who need me. So have you. You've got Zak and Cleo and a grandchild on the way. What would they do if anything happened to us?'

'They've always got Charlie. Dependable Charlie,' he said, brushing away tears with the back of his hand.

'Richard! Stop this now! You're frightening me. I want to live even if you don't. Pull over onto the hard shoulder for a minute or two and sort yourself out, you're going to end up killing some other poor soul at this rate.'

This was so reminding her of the same journey she'd had with Anna, the same fear of impending doom when she'd looked so ill.

'Okay, okay. There's a service station coming up, we'll stop there for a while. Sorry, I didn't mean to frighten you, it's just …'

'I know,' she said, giving his hand a comforting squeeze as it rested on the steering wheel, 'but just concentrate on the road for now, alright?'

'Alright,' he said, glancing at her briefly, and with gratitude. She was a tower of strength this woman, he could never have coped without her.

'Not come with Mummy today?' asked Mrs Clarke, as she helped Izzy to hang up her coat.

Charlie had this habit of depositing Izzy at the nursery door and bidding a hasty retreat, not wishing to become cast in the bad-parent saga in which Grace and Mrs Clarke appeared to be starring.

'No, Mummy's gone to London with Uncle Richard.'

'Mummy's gone with Uncle Richard?' repeated Mrs Clarke, a trifle disapprovingly.

'Yes. They were at it on the sofa this morning. Daddy was very cross,' said Izzy, wide-eyed and triumphant.

Mrs Clarke cleared her throat nervously. 'Let's go over to the drawing table, Izzy, you could do a picture for Daddy for when he comes to collect you later.'

'Daddy won't be collecting me today because he's got a lady waiting for him.'

This just got better and better.

'Oh, so who'll be coming to collect you, then?'

'Cleo. She's my sister.'

'I don't think I've met Cleo before. How old is she?'

'She's fifteen. She's my *big* sister,' said Izzy, stretching up her arms to show just how tall Cleo was.

'Is she not at school today?'

Mrs Clarke, it really would be better if you didn't ask so many questions.

'No, b-e-c-a-u-s-e … she's got a baby growing in her tummy.'

'A baby?' spluttered Mrs Clarke, eyes rounded in dis-belief, a mottled red flush suddenly creeping up her neck.

'It's growing from a seed that's in her tummy. I ate some grapes and thought a baby would grow in my tummy too, but it won't, will it Mrs Clarke?'

This poor child. Mrs Clarke looked at her with sympathy, the hot flush rising. 'No, Izzy, it won't. You can be sure of that.'

'Even though I swallowed some of the seeds?'

'It definitely will not.'

Izzy made a start on her picture, seemingly satisfied, her tongue hanging out in concentration. Mrs Clarke heaved a sigh of relief, her blush temporarily subsiding, although she couldn't help but feel a certain amount of depression when she thought of the terrible backgrounds some of her children came from. How could they hope to grow up into sensible, balanced adults when things like this were going on at home? They were scarred for life – and no wonder.

'Mrs Clarke?'

'Yes, darling,' she felt some sympathy with this poor child now.

'Do you know what my picture is?'

'You tell me,' she said, guardedly.

'It's the seed in Cleo's tummy growing into a baby,' said Izzy, delighted with herself.

'Lovely,' replied Mrs Clarke, redness returning.

'Mrs Clarke?'

'Mm?'

'How did the seed get into Cleo's tummy?'

Flushing furiously, Mrs Clarke glanced around. Several other pairs of eyes looked up from the drawing table now, crayons poised expectantly. But luckily a little boy called William inadvertently saved the day.

'Mrs Clarke!' called a small voice from the other side of

the room. 'William's weed himself.'

'Oh dear,' she sighed, with evident relief, 'let me come and sort him out.'

After that she made sure there was no time for further questions. Clapping her hands to gain their attention, she said, in the loud clear voice of a teacher in full control, 'Right, children. Everybody sit nicely on the mat please, we're going to have a story. It's called *Goldilocks and the Three Bears.*'

Izzy beamed with delight.

# 23

Finally they arrived, Battersea, SW11. The journey had been harrowing for both of them, Richard had been in pieces most of the time and definitely not in any fit state to drive. They really should have travelled by train, but once they had set off it was too late to turn back. It was only due to Grace's strength of character that they had managed to get here without major incident. Richard had been totally reliant on her and was indubitably grateful to have someone so close with whom he could share his grief. Anna had been his lover, Grace's sister; their feelings of loss could be equalled by no one ... other than Hugo, her son.

They climbed the short flight of steps up to her front door, the same door that had seemed so symbolic of good times to come only days earlier. Now it loomed before them like a harbinger of doom. It was Grace's turn to crumble. She stumbled against Richard as she fought with her emotions.

'I don't think I can face this,' she gasped, suddenly overcome by the enormity of all that had happened.

'We've got to, like you said,' replied Richard, suddenly the stronger of the two.

He rang the doorbell firmly, its sound eerily seeming to echo the gravity of the situation. Footsteps came downstairs towards them.

'Oh Richard,' Grace quivered nervously.

'Put yourself in his situation, how do you think he feels?'

said Richard, his heart going out to the young man they were about to meet.

The door opened slowly, giving them their very first glimpse of the son Anna had loved so much, Hugo.

Anna's flat seemed to be shrouded in grief. The three of them huddled in the living room, a little wary of each other, unsure of what to say. Grace could hardly take her eyes off Hugo, it was uncanny how much he resembled Zak.

'Sorry, I don't mean to stare, it's just that you look so much like Zak, my son.'

'I know, Mum said when she rang,' he answered, eyes lowering to the ground at the sudden remembrance that he would never speak to her again.

Grace's eyes welled. 'I can't believe we'll never see her again.'

'Me neither,' said Hugo, sobbing openly now, Grace's words seeming to have broken down a barrier.

Grace moved across to sit next to him and put her arm around his shoulders. 'I know I'm not your mum and never will be, but I want you to know I'm always here for you, Hugo.'

'Thanks, Auntie Grace,' he said, hugging her, as the two of them wept together. 'We just wasted so many years, Mum and I, years when we should have been together.'

'I know, I know … and I just can't believe that all that happened to my sister without me even realising what had gone on. I feel so responsible.'

'Don't be silly. How could you possibly have known? You were still only a child when she left.'

'That's what she said too, but it doesn't make the guilt any less. If only she'd told me … even a bit later, when I was older. I could have helped, done something. If only she'd made contact with me years ago instead of leaving it until now.' Grace was wrought with anguish.

'Like Mum always said, life is full of "if onlys". There's no point in looking back and torturing yourself,' said Hugo. 'I went through a horrendous time when I was younger, because of everything that had happened, I'm sure Mum must have told you.'

'She did. I feel absolutely in awe of you when I think of what it must have been like having all that burden of information suddenly thrust upon you. How on earth did you cope?'

'I didn't, basically,' said Hugo. 'I was already off the rails but I fell apart completely. I was an emotional wreck. It was a long time before I could get my head around it, I can tell you.'

'And yet you seem to have come out of it relatively unscathed. I think you're a pretty amazing young man. Your mum was so proud of you, you know.'

'I was proud of her too. She had it even harder than me in some ways.'

Richard had sat in silence throughout their conversation, wrapped up in his own grief. But suddenly a question formed in his head.

'What I don't understand is why she left it so long to contact Grace. Why now?' he interrupted. 'It's almost as though she had some sort of premonition. And not only that, there was a secret, something she seemed to be on the verge of telling me, something that was controlling her life, almost. I know I hadn't known your mother for very long, but strange as it may seem, we had fallen in love. I knew I wanted to spend the rest of my life with her – even asked her to marry me … but something was holding her back. That's why I followed her down here, to try and find out what it was, because she did love me, she even left a final message on my phone to tell me so … and, oh … I loved her so much,' he sobbed.

'I should explain. Or perhaps my mother should,' said Hugo.

'What?' a startled Richard looked up through his tears.

'She left letters for both of you, telling you her reason for making contact again.'

Grace gasped. 'But why would she have done that? Why would she have written letters? I don't understand.'

'They were by her bed,' said Hugo. 'She must only have written them after you'd left.'

'How do you know that?' asked Richard, in a state of disbelief.

'Because she left one for me too. I read it earlier.'

'This is weird,' said Grace. '*Did* she have a premonition? Why else would she have done it?'

'I'll get the letters,' said Hugo, resolutely.

They both needed privacy to read their final messages from Anna. Richard took his through to the bedroom and lay on her bed where so recently they had made love. He hugged her pillow to him, still smelling faint traces of her perfume, still hearing her voice as though she was speaking the words to him as his eyes scanned the page.

Thoughtfully, Hugo disappeared into the kitchen under the pretence of making more tea, leaving Grace alone in the lounge to uncover the secret her sister had managed to keep so well.

*My dearest Grace,*

*We lost so many years together, you and I. Growing up, sharing secrets, solving problems, supporting, just being there for each other. But it was not to be, and that was neither your fault nor mine. We lived our lives separately, coping, individuals, neither of us knowing what had happened to the other. Just a passing thought occasionally, in the back of our minds, wondering about the other but then moving on.*

*You moved on with your gorgeous family, and I love them all. Zak – so confident and kind, and with such a strong sense* of family as well as humour, he would make any mother proud. Cleo – well, what can I say? She reminds me so much of myself it's unreal, my life twin, I love her to bits. Izzy – my poppet, just adorable, a real bundle of mischief. And then there's Charlie. I know he doesn't light up your life like you might wish, but he's reliable and he loves you, and that can be enough to settle for sometimes – you could do a lot worse than Charlie. As for Mother, I can't bring myself to say anything about her at all.

Me? I had my amazing Hugo and I wouldn't swap him for the world. Please take care of him for me, Grace. The hardest thing for me throughout all of this has been the thought of him being left all alone. I know he still has Frank and Alice, but I gave birth to him, we've been to hell and back together and we couldn't be closer now. I feel like I'm abandoning him all over again, like I did years ago, and I cannot begin to describe how heart-wrenching that feels. He's had a lot to deal with in his life and, so far, has coped magnificently. No mother could be prouder of her son than I am of him.

So what made me write this letter? Why did I seek you out after all those years? I'm sure a thousand questions must be forming in your mind and I apologise for not telling you face to face but I just did not want a fuss. Anyway, the truth of the matter is, about three years ago I had breast cancer. I was petrified, as you can imagine, and almost as upset by the hurt I was causing Hugo as I was for myself. However, at the time, things turned out better than I had feared. I was able to have a lumpectomy rather than a full mastectomy and, although this was followed by six weeks of visits to the hospital for radio-therapy which wasn't pleasant, it was do-able, and I was alive! I cannot tell you the relief I felt. When it was all over Hugo and I went away on holiday for two glorious weeks in the sun. Cyprus, it was fantastic. I'm so glad we had that holiday together.

Anyway, we came back, I returned to work as did he, and

*life plodded along until two months ago, when we were hit by another bombshell. I'd been feeling a bit under the weather, tired, nothing specific. My cancer check-up at the hospital was due and I went along, nervous obviously, as you always are when it has happened to you before. Nevertheless, although you always go half expecting bad news, deep down you think it couldn't possibly have come back, not to you, not again. But it had.*

*I could hardly take in what the oncologist said to me that day. Words like aggressive, spread, treatment, prolong, whirled around my head. This couldn't be happening to me, it only happens to other people. I should have brought someone with me, he said, it helps. Helps? As far as I could see nothing could possibly help at all. He said I had six months to live at the most without treatment. Nothing could cure my cancer now.*

*He did give me an option, not wanting to leave me entirely without hope, and that was to have some treatment. More treatment. An aggressive course of chemotherapy would mean lots of hospital visits, would make me feel very sick, and would make my hair fall out, but, it could prolong my life by a few months.*

*He said I'd need support and asked about family. But who? Who could I inflict that on? Not Hugo. Not him. He'd gone through enough. And not you, I could hardly land on your doorstep and say 'Hi, I'm your sister, I'm dying but having chemo. Will you look after me for a few months while I'm bald and throwing up everywhere? I will die eventually but thought I'd just prolong the agony and let you share it.' Knowing you as I do now, you would have done it, but I could never have put you through all of that. Anyway, what would I have gained? Another couple of months? Not worth it. Final farewells stretched beyond the point of endurance.*

*However, it did stir up a longing within me to see you. I'm so glad I had a chance to get to know you again, I love you beyond words. You must have thought I was a bit of a snappy bugger at times, and I apologise for that, but now you know the pressure I was under perhaps you'll understand and forgive me. Excuses, excuses. I'm sorry, I should not have been crotchety, especially with you, my adorable sister. I love you.*

*I love your kids too, they're an absolute delight, you've done a fantastic job with them. I only wish I could have hung around for longer, seen them all grow up, seen what hand life deals them. Give them all a hug from Auntie Anna, Richard too. Take care of him, Grace, I know you will. I never expected to fall in love, and it was too late. I've broken his heart and I didn't mean to, he's an amazing man, the love of my life for what's left of it.*

*I'm writing this letter now because I know I can't have much longer and I couldn't just leave you without an explanation. Sometimes now I feel so tired, and I'm scared Grace. Not scared of dying so much, more scared of not being able to cope, becoming a burden. I've always been so independent and can't bear the thought of having to rely on other people. Losing my dignity, that's another one, having to have others to sort out your intimate bodily functions. I mean, how bad will it get? Will I reach the stage where I don't even make it to the loo and end up laid in my own piss, or worse? God, the thought of that is too much. I so wish I could die right now, get it over with before things get any worse. I know it's going to happen, so why not now? If I wasn't such a coward I'd do something about it, kill myself, end it all. But I know I won't do that, so I'll just have to wait for my final exit, fervently hoping that things don't get too messy in the meantime.*

*Enough of my ramblings, I'm always like this when something horrible is about to happen – rabbiting on non-stop, as though my never-ending chatter will prevent it from taking place. The 'something horrible' now is saying my final goodbye to you, but I know that I must.*

*So take care of everyone, Grace. I know you will, it's what*

*you do best. But, most of all, make time for yourself. Difficult I
know, but I'm living (hah, hah) proof that you just never
know how long you've got. Make the most of your life, do the
things you want to do, fly free, life is precious and so are you.
I couldn't have asked for a better sister.
All of my love forever,
Anna xx*

As Grace tearfully finished reading, Richard emerged from
the bedroom, white-faced and clutching his letter to him.

'She was dying, Grace,' sighed Richard, as he sat down
next to her looking drained of life himself.

'She was so brave,' murmured Grace. 'To have been
going through all of that suffering and yet still managing to
keep it from us.'

'She just didn't want a fuss,' said Hugo, coming back in,
bringing tea. 'I was the only one she'd told. I think her
friends thought she'd turned into some sort of recluse.'

'What a good job she had you,' said Grace with admiration. 'It must have been so difficult, I don't know how
you've coped.'

'I'd have done anything for Mum,' he said, voice quivering. 'We were so close. I just don't know what I'm going to
do without her.'

'I wish she'd told us what she was going through, let us
help,' said Grace.

'She wouldn't have wanted that, I suppose she told you in
her letter.'

'But even so …'

'She would have hated the idea of anyone else having to
go through the ordeal with her. She hated being ill, even
when it was something quite trivial. The trouble was that
she was always so strong and independent, not used to
having to ask for help. Having to be taken care of as she got
worse would not have come easily to her, in fact she would

266

have been devastated.'

Richard cleared his throat, trying to keep control of his emotions. 'I know this is a horrible thing to say but, in fact, whoever did this to her has probably helped her in a weird sort of way. Not that I wouldn't give absolutely anything to have her back here again but at least her suffering has come to an end now, without her having to endure the humiliation and loss of dignity that would have become part of her existence. She would have hated it, Hugo's right.'

'I know,' said Grace, welling eyes almost at the point of overflowing again. 'Can't stop you wishing she was still here, though, can it? Here and well.'

'That was never going to happen,' said Hugo. 'She'd deteriorated rapidly this past few weeks. I'm only glad we got on so well since we found each other again. At least I shall have happy memories of her now.'

'I missed so much of her life.'

'We all did.'

# 24

Back home in Cheshire, chaos reigned. When did anything else? They'd had a relatively peaceful night, all things considered. Charlie was just beginning to congratulate himself on the success of his organisational skills.

'Hey, Alfie,' he said, greeting the desperate dog as he came down the stairs and opened the door into the kitchen, much to Alfie's relief. It was Saturday morning and the whole family had managed to have a lie-in for once. Unfortunately, this was to the detriment of Alfie who had almost had to cross his furry legs and tie his bladder in a knot. A puddle on the floor was so demeaning to a dog. In response to his pleading brown eyes, Charlie opened the back door and he shot up the garden post-haste to sprinkle, with considerable force, the contents he'd been holding in storage, all over his favourite bush. Back he came, tail wagging proudly.

'Good dog,' patted Charlie absent-mindedly, as he took the eggs from the fridge.

Actually, Alfie thought he deserved a bit more praise than that, a reward even, for all the discomfort he'd had to suffer. After all, had he, or had he not, just prevented Charlie from having to get out the mop?

He sat, like the ever-obedient dog, looking alertly. Was the fridge door still ajar? Ever so slightly but … his nose twitched tentatively, sensing sausages. Charlie was not as alert as Alfie's mum, she had eyes in the back of her head, but Charlie … Alfie's super-sensitive nose went into over-

268

drive, he knew he had to have them, it was worth getting sent into his basket for. Go for it.

One swift move and his head was in the fridge. Grabbing the first one he could reach he gave it a tug. Easy. They slithered out like a jointed snake. He gave the snake a quick shake to make sure it was dead and then dashed up the hall with it trailing behind him.

He settled down with it to investigate, but then the one person he could usually rely on in times of duplicity chose that very moment to come down the stairs.

'Alfie! What have you done?' she shrieked, clasping her hand to her mouth in delight. 'Daddy! Daddy! Come and look at Alfie!'

Charlie abandoned his pan of scrambled eggs and raced into the hall sensing urgency. But the damage was done. What would have been their evening meal now lay in half-chewed, squashed pink blobs on the carpet.

'Alfie! You naughty dog! Get into your …'

He was already there. Doleful, but licking the last remaining bits of sausage from around his mouth. What a delightful delicacy that had been.

'Is something burning?' asked Zak, recently awakened and looking like death.

'Don't think so, the toaster's fixed now,' replied Charlie, still scraping up sausagemeat, concerned about the carpet, no idea now what they would eat tonight – certainly not sausages.

'Think this pan's had it,' said Zak, calmly, creating clouds of sizzling smoke as he ran cold water onto the blackened remnants of breakfast. 'What was it, anyway?'

'What?' asked Charlie, half-turning, carpet and sausages still uppermost in his mind. 'Oh my God, the eggs! I forgot all about them. Thanks, Zak.'

'No worries.'

'Damn dog,' grunted Charlie.

Alfie lay down, uttering a sound somewhere between a whimper and a groan. Perhaps it was best if he went to sleep.

'Me want breakfast! Me want breakfast!' chanted Izzy, banging her spoon on the table impatiently.

'I'll get it for her,' said Cleo, arriving downstairs at last but looking grumpy. It was mission impossible to stay in bed in this house when everyone else was up, unless you had earplugs. Perhaps she'd try that tomorrow.

'Where's Gran? She's usually first to the table.'

'Dunno,' said Charlie, washing his hands. 'Not seen her this morning.'

'I'll take her a cup of tea,' said Zak, carrying it through to her room together with the biscuit barrel.

'Ah, bless him,' mocked Cleo.

'Shut it! You're only jealous 'cos I'm her favourite,' retorted Zak, as he opened Gran's door.

'As if.'

'Where is she?' shouted Zak, seconds later

'Hiding from you, wonder boy,' teased Cleo.

'Seriously, she's not here.'

'She must be.'

'Check for yourself.'

'Well, where can she be?'

'Bathroom?'

'She can't get up there on her own.'

They dashed around the house in search of the elusive grandma.

'Hide and seek! Hide and seek!' chanted Izzy excitedly.

Even Alfie leapt from his basket and joined in the hunt, his misdemeanours forgotten.

'Is she in the garden?'

'No, I checked.'

'She must have gone out somewhere.'

'But she never goes out without one of us, she's not safe.'

'We know that, but does she?'

They wandered up and down the street looking for her, knocking on doors, but nobody could solve the mystery of the missing grandma. Where on earth could she have disappeared to? How far can you get on a zimmer frame, for God's sake?

Charlie rushed around like a headless chicken, Izzy hot on his heels. Grace would kill him. Every time she went away he seemed to lose somebody.

'Daddy!' shrieked Izzy.

'What?' snapped a startled Charlie, fearing she'd been run over by a double-decker bus, at least.

'Mind the cracks! You're treading on them all.'

Fearing a minor explosion, Cleo came to the rescue and took Izzy firmly by the hand. 'I'll take her back inside,' she said. 'I don't know what more we can do. Gran could be anywhere by now. We don't even know what time she went out.'

'Nine o'clock,' piped up Izzy.

'What?' they rounded on her.

'The big hand was on twelve, and the little hand was on nine on my Barbie clock and the front door went *bang*!' said Izzy innocently. They looked at her in amazement.

'That must have been Gran,' said Zak.

'But that was over an hour and a half ago,' said Charlie.

'I'm scared,' said Cleo, tears in her eyes. 'What can have happened to her?'

'I think maybe we should phone the police,' said Charlie.

'No need,' said Zak, pointing to a car that was approaching. 'They're here, and with a passenger.'

'Grandma's been arrested!' shrieked Izzy, as the police car pulled up at the pavement beside them.

'I believe this lady lives with you,' said the policeman, as he got out of the car.

'Indeed she does,' said Charlie, 'we've been looking

271

everywhere for her. Where did you find her?'

'Had a call from a gentleman a few streets away. Apparently his door wasn't locked and she just walked straight in. Said she lived there and started yelling at him to get out of her house. Poor man didn't know what to do, he'd never seen her in his life before. It was a bit disconcerting for him when she started attacking him with her zimmer frame; he tried to restrain her but when she shouted 'Rape!' he panicked and phoned us. Mind you, even that was difficult for him. She threw the zimmer frame at him while he was on the phone and it hit him squarely on the head. You wouldn't think she'd have the strength, would you? Anyway, we went to collect her and, fortunately, he was very understanding and not too badly injured – said he wouldn't press any charges, it was just a shock more than anything.'

'Is anybody going to get me out of here? I haven't got all day, you know!' shouted a familiar voice. 'It's alright for you standing around talking, you've got nothing else to do.'

'Sorry, love,' said the other policeman, with a smile. 'Here, let me help you.'

'Thank you. I'm glad somebody's got some sense.'

'Where on earth have you been, Gran?' asked Charlie, coming round to take her arm. 'We've been really worried.'

'You? Worried? I bet you didn't even know I'd gone! I only went out visiting anyway, I don't know what all the fuss is about.'

'Here, Gran, have your frame to walk with, it's easier,' said Zak, taking it from the policeman and passing it to her.

'Ah, here he is, bless him. The only one who cares.'

'Does she do this often?' asked the policeman.

'First time,' said Charlie. 'She never normally goes anywhere without one of us, she's not safe.'

'It might be as well if you could keep something with her name and address on her in case it happens again. We've been quite a while riding around with her in the car to see if she could recognise anywhere, she had no idea where she lived.'

'Sorry, she's definitely getting worse.'

'We'll need your phone number as well. You'll get a call later on to fill out an incident report.'

'Not a problem.'

'Did you arrest my gran?' asked Izzy, a thoughtful frown on her face. She'd been uncharacteristically silent until now.

'No,' smiled the policeman, 'she just came for a ride in our car.'

'But she doesn't know you, and Mrs Clarke says you're not allowed to get into cars with strangers.' She could be such a prissy missy at times.

The policeman smiled at her, impressed. 'Mrs Clarke's right, you must never get into a car with a stranger, but your gran was lost and I'm a policeman and it's my job to help lost people to find their way home. Is that okay?' he asked, eyes twinkling.

'Suppose so,' replied Izzy, still looking pensive.

'For goodness sake! How much longer do we have to stand around here gossiping?' grumbled Gran.

'Okay, we're going now,' said the policeman. 'Nice to have met you,' he said to Gran, as they got into the car and drove off with a wave.

'What nice young men,' said Gran, hobbling into the house. 'We've had a lovely day out, we must do it again sometime. They really enjoyed themselves.'

Despite their sorrow, they managed to get quite a lot organised. Keeping busy, having things to do, helped to keep them from permanently dwelling on their sadness, even though everything seemed so surreal.

Grace and Richard had both spoken to the police individually, although there was not a lot either could tell them.

Anna had been fine when they'd last seen her, despite being cross with them for leaving her, which they could now totally understand, knowing how she must have felt. She must have known it would probably be the last time she'd ever see them and yet she had still not wanted to inflict her illness and her suffering onto them. They told the police also about their phone messages from her.

Anna's phone had still not been traced – it was probably at the bottom of the Thames somewhere, nobody with any sense would want to hang on to that after a murder. Had she really only been killed for a mobile phone? Unbelievable.

'I wish I could get my hands on the bastard who did it,' said Richard, acrimoniously.

'I know. The only thing that stops me from feeling quite so bitter is when I think of how she was saved from suffering with her illness any longer. You read her letter. She would have hated having to become dependent, at least she was spared that.'

'Nevertheless, he should hang for what he did to her. As if she didn't have enough to contend with.'

Provisional arrangements had been set in place for the funeral, although it wasn't possible to confirm the actual date yet as they had to wait for the coroner's report and they weren't quite sure how long that would be. Knowing that she was terminally ill, Anna had actually planned everything herself, from the church, to the guests, to the hymns. There wasn't a lot left for them to do: the insurance, the will, her bank details, etcetera, were all there and clearly marked out for them to find. 'Typical mum,' smiled Hugo through his sadness, 'organised to the end.'

There seemed little point in Richard and Grace staying any longer other than as support for Hugo, but he assured them he'd be fine, he'd have to get used to it sooner or later anyway. And, much as he didn't know how he would be able to face it, Richard knew he would have to get back to work until the funeral. He'd need to take time off for that and he already felt he'd taken rather more than his quota. Grace too had to get back: Charlie couldn't be left holding the fort indefinitely, he had a business to run.

And so, wreathed in sadness, they said their farewells to Hugo, leaving his sad and lonely figure waving goodbye from the doorway. Despite the fact that he'd tried to assure them that they didn't have to worry about him, they could do nothing but.

'I hope he'll be alright,' said Grace in a small voice as they drove away.

'We'll be back for the funeral shortly. He can come and stay with us for a while after that. It'll be good for him to meet the rest of his family, let him know he's not totally on his own.'

'Weird how things work out, isn't it? A few weeks ago I would never have believed any of this could possibly happen. It feels like it's all been a dream somehow.'

'I know what you mean,' said Richard sadly. 'That mad whirlwind of unexpected love that blew me away ... and now it's gone.'

'At least you experienced it, Richard, that's what I keep telling myself. It could have been that she'd never come to see us, she could have been ill and died and we would have never have known until it was too late – maybe not even then. Just be glad you had that time together, short though it was.'

'I am. It's just that it seems so cruel to have found that special love and then to have it snatched away,' he said, his voice breaking.

'D'you wanna stop for a coffee? There's a service station coming up,' said Grace, her own grief surfacing.

'Mm,' replied Richard, turning in gratefully.

Izzy was in bed by the time Grace and Richard got back, but at the sound of her mother's voice she bounded down the stairs to greet her.

'Mummy!' she shouted with delight, arms outstretched as she rushed towards her.

Grace lifted her up and gave her a hug, 'Ooh, I've missed you,' she said, squeezing her tightly whilst simultaneously fending off the frantic furry frolics of Alfie as he vied for her attention. 'Okay, okay, I've seen you. I love you too,' she said to him, as he drooled with delight in his doggy devotion.

The others prised themselves away from the television and joined the greeting party in the hall.

'Grace! Good to have you home,' said Charlie, kissing her through the flurry of dog and child.

'Miss me?'

''Course we did,' he said, his love for her beaming from him.

'We lost Gran,' said little big mouth.

'Izzy!' chorused Zak and Cleo simultaneously.

'What? Where is she?'

'Oh, it's nothing, it wasn't for long. She's asleep now, I'll tell you later.'

'You coming in, Dad?' asked Cleo to change the subject, as Richard hovered in the doorway.

'Think I'll just go home,' said Richard sadly.

'Stay over if you like,' invited Grace, trying to ignore the fact that Charlie's hand seemed to have attached itself firmly and possessively to her posterior.

'No, honestly, I need some time on my own.'

'Love you, Dad,' said Cleo, hugging him tearfully as he left.

Izzy's eyes were elsewhere as Grace put her down. 'Daddy! You're not meant to pinch ladies' bottoms, it's very rude!'

# 25

A short period of normality ensued, as much normality as was possible in the circumstances anyway. Charlie and Richard both returned to work although, in Richard's case, this was anything but easy. He was still raw with grief and seemed to see Anna's face everywhere, haunting his world but out of his reach. It was so hard for him to concentrate on what to him, now, seemed like pointless tasks but he knew that work was his only saviour. It would have been all too easy to slide down the slippery slope of depression but somehow, amazingly, reason prevailed. Maybe it was Anna's voice that spoke to him, her spirit ever-present, or his own voice, dispiritedly, telling himself not to give in.

Charlie endeavoured to get his business back on track. It was hard taking a break, however short and for whatever reason, when the business was your own. He'd had to turn down a couple of big jobs this past week and knew he really couldn't afford to be doing that. Apart from anything else it wasn't good for his reputation; the business had built up its good name by being thought of as reliable.

One person who did think of him as reliable, though, was Grace. He was her rock and she seemed to have come to depend on him more and more each day. This craving for excitement she'd had seemed almost to have died with Anna. Maybe it would return, who could say? But for the moment at least, Charlie's steadfastness and solidarity were exactly what she needed. Charlie loved her and she was cocooned in his love, protected from the evils of the world.

It was, in fact, Charlie who had managed to sort out Cleo. Richard was in no fit state to sort out anyone but himself, his grief all-consuming. And, while the risk of establishing Cleo's future as far as her education was concerned would normally have fallen to Grace, Charlie stepped in willingly.

It was a problem of some immediacy. Cleo did not want to go back to school under any circumstances. Neither Cassie nor Lisa had bothered to get in touch with her whilst she'd been absent, proving to Cleo just how little they cared. She knew how much she'd be taunted if she went back pregnant; it had been bad enough before, and without the support of friends she wouldn't be able to cope at all.

The stress of simply the thought of it was making her feel ill, and that was not good for either her or the baby. As far as she was concerned it was her life and she was not going back.

Not so simple in the eyes of Grace and Charlie. She was not yet sixteen, her GCSEs were looming and, apart from anything else, it was their duty to ensure that she completed her education. It was going to be hard enough for her being a teenage mum without having the added handicap of going out into the world without a single qualification.

After several heated discussions, Charlie rose to the challenge and solved the dilemma to everyone's satisfaction. He discovered that Cleo was entitled to a home tutor, who in fact had started working with Cleo that very week. Fortunately, Cleo got on well with her tutor. Indeed, she probably worked harder now than she would have done at school, as there were fewer distractions. She actually sounded quite inspired, brimming with confidence, wanting to do well. Accepting of the fact that what was done was done, the timing of the pregnancy could not have been better. The baby was due to be born about five weeks before the start of her GCSEs and, all being well, she would be able to return to school to take the exams. Her coursework could be done at home with her tutor before then. She knew it was going to be tough, but with the support of her family she intended to give it her best shot.

The thought of the impending funeral had hovered over them like a dark cloud during this time. Until the finality of a funeral it almost felt as though it had all been a dream and that Anna was still alive and in London as before. But then today was back to stark reality; Anna was dead. And on a cold December day the three of them clung together at her graveside, Grace, Richard and Hugo, united in their grief.

It had been a beautiful service, or as beautiful as any funeral service could be, planned to the last detail by Anna herself. As it came to an end the haunting strains of Eva Cassidy sounded almost ethereal as she poured her heart and soul into 'Somewhere Over The Rainbow', a moment of such poignancy that all those present would associate the song with their lost friend forever. There was not a dry eye in the church.

Grace was relieved in a way that the rest of her family had decided not to travel down to London for the funeral. She would have been distracted by their needs, particularly Cleo's and Izzy's, and selfish though it may seem, she wanted time alone to say goodbye to her sister, with just the peripheral support of Richard and Hugo who were too wrapped up in their own grief to intrude into hers.

A slight touch on her shoulder made her turn, eyes not focusing at first, awash with sorrow. But then arms reached out to her in comfort and sympathy as, in recognition, she fell into them, overcome with gratitude for their presence there.

'I'm so sorry,' whispered Kate, her own emotions over-flowing now as she hugged her grief-stricken friend. 'I just had to come. I wanted to be here for you.'

'Thank you,' sobbed Anna, trying to regain a modicum of composure. 'Sorry I'm ...'

'Hey, you don't have to apologise to me. I was the one spilling my heart out the last time, remember? When my brother rang to tell me what had happened I knew I had to come to the funeral – I couldn't have done any other.'

'But it's such a long way...what about Jessica?'

'She's fine – my mum's looking after her.'

'I feel awful.'

'Well don't. I wanted to be here, I'm your friend aren't I?'

'The best one I ever had,' smiled Grace through her tears, hugging Kate in gratitude.

'Oh my God!' exclaimed Cleo, in her usual Cleo-like way. 'This milk's disgusting! Errghh, no wonder, it's out of date! Charlie!'

'What do you mean "Charlie"? You know where the shop is, don't you? You're just as capable as me of walking down there,' responded a much-frazzled stepdad.

'But I'm pregnant.'

'But I'm old.'

'Not *that* old.'

'And not *that* pregnant! Oh go on, I give in,' said Charlie, totally unmasterful in his own house. 'Fancy a walk, Izzy?'

'Alfie leapt out of his basket at the very mention of the word. Charlie groaned. They only wanted milk. This was going to turn into an expedition.

'To the shop?' piped up motormouth.

'Mm.' Guess what was coming next.

'Sweets?' asked Izzy, rolling her eyes expectantly. Why use more words when one would suffice?

Charlie groaned again, remembering all too clearly the sick-splattered bedsheets from the last episode. There was no way. He looked into Izzy's pleading eyes, intent on saying no.

'Okay, what kind would you like?' said Charlie, astonishing himself. Had those words really just come from his mouth?

'I'll get Alfie's lead,' said Izzy, skipping over to the cupboard where it was kept.

Alfie started to spin around with excitement. Possibility was turning into reality! 'Woof!'

'But dogs can't ...' Why did Charlie even begin to imagine that he stood half a chance?

'It's okay. When I go with Mummy we tie him up outside the shop'. Sorted.

'Oh!' exclaimed Cleo, in a surprised kind of way.

'What?' asked Charlie, somewhat disinterested by now.

'I've just found another bottle in the fridge. This one's okay.'

Charlie groaned yet again, his head in his hands. 'Cleo!'

'Sorry.'

'It's okay,' soothed Izzy, taking control of both the situation and the dog as she took Alfie's lead and they almost fell over each other in their haste to be first to the front door. 'We've got to go anyway, we need sweets now,' she said firmly.

'But ...' Who was he to argue?

'You are coming back for something to eat aren't you?' Grace asked, almost pleadingly.

She was so grateful for this unexpected and invaluable support and yet inexplicably afraid that it might disappear as quickly and mysteriously as it had arrived. Or maybe it wasn't so inexplicable. After all, Kate did make a habit of running away from situations she couldn't cope with and Grace knew how the funeral must have evoked some very sad memories for her. Simultaneously Grace herself was feeling somewhat paranoid. Anna had disappeared once before and then had come back into her life briefly only to disappear again. She and Kate had formed such a special bond, she couldn't bear it if she disappeared too.

'Well I'm not going to be turning round and going straight back to Cornwall am I? I came here to support you – staying at my brother's for a couple of days.'

Grace looked at her with gratitude 'You're so lovely,' she said, giving her a hug.

'Shut up, you'll have me in tears again in a minute,' said Kate, hurriedly drying her eyes on the back of her hand.

'Look,' said Grace, pointing up at the sky.

'What?' asked Kate, still somewhat tearful.

'A rainbow! How amazing that that should suddenly appear.'

'Well not really, it was pouring down earlier.'

'No, I mean after hearing that song in church, Somewhere Over The Rainbow – it seems sort of symbolic somehow. Like Anna's at peace, finally.'

Izzy skipped along the pavement, a bag of sweets grasped tightly in her hand, forbidden to eat any until she got home.

'Hurry up, Daddy, you're going too slow,' she said, turning to check he was still there. 'What are you doing?'

'Wait a minute, Alfie's doing a poo.'

'Yuk! Can I have a sweet while I'm waiting?'

'Just one.'

'Two?'

'Just one, I said, Izzy.'

Izzy selected one carefully and popped it into her mouth, chewing noisily. 'Yum!'

Alfie scratched at the ground with his back feet, tail wagging excitedly, mission accomplished. He shook himself happily, panted and was ready to continue.

'Oops, Daddy, don't forget to pick it up,' said little goody two-shoes. 'Mummy *always* picks it up.'

'Well so do I, normally,' he said, checking in his pockets for a poop bag. He could have sworn he'd brought one with him.

He looked at the still-steaming dollop that lay at the edge of the footpath. Perhaps he could just …

'Don't leave it there, Daddy. Somebody will get it on their shoes and it will make them all smelly. Pooh!' she said, holding her nose dramatically.

The solution was staring him right in the face.

'Okay, I'll just have to use your sweet bag, then. What a good job it's big.'

'But Daddy, it'll be all over my sweets!' exclaimed Izzy, clutching it tightly to herself in absolute horror.

'Then you'll just have to eat them up first,' said Charlie, getting impatient now.

'But you said …'

'I know what I said. Just eat them.'

Adults! They can be so hard to understand at times. Looking unusually apprehensive, Izzy took a sweet from the bag and licked it laboriously.

'Hurry up.'

'I am.' As Charlie knew well by now, the words 'hurry up' and 'Izzy' didn't go together.

'Could you spare one for me, please?' Every little helps.

'Suppose,' said Izzy, holding the bag out to him, begrudgingly.

Alfie shuffled about on his bottom impatiently. This was meant to be walkies not sitties. Walkies, however, could be delayed for a good reason. His nose twitched inquisitively towards Izzy. How had he only just noticed? His tongue dangled from his mouth, drooling desirously, his eyes fixed on Izzy's every move.

'Okay, just one,' she said, dropping what looked like a miniature version of Grandma's dentures to the ground.

What the heck … he ate it anyway.

'Izzy, come on. We can't stand here all day. Put the rest in your coat pocket for now and give me the bag.'

'But Mummy says never to put sweets in your pocket 'cos …'

'Just do it.' Charlie could be quite firm occasionally.

''Cos all the sugar comes off and makes a big sticky mess.' And Izzy could be quite pedantic.

'Do as you're told.'

'Okay,' she said, finally handing him the empty bag but simultaneously distracted by something else.

'Oooh!' she exclaimed, looking up at the sky.

'Now what?' asked Charlie, too busy pooper scooping to care even if the sky was falling down.

'A rainbow – look!'

'Mmm. Very nice. Let's go,' he said, gingerly holding the bag that was now filled with something far worse than sweets. Strewth! It was all over his hand.

Izzy skipped ahead, happy and full of sweets, singing a song that Auntie Anna had taught her:

> *Red and yellow and pink and green*
> *Orange and purple and blue.*
> *I can sing a rainbow, sing a rainbow,*
> *Sing a rainbow too.*

After the funeral, everyone went back to the bar in Battersea, the one where Grace had been with Anna, and where she had first met Kate. Had that really only been less than a month ago? It seemed like another lifetime.

It had been Anna's local, the place where she used to hang out with her mates. The owners had known Anna well and had provided a buffet above and beyond what Hugo had asked for at no extra cost, showing how much they had valued her both as a customer and as a friend. In fact there was such an outpouring of love for Anna from everyone that it brought tears to Grace's eyes. It was good to know that she'd had friends who cared.

Grace saw Hugo looking pensive and went over to him and touched his arm. 'Okay, Hugo?'

'Yeah, thanks, Auntie Grace. I'm so glad you're here, I couldn't have done it without you,' he said, a perceptible catch in his voice.

Grace gave him a hug, crumbling inside but wanting to appear strong for him. 'I'm glad we're here for each other, Hugo.'

Richard too was finding it tough. It was hard to believe it was his Anna they were talking about; it was as though it was someone else and that Anna would walk in in a minute to join them, that mischievous smile playing on her lips, her eyes searching through the crowd to find him ...'

'Ohh!' he was jolted back to the real world as his glass slipped through his fingers and smashed into a myriad of pieces on the slate floor.

'Richard, are you okay?'

He was suddenly the centre of everybody's attention, the last place he wanted to be. 'Fine. I'm fine,' he said, not wanting a fuss.

Gently, a hand caught his elbow, leading him towards the door. 'Come on outside, let's get some air, it's getting really hot in here.'

He allowed himself to be led, was grateful for the diversion from the overpowering sense of loss that had suddenly washed over him. Her voice was soft as she spoke, reaching in her bag to find tissues for him.

'Here, use these. They're a bit crumpled but they are clean.'

'Thanks,' he spluttered, almost incoherently. 'Sorry.'

'Don't be sorry,' she said, full of understanding. 'You shouldn't try to bottle it up. I know, I've been there, almost got the T-shirt.'

'You're Kate aren't you?' he asked, showing a modicum of composure.

'Yes, Grace introduced us in the churchyard. Not the best of places, I don't really think you took in a word she said.'

'Sorry.'

'Don't be sorry, it was understandable. Your mind was elsewhere. Grace told me how it was with you and Anna, I'm so sorry, you must be devastated.'

'Pretty much,' he said, his lips quivering as he tried to hold back another onslaught of tears.

'Would you like me to go? Leave you on your own for a while?' she asked, tentatively.

'No, stay, I'd appreciate your company – if you don't mind me blubbing all over you that is,' he said with half a smile.

''Course not,' she replied.

Inside, as tongues loosened with alcohol, more and more anecdotes were told. Grace found them increasingly difficult to listen to; they only served to compound the guilt she already felt about the way Anna had been forced to live her life in isolation from the rest of her family. She sought out Hugo, but saw him chatting animatedly to a young man at the far end of the bar and didn't want to interrupt; it was good to see him looking a little less sorrowful. Nevertheless, Grace had started to feel a bit panicky. Surrounded by all these strangers, who had obviously known her sister better than she had herself, it was hard not to. Missing Anna, missing all that they could have had together.

She stumbled outside, seeking solace and strength from the real world that lay beyond the bar door. Life goes on, she knew that, but as she breathed in the cold December air, she had never felt so sad and alone. The anonymity of the city life surrounded her, rushed by, uncaring of her grief. Grace was accustomed to the richness of family life, to the joy of caring for everyone, being central to their world.

No matter if she did complain sometimes, it was a comfortable place to be … to be needed, to be loved. She wished Charlie was here.

But arms *did* reach out to comfort her, familiar and strong.

'Hey,' said Richard, drawing her to him, still obviously distraught himself.

Kate hugged into them, wanting to soothe both, more distressed by their sadness than by the death of Anna who she really hadn't known. She felt so close to them, particularly Grace who she felt as though she'd known for ever, but also to Richard even though they'd only just met that day, the intensity of the situation seeming to bind them all together.

'Maybe we can say our goodbyes to everyone and make an escape, I really don't think I can face standing around in the bar making pleasantries again,' said Grace.

And so they went their separate ways, Grace and Richard back to the flat, leaving Hugo to follow, and Kate back to her brother's. Grace was loath to let Kate go, not knowing when they would see each other again, but Kate promised to come up to Cheshire for a visit very soon and meantime swore that they would keep in touch by phone. It was a friendship that neither wanted to lose.

# 26

Life does go on, it's true.

'What are you sitting there moping for?' Gran's voice cut through Grace's thoughts.

'Why d'you think?' snapped Grace curtly.

If truth be told, she was a million miles away. Well, not a million exactly, but London, far enough. She was worried about Hugo, there on his own; he'd sounded so sad when she'd spoken to him on the phone. He was used to living alone, of course, it wasn't as though he'd shared a house with Anna, but obviously her death had left a huge gap in his life.

He seemed quite a solitary person, no mention of friends or girlfriends, just work. Grace remembered talking to Anna about him briefly and her saying that, as far as she knew, he'd never had a serious relationship. Actually, that was probably true of a lot of Londoners, there seemed to be far more people who were single than otherwise. Unlike around here where if you weren't part of a couple by the age of twenty-five you were definitely past it.

Anyway, she must stop worrying about him. He was a grown man and perfectly capable. For all that, she was pleased that he'd said he'd like to come up and spend Christmas with them. Christmas! She really must get herself organised, it was only just over two weeks away and she hadn't done a thing.

A sudden realisation that something strange was happening made her turn her head, just in time to see Grandma pouring boiling water from the kettle onto the teabags in the caddy.

'Mother! What are you doing?'

'Well! What kind of stupid question is that? I'm making a cup of tea of course, I thought even you would have known that!'

'But Mother, that's the tea caddy! You've spoiled all of those teabags now – what a waste!' said Grace, scooping out the soggy brown mass and squeezing it out between two spoons before dropping it into the bin, rather too hastily, and tipping the contents of the tea caddy down the sink.

'What did you do that for?' asked Grandma, eyes un-believing of what she'd just witnessed. 'That was my tea, I could have drunk that, I was just going to.'

'That was just a mess. You take one teabag and you put it in a cup and then you pour on boiling water, okay?' instructed Grace, rather sarcastically, it has to be said.

'Think you know it all, don't you?'

'Yes,' Grace answered stubbornly, looking in the cup-board for the new packet of tea. Where had it gone? 'Where are the teabags?' she muttered to no one in particular.

'Well! And you think I'm stupid? You just put them in the bin! Even my memory's better than that!'

Grace groaned inwardly. 'I thought we had another packet,' she said, searching, but to no avail.

'Well that just goes to show,' said Grandma, revelling in what was, to her, her triumph.

'Oghh! I'll go down to the shop and get some more,' said Grace, turning to see Gran rooting in the bin, ably assisted by a four-legged friend.

'No need. Waste not, want not. These will be fine when I've given them a wash.'

'Mother! For goodness sake! Alfie! Get out!'

Gran turned, triumphant, the crumb-encrusted teabags in her hand, dropping large chunks of amazingly unsoggy

Weetabix onto the floor much to Alfie's delight. 'Told you, nothing wrong with them.'

But in true mother-never-misses-anything style, Grace had been sidetracked. Was Cleo not eating properly again? She was the only one who had asked for Weetabix this morning, but she must have sneaked it into the bin without even adding milk and attempting to eat it. There was always something to worry about.

'Grace, are you listening to me?' asked Gran. Typical. They only ever noticed her when she did something wrong, and she was right this time.

'What?' snapped Grace, her mind on Cleo.

'The teabags! Talk about *me* being confused, you want to take a look at yourself!' said Gran, running water into the sink and squirting in some washing-up liquid.

'Mother! Surely you're not going to …' Too late. They were in.

Unable to take any more, Grace went to get her coat, Alfie hot on her heels. 'Back in a minute. Just going to the shop.'

Later that night as she lay in bed next to a slumbering Charlie, Grace found sleep totally elusive. She was worried about everyone. Was her mother getting worse? Certainly she did seem to be becoming increasingly confused. How were they going to cope with her as things got worse and worse? She'd be a danger not only to herself but to them as well; she could get up to anything while they were all asleep at night, anything was possible, she'd proved that often enough. And what would happen when they couldn't cope with her, or rather when *she* couldn't cope with her? After all, it was down to her at the end of the day. Recently, every time she had a confrontation with her mother, which was very frequent, her stress levels had been sky high. She dreaded to think what it was doing to her blood pressure.

But how could she put her mother into a home? Her own mother. Just imagine the reaction if she even tried! And the guilt – that would be insurmountable.

On top of all this there was Cleo and the Weetabix in the bin. She'd had suspicions about Cleo's eating habits before and been proved wrong, but now, with the baby on the way, it was even more important that she ate properly. Baby. Grace was trying to be positive about it on the surface but underneath she was concerned. How on earth would Cleo manage to look after a baby? She could hardly look after herself, never mind a baby as well.

Wasn't it great being a mother? Worry, worry, worry, that's all Grace ever seemed to do. Poor Hugo, he didn't even have a mother now. But Anna had asked Grace to take care of him for her, and that was the least she could do. He was obviously going to be feeling down, but thankfully he'd agreed to come and spend Christmas with them so that would hopefully give her a chance to find out how he was coping.

But Anna. This would have been their first Christmas spent together since they were children. How good would that have been? Anna, Hugo, Richard, all with them. One big happy family. Oh Anna!

She tried to weep silently so as not to disturb Charlie, but it was impossible. Grief wracked her body, as it convulsed with unplumbed depths of sadness and pain. Charlie was soon awake and perceived the situation. There was no need for words as he turned towards her and held her in his arms, his strength and the warmth of his body making her feel so loved. Her sobs subsided eventually, his very presence bringing comfort. For all of her complaints about feeling trapped in a cage and wanting to escape and fly free, she knew she was safe with Charlie. She was the centre of his world and he would never let her down. He would always be there for her, idolising her, praising her, keeping her secure. What more could anyone ask?

She raised her head and gazed into his warm brown eyes, eyes that were filled with such love and devotion that she could almost have wept again.

'Charlie, I do love you, you know.'

'Well I should hope so, you're my wife,' he teased, his smile filled with adoration.

'Doesn't always follow,' she responded pensively. 'Just because you're married it doesn't necessarily mean you love someone, people change.'

'Are you trying to tell me something?' he asked, paranoia pitter-pattering in.

'I'm just trying to tell you how much I love you, that's all.'

'All? Grace, that means everything to me, *you* mean everything to me, you know that,' he said, love for her beaming from his every pore.

His mouth came towards hers, tentatively at first, lips brushing, butterfly kisses, eyes half-closed in the blissful state of loving her so. Comforting calmly, taciturn and tranquil, warmly filled with wonderment that she chose to be with him above all. His Grace.

But his Grace suddenly took on a whole new persona. Maybe it was just to drown her sorrows and draw comfort from her man or, possibly, because she'd experienced another way of living that said there's more to life than housework and kids. Perhaps, even, she'd realised that life is too short and that you should make the most of what you've got. But, whatever it was, she took Charlie completely by surprise as she opened her mouth and almost devoured him whole.

'Jeez!' he spluttered, briefly coming up for air and almost in need of resuscitation. 'Wassallthisabout?'

'You complaining?' she gasped, conversation being the last thing on her mind.

Her tongue flicked down the length of his torso, tormenting, tantalising. She wanted him inside her, wanted, needed, but wanted to please him also. As she took him in her mouth he gasped with pleasure as her lips moved slowly up and down the length of him, sucking, squeezing, tongue forever teasing. He wanted to pleasure her too, simultaneously, but found himself rendered almost incapable of speech or movement, such was the intensity of feeling. His sensuality had gone into overdrive. With difficulty, he managed to rein himself back in a little and, surprised that he still had use of his limbs, reached out a hand to her buttock as she knelt over him. His hand moved slowly around the curve of her, his fingers homing in on the warm, wet place of his intent. Grace shuddered as his fingers explored her; she was soft and yielding in his hand. She whimpered almost, wanting more but not wanting to let him go.

'Move round,' he said, withdrawing his fingers and urging her buttocks towards him.

She didn't require much urging, her body was screaming out for more as, still enclosing him in her mouth, she straddled her man. The sensation of his hot breath against her was electrifying and, as his tongue slid softly to probe within her, she reached heights of sensual satisfaction that she almost couldn't bear.

Vaguely aware, in some remote corner of her mind, that at this moment she had the capacity to awaken the entire household if she was to give vent to the excruciating pleasure she was feeling, she made a concerted effort to repress the cries of ecstasy that attempted to fall from her mouth along with Charlie's appendage.

Charlie could wait no longer, and as he scrambled out from beneath her, breathless and desirous, she needed him too. Needed. Wanted. Had to have. She flipped herself over and lay on her back, legs wide and welcoming, winding them around him as he entered her, lifting her buttocks to feel him deeper and deeper inside.

'Oh Charlie,' she gasped, moving rhythmically with him as mind-blowing sensations rippled through her body, building and building.

Charlie was practically rendered speechless. He loved this woman beyond words. He loved her, he loved her, he was seeing stars ... exploding ... he was ...

'Oh Grace!' he gasped, as they reached their eventual climax and he fell down into her arms.

They lay motionless for a while, powerless and perspiring, their desires fulfilled. Then Charlie lifted his head and kissed the tip of her nose before rolling off and lying adjacent, his head next to hers on the pillow.

'That was unbelievable,' he sighed.

'Mm?' she asked, from a world beyond.

'What was all that about?' he asked, still wondering if it had been a dream.

She dragged herself back from that pleasurable place to the here and now. 'Don't know, but it was good, wasn't it?'

Not surprisingly, they both overslept the next morning. But when Grace came downstairs still wearing her post-coital glow, Cleo seemed to have everything under control.

'You should have woken me,' said Grace. 'I didn't realise the time.'

'It's okay,' said Cleo, busily buttering. 'My tutor rang, he's not coming until this afternoon now so I can take Izzy for you if you like. Thought you deserved a lie-in. You look much better for it, actually,' said Cleo, glancing up at her mother, not realising the real reason for Grace's glowing countenance.

But suddenly the truth dawned as Charlie came into the kitchen, slid his arm around Grace and kissed her rather over-affectionately for the middle of the family kitchen at this time of the morning. Ugghh. Gross. Old people shouldn't be allowed to do that sort of thing, it was disgusting.

'Not really hungry this morning,' said Cleo, somewhat turned off the idea of food and getting up from the table.

'Cleo, you've got to eat,' said Grace, attempting to disentangle herself from Charlie who seemed to have grown extra hands.

'I'll have something when I get back,' said Cleo, averting her eyes. 'Come on, Izzy, let's get you ready.'

'But I want Mummy to do it,' said Izzy, petulance prevailing.

'Race you up the stairs,' said Cleo with a persuasive smile. It worked. They were gone.

'Where's Zak?' shouted Grace after them.

'Gone early,' Cleo's retreating figure replied.

Charlie nuzzled Grace's neck. His libido had been given such a boost after last night.

'Toast?' asked Grace.

'… wasn't what I had in mind, no,' he said, pressing himself up behind her.

'Alright, alright!' said Grace, a little firmly.

'What? You mean we can? Here?' asked Charlie in amazement. What had happened to the Grace he knew? She'd always been so, well, almost prudish before.

'Charlie! I'm talking to Alfie, he's scratching my leg. Let him outside, could you?'

Deflated, Charlie opened the door, the cold air from outside rushing in to cool his ardour. Passion-killer. Just as well, really, he had a job to go to.

Grace felt equally as invigorated by last night's lovemaking, but had shopping in mind rather than sex. Hmm. Chocolate, shopping, sex, which order would she put them in? Which order would most women put them in? Depends what mood you are in at the precise moment of the question, she supposed. Last night, for instance, if someone had offered her a whole boxful of her very favourite chocolates or a shopping trip to Cheshire Oaks with £50 to spend on herself, would she have been tempted to leave that hotbed of lust and head for the door? Not a chance. Last night had been amazing. Probably – and this was a weird thing to say because of the length of time they'd been together – but nevertheless, probably the best sex she'd ever had with Charlie, who was normally such a plodder.

Actually that was a bit cruel. She couldn't blame Charlie for the lack of excitement in their sex lives, or even in their lives in general; she was equally at fault. Feeling weighed down with responsibility, taking on other people's problems, keeping everyone happy but herself. Thinking back, that was exactly what had gone wrong in her last marriage and she did not want it happening again. Ogghh, life could be so complicated. She'd felt really trapped before her trip to London and had wrongly convinced herself that Charlie was a big part of those feelings of boredom and lack of excitement. She'd flown free and experienced a small portion of another world, but really, whatever she did would not be the same without Charlie by her side. He was her rock, and she was only just coming to realise that.

'Could you hurry up?' shouted Cleo crossly as she turned, yet again, to wait for her dawdling sister to catch up.

'What?' asked Izzy, from her own little Izzy-world of snails and spiders and cracks in the pavement and worms and … 'Ooh, look what I've found!' she exclaimed, bent over studiously, bottom in the air.

'Never mind what you've found, you're going to be late. Mrs Clarke will be cross,' reprimanded Cleo, not the most patient person in the world at the best of times.

'But look,' insisted Izzy, totally unfazed by the prospect of an angry Mrs Clarke.

'Oh, for goodness sake,' snapped Cleo, her authority

thwarted. But realising it was the only way forward, she retraced her steps. 'What?' she asked, following Izzy's gaze and expecting to see the crown jewels at least. 'What?' she repeated, unimpressed by what she saw.

'There,' pointed Izzy, a rapturous expression on her face, as if she was looking at an object of sublime beauty.

A pebble.

'It's a pebble,' said Cleo, somewhat disdainfully. 'Just a pebble,' she repeated, unimpressed.

'But it's got eyes, look! Eyes staring at me! Shh!' she whispered in wonderment, totally transfixed.

'They're just white marks on the pebble, pea-brain,' said Cleo, crushingly destroying Izzy's magical mystery, insensitive to it, in a rush. 'Come on! We're going to be late, stop messing about,' she said, grabbing Izzy by the hand and dragging her along unwillingly.

'Ow! That hurts!' screamed Izzy, furious at the intervention. 'Let me go, let me go!'

For one so small she had an amazingly powerful pair of lungs.

'Shut up,' snarled Cleo, still dragging, afraid to let go now but embarrassed by the strange looks they were getting. 'For God's sake, Izzy! Be quiet and walk properly!'

'Let go of my hand then.'

'No.'

'Yes.'

'No.'

'I'll tell Mrs Clarke of you. And Mummy.'

'Please yourself.'

Finally, thankfully, the building loomed ahead.

'I go in by myself now,' said Izzy, petulantly.

'No you don't.'

'Yes I do.'

'No you do not!' said Cleo firmly, getting angrier by the minute.

'Cleo!' shouted a familiar voice.

She turned in its direction. Huh! That's all she needed this morning.

'Hey,' she said, her voice as unenthusiastic and unwelcoming as it was possible to get.

'Hey, how's it going?' said Pete, eyeing her up and down, eyes resting on her swelling stomach, which made a change at least from where they usually rested. 'Not seen you around.'

'Well …' she said, glancing down at herself … and feeling and sounding down too.

'Zak reckons it's my kid,' he said. 'Is it?'

'Zak had no right to say anything, it's none of his business.'

'But I've got rights if it is. Quite like the idea of being some kid's dad. Proves I'm not firing blanks anyway,' he smirked.

'For fuck's sake Pete, sod off! You're not the only bloke I've slept with, you know, and of all of them you're probably the least capable,' she said, cuttingly.

But Pete was too cock-a-hoop with himself to be cut down to size easily.

'I could help,' he said, sliding his arm around her shoulder, eyes alighting on her boobs which were indeed looking quite magnificent. 'Being up the duff suits you,' he said sleazily.

'Gerroff!' snapped Cleo crossly, pushing away his arm and wriggling free. 'I know exactly what sort of help you've got in mind, and it's got nothing to do with the baby.'

'Aw Cleo, c'mon. You know I like you. I wanna be its dad, I wanna …'

'*Izzy!*' screamed Cleo, in sudden realisation that her sister was no longer there. 'Where's she gone? She was here a minute ago! This is all your fault, Pete. Mum'll kill me!'

Head in a whirl, Cleo rushed off in the direction of the

school, praying that that's where she'd gone, not even daring to think of the alternatives. Izzy, Izzy, Izzy, what have you done?

As if she hadn't got enough to worry about, the sound of Pete's voice echoed in her ears as she ran, holding her protruding belly with one hand.

'Well I reckon I'm its dad and I can find out. There's paternity tests, you know!'

Breathlessly, she opened the nursery school door, desperately casting her eyes around the room in search of her missing sister.

'O-h-h-h.' Panic set in.

Mrs Clarke hurried towards her, several little hangers-on holding onto her hands and skirt.

'Can I help you?' asked a sarcastic Mrs Clarke, knowing full well that she could. She blocked the doorway with her considerable frame, protecting her children. Anything was possible with this riff-raff. Just look at the state of the girl, showing off her bump as though it was something to be proud of. What was the world coming to?

'Can I help you?' she repeated slowly, using exaggerated mouth formations as she spoke the four words, implying that Cleo was some kind of imbecile.

'Um, I'm looking for Izzy, my sister, um …,' gabbled Cleo in a state of panic, and now doubly so, having been intimidated by Mrs Clarke.

'Well, *your sister*, poor child, had to walk to school all by herself this morning. In all my …'

'Is she here?' gasped Cleo, with an enormous sense of relief.

'Do not interrupt when I'm speaking!' snapped Mrs Clarke.

'Well where …?'

'Did you not hear what I said?' cut in Mrs Clarke, acidly.

This entire family seemed to be without any discipline what-soever. 'As I was saying, before I was so rudely interrupted, in all my years of teaching I have never ever known of a case where a three-year-old child has to walk all the way to school on its own before.'

'But ...'

'Stop!' commanded Mrs Clarke, holding up a hand emphatically, after disentangling it from a wide-eyed child. 'I shall be speaking to your parents about this, it may well be that Social Services have to be informed. Do you realise what could have happened to her? Do you even care? All I can say is that it's fortunate that Izzy is such a good and sensible child.'

The good and sensible child chose just this precise moment to sidle up to Mrs Clarke, unfortunately lacking a halo, but in every other way looking the picture of angelic innocence.

'Oh there you are, darling. Are you alright now?' said a transformed Mrs Clarke, bending over Izzy and taking her small hand in hers in a 'sorry for' way.

Izzy managed to produce a dramatic sniff. 'Yes thank you, Mrs Clarke.'

'Izzy!' Cleo could contain herself no longer. 'What do you think you were doing, running off like that? Just wait until I get you home. I ...'

'Dear, dear, dear! We don't want any of your idle threats around here young lady! May I suggest you take yourself home and learn to control that temper of yours. It strikes me you've got enough problems, without adding to them,' said Mrs Clarke, her eyes coming to rest on Cleo's bump, her face registering disgust.

With a stifled sob of frustration, Cleo turned and rushed out of the door, a sea of eyes watching her go.

'Alright, darling?' asked Mrs Clarke, pityingly.

Maybe, in future years, Izzy would become an award-winning actress. Certainly she managed to produce her second dramatic sniff with relative ease.

'Come on, let's go and read a story,' soothed Mrs Clarke.

'The three bears at it in bed?' asked Izzy.

'*Pardon?*' asked Mrs Clarke. Did she really want that repeated?

# 27

Christmas. The countdown had begun. Although she didn't feel in the Christmas spirit in the least, she knew she would have to make an effort for everyone else. It was going to seem strange having Hugo here, and Anna just a memory. Richard was going to spend it with them too; she couldn't just leave him on his own, not this year, despite Charlie's reservations. Actually, any reservations Charlie had had were becoming increasingly diminished now. Thankfully, with the improvement in their sex life, he was finally coming to realise that he was the one she wanted to be with. His jealousy was becoming a thing of the past – most of the time, anyway.

The one person Grace worried about most, at the moment, was Cleo. She seemed very up and down – hormonal probably, but nevertheless … The confrontation with Mrs Clarke when Izzy went missing hadn't helped, it had knocked her confidence. Stupid woman. What did she know about raising children? Grace had had a real go at Mrs Clarke when she'd been asked to go in and see her about it. Put her in her place, hopefully. Social Services hadn't been mentioned again, anyway. Surely there were more problem children than hers for them to be worrying about? Problem children? What was she on about? She didn't have problem children: hers were perfect.

Poor Cleo. She was worried about Pete too, with his idle threat of a paternity test. Had he been serious? They'd just have to face that one if and when it happened, she supposed.

Anyway, back to the Christmas check-list, if she could stop her mind wandering for five minutes. She was actually quite proud of herself. Two and a half weeks was all she'd had, in between all of her other jobs of course, to organise Christmas for eight people – and she was doing well. Cards written and posted, presents ... um, well, turkey ordered ... So, just more presents to buy and wrap, decorations to go up, food to buy. Cleaning? That was the old Grace. She seemed to have given up on that one since she flew out of her cage.

Flying in through the door came Charlie, in the form of her fairy godmother. Well, less of the fairy actually, as he came up behind her and pressed himself up against her while she stood at the kitchen worktop studying her list.

'Hey,' he said, nibbling her earlobe, knowing she liked it.

'What are you doing home at this time?' she asked, turning, surprised.

'Pleased to see me?' he asked, pecking her lips, anticipating.

'You know I am but ...' she turned and wrapped her arms around his neck, welcoming his kisses.

Charlie was beginning to feel quite amorous and ... in walked Grandma.

'What on earth is going on in here?' she asked, her face wrinkling with disgust. 'We don't want any of that sort of behaviour, thank you very much, there's enough of that on the television.'

'Oh! Been watching blue movies have you, Gran?' joked Charlie, despite his frustration.

'Blue? Pink? Doesn't matter what colour they are, they're all the same as far as I can see,' said Gran, parking herself firmly at the table. 'Tea?' she asked, expectantly.

'Oh, I'll make it,' said Grace. 'What did you come home

for anyway, Charlie?'

'To give you, my love, the chance to go and get your Christmas shopping done. I've decided to take the rest of the day off, so I'll pick up Izzy from school and take her to buy the tree.'

'Oh Charlie, you really are my Prince Charming, that's fantastic!'

'Glad to be of service, Cinderella.'

Grace poured out Gran's tea. 'Just got to go upstairs and get ready,' she said, a smile on her face. 'Follow me up, Charlie, there's something I want to show you.'

Cleo wandered in as Gran was sipping her tea. 'Where's Mum? I thought I heard Charlie.'

'You did,' slurped Gran. 'They've gone upstairs. She wanted to show him something.'

'Errghh! That is so gross!' exploded Cleo, stomping back out again.

'What?' asked Gran, removing her dentures and using them to shovel sugar into her tea to save having to get up for a spoon. The service around here was abysmal.

Grace did eventually manage to get to the shops, although it wasn't exactly a pleasant experience, not as pleasant as the one she'd just had, anyway. She smiled when she thought about Charlie, so caring and thoughtful – and such a stud just lately! Their sex life had certainly improved recently. It was true what they said about marriage, you had to work at it.

She was almost carried along by the crowd of bustling shoppers, last-minute present hunters like herself, anxious to find that perfect gift. She was like this every year, always meaning to be organised but never quite succeeding. At least this year she had an excuse. Thinking of Anna brought tears to her eyes unexpectedly. Strange how grief seemed to wash over her suddenly, unannounced. She'd been quite happy a minute ago, head in the clouds, thinking of Charlie.

'Hey! Watch where you're going!' mouthed off some face-less buggy-pushing yummy-mummy.

Too late. She was definitely back down to earth now, liter-ally. Grace tripped over the swivel-wheeled state-of-the-art buggy and hit the ground with a bump, tears still on her face.

'Don't know what you've got to cry about, you should watch where you're going. You could have hurt my Precious Pumpkin then,' she said, making cooing noises at her designer baby, unconcerned that Grace was in a decidedly non-designer heap on the floor.

'I didn't though, did I? Hurt him, I mean?'

'Her. You didn't hurt her. No, she seems to be okay, for-tunately for you.'

'What's her name?'

'You trying to be funny or what? Come on Precious,' said the yummy-mummy, flicking back her bleached blonde hair with her bejewelled acrylic nails and giving Grace a final scowl from her fake-tanned face before tottering away on her Jimmy Choos, pushing Precious Pumpkin along the road towards the fame-filled world of celebrity, the world of her dreams and aspirations.

Grace, meanwhile, was still in a heap, a crumpled heap at that, amid her bags full of Christmas shopping on the ground. She could only feel gratitude towards the carrier bags, actually: at least they'd broken her fall and prevented her fall from breaking any bits of her. That stupid girl! She could at least have had the decency to help her up.

'Are you alright, love?' asked an old lady, hobbling up to her, leaning heavily on a walking stick. 'Can I help you?' The poor woman looked in a worse state than Grace.

'No, I'm fine thanks, honestly. Thank you for asking though.'

Embarrassed more than anything, Grace struggled to her feet, ran a hand through her hair and smoothed out her clothes before retrieving her shopping, some of which had spilled out of the bags and was strewn across the pavement.

'Mum?'

Zak.

Why is it that when you do something embarrassing, somebody you know always sees you?

'What happened?' he asked, running up to Grace in a state of panic. 'Are you alright? I saw you sprawled all over the floor.'

'Ogghh!' she groaned, not wanting a fuss. 'Don't make it sound worse than it is. Just tripped over some stupid woman's buggy, that's all. Help me pick these up, could you?' she said. She hadn't needed to ask, Zak was already down on his hands and knees doing just that.

'So why are you crying?'

'Crying? I'm not crying! Oh! Fancy a coffee somewhere? Sorry for snapping.'

'Sure, or something stronger if you like, you look in need,' smiled Zak, linking arms with Grace and picking up the heaviest of the shopping. 'Come on, there's a really nice bar just along here.'

'How would you know about things like that?' asked Grace, returning his smile.

'Haven't a clue, Mum,' he responded, with his usual cheeky grin.

'I'm really enjoying this,' said Grace, settling back on the comfortable sofa, sipping her gin and tonic.

'Looks like it,' said Zak, enjoying spending some time alone with his mother for once.

'No, I mean it's good for us to be able to make time for just the two of us. Never get a chance usually, do we?'

'I know, I was just thinking the same thing.'

'I keep meaning to ask you: what happened with Genevieve?'

'Oh, nothing. Still see her around but I'm better off without her. That whole drugs scene, it's crazy.'

'Sensible lad. Pity. You really liked her, didn't you?'

'Yup. Don't wanna hang around with that crowd though. Maybe one day she'll come to her senses.'

'Anyone else on the horizon?'

'Mum!'

'Just asking.'

'Nope. I'm enjoying hanging out with my mates for now. Don't want to get tied down with anybody anyway, got uni coming up soon.'

'Mm, I know. It's going to seem weird not having you at home. Looking forward to it?'

''Course I am. Gonna miss everyone though.'

'I expect you'll be back – dirty washing, food refills, all of that,' smiled Grace.

'Hey, I'm not that bad!' retorted Zak. 'I'll be back 'cos I love my mum!'

'Aww, Zak, you say the sweetest things.'

It was dark by the time they got home. Charlie had been beginning to wonder what had happened to her.

'Phew! You smell of booze,' he said, greeting her with a kiss. 'What have you been up to?'

'I found her sprawled on the floor,' grinned Zak.

'Was this before or after you went to the pub?' asked Charlie, faintly amused and unaccustomed to having a tipsy wife.

'Don't ask, it's a long story but I'm absolutely, absolutely fine now and I have a be-au-ti-ful son,' slurred Grace, kissing Zak on the cheek.

'It was good,' said Zak. 'It's not often Mum and I get a chance to spend time together.'

'Probably as well,' smiled Charlie, fascinated.

'What's for tea?' asked Cleo. 'I'm starving.'

Typical for one who's not usually hungry at all.

'Tea? Oops, I forgot all about tea!' sniggered Grace, in a totally uncharacteristic way.

'Tell you what, I'll go and get a takeaway,' said Charlie. Problem solved.

'Well don't lose it on the way home,' Zak spluttered hysterically.

'Lose it? How can you lose a takeaway?' asked a mystified Grace, yawning. This was all too much.

'Don't ask,' said Charlie; his turn now.

But mini-motormouth was back.

'Daddy lost our burgers when he made me fall off the wall and cut my knee. And he lost Cleo as well.'

Nice one, Izzy. What a good job your mummy is in her own little happy world this evening.


Morning dawned. Grace had a headache. Izzy bounded up the stairs and leapt on top of her as she lay in bed trying to convince herself that she wasn't going to die.

'Hurry up, Mummy, we're going to put the Christmas tree up today.'

Did she usually shriek so loudly? Yes, probably. Just more noticeable today to Grace.

Charlie followed with a welcome cup of tea. 'Izzy! I told you not to disturb Mummy, she's having a lie-in.'

'But ...'

'How's your head?' he asked, putting the tea by her bed.

'Like an army band is marching around inside it, trying to find its way out,' breathed Grace, eyes closed.

'But I ...'

'Paracetamols?'

'Please.'

'But I th...'

'Here.'

This must have been the longest time ever that Izzy's demands had been kept at bay. But not for much longer. She tried a new tactic.

'M-u-u-mmy,' she said, sidling up to Grace and rolling her eyes pleadingly, despite Grace's eyes still being closed. 'Please can we put up the Christmas tree?'

'In a minute.'

Even Charlie didn't believe that one.

'But when you say "in a minute" it always means "no".'

One of Grace's eyelids flickered up, exposing half an eye, giving her a pained expression. 'It does not,' she said, sounding unconvincing even to herself.

'Take your paracetamols, you'll feel much better,' said Charlie, Miracle Man. 'Come down when you're ready.'

It was late afternoon before the tree was finally done. It stood in the corner of the living room, resplendent in all its glory.

'Wicked,' said Cleo. A compliment, apparently.

Grace loved it when they all put up the decorations together, it was a real family occasion. Even Grandma joined in. They put a second, much smaller tree in her room to keep her in the festive spirit – hopefully. Grace watched as Grandma decorated it herself. She could be infuriating at times but today she'd been on her best behaviour. Would all that change with Hugo's arrival? He was coming to spend Christmas with them and she hadn't even had the nerve to tell her mother yet. Maybe today was the day, while she was in such a good mood.

'Mother,' she started.

'When is Hugo coming?' asked Cleo. Could she read her mind?

'What?' said Grandma, astounded.

'I'll make some tea,' said Charlie the chicken.

'Hugo's coming here for Christmas,' said Zak (bless him). Maybe Zak was the correct choice of person to break the news – he was Gran's favourite, after all.

Silence reigned for several seconds.

'Did you hear me, Gran? I said Hugo's coming to spend Christmas with us.' Brave boy.

'I heard you,' she said, stuffing the top branch of her Christmas tree up the fairy with some considerable force.

'Hugo's your other grandson,' said Zak, going in where angels fear to tread.

The ground shook.

'I know who Hugo is,' stated the fairy impaler to her mesmerised audience, who had grown even paler.

She turned from her task to face them. 'What's the matter with you all?'

'N-nothing,' stammered Grace.

'Tea?' asked Charlie, entrance timed to perfection from his place in the hallway from whence he'd been listening outside the door. One little old lady. Why were they scared of her? He wasn't. He was a man. 'Tea?' he repeated. 'In the kitchen, no spills then.' Firmness itself.

'Bring it in here,' commanded the one who reigned supreme.

'Okay,' squeaked Charlie, bowing to her every need.

All in all it had been a good day. Grace loved times like this when all of the family were together. It didn't happen very often these days, everyone was usually out doing their own thing, and she knew it would happen even less as the children got older and moved away. She couldn't even begin to imagine what that would be like, not having her family around her. She'd still have Charlie though, the two lovebirds in their nest, free to fly together. Strange how her attitude had changed now. Only recently she'd been wanting to open her cage door and fly off to freedom and adventure alone. Now, with only just a little taste of it, she knew she wouldn't want to fly anywhere without her man.

She turned to watch him sleep, his mouth partially open, emitting little noises every time he breathed in, as his head lay on the pillow next to hers. She snuggled up to him, feeling an overwhelming sense of lust, snores or not. Under the bedclothes, her hand explored his body, slowly, sensuously … With a sudden intake of breath, Charlie's snoring ceased and was replaced by a groan of pleasure.

'Sorry to wake you,' she said, her hand pausing, her mouth dry, her body crying out for him.

'Uh … don't stop … and don't say sorry,' he gasped, his hand reaching out for her also, his fingers sliding easily into her more than ready flesh.

She gave a sudden gasp as his fingers hit the spot and moved rhythmically, creating a myriad of sensations that rippled through her body and left her floating on a sea of delight. From somewhere beyond, she heard a voice.

'Mummy.'

'What? Where …?' Grace battled, with a great deal of difficulty, against her imminent clitoral climax and struggled to open her eyes, still panting with the urgency of it all. Her eyes opened. And focused. Izzy.

'Izzy!' she gasped, clutching onto the bedclothes, unable to believe what she was seeing. How long had she been there?

'Mummy, what are you doing?'

'What?'

'You looked funny,' said a worried-looking Izzy.

'I was asleep, that's all. People do look funny sometimes when they're asleep,' said Grace breathlessly.

'But …'

'What are you doing here anyway?' interrupted Grace, whose head was in a whirl of confusion despite her body still being in meltdown. 'You're meant to be in your own bed.'

'I heard a funny noise.'

'What kind of a funny noise?' Grace hardly dared to ask.

'Woo-oo … like a ghost,' said a scared-looking Izzy.

Grace was mortified. She didn't usually … She hadn't realised … How loud had she …? 'I'm sure there isn't a ghost,' she said, knowing this full well to be true but still not convincing Izzy.

'Can I get into your bed?'

'I suppose,' sighed Grace, her body that of a lover, her head that of a mother.

Charlie groaned with frustration and turned on his side to make more space in the bed. Grace turned her back on him and shuffled along to make room for Izzy, her naked bottom coming into contact with Charlie's dampened ardour which twitched a rapturous welcome.

'Charlie!' warned Grace, shuffling away from him in disgust.

'Hardly my fault, is it?' he asked, deflated.

Izzy climbed into the bed and snuggled up to Grace. 'Pooh! You smell funny!' she said, clutching her nose.

'Izzy!' said Grace. 'I'm a bit sweaty, that's all. Now go to sleep.'

Izzy cuddled up next to her, stopped wriggling about and closed her eyes. Charlie turned over, his back to Grace, plumped up his pillows and settled down.

Okay, so that only left Grace still feeling frustrated then. Bit of a déjà vu, really. This was how she'd felt half an hour ago, before she'd woken up Charlie and set off the whole sequence of events. Ogghh! It could have been so much worse. What if Izzy had walked in on them five minutes later? Goodness knows what she would have seen. At least they'd been under the bedclothes, she couldn't have seen too much … could she? They really should be more careful. They'd talked about fitting a lock on the bedroom door before and they definitely must do so, this had taught them a lesson.

Grace squirmed about in discomfort, unable to settle down. Squashed in between two bodies, hot in more ways than one. Eventually, like music to her ears, the sound of snoring drifted in from both sides. Never had she thought she would welcome it so much.

'Charlie!' she whispered, turning and poking him in the ribs.

'Hallelujah!' he exclaimed, obviously not as asleep as she'd thought.

'Could you carry her back to bed, then? I'm a bit stuck in the middle.'

'Suppose,' he said, an aura of rejection still surrounding him.

'I'll make it worth your while,' she said temptingly.

'I'll be back,' he said, scooping up his daughter and returning her from whence she came.

Grace threw back the covers to cool herself down, legs splayed, touching herself, waiting for her man. She didn't have to wait for long and was more than ready on his return but …

'What if she comes back?' he asked, as obviously desperate for her as she was for him.

'Bathroom! Now!' she commanded, almost dragging him in and bolting the door.

'Ooh, I like you being masterful,' he said, pumping away, loving his Grace. 'We've never made love in here before.'

'I know,' she gasped. This had definitely been worth waiting for. 'It's good to be adventurous.'

She closed her eyes and arched her back, pleasure mounting inside her, rippling through her body, building, rising, lasting forever, until that explosion of orgasmic delight blew her mind and body and almost made her cry out again with the thrill of it all.

'Oh Gracie, I do love you,' gasped Charlie, coming within seconds of her. 'That was amazing.'

313

'At least we had privacy this time,' she smiled, almost too exhausted to speak.

Privacy? Maybe. But not for long. Someone tried the door handle.

'Anyone in there?'

Cleo.

'Yes. Me,' said Grace.

'Will you be long?'

'Um, no,' she said, giggling with Charlie.

But that didn't last long either.

'Could you hurry up, Mum? I'm pregnant, and when you need a wee, you need a wee. Can't wait any longer, you've been ages.'

Grace and Charlie looked themselves up and down in sudden realisation. They'd been so intent on rushing to the bathroom to ravish each other that the fact that they were completely naked had never entered their minds. Solution? Obviously there was only one.

Grace slid back the bolt and opened the door. 'Sorry to keep you waiting,' she said to Cleo as, starkers, they walked across the landing to the so-called privacy of their bedroom, cries of 'Oh my God, that is so gross! Old people – that's disgusting! How can I use the bathroom now? It needs fumigating!' ringing in their ears.

# 28

It was only two days before Christmas and Hugo's arrival was imminent. Richard had said he would go and meet him from the station and, when Grace had hinted that she would like to go too, Charlie had agreed that it would be a good idea. (Had he had a personality transplant? No, just more sex!)

Grace had been feeling quite guilty about Richard and was glad that she was going to be able to spend a little bit of time with him on her own, even though it was only a short distance to the railway station at Crewe. Since they'd come back from London they'd only had contact by phone. He seemed to have immersed himself completely in work, keeping busy to prevent any thoughts of his life as it might have been.

Richard was right on time as he drew up outside the house to collect her. She had a send-off fit for a queen from her family, who were waiting in eager anticipation to meet this new relative, about whom they had heard so much. She rushed up the drive to the waiting car and got in. She wanted to give Richard a hug – he did look in desperate need of one – but was aware of Charlie's eyes boring into her, and resisted.

'Hey,' she said, her warm smile melting his icy heart just a little. 'You're looking well.'

'Don't lie, Grace,' he said, even managing a little smile himself without his face cracking. 'I know you too well, you're just trying to make me feel better.'

'Sorry. Am I that transparent?'

'Sometimes, yes. But look, you've made me feel better already – I'm smiling,' he said, his face almost aching with the effort.

'You should have come round. I don't like you being on your own.'

'I know, but to be honest I've not felt much like playing happy families. It's just been a case of work, work, work – oh, and eat and sleep too, whenever I've been able. It's been all I could cope with. How've you been?' he asked, suddenly feeling selfish in his grief. After all, Grace had lost someone too.

'Ogghh! The trouble with me,' said Grace, 'is that life is so busy in our household that I really don't have time to grieve. Consequently, it just seems to wash over me at inopportune moments, great tidal waves of grief leaving me wailing like a banshee in the middle of the street, like the other day.'

'What happened?'

'Oh, I don't know,' said Grace, embarrassed now even to remember. 'I was out shopping, thought of Anna, burst into tears, tripped over some stupid woman's buggy and landed in a heap on the floor. Glad you find it so funny.'

'Sorry, it's just the vision …' he smiled, on the brink of the first laugh he'd had since Anna's death.

'Well it gets worse,' she said, smiling herself now, enjoying cheering him up. 'Along came Zak completely out of the blue, rescues me and my shopping, and escorts me to the nearest pub! You can imagine the state I was in by the time I got home.'

'Oh Grace, thanks for making me laugh again, I was beginning to think I never would. Maybe you're right, I have been spending too much time on my own.'

'Well now's the time to rectify that. Hugo's going to need some support in that madhouse of mine, he'll wonder where he's landed.'

'Richard! Auntie Grace!'

They heard his voice before they saw him as he rushed towards them from a different platform. They'd been so deep in conversation that they hadn't heard the announcement over the tannoy; it was always so muffled that it was easy to miss.

'Hugo!' shouted Grace, running to greet him. 'Sorry, I bet you thought we'd forgotten you.'

'Not a problem,' he said, hugging them both. 'I thought maybe you'd be waiting in the entrance but then I spotted you as I was about to go up the steps.'

He looked so young and vulnerable away from his own environment, much more so than he had in London. It seemed awkward between them as well, strained, with everyone on their best behaviour, overly polite. But it was bound to be difficult at first. They were related in the family sense, but relating to each other was a whole different thing. After all, they hardly knew each other, really; the only time spent together so far had been after Anna's death and at the funeral, when they'd had common ground. Now that was gone.

'Let me carry your case,' said Richard, wanting to feel useful.

'No, it's okay, thanks. Honestly, I can manage,' said Hugo, moving towards the steps.

Grace and Richard followed until they reached the top, then Grace moved to the other side of Hugo and linked her arm through his.

'I'm so glad you've come to spend Christmas with us,' she said, maybe a trifle overexcitedly, glancing up at him.

Was that a tear she saw on his face? She gave his arm an affectionate squeeze. Poor boy, he was grieving too. What an ordeal he must be going through, trying to come to terms with the loss of his mother after all he had already gone through in the past.

'They're here! They're here! They're here!' Izzy bounced up and down like a mad thing, unable to contain her excitement as she heard the car pull up the drive.

Alfie barked a rapturous welcome also, no idea to whom, but Izzy's enthusiasm was as infectious as chickenpox so he thought he should. Hang on a minute, did somebody mention chicken?

Charlie went to the door to let them in, Izzy clinging round him like a pear on a tree, suddenly shy – although probably not for long. Zak and Cleo hovered behind him, curious to see their new cousin.

Gran, amazingly enough, did not disappear to her room as she had with Anna's arrival, and as they'd expected she might. Instead, she decided to take a stance and mark her position as the head of this family. She remained firmly seated in the living room where she intended to study this young man, Hugh, or whatever his name was. After all, he was her husband's son and now, with the fortunate demise of that ... that disgrace, that almost made her his mother!

'Oh, quite a welcoming committee,' said Hugo, somewhat nervously, as he approached the open door and was met by a sea of unblinking eyes.

'For goodness sake! Move and let the poor lad in,' instructed Grace, sensitive to how he must be feeling.

Move? Alfie didn't need telling twice. He leapt all over Hugo, lavishing him lovingly with licks.

'Alfie! Get down!'

Huh, a dog just can't win.

'It's okay, Auntie Grace, I like dogs.'

Okay, maybe sometimes they can.

'You must be Izzy,' said Hugo, to the shy little pear that still dangled from the tree.

'Say "hello", Izzy,' said Charlie.

Uncharacteristically, Izzy lowered her head and whispered 'Hello' in such a quiet voice that they were all stunned.

'Make the most of it, Hugo,' joked Charlie, 'it won't last for long! I'm Charlie, by the way. Welcome to the madhouse,' he said, stepping aside to let Hugo in.

'God! It's like looking in the mirror!' said Zak, greeting his cousin. 'Your mum said we were alike.'

Cleo gave him a welcoming hug. 'So sorry about your mum,' she said, sensing his sorrow at the mention of her.

'Thanks,' he said gratefully. 'Shall I just put my case here?'

'Yes, leave it in the hall for now. We'll show you your room when you've had a chance to catch your breath.'

Wriggling free from Charlie's arms, Izzy wormed her way into Hugo's affections in an instant, as only Izzy could. Sidling up to him, she put her small hand into his much larger one and gazed up at him, eyes wide and angelic.

'I like you,' she announced, as though she'd been studying him intently for the past few minutes and had finally reached a conclusion. 'But you have a very funny name,' she said, wrinkling her nose with some distaste.

'Izzy!' said Grace, embarrassed by her outspoken daughter.

Hugo winked at her and smiled.

'What do you think I should be called?' he asked, turning his attention back to Izzy and seeming surprisingly at ease with her.

'Um ... Sam!' she said, enjoying this game.

'Do I look like a Sam?'

'No,' she giggled, hand over her mouth.

'What a-a-bout ... Bertie?' he asked, playfully.

'No!' she squealed, laughing at the thought.

'Perhaps I should just stay as a Hugo then, should I?'

'Okay,' agreed Izzy, friendship cemented, as she did a little dance of delight around him before taking his hand again. 'Hugo, come and see Grandma.'

The innocence of a child. To the others it felt as though their panic buttons had been pressed. This was the moment Hugo had been dreading. He didn't know how he was going to react. This was the woman who had sold him, taken money for herself. More importantly, the woman who was responsible for him being separated from his mother for more than half of his life, the woman who had banished her own child and then forced her to get rid of her baby.

He felt the colour drain from his face and wanted to bolt, but with Izzy's hand clasping firmly onto his own, other than making an absolute exhibition of himself there was no way but forward.

Cleo was overcome by the need to protect him, touching his elbow lightly at first, following, but then grasping his arm within her own two, hugging in to him. She glared at Gran as they approached, beaming warning signals eye to eye. The others advanced like the back-up squad, but felt they were in some kind of earthquake as the ground seemed to shake beneath their feet.

'This is Hugo,' said Izzy, unfazed.

'I'm quite aware who this is,' said Gran, beady eyes un-wavering. 'I only hope you never bring as much disgr…'

'Grandma!' reprimanded Zak, stepping forward with a timely interruption. And who better for the job? Bless him.

'You look like twins, you two!' said Gran, astonished by their similarity, sidetracked in her train of thought.

Zak smiled, issue averted. Hugo did not. How could he?

Cleo squeezed his arm. 'Come and sit down, you must be exhausted.'

'Tea anyone?' asked Charlie, in his usual problem-solving way.

Richard decided to make a quiet exit. He'd been quiet altogether since Hugo's arrival today and, in the family chaos, it took a while before anyone realised that he'd gone. He sat in the car for a while, brooding, not wanting to go home but not wanting to stay here either. Perhaps a pub would be a better option, out of town where nobody knew him. He could sit in a corner somewhere, be anonymous. Life viewed through the bottom of a pint pot never looked so bad – not usually anyway.

He started the engine, glancing nervously at the house, expecting to be heard and not wanting to be. He needed to spend some time on his own. Amazingly they didn't notice. Curtains remained untwitched, doors closed. He turned the wheel, the car seemingly on autopilot, driving out towards Middlewich, driving anywhere but here. He turned on the radio, Cheshire FM, Duffy, 'Warwick Avenue'. Did they not know that was her favourite song? It was Anna's voice that he heard singing those words, not Duffy's, echoing around inside his head as tears trickled down his face unchecked.

He drove out through Middlewich, along the side of the canal, passing narrowboats moored along the bank. Passing happy families, dog walkers, shoppers returning home. If only they'd had more time together …

His phone vibrated in his pocket, he'd been missed. Should he stop and answer, or just drive on, escape to the bottom of a pint pot in some faceless pub like he'd promised himself? There it went again. Coming into Elworth he stopped outside the pub and looked at his phone. Three missed calls. Zak.

'Hi,' he said, phoning back. No point in worrying them. No point in making their lives miserable just because he felt so depressed. Grace, Hugo – they were coping. He had to too.

'Dad? Where are you?'

'Just had to get away, sorry. Looking for a pub to drown my sorrows in if you must know. Don't fancy joining me, do you? Although I don't want to drag you away from the big family reunion,' he said, realising he was being a bit selfish.

'Nah, they won't miss me, there's enough going on here. Pick me up in about ten minutes?'

'Fantastic,' said Richard, feeling decidedly happier. He still had his kids, whatever.

After a long drawn-out afternoon and evening of stilted conversations, Cleo and Hugo were left alone together. It had been difficult, due entirely of course to the foreboding presence of Grandma. There was, understandably, an enormous amount of tension between Hugo and Gran, and everyone around them seemed to be walking on eggshells to keep it at bay.

But finally Grandma hobbled off to her room, exhausted by the day's events. Shortly afterwards, Grace went to get Izzy ready for bed and Charlie took an overexcited Alfie for a long walk to get rid of some of his excessive doggy energy.

'I apologise for my family,' said Cleo, embarrassed by their behaviour.

'What d'you mean?' asked Hugo, smiling knowingly.

'Well, Gran mostly. But Dad and Zak both going out, Izzy being a motormouth, Charlie scared there was going to be a confrontation, and Mum … Well, Mum trying to keep the peace, like always.'

'She's okay, your Mum. Well, everyone is, except Gran. Don't know that I can ever forgive her.'

Cleo looked at him anxiously.

'Don't worry, I'm not here to cause trouble. Anyway, they're my family too now, no escape,' he said, smiling at her, feeling a bond between them already.'

'Sorry, I keep forgetting! It's kinda weird, isn't it?'

'Tell me about it,' he said, shaking his head in bewilderment.

Morning dawned quite late for Cleo. She'd sat up until the

early hours talking to Hugo. It was so good to have him here, good to have someone who would listen to her. He reminded her of Auntie Anna, his mum, in a lot of ways and he'd seemed pleased when she'd told him that. He treated her as an adult, as Auntie Anna had, really listened to what she had to say instead of still treating her like a kid as everyone else around here seemed to do.

'*Christmas Eve is here, And we go off to bed, As we climb the stair, Nod each sleepy head,*' sang Grace and Izzy together, as they filled pastry cases with teaspoonfuls of mincemeat from the open jar.

'Christmas Eve already? Oh yes, I suppose it is,' said Cleo, sounding totally disinterested.

'Seen the Rice Krispies?'

'There. Use your eyes,' said a flour-flustered Grace. 'How could you have forgotten it's Christmas Eve?'

'Father Christmas is coming tonight 'cos I've been a good girl, but you haven't.'

'I'm always good.'

'Mrs Clarke says you're very naughty.'

'Pea-brain.'

'Pea-brain, pea-brain, Cleo is a …'

'Izzy! I thought we were singing Christmas songs: *Take our stockings off, Hang them in a row …*'

Cleo could stand it no more and retreated to the garden, despite the cold, taking her bowl of Rice Krispies with her. Zak and Hugo were out there kicking a football around, Alfie dashing dementedly from one to the other aiming to transform himself into Wayne Rooney.

'Fancy coming to the pub with us in a bit?' asked Zak.

'Der! Not old enough, am I?'

'Nobody's gonna say anything, you'll be with us. And you're not gonna be drinking anyway.'

'S'pose.'

'Go put your slap on then. Give you five minutes.'

Cleo dashed back through the jolly festive spirit of the kitchen.

'Where are you off to?' queried Grace.

'The pub,' said Cleo, waiting for the reaction.

It came.

'Cleo! You can't go to the pub! You're not old enough!'

'Mum! Stop treating me like a baby. I'll be sixteen soon, I'll be with Hugo – is he old enough for you? I'm not going to be drinking alcohol anyway, am I? Not when I'm pregnant.'

Cleo sat in the pub, still fuming about her mother.

'She just wants to keep me as her little girl, that's her problem. Well she needs to get it into her head I'm an adult now. I'm having a baby of my own, for God's sake, how's she gonna react then?'

'Like she always does, I reckon,' said Zak, sipping his drink – a Coke actually, Hugo had insisted. 'Add it to her brood, another one to worry about.'

'Yeah, but it won't be,' spluttered Cleo, getting angrier by the minute. 'That's my whole point. This is my baby and I'll want to look after it my way.' She was surprising even herself by how maternal she was feeling all of a sudden. How protective she was feeling towards her unborn child.

'Watch this space,' said Zak, knowingly.

'Well I think Auntie Grace is fantastic. Don't know what you've got to complain about – honestly.'

'Sorry, Hugo, that was a bit tactless,' said Cleo. 'I didn't mean to …'

'It's okay. I need the Gents anyway,' said Hugo. 'Any idea where it is?'

'Follow me, I'm going too. Sorry sis, back in a minute.'

These were turbulent times for Cleo, her emotions were all over the place. Mum had been fantastic in the way she'd accepted the news of the pregnancy and in the way she'd supported her, but she really did have to stop all this molly-coddling and let her grow up. Cleo felt as though, if she didn't take a firm stance on this now, she'd have no say in anything once the baby arrived.

So deep in thought was she, in fact, that she failed to notice who'd taken occupation of the seat next to hers.

'Can we talk?'

It was the voice of the sleazeball himself.

'Talk to *you*?' reacted Cleo, turning to look down her nose at him with disgust.

'Aw Cleo, c'mon. I really like you, you know I do,' he said, his eyes unable to resist moving down from her face to …
'Fuckin' hell!' he exclaimed, reducing any chance he might have had down from zero to minus ten zillion. 'Look at the size of your baps now!'

It took all of Cleo's self-control not to slap him across the face there and then. The only thing that stopped her was the thought of being ejected from the pub and sent home to mummy – like the naughty kid mummy expected her to be.

'Lay off, Pete,' retorted Cleo, haughtily.

'Rather lay on, if it's all the same to you,' he said, eyes unwavering, hands itching for a quick grope, mouth drooling at the prospect.

'He bothering you?' asked Hugo, returning and sussing the situation.

But Pete was in his own fantasy world, didn't hear a thing. In fact, in his mind, he had two massive handfuls already, his head buried in-between – maybe that's why he couldn't hear. Reluctantly, he had to let go to adjust himself before there was a massive break-out in the skinny jeans depart-ment; this zip wasn't great.

'C'mon, Cleo. Come down the park. You can see what you do to me – feel this,' he said, rubbing himself, expect-ing her to look impressed. 'The baby bump doesn't bother me, quite a turn-on if you must know, bet not many blokes would say that.' She must be gagging for it by now.

She gave Hugo a conspiratorial glance. 'You met my boyfriend?' she asked.

Pete turned to follow her glance, and suddenly shrank beyond recognition in more ways than one. Hugo, in comparison, breathed in and stood tall, growing beyond recognition in all ways *but* one. But Pete *did* have a brain cell, or maybe even two. He left. Quickly.

# 29

Christmas Day and all was tranquil … What?

The day did start off quite peacefully, it has to be said, apart from the fact that a hurricane swept through the house at 6 a.m. But then, Izzy was Izzy, what more could they expect?

'It's Christmas Day! Wakey, wakey!' she informed the world and its dog, skipping around the house, in and out of everyone's rooms, oblivious to sleeping bodies and hang-overs.

Alfie joined in the fun, bounding in to see Grace, giving her face its first wash of the day.

'Ogghh!' she groaned, pushing him away, forcing her eyes to open. 'Izzy! He needs to go outside first before he can come up here, he's dribbling all over the carpet.'

'But it's Christmas Day,' said Izzy, smile turning down at the edges.

'That doesn't stop dogs from needing a wee, or anybody else for that matter,' she said, her own bladder beckoning her to the bathroom.

Izzy was back by the time she returned. 'Hugo's let him out,' she said, smile upturned once more.

'He's up already?' questioned Grace.

'I woke him first. He's in the kitchen with Grandma.'

The words 'Ding-dong merrily on high' or just plain 'ding-dong', galloped into Grace's head and she rushed downstairs in her dressing gown with a distinct sense of foreboding. Amazingly, however, 'Peace on earth, goodwill to all men' seemed to have taken up residence in the kitchen. Sort of, anyway.

'Hugh is making me a nice cup of tea,' said Grandma. Was that a smile, or a flicker of one?

'Hugo,' corrected Hugo, squeezing the teabag with considerable force.

'Me go where, dear?' asked Gran, puzzled.

'No, not "you go", Hugo. My name's Hugo,' he said, stirring the cup and bringing it over to her.

'Well I know that, dear, but I still don't understand where you want me to go.'

Frustration, thy name is Grandma.

'But ...'

Just drop it Hugo (the subject, not the cup!) and save yourself the stress.

Izzy, for once in her young life, chose an opportune moment to bounce in through the door.

'Come into the living room, everybody's downstairs now. We're ready to open our presents!'

'We can't yet, Uncle Richard's not here,' said Grace, sorry for having to pre-empt her daughter yet again.

'He is, he is!' said Izzy, bouncing up and down impatiently. 'Zak rang him up and he'll be here in one minute – come on!'

With the family gathered around the living room, gleefully unwrapping their gifts with shrieks of delight as presents were marvelled over and paper discarded, it would have been easy to forget about the one person who should have been with them this year, the missing link – Anna. Not so easy for Hugo and Richard, though. They thought about her constantly. Hugo was remembering Christmases past, the fun they'd had together. Richard caught his eye and gave him a wink of moral support, understanding what he must be going through. Hugo gave him a half-smile in return, appreciative, knowing how much Richard had loved his mum, how much he must be missing her too.

Nevertheless, they did their best to enter into the spirit of things, and with Izzy around it was hard not to. It would probably take her the entire day to open all of her presents; she stopped to play with each one of them for a while before moving on to the next.

'Uncle Richard, please can you show me how to do this?' she asked, for the umpteenth time.

'You can say "no", you know, when you've had enough,' said Grace to him, feeling guilty. 'Go and ask someone else, Izzy, give Uncle Richard a rest.'

'But I love Uncle Richard,' said Izzy, determined in her choice.

'It's okay, Izzy, bring it over here,' said Richard. 'It's good to be loved,' he said to Grace.

That was the first time Grace had even thought about Anna today, which made her feel even more guilty. She excused herself and went into the kitchen to make a start on dinner. Poor Anna, it would have been so good to have her here with them today. No wonder Hugo and Richard were quiet. Tears blurred her vision as she tried to check on the turkey which she'd put into the oven earlier.

'Ow!' she cried, jumping back as she caught her hand on the hot oven door.

'Here, let me do that,' said Charlie, coming to her rescue, putting the foil back over the turkey. 'Run your hand under the cold tap … What's the matter?' he asked, suddenly aware of her sadness.

'Anna. It just comes over me sometimes,' she said tearfully, drying her eyes.

'Bound to,' he said. 'Here, you go and sit down, I'll do the veg.'

'Aww Charlie, you're so good to me. No, I'm fine now, honestly. Let's do them together.'

'Want any help?' asked Cleo, drifting in.

Now there's a first!

'Have you had any breakfast this morning, young lady?'

Wrong reaction.

'Mum! Stop fussing over me. I've had some chocolates haven't I?'

'Chocolates? That's not what you should be eating for breakfast! You've got a baby growing inside you, you need a substantial meal!'

'*Grrr!*' exploded Cleo. 'Just leave me alone!' she said, stomping up to her bedroom and slamming the door with a resounding thud.

Haven't we been here before?

'Nice one, Grace,' said Charlie.

A criticism from Charlie? It must be bad.

The rest of the Christmas holiday followed in a similar vein, tension mounting all the time between Grace and Cleo. It was disappointing to Charlie as they had been getting on so well and there was nothing he liked more than a peaceful existence. He could understand Grace in a way, he supposed: Cleo was pregnant and she had to take care of herself. But at the same time, Grace had to let her grow up and take some responsibility for herself. He didn't know what on earth Hugo must think of them, he must feel as though he'd stepped into a war zone at times. But at least Hugo was a sensible lad and seemed to have a calming influence on Cleo when she wouldn't listen to anyone else.

Cleo and Hugo had certainly formed a special bond. It was unusual for Hugo, as he didn't form friendships easily. A matter of trust, probably, after all that had happened to him in the past. There was a big difference in their ages, Cleo still being a tantrum-torn teenager at times, much to Hugo's amusement but in spite of that they seemed to complement each other. Cleo reminded him of his mother in many ways, which is probably why he had felt so drawn towards her. It was strange how Cleo's life seemed to be echoing Anna's – pregnant at sixteen, as she had been with him. At least, in this case, mother and child would not be forcibly parted. Maybe it was for this very reason that Hugo had already begun to feel quite protective towards Cleo. He didn't want her to have to struggle through life as his mother had done. Obviously it was different for Cleo, she had her family around to support her, but that in itself could bring problems of its own. Sixteen. What an age to take on the responsibility of a baby, and Cleo wasn't even quite sixteen yet, not for another couple of weeks.

Looking at Cleo, Hugo tried to picture his mum at that age, pregnant with him, dumped with relatives she didn't really know, panicking about giving birth and having her baby taken away, wondering what was to become of her. However had she coped? Dumped in London, her baby gone, no one to turn to, no means of support – and only sixteen. He'd known the full story for a long time now, but somehow seeing Cleo pregnant at the same age made it seem more real to him.

Sitting next to him, Cleo sensed the tension, and his sadness. 'You okay?' she asked, giving his hand a comforting squeeze.

'Not really, no,' he said, tears welling despite not wanting to make an idiot of himself.

'Let's go for a walk,' she said, full of understanding. That's why he liked her so.

'Where are they going?' questioned Gran.

'For a walk,' said Grace.

'Together?' asked Gran, registering suspicion.

As they walked through the park, Hugo remained quiet and thoughtful.

'It is alright to cry, you know,' said Cleo.

'Not in front of a roomful of recently acquired relatives it isn't,' Hugo replied with a watery smile.

'Oh don't be daft, that's just a man thing. Everybody understands; you've just lost your mother, for God's sake.'

'I know. It was looking at you, pregnant like she was, thinking how it must have been for her … sorry,' he said, wiping his eyes on the back of his hand.

'Hey, you've got nothing to say sorry for. Here, have a tissue, it's clean,' she said, smiling as she passed it to him.

'Thanks.'

They walked on in silence for a while until Cleo saw a group of girls from her school year walking towards them.

'Shit. That's all I need.'

'What?'

'Don't say anything. Just keep walking,' said Cleo, head down.

'Ooh, look girls, if it isn't the slag!'

'Up the duff and still managin' to pull, eh?'

'Bit old, though.'

'How much is he payin' yer?' they shouted, seeming to find the whole thing hysterical, running away down the path in fits of laughter.

'Has this happened to you before?' he asked, understandably concerned.

'Only every time I step outside,' said Cleo, embarrassed by the whole thing.

'You should have let me say something.'

'That just makes it worse.'

Cleo left his side and walked over to the swings, the place she always went to when she was troubled. She sat down on one, sideways, holding on to one chain with both hands, her head leant back against the other. Hugo followed, sitting down gingerly on the swing next to hers.

'It's been a while since I sat on one of these things,' he smiled, looking at her for a response.

None was forthcoming.

'Why are they like that?' he asked, really not understanding at all.

'Small-town mentality. They don't like anyone who dares to be different,' she said, her face blank, staring into the distance.

'But surely you're not being *that* different. Lots of teenage girls end up getting pregnant these days.'

'Not amongst my mates they don't. Or *ex*-mates, anyway.'

Grace tried to concentrate on the crossword in the Sunday paper but it was to no avail. There was a niggle of concern that persisted in wriggling around inside her head, making it difficult to concentrate. Twenty-five across: 'An extensive grassy plain usually without trees'. Six letters. She chewed the end of her pencil thoughtfully. Maybe it was just her imagination running riot, but nevertheless ...

'Charlie?'

But Charlie was lost on a grassy plain of his own. 'Come on ref, for goodness sake! That was a foul! Surely even you must have seen that?'

Why do men do that? Shout at the television as though the people on it can hear.

'Charlie!'

'Mm? Ogghh!' he gasped, throwing his arms and legs up into the air in exasperation. 'What?' he asked, sensing her eyes boring into him.

'I'm worried about Cleo.'

'Huh! Tell me something I don't know.'

'Charlie! I'm being serious.'

'That's it Ferdinand. Get it! Get it! Go, go, go ... ogghh!'

Man U were 1:0 down and Charlie was not happy.

'I think she's getting ...'

'Could this not wait until the end of the match? It goes off in five minutes.'

'I suppose.' She was obviously not going to get anywhere until then.

Grassy plain, she thought, staring blankly at the football pitch and yet another spitting player. No wonder the grass is so green.

'Yes! Come on ... come on ... *Yeay!*' yelled Charlie, leaping to his feet as Rooney scored the equaliser just as the final whistle blew. 'Phew!' Charlie fell back down onto the sofa, exhausted. 'That was a good match.'

'Apparently so. Looks like you played it yourself.'

Charlie smiled, noticing her at last. 'Did you want something?'

'Mm, yes I did actually. I wanted to talk to you about Hugo and Cleo.'

'What about them?' he asked, turning off the television with the remote, bringing his head back to the real world.

'I'm just worried they might be getting a bit too close.'

'Too close? How d'you mean?'

'Well use your imagination, Charlie,' she snapped, somewhat sarcastically. 'Close as in girl–boy. Sex even.'

'But she's not even sixteen yet, she's pregnant, and they're cousins or whatever!'

'Precisely.'

New Year's Eve. Zak was off to a party of course. He asked both Cleo and Hugo to go with him. Cleo declined – she didn't want to go out anywhere, she was afraid of people's reactions. Hugo declined, full stop. Now why would a young man like Hugo prefer to stay in with a sixteen-year-old girl and her parents on New Year's Eve, rather than going out to a party with his fun-loving cousin? Grace had asked herself that question a hundred times. She really only needed to have asked it once. The answer was always the same.

It was an evening of innocent fun. They played Trivial Pursuit, Articulate, watched *Mamma Mia*, even had a sing.

And then the clock struck twelve.

'Happy New Year, everybody!'

Charlie took Grace in his arms to kiss her, but her mind was elsewhere, one eye open, peering suspiciously over his shoulder. Miss Marple? Jessica Fletcher? They had nothing on her. How would they kiss, Cleo and Hugo? With passion? A snog? But no. Surprisingly, a chaste hug and a peck on the cheek. Suspicions unfounded? Grace felt mildly disappointed. She'd been about to confront them but now she'd just have to wait. A cover-up, obviously.

And so she waited … and waited. Two days, to be precise. Cleo's tutor was back, full of post-Christmas enthusiasm as well as turkey. They were working on Seamus Heaney in the living room. Grace had suggested to Charlie that he might like to take this opportunity to have a word with Hugo. But Charlie turkey-trotted out of the door in a state of utter chicken-ness to take Alfie for a walk. Down to Grace, then.

How to broach the subject? Not an easy one, that. But he was going back to London tomorrow, so it was now or never. 'Never' sounded like quite a good option at this precise moment. Grace gave herself a little shake and mustered her courage. It had to be done and she was the one for the job … and he was coming down the stairs!

'Hi,' her voice sounded as if she was on helium. She felt more in need of valium.

'Something wrong?'

Huh! Straight for the jugular. She'd been vain enough to think he wouldn't notice.

'No. Why?'

Seize the moment Grace, for goodness sake.

'You've got that same look Mum used to have when I'd done something she didn't approve of.'

Absolutely no going back now.

'Okay, you're right. I *am* worried about something. Sit down for a minute.'

'This sounds serious,' he said, coming to join her at the kitchen table, an anxious look on his face. He wasn't aware that he'd done anything wrong, but something had obviously upset her.

'You seem to be getting on really well with Cleo.'

'Yeah, we've been a support for each other. We've both had our problems just lately and it's been helpful to have someone to talk to. She's a good kid.'

'But you do remember that's all she is?'

'What?'

'A kid. She's not even quite sixteen yet and, not only that, she's your cousin – doubly related, in fact.'

'I know that, but … ohhh!' he gasped, in sudden realisation of what she was meaning. 'Oh Auntie Grace! No! You thought we were getting together? There's no way!'

'You're sure about this?'

'Never been more sure about anything in my life! Honestly, we've just been talking. She's really cut up about her mates at the moment, the way they've all turned on her, and she's so lonely, not mixing with anybody at all.'

'Until you came along – her knight in shining armour.'

'Auntie Grace, you have to believe me. I would never, ever do anything to her. It'd be … I don't know … incestuous, paedophilic, following the same path as my grandfather, almost.'

'Which is what worries me, I suppose, if I'm honest.'

'Oh Auntie Grace,' he said, disheartened by the fact that she could have thought so little of him.

'I'm sorry, I shouldn't have said that,' she said, ashamed of herself for having done so. 'I had to know the truth with absolute certainty but I should have gone about it a little more tactfully. I hope you'll forgive me.'

'Of course I will. You had to know.'

'If you don't mind my asking, what do you get from this friendship? Cleo is so much younger.'

'But she's got a wise head on her shoulders. It's helped me a lot, being able to talk to her – not just about Mum but about other stuff as well, things I've never been able to talk to *anyone* about. She actually reminds me so much of Mum, though, she really does.'

'I know what you mean. Your mum even remarked on it. Kindred spirits.'

'Weird, isn't it, to think that we'll never see her again? I keep thinking she's at home and she'll be waiting for me coming back and then ...' grief overflowed as he covered his face with his hands, his shoulders shaking with emotion.

Grace moved from her seat to cradle him in her arms.

'Sorry,' he said, never wanting anyone to see him like this.

'Hugo, it is okay to cry, you know.'

'That's exactly what Cleo says,' he said, attempting a smile through his tears. 'I told you she was wise.'

'Do you really have to go home tomorrow? Couldn't you stay for a bit longer?' asked Grace, becoming filled with a new-found respect for this troubled young man, wanting to help him, take him under her wing, all the things she did best.

'Thanks, but I honestly can't, I have to get back. There's work and there's ... well, there are people expecting me,' he said, caught off-guard for a moment. He looked pale.

'Are you okay?' Grace asked, feeling something was not quite right.

'Mm,' he said, a faraway look on his face. He paused for a while, lost in his thoughts, but then, looking her straight in the eye he said, 'Auntie Grace, there is another very valid reason why I would never become involved with Cleo, but it's a secret and it has to remain that way. You have to trust me on that one, okay?'

Weirdly, Anna's voice seemed to echo inside her head.

'I can never have another relationship,' she'd said. So hauntingly similar.

'You're not ill too, are you?' Grace asked, unable to contain herself.

'What?'

'Like your mother. She said she could never have a relationship and would never tell me why, then it turned out that it was because she had cancer and knew she was dying.'

'No, no, sorry. I didn't mean to freak you out. It's nothing for you to worry about at all. Just something I can't talk about, never did, even to Mum. But believe me, I could never become involved with Cleo, she's perfectly safe with me.'

# 30

They were all sad to see Hugo go – even Gran, amazingly – but it was Cleo, understandably, who missed him most of all. She tried to throw all her energy into her studies but somehow her heart wasn't in it. The exams would come around really quickly after the baby was born and she knew she should be cramming in extra work towards them now while she had the chance but she couldn't seem to work up any enthusiasm whatsoever. It didn't help that she seemed to be getting bigger and bigger with every passing day, reminding herself almost of Mr Greedy from Izzy's Mr Men books ... or the snake in Charlie's natural history DVD that swallows something live and whole and ... yuk!

It was hard to think of herself with a baby, even harder to imagine giving birth to it. What a horrendous thought! Laid on a bed with your legs splayed everywhere, complete strangers gawping at your bits. She was dreading it, all that pain. Mum would be in her element, taking charge – she could picture it now. How on earth had she got herself into this mess? Trouble was, there was no going back now. The baby was well and truly in there and, unfortunately, there was only one way out.

'Cleo?' Mum.

'What?'

'D'you want to come with me to collect Izzy?' asked Grace, coming into Cleo's room.

'Wuppy doo, best offer I've had all day,' replied Cleo sarcastically. The sad thing was ... it was.

'Thought a walk might do you good. You've been cooped up in here for ages.'

'Well I've got work to do, haven't I? Exams this year, as you keep reminding me.'

'A break'll do you good. Come on, it's a lovely day.'

'Glad you think so.' Cleo buried her head in *To Kill A Mockingbird* to try and make herself feel less like killing someone else. 'Thanks, but no thanks. I've got stuff to do.'

When it came to trying to cheer Cleo up, Grace was definitely persistent. 'It's your birthday next week, do you want to do anything special?'

'What, like go skydiving maybe? Or ice-skating, how about that? Get real, Mother.'

'I was thinking more of a party maybe. We could invite …'

'You keep forgetting, I'm Billy-no-mates now. Who were you thinking of inviting?'

'Well, there's us for a start.'

'Great party, eh?'

'And Lisa and Cassie …'

'Forget it, Mum, not a chance.'

'So what do you want to do?'

'Nothing. It's not worth it. Could I not just have the money instead?'

'If that's what you want.'

'It is.'

Zak was on his way home from college when he bumped into Pete.

'Hey up.'

'How's it goin'?'

'Not bad. How's yer sister?'

'Okay.'

'Still with that bloke?'

'What bloke?'

'Boyfriend. She introduced us in the pub the other week … whatsisname.'

'Oh, Hugo. No, he's not her boyfriend, he's our cousin.'

'But she said …  Oh, right,' said Pete the ever hopeful.

Cleo was in the kitchen with Gran when Zak got home.

'Ah, here he is, bless him. Just in time to make his old gran a nice cup of tea.'

'I asked you if you wanted one, Gran,' said Cleo.

'Yes, but you don't make it as nice as Zak does,' said Gran, beady eyes beaming adoration on the blessed one.

Cleo tried not to feel hurt. She should be used to it by now: Zak had always been Gran's favourite. She moved around the kitchen tidying things up a bit before Mum got back.

Gran's beady eyes transferred their attention to Cleo. 'Just look at the state of you! The length of that skirt's disgusting, especially for somebody in your condition. We'll be able to have a conversation with the baby if it gets any shorter!'

'Gran!' said Zak, springing to his sister's defence. 'Don't be so rude!'

'If anyone's being rude it's her,' said Gran, indicating Cleo with a nod of her head. 'Go and cover yourself up, for goodness sake! She gets more like that disgrace every day, she does.'

Cleo put on her coat and went for a walk. She just had to get out of the house, she couldn't stand it any more. Head down and rushing along the road, who should she bump into? Mum. Great.

'Hey, where are you off to in such a hurry?'

'Just for a walk, that's all. You keep telling me to get some fresh air.'

'Want some company? I'll come with you if you like.'

'No.'

'Suit yourself. Have you been crying?'

'No.'

'You okay?'

'Yup.'

'Okay. See you later then.'

'See ya.'

As usual, in times of stress, Cleo headed for the park and took a seat on what she'd come to think of as 'her swing'. Please don't let anyone from school walk past and see me today, I can't take any more of their name-calling. She rocked back and forth, drawing some comfort from the motion, but feeling very alone. She just couldn't see a future, somehow. What would it take to find friends again? Was she doomed to be alone forever? Would nobody ever like her again? As for lads … she'd blown that one big time.

Grace just could not get to sleep. She lay in bed staring at the ceiling, wishing morning would come. Nights like this were horrible, worries going round inside your head and keeping you awake, but not daring to move for fear of waking anyone. She would have gone downstairs otherwise, and done the ironing or something. At least when you were busy it took your mind off things – a bit, anyway. The ticking of the clock and Charlie's rhythmic snoring were like torture. She tried to lie still but had twitchy legs on top of everything else.

She was worried mostly about Cleo. She'd seemed to be coping really well before Christmas – trying hard with her schoolwork, facing up to how her future would be. She'd seemed a happier person altogether, in fact; a nicer, calmer person, getting on so much better with them all, being a pleasure to live with. Grace had felt so close to her again, like in times past. But now it all seemed to be changing.

The secretive Cleo was back – grumpy, not wanting to talk, shutting herself in her room.

It was understandable, Grace supposed. It must be so difficult for her not having any friends she could talk to or hang around with. It was terrible the way they all just seemed to have abandoned her simply because she was pregnant. Would things change after the baby was born? Probably not. But at least once her exams were over Cleo could get a job and, hopefully, go on to college or uni while they looked after the baby for her. Ooh, she was really excited and looking forward to there being another baby in the house to care for. It'd almost be like having her own, a little brother or sister for Izzy!

She had visions of pushing it along in its pram, Izzy walking proudly by the side holding onto the handle. Complete strangers coming up to them to admire their angelic sleeping baby, saying they'd never seen one more beautiful, as people always do. She couldn't wait! Cleo wouldn't have to worry about anything at all, she'd be able to get on with her own life and leave her mum to take care of the baby. She'd be so much happier then, sixteen was no age at all to be tied down with a baby.

In the meantime, Grace had to think of something that would cheer Cleo up now. All this stroppiness she had reverted to would be doing the baby no good at all. What if she were to have a word with Cassie and Lisa herself? They seemed like such nice girls and they'd all been best friends for a long time. This had probably been a simple misunderstanding, blown up out of all proportion. After all, Grace knew what teenage girls could be like, bitching at each other one minute and best of friends the next. It seemed like the perfect solution. She wouldn't go round to their houses, that would be too embarrassing, but the next time she met them in the street … She'd warn them not to tell Cleo, of course.

After such a restless night, Grace overslept. 'Why didn't you wake me, Charlie?'

'You looked so peaceful.'

'That's beside the point, I've got to take Izzy.'

'Don't panic, I've got her ready and Cleo says she'll take her this morning.'

'But …'

'No buts. Turn over and go back to sleep. I only wish I could get back in there with you.'

'Mm. Me too,' she said, beginning to relax again. 'You're too good to me Charlie,' she said, holding out her arms to him for a hug.

Tempted, fully clothed and late for work already, he crawled onto the bed on top of her. 'This is cruel,' he said, kissing her longingly.

'Daddy!' shouted Izzy, as she bounced round the bedroom door to say goodbye. 'You're squashing Mummy, stop it!'

Back to reality. Charlie moved aside and stood up with a heartfelt groan. 'Just kissing her goodbye, that's all.'

'You're too big,' said Izzy, pushing him.

'In more ways than one,' he said, winking at Grace as he reluctantly left for work.

''Bye Mummy, see you later,' said Izzy, kissing her before running back down to Cleo.

Mrs Clarke was surprised to see Izzy arrive on time for once. 'Not with Mummy today?'

'No, Mummy's still in bed.'

'And Daddy?'

'He was on top of her.'

Mrs Clarke cleared her throat nervously. 'Um, let's go over to the drawing table Izzy.'

What more could she say? This poor child, it was amazing how she seemed so relatively normal when she came from a family of such immoral standing. One only had to look at

344

the sister for a start, pregnant at such a young age. They didn't stand a chance in life. Drugs, teenage pregnancy, mother up to all kinds of loose behaviour … what a household to grow up in! And there was little Izzy, so sweet and innocent. It just made one feel so protective towards her, wanting to save her from the den of iniquity she had to live in. Of course, this was the reason she herself had gone into teaching in the first place. In this troubled world if you can bring hope to the occasional person, help them along the path of righteousness …

'Izzy, what are you drawing?' she asked, coming back over to the table to talk to her. Poor child, she probably never gets any attention at home.

'It's Cleo and Hugo,' said Izzy, sitting back proudly so Mrs Clarke could see more clearly. 'They're kissing,' said Izzy, covering her mouth with her hand as she giggled, eyes alight with mischief.

'Is Hugo Cleo's boyfriend?' asked Mrs Clarke, a question borne of a certain amount of morbid curiosity.

She wasn't disappointed.

'No, he's our cousin,' said Izzy, glaring at Mrs Clarke as if she was stupid.

Izzy continued with her colouring-in, her tongue sticking out of the side of her mouth in concentration. Mrs Clarke stood and watched, her feet stuck to the floor in horror. This just got better and better.

'Mrs Clarke?'

'Yes, darling?' She'd do whatever it took to help this poor child.

'How does the baby get out of Cleo's tummy?' asked Izzy, still colouring. And with a crayon the same shade of red as Mrs Clarke's face, strangely enough.

'Erm … well … erm …'

'Because,' Izzy interrupted, 'if the baby comes out of Cleo's mouth when they're kissing then it will go into

Hugo's mouth. Then he will swallow it and have a fat tummy instead! That's funny, isn't it?' she giggled.

Hysterical, Mrs Clarke. Don't you think?

# 31

Winter passed. Spring bloomed. So did Cleo. She'd never expected to look this fat; it was gross. Remember skinny jeans? Would she ever get there again? No wonder she hadn't had any friends to party with and her sixteenth birthday had been the non-event of the year. Who'd want to be friends with a big fat blob? She viewed herself sideways in the bedroom mirror, feeling her baby as it moved inside her, its foot kicking as if it was trying to get out.

'Hey, not time for you yet,' she said to it, stroking her stomach gently. 'Another three weeks, be patient.'

At least she could talk to the baby. It seemed to be the only person she could talk to just lately, her only friend. Zak was okay but he had his own life, he didn't want his elephantine sister hanging round with him all the time. She had gone out with him last night but she'd just felt in the way, all his mates staring at her as if she was some kind of freak. Well, she was, as another look at herself in the mirror confirmed.

One person she could always rely on was Hugo. He phoned her regularly and always managed to boost her spirits. She helped him too of course. Cleo was the only person he'd ever confided in. Not intentionally, he'd never meant to tell anyone, but one day over Christmas when they'd been exchanging confidences as well as gifts, he'd broken down and told her the truth about himself and his life. This was probably what had drawn them so much closer together.

'Cleo?'

Grrr. Mum again.

'Can I come in?'

'Yup.'

'Oh,' said Grace, looking around for evidence and finding none. 'I thought you were revising.'

Was that a question or a statement?

'Nope.'

'Cleo, the baby's due in three weeks, you won't have much time for revising after that. Get on with it while you've got the chance! Exams are only nine weeks away, they'll be here before you know it.'

Nag, nag, nag.

''Kay.'

It was easier not to argue sometimes.

'Fancy a little walk before you start?'

'Nope.'

'Okay. Well, I'll leave you to it then.'

''Kay.'

Actually she *would* have a walk. Go to the park, sit on her swing, have a think.

'Oh, I thought you were revising,' said Grace, as Cleo came downstairs wearing her coat.

'Going for a walk.'

Four words, Cleo – quite a conversationalist.

'But I thought you didn't want to.'

'Changed my mind.'

'Shall I …?'

'See ya.'


Perched on the swing, a glimmer of an idea hovering on the horizon, Cleo's worst nightmare came true. Walking towards her through the park, beaming hostility, were Cassie and Lisa and another girl who they now deemed to be their new best friend. Simultaneously, in the distance, from the opposite direction walked Pete.

'All on your own then Cleo?' asked Cassie, taking a confrontational stance, arms folded in front of herself.

'Waiting for someone – not that it's any of your business,' said Cleo, moving the swing slowly, examining the chain as though her life depended on it. Maybe it did.

Lisa blew a large pink bubble, popped it, and sucked the gum neatly back into her mouth. 'Liar. You ain't got any friends.'

'Yeah, like you'd know,' said Cleo, watching Pete from the corner of her eye as he sauntered towards them, hands in his pockets.

Cassie eyed her up and down with some disdain. 'Your mum told us.'

'What?' Cleo stopped swinging and stared at her in disbelief.

'Your mum said that you hadn't got any friends and that we should call round for you sometime.'

'Well she's lyin'. I've got loads of friends,' snapped Cleo, understandably furious.

'Yeah, looks like it.'

'Pete!' shouted Cleo. 'What time are you coming over tonight? Can you make it about eight?'

'Yeah, sure babe,' he said, walking quickly across to them and putting his arm around her shoulders.

Cleo stood, turned and kissed him full-on. He reciprocated, naturally, couldn't believe his luck. He was gobsmacked ... his gob was smackered, his hands were ... stopped.

'Later,' she said, her eyes full of promise.

He was on a promise! He continued with the snog.

Cassie, Lisa and their new best friend watched, but only for a minute; their fun had been spoilt. If the truth known, all three were jealous. He may have been thought of as a sleazeball by Cleo, but to them he was testosterone on legs. Eighteen and built – what more could they want? He was well fit.

Watching over Pete's shoulder until the defeated trio had left the park, Cleo was finally able to eject his tongue from her throat.

'Thanks.'

What? He was getting thanked for doing something he'd been wanting to do for ages? 'That's okay. About eight o'clock, then?' he asked, wanting to confirm it. He could hardly believe what had just happened, it was like all his birthdays had come at once.

'What?' she asked, giving him short shrift now. She had more important things to deal with – like her mother.

Surely she couldn't have forgotten that quickly, although he had heard somewhere that pregnancy can make you more forgetful. 'Tonight. Remember? You said for me to come round.'

'Pete! Surely even you can't be that thick! I was just using you to get at them, making out we were together so they wouldn't think I was a complete Billy-no-mates.'

Pete looked dumbfounded, and somewhat annoyed. 'You know there's names for girls like you – you shouldn't mess people around like that. And don't think I've forgotten about that paternity test,' he said, lowering his eyes to her bump, ''cos I haven't!'

With a final cold glare, Pete turned on his heels and stormed off, leaving Cleo in a state of despair. Okay, her friends hated her, Pete hated her, and as for Mum … that was unthinkable. The glimmer of an idea that had been forming in Cleo's mind when she came into the park today suddenly burst forth like a Catherine wheel, sparks flying as it whirled around inside her head.

Saturday morning and all was well. Grace was up before Charlie today, making breakfast for everyone when he finally came downstairs.

'Like some bacon?' Grace asked with a smile.

'Mm, yes, that would be lovely. What have I done to deserve this?' he asked, standing behind her, resting his chin on her shoulder, his arms around her waist.

She disentangled herself, wanting to get on, giving him a kiss on the cheek and a knowing smile. 'Plenty,' she answered, adding more bacon to the pan. 'Eggs anyone?'

'Please,' said Zak, up early for once, getting ready to meet a fair-haired girl he'd been talking to the previous evening. Or rather, desperate to see this well fit blonde bird he'd pulled in some random club last night. 'Where's Cleo, still in bed?'

'No, she was up and out early this morning. Gone to spend the day with your dad, he's taking her shopping.'

'That'll be right. Shopping's the only thing that'd tempt her to go out this early.'

'Richard's been here this morning?' asked Charlie. He still couldn't help himself sometimes. The thought of them together, Grace probably still in her dressing gown …

'No, no, I didn't see him, he didn't come in. Cleo just ran out to the car. You know what she's like at the prospect of shopping.'

'It should cheer her up, anyway.'

'Hopefully.'

'Let's go out somewhere today, just the three of us: you, me and Izzy,' said Charlie.

That made Grace look up from the frying pan, it was so unlike Charlie to suggest them going out somewhere.

'What about Mother?'

'She'll be alright for a few hours. Probably be asleep anyway.'

Grace, Charlie and Izzy had a lovely day. They settled for a trip to Cheshire Oaks in the end. Charlie hadn't been overly delighted by the prospect at first, shopping not being his favourite thing, but he'd do anything to make Grace happy, and in fact he really enjoyed himself. Izzy had been growing out of everything recently so they managed to get her kitted out with some new clothes. Later, after treating themselves to a pizza, they went to the toyshop where Charlie, despite Grace's objection ('It's not her birthday, Charlie!'), bought a baby doll for Izzy that she'd fallen in love with. Finally, they spent rather a long time in the bookshop, just browsing, and after having coffee and muffins there, they set off for home.

'I hope Mother's been okay,' said Grace, suddenly realising how long they'd been out.

'She'll have been fine,' Charlie reassured her.

Mother had indeed been fine-ish. Alfie had caused her a bit of a problem when she'd forgotten to let him out and he'd done a puddle on the kitchen floor but she'd managed to mop it all up with the tea towel, so Grace need never know. And then there was the other puddle – a mystery that one. The fridge seemed to have defrosted itself for no apparent reason until she'd discovered that somebody had pulled out the plug. Who would have done that? She could only presume it must have been Zak. He must have sneaked back in and done it without her knowing and yet it was so unlike him, he was usually such a good boy, bless him.

Oh, and then there was the tea. Why on earth didn't it come ready done in packets like it used to? Well, it did come in packets of course, but then the tea was all divided up into stupid little bags. Anyway, she thought she could save Grace some time by emptying it all out of the bags for her. She'd been hours. Hours! Cutting open each bag, tipping tea leaves into the caddy, what a monotonous job it had been. But then, just when she'd nearly reached the end, she'd turned to go and answer the phone and caught the caddy with her elbow, tipping its entire contents into the sink. Could she get it out? Well she had managed to retrieve some of it, Grace would be pleased about that. She'd scooped and scooped until she was blue in the face, but the rest … well, she'd just had to wash it all down the sink, hadn't she?

And that had created the next problem. The sink was blocked. Sinks these days, they don't make them like they used to. Actually, she thought she'd been quite clever with this one, using the brain that no one seemed to think she had any more. She'd remembered seeing a piece of hose-pipe. Charlie must have had it for something, it was in the cupboard underneath the stairs, on top of the laundry basket. Anyway she'd got it, connected one end to the kitchen tap, pointed the other end towards the plughole, turned on the tap and … whoosh! Now, unfortunately this is where something seemed to go wrong. Water, with tea leaves in it, mysteriously splattered all over the kitchen window. Meanwhile the sink, which she had been expecting to empty, seemed to get more full than ever – in fact it was in serious danger of overflowing. She'd thought it was prob-ably best, at this point, to turn off the tap and leave it for Charlie to sort out when he got home. At least they couldn't say she hadn't tried.

The tea leaves stuck to the window she could do nothing about at all. She had tried wrapping a tea towel around the end of her walking stick and reaching up to wipe it that way, but somehow the walking stick had caught Grace's vase on the window sill, knocking it and its contents onto the floor where it had smashed into a thousand pieces. She was fairly sure that wasn't the vase Grace's aunt had left to her in her will … it was probably just a cheap one she'd had from somewhere, so she'd probably be quite glad to be rid of it.

Anyway, the broken vase had started off a whole new saga. No sooner had the broken pieces of china scattered themselves all over the floor, when along came Alfie to investigate. What a silly dog. Now if he'd just been careful where he'd put his feet he would have been fine, but no, he trod on the sharpest piece and cut his foot. Well, for a dog, she had never heard such a wimp – talk about howl! Admittedly it did bleed quite a lot. In fact, try as she might, she could not stop it. It might have been easier if she could have caught him, but he was skittering about in a state of panic, howling like a banshee.

So what was she meant to do? Obvious. Dial 999. Police? Fire? Ambulance? Well she couldn't really send him off in an ambulance, and he wasn't on fire, so the police would have to do. She amazed herself by remembering her address, especially with all this pandemonium going on. She really was quite proud of herself today.

It was surprising how quickly they arrived, siren blaring, blue light flashing, like something from that series on the television. She was standing by the door watching, waiting to let them in. But then she had another surprise – they knew her, name and everything! How could that be? They said she'd been for a ride with them in their car a few months ago. They were taking her for a ride now: as if she'd get into a car with two complete strangers – men as well! At least she thought they were men, one she wasn't altogether sure about.

But back to the dog. She'd done the right thing to call them, they bandaged him up a treat. And then, even better, the one who looked like a woman (and this possibly proved it) offered to make them all a nice cup of tea. They were quite interested in hearing all about the family as well and it was nice to have someone to talk to. She told them that Grace and Charlie had gone for a day out and left her all on her own, but that as she always had to do everything around here anyway, it really didn't make that much difference. She told them seventeen-year-old Zak was at the pub and Cleo, only just sixteen, was pregnant and staying with her dad like she often did – overnight sometimes. She thought it was disgusting: it was obvious what they were up to, there'd been incest in their family before.

The policemen looked both dazed and amazed. The man/woman one had a bit of trouble finding the tea, but she helped him, and he managed to make a pot full eventually, even though it did seem to have an unusual taste. She supposed even policemen/women couldn't be good at everything. In fact they were just sitting around drinking it, a freshly bandaged and now tranquil Alfie back to begging for biscuits, when the front door burst open with a sudden hullabaloo.

'Mother! Mother! What's happened?' shrieked Grace, in a flurry of worry, carrier bags and child.

Charlie followed at a more sedate pace but still with an anxious face having arrived home to find a police car parked outside his house. Alfie limped over to greet them, playing for sympathy. This could be worth loads of biscuits – a whole packet to himself ...

A pat on the head. That was all? He rolled over on his back. Dead dog. Feet in the air (and one with a bandage!) – they'd have to notice now ... It failed.

'Mother, tell me what happened!' repeated Grace, her eyes darting nervously around the disaster that vaguely resembled her kitchen. There was blood everywhere! 'Did somebody break in? Did they hurt you?'

Did she hurt my foot? Alfie gave a little whimper, but still to no avail.

'Just in time for a nice cup of tea,' said Gran. 'Get a chair and sit down Grace. We've been having a lovely chat, haven't we?'

'Never mind that, what's happened?' asked Grace, becoming more anxious by the minute.

'Nothing to worry about,' said the policeman, vaguely

amused, but also concerned that they had gone out and left this poor old lady home alone when she clearly couldn't cope.

He explained how they came to be here, Alfie finally getting some attention, although exactly how the kitchen had come to be in such a state remained a mystery. What a pity dogs can't talk, although Alfie did make a very plausible attempt at 'Sore foot', 'Biscuits please' and 'More'.

As for Gran, she simply blamed the burglars for everything.

'But there weren't any burglars,' said Grace.

'Yes there were. You said somebody broke in,' said Gran.

'No! I just asked whether somebody *had* bro ... oh, never mind,' said Grace. It really wasn't worth it.

Acknowledging cries of 'Call again' from Gran, the police officers made their way to the front door, explaining to Grace about the incident report forms before going on their way. As the door closed behind them they came face to face with a young man – both of them did, as he swayed from side to side, first seeing one face and then the other.

'Are you one p'liceman or two?' he slurred, mesmerized, and obviously out of his skull.

'Think you've had a bit too much to drink, young man. I should get in the house if I were you.'

'I will, I will officer. Thank you. Going in ... going ... now,' said Zak, leaning heavily on the doorbell ... and throwing up simultaneously.

The two police officers left, the sound of Grace's raised voice ringing in their ears.

'Didn't the old lady say he's only seventeen?'

'Yup. But if you think I'm going back in there ... It's a madhouse!'

'Saturday night or not, any calls we get tonight'll seem simple after that lot. Roll on the end of our shift, my head feels as though it's been run over by a ten-ton truck.'

With all the chaos that had been going on, it was nearly half past ten before Grace gave a thought to Cleo. She was probably staying overnight with her dad, but she hadn't let them know. She rang Richard's phone and Cleo's mobile but there was no reply from either of them.

'Oh Grace, stop worrying,' said Charlie. 'She's with her dad, he's perfectly capable of taking care of her, and anyway she's sixteen now, she's not a child any more.'

'But neither of them are answering their phones,' said Grace, the ever-worrying mother.

'Probably been to the cinema or out for a meal or something with their phones switched off. She'll be staying overnight, more than likely, and just forgot to mention it. Anyway, it's only early yet.'

'But …'

'Grace, forget them, they'll be out enjoying themselves,' he said, snuggling up to her on the sofa, kissing her on the cheek, kissing her neck, wishing she'd relax.

She shuffled away slightly, Cleo on her mind. But Charlie was persistent. He waited a while and then snuggled up to her again, nibbling her ear, her neck, her …

'Charlie! Stop it! How do I know she's alright?'

'Because we'd have heard if she wasn't. She'd have rung, or Richard would. We've been here since teatime and I had my mobile when we were out.'

'Suppose,' she said, only slightly reassured.

Try as he might, there was only one thing on Charlie's mind – and it wasn't Cleo. He tried again, kissing, fondling, fearing another rebuff, but when none was forthcoming his hand seemed to take on a life of its own, moving up the inside of her thigh, fumbling with the zip on her jeans, his fingers slipping inside, teasing her, firing her passion.

'Charlie, somebody could come!' she gasped, aroused herself now.

'Well you – hopefully,' he breathed, feeling so horny by now that he didn't care if the Queen herself walked in at this moment.

As for Grace, Charlie's fingers were working such magic that any worries she'd had seemed to have flown right out of the window along with her modesty. Unfastening Charlie's trousers, she guided him towards her, moving to lie on her back as he slid inside her.

'Oh Grace, that feels so good,' he sighed, as he moved slowly on top of her, his naked posterior bared to the world …

… and Grandma. 'Saints preserve us! What on earth is going on here? I've never seen anything like it in my life!'

A flurry of clothes and naked flesh scrambled about on the sofa. Never had an erection been so rapidly deflated, nor modesty covered. One would have expected Gran to avert her eyes, but the little beady things were everywhere.

'What do you think you were doing? There's names for things like that!' she said, her face filled with disgust.

'Yes Gran, it's called sex,' said Charlie, rising to the occasion. Well, not literally of course, not any longer.

Grace was mortified. What on earth had they been thinking? Well they hadn't, that was the problem.

'Sorry, Mother,' she said, shamefaced and unable to look at her as she fastened her jeans.

'Get to your room,' commanded Gran, taking a mother stance, disciplining her child.

'Don't worry, we're going,' said Charlie, not wishing to be chastised by a senile old lady. 'But we weren't doing anything wrong, you know, we are married. You should have stayed in bed instead of sneaking around like some kind of peeping Tom.'

'I've never seen anything so disgusting,' muttered Gran as she made her way back to her room. 'Disgraceful. You're getting just like that sister of yours. The world's gone mad!'

Grace and Charlie went up to their bedroom, dignity eventually restored.

'I felt just like a naughty schoolgirl,' laughed Grace, as she got into bed.

'Mmm,' said Charlie, standing to attention at the thought, 'I like that idea, you as a naughty schoolgirl …'

# 32

Sunday morning and all was right with the world. Why did that sound ominous?

Grace yawned, stretched and opened her eyes. She'd had the most delicious sleep. Not surprisingly. Charlie lay on his side, his head propped up on one elbow, gazing at her. He ran his hand over her body, leaned over, and kissed her gently on the forehead.

''Morning, gorgeous.'

'Charlie,' she said, 'how long have you been awake? Why are you looking at me like that?'

'About ten minutes. And because I can't take my eyes off you, you're so beautiful.'

'Is anyone up?'

'No, only me.'

'Charlie!' she giggled. 'Don't start that again.'

'Better go for a cold shower then,' he smiled. 'Mind if I go first?'

'No, go for it,' she answered, still trying to wake herself up.

As she lay listening to him running the shower she heard the distant sound of the doorbell and reluctantly forced herself out of bed and into her dressing gown to go and investigate.

Richard.

'Hello?' she said, intrigued, it was still quite early yet.

'Hi. Sorry to disturb you so early but it's such a lovely day and I thought Cleo might like to go for a trip out with me

360

somewhere. It'd get her out of the house for a bit anyway.'

Grace's brain certainly wasn't in gear this morning, she was still not fully awake yet.

'Good idea. Yes, I'm sure she'd love to. I'll just go and give her a shout, come in for a minute,' she said, going up the stairs. 'Cl...! Hang on a minute, Cleo isn't here. She spent the day with you yesterday, she stayed at yours last night ... didn't she?'

One look at Richard's face provided the answer, and the colour drained from her own with shock.

'I haven't seen her this weekend, Grace.'

'But she said ... you picked her up yesterday morning.'

'Honestly, that's why I came round now.'

'So where was she last night, then?'

'I have no idea, but she wasn't with me. Have you checked her room?'

Grace seemed incapable of movement. Richard pushed past her and ran up the stairs, coming face to face with Charlie in his boxer shorts at the top, toothbrush in hand.

'Wassup?' mumbled Charlie, still brushing.

'Cleo's disappeared,' said Richard, pushing open the door to her room to double check. 'Not here,' he shouted back to Grace.

Suddenly the whole household was awake and everything turned into chaos. Gran with her 'I told you so's', Izzy crying for her missing sister, Zak with a humungous hang-over and thinking he was going to die, Alfie barking, and the three supposedly sensible adults running around like headless chickens. Where *was* Cleo? How could this have happened? Why wasn't she answering her mobile?

Breaking through the bedlam came the sound of distant bells.

'Phone,' said Zak, clutching his head.

'Well get it, then,' snapped Grace, brain still not fully functioning.

361

'It might be Cleo,' said Zak, still some logic despite the hangover.

Grace's limbs were miraculously remobilised, and she nearly knocked him down in the rush. 'Hello?' her voice tremored in apprehension.

'Auntie Grace,' said Hugo at the other end of the line. 'Nothing to worry about but Cleo is here in London. She gave birth to a baby girl in hospital about half an hour ago.'

'Oh my God,' said Grace, clasping her hand to her mouth, rendered almost speechless, as the others looked on in fear of what had happened.

'I couldn't ring earlier as she wouldn't let me and I didn't want to upset her, she was already in a bit of a state. She came down on the train yesterday and rang me from Euston – lucky I answered or I don't know what she would have done. I went to meet her and then she started in labour when we were on our way back, on the Tube actually, it was horrendous.'

'Oh what a silly girl, anything could have happened!' Grace was stunned, hardly able to take in what he was saying. 'Is she okay?'

'She's a bit shattered obviously but absolutely fine now. The baby too, she's gorgeous. Cleo wants you to know she's sorry, though. She didn't mean to worry you and she hopes you're not too cross with her.'

'Cross? Of course we're not cross. We'd just been really worried, but I'm relieved to hear she's okay, that's all. Give her our love and tell her we'll be down there as soon as we can. I can't wait to see her!'

So the chaos continued, but born of excitement now rather than fear. Grace couldn't wait to see the new baby, hold it in her arms. She wondered if it would look like Izzy – she'd been a beautiful baby. Charlie couldn't help but be the voice of reason, wondering where she'd had the money from to pay for her train ticket, wondering where they were all going to fit in this ever-expanding house.

'Charlie, don't be such a killjoy. She had money for her birthday, didn't she? I expect she used that.'

Once again, Charlie was going to have to be left behind to look after everyone. He did tentatively suggest taking Izzy down with them and leaving Zak to cope with Grandma, but Grace was having none of it. After the performance Gran had given when they'd left her the previous day, she thought it would not be a very wise thing to do. Charlie hoped that was her only reason, although he did feel a lot more confident of her love now than he had the last time she'd gone away with Richard.

Richard went home to pack while Grace sorted herself out. She wasn't good at throwing a few things in a bag; she had to make sure she was prepared for every eventuality, remembering to pack some of the baby stuff they'd bought, not knowing what they were going to need, when they'd be back, anything. Hugo had said they could use Anna's flat, there was a key under the plant pot by the front door. Oh, it was so exciting! A little baby girl! She couldn't wait to bring them both home. In her head they were here already, one big happy family.

St George's. As they walked into the maternity ward, Grace spotted them before they saw her: Cleo sitting up in bed cradling the baby in her arms, Hugo looking on like the proud father he wasn't. Sensing their presence, Cleo looked up, her face pale and exhausted and yet radiant at the same time.

'Mum!' she gasped, her face lighting up, but then fading again with sudden remembrance. 'I hope you're not too cross with me. Sorry,' she said, biting her bottom lip anxiously.

'As if we could be cross with you when you've just given us

this gorgeous grandchild! Look at her, Richard, she's absolutely beautiful, so tiny.'

Richard could hardly speak, he felt so emotional. 'She's perfect,' he said, touching her soft little hand gently with his own.

'How are you feeling?' asked Grace.

'Not too bad. Just a bit knackered, that's all.'

'Bound to be.' Grace couldn't take her eyes off the baby. She could hardly remember her own three being that small. 'Well done you,' she said to Cleo, giving her a hug.

'I couldn't have done it without Hugo,' said Cleo, beaming at him. 'He's been amazing.'

'Thanks, Hugo, I don't know what would have happened to her if you hadn't been there,' said Richard. 'It was a bit of a crazy thing to do.'

'I know, sorry,' said Cleo, 'But it all worked out in the end.' She gazed down at her baby in wonderment. She found it hard to believe that she could have produced anything so perfect.

'I hope you don't blame me at all,' said Hugo anxiously. 'I didn't even know she was on her way here.'

'Of course not. You've been a really good friend to her, Hugo, she's lucky to have you,' said Richard.

'Which is why,' said Cleo, with a sudden look of determination, 'I've decided to …'

'Cleo!' exclaimed Hugo. 'Now is not the time. Let's talk about this later, when you come home.'

'Ooh yes, I can't wait to get her home,' exclaimed Grace, so baby-besotted that she was completely oblivious to any underlying tension … which was unusual for her. 'Can I hold her?'

''Course you can,' said Cleo, relinquishing her precious bundle for the moment.

Richard, however, was aware that something had remained unsaid. Something very important from the look on Cleo's face. She was about to drop another bombshell, no doubt, and would leave them picking up the pieces yet again. He really could not cope with any explosions tonight, he just wanted a bit of peace so they could all bond with this beautiful new baby.

'Have you thought of a name for her yet?' he asked.

'I'm going to call her Daisy, but I want her second name to be Anna, so she'll be Daisy Anna,' she said proudly.

'That's lovely, Cleo, and what a lovely thought,' said Grace, tears welling as she gazed at her baby granddaughter with overwhelming happiness.

Richard and Hugo looked on with mixed emotions, remembering with love the woman they had lost.

'I felt so close to Auntie Anna. I always knew I would call my baby after her if I had a girl. It seems like a fitting tribute somehow.'

Cleo was allowed out of hospital the next day. They collected her in Richard's car and drove back to the flat. It was a happy day and yet poignant at the same time to be bringing the new baby, Daisy Anna, home to the flat where Anna had lived.

And home it really was going to be. Cleo had finally dropped her bombshell and broken the earth-shattering news – she was going to live here in London, right here, in Anna's flat.

Home sweet home? I don't think so somehow.

'I have never heard anything so ridiculous in my entire life!' exploded Grace. 'You're sixteen, for God's sake! You can't look after yourself, never mind a baby as well. What d'you think you're going to live on? What about your exams? You're coming back with us and that's final!'

Did you really expect any other reaction?

'But Mum, you can't tell me what to do. I'm sixteen, I've got a baby of my own. What sort of a life d'you think I'd have back in Cheshire? I haven't got any friends and I've got the reputation of being the village bike. Everybody'd just be talking about me and, I'm telling you, I've had enough! At least this would be a fresh start. Hugo says I can live here, rent free, for as long as I want and there are all sorts of allowances I can claim, I've looked it up on the Internet – I'm not just going into this blindly you know. I could even get a part-time job later on if I can find someone to look after the baby ... maybe even go to college and take my exams next year, who knows? Hugo says he'll help me in any way he can, he's not that far away, and he's got friends nearby who'll help me too. Please don't blame him for any of this though, it was all my idea. He's just being supportive, that's all. I really, really want to do this, Mum. Please don't try and stop me.'

'We can't always have what we want, Cleo.' Grace was not to be convinced. She could feel her whole family slipping away from her.

Richard interrupted. 'What if you tried it for six months? Come home again if it doesn't work out?'

'Huh! Thanks for backing me up, Richard,' said Grace sarcastically.

'Yeah, that's what *she'd* love, isn't it?' said Cleo. 'Things not working out for me so I'd come back home with my baby.'

'Cleo!' warned Hugo.

'Well that's what this is all about, isn't it? Nothing to do with me not coping, it's about her not coping with an empty nest. Zak'll be gone as well soon, he's got uni. She just wanted my baby all for herself and me back home to stop the place looking empty and to give her a purpose in life.'

'Cleo!' shouted the three of them simultaneously.

'I'll take the baby and sit in the bedroom with her for a while,' said Hugo, ever thoughtful, wanting to give them some space. 'It can't be good for her, all this shouting going on.'

'Thanks Hugo,' said Cleo, a little shamefaced.

A wall of silence had been built. Amazingly enough, Cleo was the first to chip away at it.

'Sorry, I shouldn't have said that.'

Grace came across and gave her a hug. 'No, you're right – partly, anyway. I *was* looking forward to having a baby in the house again and I *am* dreading the thought of both you and Zak leaving home. Nevertheless, I still feel you're too young to be living on your own and with a baby to look after – especially here in London, not knowing anybody except Hugo.'

'Mum, how old was Auntie Anna when she was forced to live here on her own, having just had her baby taken away and probably in a lot worse state than I am now?'

'Sixteen like you, I know, but it doesn't make me worry any less. Anyway, times were different then.'

'Not that different. And I've got Hugo, she had no one.'

Grace looked thoughtful for a moment. 'Well, that still worries me too, actually – you and Hugo.'

'What about us?'

'Oh come on, Cleo, don't play the innocent. What if it develops into something more than a friendship?'

'Mum! He's my cousin!'

'Yes, precisely, and your uncle too, given our family background. It could have all sorts of repercussions.'

'I know, I'm not stupid. But there's no chance I could ever fancy him. It'd be like … well, like going with Zak!'

'It's just that when you spend a lot of time with someone feelings can change. What starts off as a friendship can turn into …'

'Mum, stop! You're making me feel sick at the thought of it! No way! Hugo's my friend and that's all he'll ever be.'

'And you're sure he feels that way too?'

'Absolutely positive. He has issues of his own to deal with anyway,' said Cleo.

'Like what?'

'Not up to me to say,' she replied, with an air of mystery.

Richard was a saint when it came to pouring oil on troubled waters. He stayed in London, sorting out Cleo's finances for her, making sure everything was set up. He also said he'd pay her an allowance each month for now as he didn't want to think of her struggling for money; she'd have enough to contend with looking after Daisy. Cleo couldn't thank him enough. She was really going to miss her dad, and he her, although he did warn her that he'd be down to see her whenever he could; she'd have trouble keeping him away.

Grace was still not convinced this was going to work, but she was in the minority and had reluctantly agreed for Cleo to give it a trial for six months. However, she had insisted on staying with Cleo for the first two weeks to help her adjust to her new life and make sure she was coping. Cleo was actually really glad of the help; being a new mum seemed like a mammoth task.

Charlie was not overly happy left trying to juggle work, Izzy and Gran yet again, but what other choice did he have? Richard had, however, said that he'd come and look after Gran for the weekend when Grace was ready to come home. That way, Charlie could drive down to collect her, with Zak and Izzy, and they'd all be able to have a bit of a break. Did Richard know what he was letting himself in for? And would Gran really stay alone in the house with a *man*! That remained to be seen. Richard had also promised to go over and help Charlie as much as he could while Grace was away. Had he? Seriously? Had they become best mates now, or what?

It was lovely for Grace and Cleo to have this time together – alone except for the baby, and she was an absolute angel. Cleo had taken on a whole new persona, that of a mum, and amazingly it suited her. Grace had never expected her to adapt so well to her new role. The teenage angst seemed to have flown out of the window and it both surprised and delighted her.

The only niggle of doubt lurking in the shadows for Grace now, was about Hugo and his feelings towards Cleo. He had tried to reassure her before, but she really needed to know the full story if she was ever to feel remotely relaxed about the situation. Cleo knew how she felt, but could only suggest that she talked to Hugo about it. He had confided in her and she was not going to break that confidence.

# 33

Hugo had been expecting her call. He knew she'd never believe him unless he told her the full story. And who could really blame her? She was entrusting her sixteen-year-old daughter to him, and she obviously didn't want him jumping her as soon as her back was turned. With one case of incest already in their family's past, she had every right to be concerned, it was perfectly understandable.

The doorbell rang and he went to let her in. It was the first time she'd visited his flat and she was impressed. Interior design at its best.

'You look surprised,' said Hugo, as her eyes gazed around the open-plan room.

'Well, yes. A young man living on his own … I never expected it to look this good.'

'I did have a bit of help, I suppose,' he said, pouring her a drink.

'From your mum?'

'No,' he said, handing her the glass.

She looked up, expecting him to continue the sentence, but he didn't. She sipped her drink.

'So,' he said, 'how are they doing?'

'Really well, actually,' said Grace. 'Cleo's surprised me. She seems to have taken to this whole motherhood and independent woman thing like a duck to water.'

'I never doubted it,' said Hugo. 'Cleo has an inner strength. She's so mature for a girl her age, I really admire her.'

'Well you certainly seem to have brought out the best in her, Hugo. I can only thank you for that.'

'So long as you don't blame me for everything.'

'Listen, Cleo has a mind of her own, as I'm sure you've noticed. Once her mind's made up about something, there's no stopping her.'

Grace took a gulp of her gin and tonic – as opposed to a sip. Enough of the trivialities, she had to move on to the point in question. Was he gay? Is that why he'd never have a relationship with Cleo? It was the only explanation she could think of. He didn't look it, though, but then, you can't always tell can you? Look at the man Kate had told her about, he was married and even his wife didn't know. … Maybe Hugo was a transvestite or some other sort of gender-bending thing? Dressing in women's clothing? Hardly. She could picture him more in leather, or rubber, or … oh my God, what was she thinking!

'Top up?'

What?!

'Sorry,' she mumbled, somewhat hot and flustered. 'Sorry, I was miles away then.'

'Your drink – another gin and tonic?'

She looked down at her glass and was surprised to see it empty. No wonder her mind was on a rampage, she'd drunk that far too quickly and she should definitely not have any more. However, 'Thanks, don't mind if I do,' were the words that actually came out of her mouth.

'I expect you're here for an explanation,' said Hugo, refilling her glass. 'I can hardly blame you. I should have told you before but it's just that some things in life are private, and this is something I'd never discussed with anyone until I met Cleo. I've always kept it secret, thinking it was the best thing for all concerned.'

'You're gay, aren't you?' blurted out Grace, totally not meaning to do so.

371

'Gay? Whatever gave you that idea? Do I look gay or something?' asked Hugo, taken aback, amazed and suddenly sensitive to the fact that maybe this was the impression people had of him.

'No, no, of course you don't. I just thought it might explain why, that's all,' said Grace, somewhat embarrassed now. Transvestite? Don't even go there.

'It's okay,' smiled Hugo, 'I can see where you're coming from. It would have been a logical explanation. But no, I do have a girlfriend – sort of, anyway.'

'Sort of?' thought Grace. Transexuals, trans-allsorts were running through her head. She looked at him, intrigued, waiting for him to continue.

'Her name's Rose,' he said with a shy smile. 'Classic case really, we met at the cheese counter in Sainsbury's. She had her son with her, just a toddler then, in his buggy. He dropped his toy, she hadn't noticed, he was staring at it and I bent down and picked it up for him. She saw me and said thank you. Our eyes met, and I can honestly say there was instant attraction. But obviously she had a child, and I noticed her wedding ring. I walked away.

It was only a few days later when I bumped into her again, walking on Clapham Common with the buggy, no man with her. I said hello and she stopped and chatted, just generally. There was something about her … but she went on her way.

Weeks past before I saw her again, sitting on a park bench, the boy eating ice-cream. She had a sad, faraway look on her face but it brightened when she saw me. I sat down and, before I knew it, she was telling me her whole life story.

Yes, she did have a husband. They'd been happily married, overjoyed when Jack was born, but then one day as they'd been out walking with the baby in his buggy, there had been a horrendous accident. A car had mounted the pavement, heading towards them. Her husband, Daniel, had grabbed both herself and the baby and pushed them to safety but, in doing so, had found himself right in the path of the oncoming car.

Rose and Jack had been left completely unscathed by the accident, all due to his bravery. Everyone said it was a miracle that Daniel had survived at all, but he had. The tragedy was, he was now paralysed from the waist downwards. Rose just feels never-ending guilt. He had almost given his life to save them. He spent months and months in and out of hospital and knows he will never walk again … nor make love. For the rest of his life he'll be confined to a wheelchair. Rose knows that she will never leave him. Not only is the guilt too great, but she loves him. And he's Jack's dad.

We were just friends for a while, strongly attracted to each other but too guilty to do anything about it. She had a husband, he'd given everything for her … But eventually we succumbed, it was virtually impossible not to. We were like two magnets drawn together, unable to be prised apart. I love her utterly and completely, Auntie Grace, she is my world. I know we can never live together; her place is with Daniel and I understand that. She has to live with him and care for him, and she still loves him. But she loves me as well, it's a complicated situation – but proof that you can love two people at the same time, just in different ways.

'So you see,' he said, dragging himself back to the here and now, 'I could never form a relationship with Cleo, because my heart and soul and everything I am already belongs to my Rose. Life is complicated enough.'

Grace had to choke back the tears. 'Oh Hugo, I had no idea.'

'Neither has anyone else, apart from Cleo. We prefer it that way, it's for the best.'

'Thank you for telling me, I'm so glad you did. It's made me feel even closer to you, having a more complete picture of your life.' She moved over to give him a hug.

'I hope you don't think that makes me a horrible person, sleeping with another man's wife.'

'I could never think that of you, Hugo. I think you're a very caring and compassionate young man – you've shown that with Cleo. I think Rose is very lucky to have found you.'

'I'm the lucky one, Auntie Grace.'

It was a reassured Grace who let herself back into the flat that night. She peeped around the door of Cleo's bedroom to see her sleeping peacefully, a contented baby in the Moses basket by her side. It was strange how life had gone full circle almost: Anna – Hugo – Cleo – Daisy Anna ... If this baby grew up to be as good as Hugo she would have done well. He was a fantastic young man, no one could have a better role model.

Now all that remained for Grace to worry about was her own empty nest. But in fact, what was there to worry about? It wasn't long ago that she'd wanted to escape from her cage and fly free. That time was coming now. She still had her Charlie and Izzy too, but there would be more time for herself, for the things that *she* wanted to do. In fact she'd had a phone call today from Kate, asking whether she could come to stay for a while. What was all that about? She couldn't wait to find out.